HOME TO
PLEASANT
PASTURES

A PASTOR JOHN AND WENDY NOVEL

Greg Chantler

Contents

Prologue

D O YOU WANT TO KNOW WHAT'S REALLY weird about the story I'm getting ready to tell you? Here I am, a big 6 feet-2 inches-210-pound Swede, and I feel like a little kid. It's like my emotions are trapped in a Star Trek episode and they're set on warp speed. There's this really cool futuristic navigation system that's supposed to guide me all over the galaxy in a logical way, but instead it's sending me in a hundred random directions. One minute I'm scared and shaking in my boots; my insides quivering like grandma's Jell-O and fruit cocktail salad. But then, just as I'm wondering seriously about following through with my plan, this shiver runs up and down my spine and I'm so excited I'm ready to run out on the lawn and turn cartwheels. And believe me, that's not an easy feat for a guy my size. In between bouts of fear and episodes of spine tingling excitement come tiny doses of absolute bliss. They're so blissful, in fact, I'm not convinced I should even be having them. When you're a pastor I'm not sure people expect you to have these kinds of feelings. People want their pastor to be self-controlled and not given to these moments of ecstasy. It somehow tarnishes the image of what they think a man of the cloth should be. But still? What am I going to do? The feelings are there in all their glory and to try to pre-tend otherwise would be pretty much impossible. And these random thoughts that have been plaguing my emotions are there because of a person. A woman. A beautiful, sensitive, loving woman who I want to spend the rest of my life with. That may be poor sentence structure and might make my old high school English teacher turn over in her grave, but that's exactly how I feel. I want to spend the rest of my life with this sweet, caring, impossibly stunning young woman by the lovely name of Wendy. When she walked into church our eyes met for a split second, before Virginia Crupp began telling me about the latest mis-sionary project for the ladies of the Martha Circle; a group dedicated to patterning their projects after the hospitality gifts that Martha of the gospels displayed. It's all very good and normally I would stand there listening to Virginia for several minutes. I'd then place my hand on her shoulder and say something spiritual like, "You ladies are doing such a great job and you're changing your little corner of the world in such wonderful ways. I know that brings joy to God's heart." Now those aren't just spiritual words, I really believe that. I do. But at that moment I didn't really care if they had set a goal of rolling 50,000 bandages for medical missionaries overseas. As selfish as this sounds, I just wanted to talk to this stunning creature that just came through the doors of the Pleasant Pastures Community Church. And so, I excused myself as soon as I could do so without offending Virgie, and made my way over to the young woman who I would soon find out was Wendy Baker, from back east. My first thought was, "Well, Baker is a nice name but Wendy Larson sounds a lot better." She looks like a Wendy Larson with her long blonde hair and beautiful blue eyes. I could get lost in those eyes, and I would have, if it wasn't for her smile. I know it sounds weird because people always talk about the eyes being the "window to the soul", but to tell you the truth, I've always been more of a mouth person. The first thing I usually notice is a person's smile. And Wendy's was delightful. When I introduced myself as John her smile lit up the room and I think I experienced something that I had read about but seriously doubted if it actually existed. I think I experienced the phenomenon known as "love at first sight." I've always looked at that idea with a large dose of skepticism. Now I know all about loving people in general, the whole "loving your neighbor" idea, but falling in love was in a whole other realm. How could "love at first sight" be even remotely possible? My pastoral training and theological studies led me to believe that love is a choice. We choose to love someone as we get to know them. And we get to know them by spending a lot of time with them, understanding their deepest thoughts and dreams, their hopes and aspirations. And that's all true. But when Wendy came walking through the door of the church that Sunday morning, all my years of pastoral training and theological study on love flew right out the window. I fell head over heels, madly, passionately in love with Wendy Baker before I even knew her name. Just being around her for those few minutes provided more joy than I think I've ever experienced in my life. Now, I've had wonderful times, don't get me wrong. I've found joy in so many of life's experiences, but this was different. Vastly different. Amazingly different. I looked at this beautiful young woman and suddenly had visions of the two of us standing in the church at the altar. Wendy's wearing a lovely white dress with lace trim and tiny pearl buttons and I'm in a powder blue tux and ruffled shirt, a look that is very popular in this fashion conscious decade of the 70s. We're saying our vows, and in all honesty, I've never felt so happy in all my life. And if I have anything to say about it, I'm going to make that vision come true. You see, after three months of dating, I'm going to ask the girl of my dreams to marry me. I'm going to ask her to make me the happiest man on earth by becoming Mrs. John Larson.

So here I am trying desperately to plan the perfect evening, in the perfect setting, for the perfect proposal. I know from experience that oftentimes everything doesn't go exactly as planned, but that doesn't mean I'm not going to give it my best shot. Maybe it'll be by the little brook that runs through the lush green pasture land behind the church; maybe on the little bench where couples have sat for years, just staring into each other's eyes, whispering promises of love for one another. I even found myself praying about the weather. I know there's a 0% chance of rain, but I'm concerned that the Eastern Washington heat at this time in the summer might be a bit over the top. Think about it. Nothing says romance like sweat stains on your freshly laundered shirt. I try everything I can think of to make this night one of perfection. I know I could do the usual thing of taking her out for a beautiful candlelight dinner in the charming little Bavarian style town of Leavenworth, just a few miles up the road. That's what a lot of soon-to-be-married couples do around here. And sure, that would have been nice. Easier too, in that I would have a little more control over the setting and the weather. But I just felt that this very special moment in time should be for Wendy and me alone. I didn't want a bunch of tourists looking in on this very personal profession of my undying love for Wendy. This was our time and I wanted to be alone with her. I had a box in my pocket that was kind of bulky and was driving me nuts, so I was thinking about just keeping the ring in my pocket without the box, but I decided against that. It would be too easy, in my current state of emotional fluctuation, to absentmindedly put my hand in my pocket and accidentally cause the ring to fall out when I withdrew my hand. So, as you can see, I'm really trying to think this all through very carefully. I want this to be a perfect night, for the perfect couple.

I started walking from the parsonage to Maggie's Country Diner where Wendy not only worked, but also lived in the apartment upstairs. I had arranged with Maggie, several days before, to watch Travis for the evening. Maggie, never having had children of her own, was delighted for the opportunity to play substitute mom for this little boy she had grown to love dearly. For never having had children, she was a natural, and Travis loved spending time with Maggie. Of course, part of that on Travis's part might have been the cake. Not only was Travis learning that other adults besides just his mom could be loving and caring, he was also learning about cooking and baking. I never thought a little eight-year-old kid would be interested in that, but Trav was. Who knows? Maybe someday Travis will be the owner of Maggie's Country Diner –The Sequel. He was getting pretty good and both Wendy and I had enjoyed some of the dishes he helped Maggie create.

I arrived at Maggie's diner at 6 o'clock on the dot. I never wanted to be late for anything. I think that probably becomes a habit when you're a pastor. I mean, it's not like you can have a service scheduled for 11:00 AM on a Sunday morning, and come waltzing in at 11:10 AM saying how sorry you were for oversleeping. First of all, who in the world sleeps that late anyway? And secondly, being late like that would give people the impression that I consider my time more valuable than theirs. That just doesn't fly if you're a pastor trying to care for his flock with love and respect. And you've got to respect your flock, even if there are some rather quirky, and at times, cranky characters. Yep, I hate to burst your bubble but even born-again, Bible-believing, "going to heaven" Christians can be cranky and out of sorts, and believe me, I've met my share of them.

I went upstairs to Wendy's apartment and knocked on the door. I don't know which was louder, the knocking on the door or the knocking of my knees. I'm not kidding you. The warp speed of emotions, from here to there and back again, were still present, and probably were intensifying by the second. Wendy came to the door dressed in a pair of soft, acid-washed jeans and a loose, flowing top with those long, puffy "hippie" sleeves. I love that look on her; free and light. Maggie was already talking with Travis and I could hear them planning their next excursion into the culinary arts. We said goodbye and started walking down the street towards the church. Wendy asked me where we were going and I told her that I'd like to go sit on our bench for a while. We had been there several times over the past three months, just enjoying the beautiful setting. In fact every time we had gone, the bench and the surrounding area were free of people. So the bench by the little babbling brook, in essence, became *our* bench. And sure enough, heaven smiled down on us because, when we arrived at our very special setting, once again we were the only ones there. I put my arms around Wendy and kissed her gently on the lips and then pulled her slowly to the bench. We sat down and kissed some more, each kiss reminding me of why we were here in the first place. This sweet, lovely woman was turning me inside out. I told her at that moment that I loved her and that she was the most beautiful person that God had ever created. Wendy blushed in her familiar and humble way and told me that she loved me too. We sat there just holding each other and enjoying this very special moment, a moment of intimate connection that I was convinced no other couple had experienced with such intensity in all of history. This was a very special, one-of-a-kind love that only reaches Earth every thousand years or so. And even then, it couldn't possibly reach the level of love I was feeling at that moment for my precious Wendy. I whispered a silent prayer in my heart and slowly slid down to one knee, while at the same time removing the box from my jeans. I looked into her bright blue eyes, now glistening with tears and I said, "Wendy, I love you". She looked at me and her face began to scrunch up with emotion. My throat began to feel thick, and my voice wavered with the intensity of my feelings. I looked into those beautiful eyes and I said, "Wendy, will you do me the honor of becoming my wife? I love you so very much."

She looked at me with that adorable face, scrunched up with emotion and said the words that were destined to change my life. Wendy looked at me and said, "No John, I'm so sorry, I just can't." And with a huge sob she jumped to her feet and ran away. I sat there stunned and I began to cry uncontrollably. My life was shattered and all hope was gone.

Chapter 1

John

WHEN WENDY RAN OFF THE WAY SHE DID, something died in my spirit. I experienced something that was brand-new for me; suddenly I felt very alone. But it was something more than that, it wasn't just feeling alone. I mean, I certainly felt alone at various times throughout my life, particularly when I'd gone to a new school, or more recently was called to a new church. And please understand, it's not that people at Pleasant Pastures weren't friendly, it's just that most of them were quite a bit older than me and probably were wondering how this young, 27-year-old kid was going to lead the church. It was also pretty apparent to me that, according to their view of the world, being single at 27 didn't seem normal to most of them. Most of the members probably got married at age 19 or 20, that's just what their generation did. And so, being young and single in a church of predominantly older, married folks, left me feeling uncomfortably alone, even though they tried very hard to include me in all aspects of church life. So, when Wendy ran off I suddenly felt very alone, but as I said previously, it was more than that. I felt totally abandoned; not just by Wendy but also by God. And that left me quite shaken because I've never experienced that before. For as long as I could remember God had been my Rock, my Fortress, my Shield, my Protector and so much more. Ever since I was a skinny little kid riding my bike around the neighborhood in my hometown of Duluth, Minnesota, I just somehow knew that God was with me, but now I wasn't so sure. How could this have happened? How could I so drastically have missed what I thought was God's "perfect will" for my life? Did God even have a "perfect will" for my life? I never would have questioned that before but now the idea seemed like it had implanted itself in my mind and spirit and, as far as I could tell, it was there to stay. Believe me, I was suddenly walking in uncharted territory and I didn't like it one bit. I wanted to go back into my childhood when everything felt safe and secure. God was up in heaven watching over me and nothing could happen that wasn't a part of His plan. Of course, as I grew older and matured spiritually, I began to realize how that bit of comfortable theology wasn't as simple as I once thought it was. When I began to really talk with people, as their pastor, it didn't take me too long to realize that most of them had been through periods of deep despair and heartache. They went through troubles and trials that I could never blame on God. To blame God would be to disparage

His loving character and nature and I just couldn't bring myself to do that, no matter how upset I was. But still, this sudden departure of the woman I deeply loved left me with more questions than I would have ever imagined.

Growing up in Duluth, Minnesota certainly wasn't perfect. We often had weather so cold that they had to suspend classes sometimes because it wasn't safe to walk and breathe the air on your way to school. There were times when the wind chill would send the temperature plummeting to 30° below zero. Now that's cold, in fact, that's crazy cold. But because most of my school friends and I had lived there all of our lives, I guess we just figured that's how everybody lived. And of course, in the summer, it could be quite warm, relatively speaking, and we'd find ourselves swimming in Lester River or laying on the sandy beach at Park Point. During the day that sandy beach on Lake Superior was a favorite picnic and swimming destination for families looking for a way to cool off. When you're used to months of below zero temperatures, climbing to anything above 75 or 80° felt like a heat wave, straight from the Sahara Desert. When you go to Duluth you find a pretty hardy bunch of folks who go through any winter with hardly a thought, but when the temperature starts going up, that's when you'll hear a few folks grumbling, anxious for fall to come soon. I know it's weird, but that's how we sons and daughters of Duluth are.

I went through Lester Park grade school, Ordean Junior High and finally graduated from East High School. I know some people found Junior and Senior High School to be very hard, not so much academically but socially. Kids can be pretty cruel, can't they? I still remember the time when some girl, who I used to like in grade school, started spreading rumors about me when we got to Junior High. I

won't tell you what the rumors were about but they were embarrassing enough that I convinced my mom I was sick for almost an entire
week. I think that's when I realized I had a talent for acting. It's not
easy to fool a mom about being sick, especially for close to a week. But
I did. You wouldn't believe the painful expression I could get on my
face when she'd come into my bedroom in the morning to see how I
was feeling. She'd come in with her morning cup of coffee always in
her hand. Remember, I'm from a family of Swedes who viewed coffee
like it was liquid gold. Don't mess with the Swedes and their coffee
if you value your life. She would put her coffee on the little table by
my bedside and she would lean over me and place her hand on my
forehead. And she'd say, "Well, you don't feel particularly warm but
maybe I should take your temperature just in case." And so, she'd reach
for the thermometer that she kept on my bedside table for the duration
of my illness. She'd put it in my mouth and wait the requisite amount
of time and then be startled when my temperature was about 101 or
102; high enough to indicate that I was still sick but not high enough
to go to a doctor. We Swedes are a hardy bunch and refuse to go to
doctors unless were bleeding out our eyes. So, I had an elevated temperature for several days in a row. However - and this is where I feel
kind of guilty - when she would lean over to me to feel my forehead,
and sometimes to pray a short prayer for me, my left hand would reach
out, take the thermometer, and carefully dip it into my mom's coffee
cup for just a second or two. I would then put it back on the brownish
doily on the table by my bed and, within a few seconds, she would
take my temperature and, lo and behold, it would be elevated. Sneaky
trick, I know, but I was desperate. But as the Bible says, "Be sure your
sins will find you out." On my last sick day, I kept the thermometer in
the coffee a few seconds too long. And when she took my temperature

and it read 108° and I was obviously still alive and not convulsing, I knew it was over. I was caught and there was no way I could act or talk my way out of this one. So, I confessed everything, including my embarrassment over the rumors. I thought I'd be on restriction for a year, but my parents surprised me. They sat me down that night and let me just talk about my fear of going to school and having kids point at me and laugh. They told me that nothing is ever solved by running away from a problem but a great deal is accomplished when we stand up and face it. And that's what I was going to do, but they would pray the next day for things to work out all right. So, I went to school the next day, ready to stand strong in the very face of ridicule and, believe it or not, nothing happened. The attention span of a Junior High kid is about a millisecond and I realized that the rumor mill had shifted and moved on without me. I also realized that my parents knew how much I had suffered, not only by the embarrassment from the rumors, but also the guilt of having lied to them that whole week. There wasn't going to be a punishment or restriction. I had expressed my shame at having lied to them and they received my apology graciously. I think that's the first time I came to begin to truly understand God's love and forgiveness. And it's had an impact in my life and ministry ever since. So, I went through Junior High and High School and every-thing was pretty smooth after that. I got involved in various sports, one of which I seemed to have a real talent for and I'll talk about that later. I also wound up taking a speech and drama class, not because I wanted to be up in front of people, and certainly not because I thought I was going to become a pastor and felt the training in public speaking would be good. Those might have good reasons to take the class but my motives weren't quite so high and lofty. The reason I took the class is because Shelley Whitney was also going to take it. And as far as I was concerned, anyplace Shelley was, I wanted to be there too. If she would have asked me to go to a knitting shop and spend the afternoon looking at skeins of yarn, I would've been there in a minute. Motivation. So, I signed up for speech and drama but sadly, when I came to my first class, I discovered that Shelley was in second period and I was in fourth. Oh man, why didn't I pay attention to the details? I had no idea there were two classes. I tried to transfer to the second period class, but it was full. I almost dropped the class, but then I heard they always did an all-school play with kids from both classes participating. So once again, my heart was full of hope. And sure enough, Shelley and I had two of the lead parts in the spring play. I was hoping we'd be cast as lovers, but she was the grandma and I was the pastor of her church. It might have been prophetic, to a certain extent, but I still would've rather been her lover. I know that's not particularly deep and spiritual, but hey, you know how hormones are.

Anyway, Shelley Whitney and I never did get together. It seemed as though she was always dating someone else, and I just couldn't seem to time my approach right. When I would hear she had broken up with someone, by the time I got up the nerve to ask her out, after having given her a few weeks for mourning the loss of her previous relationship, she had already been snatched up. Finally, I got smart. When I heard that she was free from her most recent relationship, I moved in right away and asked her out. I was so excited I thought my heart was going to explode. I asked her out for that next Friday night to go see the double feature at the Skyline Drive-in Theater, which was a popular place for High School kids. I didn't even think to find out what was playing that weekend. It could have been a documentary on the "Magical World of Arts and Crafts" and I wouldn't have cared a bit. I was going to be the lucky guy who got to take Shelley Whitney to the Skyline Drive-in. I kept counting down the hours until I picked her up for the maiden voyage of what was going to be a long and exciting cruise of earth shattering, heart-hammering love. This date was absolutely going to change my life and I was pretty sure it would lead to a life of wedded bliss. Well, finally Friday came and I counted down the minutes until I could pick her up at 7:30. Of course, the movie didn't start until about 9 o'clock that time of year, but I certainly couldn't wait that long and remain at least somewhat sane. So, I made arrangements with her to go early and hit the London Inn for burgers, onion rings, and shakes. I also knew that a lot of my friends would be hanging out there, since it was the favorite burger joint in all Duluth. I was excited about showing up with Shelley. I just figured that a little posing with one of the most popular girls in school would do wonders for my reputation. Okay, I admit that was kind of selfish and shallow of me but I wasn't exactly Mr. Popularity. Now it's not like people hated me or anything, in fact it was probably quite the opposite. I think I was just known as this nice, easy-going, tall, Swede who people knew but didn't get too excited about. I was probably like the cream sauce my mom made for some of her Swedish dishes. I was just kind of white and bland, nothing too colorful that would catch your eye. And I certainly would never have been termed spicy. The one and only Taco Bell in town served the city's spiciest foods and most people were kind of nervous to go there. Who knows what kind of trouble you could get into if you had an extra hot sauce packet on your taco? I think people would describe me as Swedish cream sauce and that didn't exactly give me personality plus. But tonight, all that was going to change. I was going to show up at the London Inn with Shelley Whitney and subtly make it known that we were heading for the Skyline. Oh, what a night this was going to be.

At exactly 7 o'clock that evening I was just ready to jump into my dad's 1965 Chevy station wagon and drive the 20 minutes to Shelley's house. I'd have to circle the block a few times because I always prided myself on being annoyingly punctual. Just as I was getting ready to leave my house, having brushed my teeth, combed my hair in the popular surfer cut of the pre-hippie days and double checked my wallet for money, the phone rang. I picked it up and said "Hello" and a very scratchy sounding voice said, "Is this John?" And I said "Yes", not liking what I was feeling inside. Scratchy Voice said "This is Shelley. I'm so sorry John, I came down with a bad cold and cough and I'm not going to be able to make our date. I'm sorry that it's such late notice but it just came on this afternoon. I wouldn't want to give this to you, it's pretty bad. I hope I can see you at school next week." So, I said, "Sure, that's all right Shelley, I just hope you're going to feel better." We said our goodbyes and I sat there for several minutes trying to understand why the whole universe was against me. I could've been on a date with Shelley Whitney but instead I'll probably just stay at home and watch reruns of "I Love Lucy." Now there's an exciting way to spend a Friday night. John Larson aka "Bland White Cream Sauce" strikes again.

But just as I was going to take the final plunge into the pit of despair, a brilliant idea flashed through my mind. I know she can't go out of the house, but that doesn't mean I can't go over there. I don't mean to stay or anything like that, I just mean to make a very quick, but endearing sick call. I'll pick her up a small box of chocolates and a beautiful "get well "card and I'll just drive over there and drop it off. Maybe I'll at least get to see her for a couple of minutes, but even if I don't, I'll have accomplished a great deal. Shelley will realize what a thoughtful and kind guy I really am and perhaps come to think of me as a good catch, sweet and endearing. And if her mom answers the door and I tell her that I'm John and that the candy and card are for Shelley, her mother's heart will melt and I will have won her over in a second. And when you've got mom on your side, that's a very good thing. This idea was a strategic move of pure genius. And so, I went out and got a card and a box of candy. I wrote a nice note on the card, nothing too mushy, but just enough that it would pull at her heartstrings. I drove over to Shelley's house, hoping that either Shelley or her mother would answer the door. As it turned out, after knocking a couple times, a very nice-looking lady opened the door, and smiled at me. Now I could understand where Shelley got her looks. Her mother was very attractive and interested in what I was doing there. I introduced myself and said, "Hi Mrs. Whitney. I wonder if I could see Shelley for just a minute or two?" I was about to say that I'd heard she was sick. But before I got the chance Mrs. Whitney said, "Oh, I'm sorry John, she's out on a date. She just left about 15 minutes ago." Well, the bottom fell out right there. But a funny thing happened, something I wasn't quite expecting. I suddenly felt something stirring inside of me, something I wasn't really used to feeling all that much. The best way to describe it is that I went from being a "bland white cream sauce" to being a packet of Taco Bell Picante in a split second. In other words, I was ticked. Shelley Whitney stood me up and is probably on her date thinking she really put one over on me. So, I was mad, but I didn't let it show. I just asked her mom to please give Shelley the box of chocolates and the card. When her mom looked puzzled I said, "Oh, she'll know what it's about." And she said "Okay, I'll be sure she gets this. It was nice to meet you John." "It was nice to meet you too, Mrs. Whitney." She was so pretty and nice I almost wished I could take her to the Skyline Drive-in, but I suppose there was a husband in the picture some place, so what are you going to do?

As I drove home I was processing the whole evening, trying to figure out what had happened. Why couldn't it have worked out? I thought about it over the weekend and came to understand something that actually bothered me a bit. What I was feeling for Shelley wasn't love or anything like that. It actually boiled down to three things. She was pretty, she was popular and she could do wonders for my reputation. Instead of being bland, I could be spicy. When this revelation came to me I felt badly and asked the Lord to forgive my selfishness. I didn't like that she had deceived me, but was her deception worse than mine? Of course not. Over the next several days at school I would see Shelley in the halls and just say a friendly "hi." She would return the greeting and walk on. As strange as it sounds, we never even acknowledged what had transpired on that very weird Friday night in early May. I never mentioned her standing me up for another guy, and she never mentioned the chocolates or the card. Why we never talked about that I don't know. Maybe on some level we were both too embarrassed. I came to find out a few days later from a buddy of mine, who's dating Shelley's best friend, why Shelley stood me up. Get this: she heard that I didn't drink or smoke pot and she just felt that I would be too boring for her. And so, she decided to go out with another guy instead, someone who did all of that and, I suspect, more. Maybe she was just too much woman for me. Well, that's all right, maybe God had His hand on me after all. Maybe He cared about everything in the world; even a person's dating life. I didn't hate Shelley and she didn't hate me. We even signed each other's yearbooks just before graduation in June. I've never seen her since and that's all right. But I will say this; it was a pretty long time before I actually asked another girl out, and that wasn't until I got to college. I guess I just learned that relationships have a great potential to break when they take a wrong turn. I didn't want to experience that again, so I pretty much backed off from relationships. At least I did, until I met Wendy. Shelley standing me up hurt and embarrassed me, but Wendy turning me down and running away just about did me in. And after she left, every time I got up to preach was a struggle. How could I preach to my flock about the hope that is theirs in Christ, when I feel absolutely hopeless? I knew I was in crisis and I honestly didn't know if I was going to pull through.

Chapter 2

Wendy

WHEN JOHN DROPPED TO ONE KNEE I SUD-
denly felt a wave of panic work its way through me
like an emotional tsunami. We had talked about marriage, but there's something you need to understand about me. I'm
what you might call "damaged goods." Now, I know how I come
across. I'm a fairly pretty blonde, blue-eyed woman of 27 years and I
have a nice personality. John would say that I'm absolutely stunning
and I'm the sweetest person he's ever known. He would say that I'm
God's most wonderful creation and that I always make his heart skip a

beat. John says all kinds of things about me that are both a little embarrassing and yet, at the same time, wonderful to hear. In fact, whenever he says those heartfelt words of what I can only conclude have to do with the whole "love is blind" thing, I feel kind of warm inside. I don't really believe those things about myself, but I'm glad he does. And I'm also glad he shares his thoughts with me so openly, because in all reality, it makes me feel like maybe I'm really worth something. It gives me a measure of hope that maybe my purpose on earth isn't just to be someone or something that's to be used for a while in various, rather tawdry ways, and then cast aside when something better comes along. You see, I've heard those kinds of words all my life. A lot of men, over the years, have said some of those same words and phrases to me and, as much as I wanted to believe them and feel like I'm worth something, the words, feelings, the hope that began to take root never lasted. I learned pretty early on that when a man was done with me and he had gotten everything he felt I could give him, he just discarded me like a piece of trash. And honestly, that's what I've felt like for most of my life. A used up, discarded, piece of trash. Whenever someone new came into my life and expressed words of love and devotion, I'd begin the cycle all over again. It would start with the exciting hope of a new relationship and then just keep progressing until I felt that this was the real deal; this man really loved me. I would have visions of our wedding and of the life we'd have together. The future would begin to look a little brighter, the love a little stronger, and the hopeful dreams a certain reality. But that was all a pipe dream, an emotional sham. A cruel joke. Whatever you want to call those dreams and visions, always in the back of my mind was this nagging thought of being used. This new guy wasn't going to hang around long enough for us to make a life together. What a joke. He was going to be like everybody else in my life. He was going to get what he wanted from me on every level and then, when the novelty and excitement of whatever we had together wore off, he'd be on to the next conquest and I'd be left crying in my sheets. Well, it doesn't take too long before you begin to see that as normal, at least normal for you. And who knows, maybe that kind of life, that kind of selfishness is common to everyone, not just me. Sometimes it makes me wonder why I even bother getting up in the morning. Why should I drag myself out of bed and face the cold, cruel world that's absolutely sucking the life out of me? I'm on a merry-go-round but there's nothing merry about it. It's just the idea of going round and round, seeing the same scenery every few seconds, and recognizing that there's no way off. I don't know how to stop it and that scares me to death. There's a real difference being on a merry-go-round by choice and being stuck on one. When you have a choice, that merry-go-round can be fun and exciting, but being stuck on one brings a desperate panic. You want to jump off, but you can't. And when the realization hits you that you're stuck there forever you slowly, agonizingly, began to die inside, until one day you know you're dead. You're still breathing. You're still doing some of the same basic things that other people do, but you know, beyond a shadow of a doubt, you're absolutely, positively, 100% dead. And believe me, it's not a place you want to be. I knew there was no resurrection in my future. There was nothing but the cold, empty tomb of my broken life. That was my purpose, that was my destiny.

I grew up in Chicago and from the very beginning my life was chaotic. My mother was a beautiful woman at one time, but by her 30th birthday she developed a very cold and harsh demeanor. She didn't trust anybody and she definitely never forgave anyone. She held onto her anger and her unforgiveness all of her life and it prematurely aged her. At 30 she looked 45, at 45 she looked 65. She had a hard life and really didn't know the first thing about being a mom. In reality all she was doing was repeating what she had grown up with. Her mom was the same way. It's not like her mom didn't love her, it's just that her mom couldn't get out of the chaos of the consequences of frequent bad choices. There were men that would come in and out of my grandma's little apartment all the time. According to my mom, when she and I would have the occasional talk, my grandma always thought the new guy was the answer to all her problems. He was going to love and care for her and her kid, and her life was going to be better from that point on. But, of course, it never was. Mom remembers a fairly constant stream of guys going in and out of her life as a little girl. Some were nice but others were not. In fact, my mom would sometimes describe them as pure evil and they would bring a dark presence to the place. My mom hated growing up like that. She hated the chaos and the drama. She hated that she could never seem to obtain the one thing she desperately wanted. And that one thing was a sense of stability, a sense of security. It wasn't the latest gadget, or the latest fashion, or the latest movie idol that mom longed for. It was simply the desire to feel safe and secure, to feel genuinely loved and cared for. But she never got it. The elusive gift never came. And because it never came, mom had no choice but to find a way to make it on her own. And so, she did. Being beautiful helped, at least for a while. But mom discovered something early on. Being beautiful is both a blessing and a curse. It can open up a lot of doors, yes, but when the beauty isn't controlled properly, when it's used in the wrong way, the doors that are opened can wind up being very scary indeed. Mom grew up in a chaotic household, where they seemed to live from crisis to crisis with never a happy-ever-after ending in sight. Mom hated it and struck out on her own early in life. She hated her life growing up, and yet, that was the same world she brought me into. I never knew my father; he could have been one of many men that drifted in and out of her life. That was always hard for me, and yet, as I look back, maybe it was a sort of backward blessing. Who knows what my father might've been like. Maybe it was good that he wasn't in the picture. Oh well, I haven't even thought about him in years.

Life with mom was pretty crazy. Sometimes things seemed to be better, less wild, less filled with stress. Mom worked as a waitress at a little 24-hour diner down the street. Guys would get off from the late shift at one of the large factories in the area and drop in for a late dinner or early breakfast. She made minimum wage, plus tips, but people in that poor, rundown neighborhood were lousy tippers. Sometimes she'd turn on the charm and some guy would leave a bigger tip, but that really didn't happen too often. For the most part we just barely made ends meet and mom felt that her only way to truly escape this life was to meet a man. Not just any man, but a rich, successful man who could rescue us from this hell on earth. And, believe me, there were lots of men. But her knight-in-shining-armor never did come and rescue her. And, even to this day, she's still hoping to be rescued. I feel sorry for her but there were some things that happened that finally made it impossible for me to stay in Chicago. I know mom didn't want me to leave, especially not knowing where I was going. But all I could say, in the note I left on her nightstand was that things had gotten a little out of control and I needed to head out, at least for a while. Travis and I would be safe and we would contact her when we could. But other than a couple of phone calls while we were running to what seemed like the other side of the world, I really hadn't contacted her. I didn't want her to know where we were. It was just better all-around if nobody, but me, knew our whereabouts.

Chapter 3

John

AS YOU CAN PROBABLY TELL FROM MY EXPERI-
ence with Shelley, I wasn't exactly excited about getting
my heart crushed again. Being stood up by Shelley wasn't
that big a deal, but it hurt my pride and left me wondering why being
a little conservative was a bad thing. You'd think they'd want a guy
who didn't drink or smoke pot or expect a girl to jump in the sack with
him on the first date. But it was the late 60s and the whole hippie thing
was just beginning to become a genuine worldwide movement. Guys'
hair was getting longer, peace protests were popping up in major cities

around the country, young men were burning their draft cards and slogans like "Make Love Not War" were gaining in popularity with the younger hippie crowd. The older folks hated all of it because it seemed to cast disdain on their fervent patriotism and common sense view of right and wrong. Let's just say that the whole movement did indeed bring some sweeping changes to our world, some good and some not so good. We were kind of stuck in this war that was being fought in the rice paddies of far off Vietnam. I'm not sure I could have even pointed Vietnam out on a map until my high school World Problems class taught me to begin to look outside myself.

I knew the world was in turmoil, but I didn't really know how to fix it and so I just continued on doing my own thing. They were doing a lottery draft by this time and because I drew a very high number I escaped. I felt bad about that in one way, but I just figured that wearing a military uniform just wasn't meant to be in my future. But then I thought about all the guys who had served their country, and so, after much thought and prayer, I decided to enlist in the Army as soon as I got out of high school. My mom was very anxious about this move and couldn't understand my reasoning. My dad, on the other hand, was proud of me and yet was anxious as well. To make a long story short, I went to enlist and wound up flunking the physical of all things. I had a condition that I can't even begin to pronounce but, suffice it to say, they didn't want me. I couldn't believe it. I'd always heard that the Army would take anybody as long as you were breathing. Well, I was breathing all right, but evidently not good enough and that was part of the problem. I'd always battled asthma and took medication to control it. But it especially flared up during strenuous physical workouts and, being in sports early on, just brought my condition to the forefront.

So I chose sports where I wouldn't have sustained periods of running like track or basketball. I stuck with those sports where I would need to run for just a short period of time, like baseball, boxing and even some weightlifting. I was in pretty good shape, but the Army wasn't about to take a chance on a guy who had what they considered pretty severe asthma. I walked out of the enlistment office and began to seek guidance about where to go from here. I was disappointed on one hand, but I've always figured that things happen for a reason. And so, I began to plan the next part of my life. Without the draft hanging over my head anymore, I was free to pursue my own personal dreams and goals. But honestly, I had no idea what my dreams and goals were. I'd always gone through high school figuring I'd be drafted for a couple years of service. But after the lottery drawing I knew I was off the hook. So after being out of high school for a few months and finding out that my military service wasn't required, I suddenly had my whole life ahead of me and didn't have the foggiest notion what to do with it.

I'd always received pretty good grades in school, but hadn't really decided what I wanted to pursue for a career. And so I just continued to work at "Gunner's Mighty Fine Junk". I know that's an odd name but that's what it was. Gunner was this old, crusty guy who had been in the junk business for over 40 years. You can't believe what Gunner had around his place. If they didn't have it, it was a pretty sure bet nobody did, at least not in Duluth. They had a huge yard full of cars that had either been totaled or abandoned. People would come in looking for a specific part from a vintage Chevy and sure enough Gunner would find the part for them. But he didn't just deal in auto parts. He also had a store that stocked items that people either had given him to get them out of the house and clean up years of clutter, or they had sold to him for a few extra dollars cash. And interestingly enough, if you knew what to look for, you could get some pretty good deals at "Gunner's Mighty Fine Junk." I still remember the guy who came in looking for some used records and Gunner had six or seven shelves of them. This guy stood there methodically looking through every record on the shelves and, when he was done, he bought several. Some were just the typical artists you'd expect to find in a place that dealt in used items. But one record didn't have a cover and was just standing there on its own. Over the last year or so nobody really had paid much attention to this lone record, with the hand-written label attached. Imagine Gunner's surprise, when a year or two after the sale, an article appeared in the paper about how this guy had found a record that turned out to be quite valuable. That unmarked record that every-body skipped over turned out to be a demo by some unknown guy who was born in Duluth and grew up in nearby Hibbing. This demo was the first recording ever made of a young Bob Dylan, one of the most provocative voices of the hippie generation. That record even-tually sold for thousands of dollars and when Gunner found out about the article, and the treasure he had let slip through his hands, he said, "Huh, who knew? Who's Bob Dylan anyway?" I guess there really was a generation gap.

But that article about Bob Dylan's record hiding in the middle of all that other junk began to eat away at me. There it was, hiding in plain sight. If Gunner had recognized the value of this gift he could have made a great deal of money. But that was the problem. He didn't recognize the value of what was there right in front of him all the time.

So, I'm thinking about that one Sunday night while sitting in the evening service at the Our Savior's Baptist Church my family had attended almost my entire life. I had given my heart to the Lord and had been baptized early on in my elementary years. And my faith was quite important to me. That's one of the reasons that I didn't do some of the things that Shelley Whitney wanted in the guys she dated. I mean, I wasn't crazy religious or anything like that, but I was strong enough in my faith that I knew I wanted to live in such a way as to be pleasing to the Lord. I didn't want to do anything that would bring sadness to His heart. And so, I just tried to live in a way that would honor Him.

But as much as I was committed to my faith and wanting to live it out on an everyday, practical level, the idea of my faith determining my future didn't really compute with me for some reason. As odd as it sounds, I never really asked the Lord what His plans were for my life. What did He want for me in these short 70-80 years here on earth? I just figured that I was simply an ordinary guy with some gifts and talents like everybody else, but what does that have to do with my future? Things weren't connecting, at least not until that night sitting in church.

So here I am, sitting in the pew while the pastor is delivering his sermon but my mind is wandering. I'm still thinking about that record that Gunner had sold for $.50 and was now worth several thousands of dollars. And as I'm thinking about that a thought came to me that was destined to change my life. Looking back on it, the thought I had was what I would later call the "still, small voice of God." But the voice that spoke to my spirit said, "You are just like that record. You're very valuable, you just don't know it. You've been spinning round and round, not really knowing where to go and what to do. You're hiding in plain sight, but that needs to stop. Let me reveal your true value.

Let me show you what I've always intended for your life. Quit going round and round like a record. I've already purchased you; now let me take you off the shelf." Well, let me just say this: When the Lord tells you things like that, you sit up and listen, believe me.

I left the service that night in a bit of a daze. It wasn't an unpleasant daze and it wasn't like I was walking around like a zombie, I just mean that I knew I had encountered God in a marvelous way. Now, it's not that I'd never heard God's voice before leading and guiding me through thoughts and impressions. That was pretty common actually. I suppose a lot of others would describe that as being the "voice of God," while I would simply say "I just feel that God is leading this way" or "I just feel that this is what God wants me to do." Do you see? I would get impressions inside me and I would oftentimes make decisions based on those feelings. And, sure enough, when I would follow those impressions, things usually worked out pretty well. I mean life wasn't perfect, but I never felt I was trapped in a chaotic world that was spinning out of control. But what I heard that night in church was something different. It really was like the voice of God speaking directly into my head. I couldn't have missed it if I'd tried. As secure as I felt at that time in my life, God let me know clearly that I needed to stop going round and round like a broken record. And neither was He going to let me just sit on the shelf hiding out. He wanted to take me down off that shelf and actually use me, because I had more value than I thought I did. And when I heard those thoughts in my head they were rather confusing. I wasn't sure I really saw the value that God seem to be referring to in me.

Now part of me, the timid, kind of "inferiority complex" part of me, tried to argue with the thought of being valuable. It's not like

I thought I was a horrible person. It's not like I felt stupid or incapable of doing anything worthwhile, it's just that I was still stuck in this "bland, white cream sauce" mentality. Yeah, I could add a little flavor to a Swedish dish, but I would never be seen as incredibly delicious and absolutely essential for culinary success. I guess another way to say that is I was just a pretty ordinary guy who wasn't exactly tearing up the track in any area of my life. And as I thought all of this over, I kept landing at the same spot. God's still, small voice let me know that I was valuable to Him. That wasn't a new thought necessarily because I grew up knowing that God loved me. At the risk of sounding sacrilegious, I guess I always thought of the idea of God loving me as being His job. That's just who He is and what He does. He loves everybody, all over the world. "God is love." Everybody knows that, it doesn't take a genius to discover that in the Scripture. I guess I just always felt that God was like your mom. She had to tell you what a fine boy you were and how much she loved you. And yeah, it was good to hear it but it wasn't exactly earthshaking because she's your mom, that kind of stuff was in her job description. That's how I viewed God, I guess. But that night in church and hearing God so clearly kind of shook me up. I couldn't get those thoughts out of my mind. God wanted to take me off the shelf. He didn't want me hiding out up there. But neither did he want me to spin round and round like a broken record, never really getting anywhere or completing anything. He had other plans for my life. The big question, of course, was whether I was interested enough to go along with His plans. You see one thing I learned early in Sunday school is that we have a free will. In other words, I can choose to go my own way, make my own decisions and set my own path to the future. I think my pastor used the term "free moral agent," meaning that I certainly had the power to choose my own way and make my own destiny. But as I considered what the Lord had spoken to me clearly that night, I came to a very important conclusion. In fact it was a conclusion that was going to set the direction of my life. I very wisely came to understand that I'd be an idiot not to take God up on –His offer. If He wanted to take me off the shelf, whatever that meant exactly, who was I to argue? Why wouldn't I want God to do that? Who wants to be stuck on a shelf? Or who wants to spend their life going round and round, but never completing anything? I finally got it through my thick skull that maybe I needed to spend some time alone with God. So that night I went up to my bedroom and simply sat there, thinking about what I'd heard Him say. And finally, I slid from the edge of my bed to the floor. I leaned my elbows on my bed, closed my eyes and began to pray what would turn out to be the second most important prayer of my life. The number one prayer was asking Jesus to be my Savior. But this prayer went further than that. I was now asking Jesus to be my Lord. I'm not sure I had fully understood that concept before. In fact, I'm not sure I fully understand the concept now, even as a pastor, but I'm learning more about it every day. I said, "Lord, I love you. I've always loved you. But I just want to say something. I will do anything, be anything, go anywhere you want me to go but please, just use me. Please God, take me down off the shelf and just use me." And that was it. No long prayers. No flowery King James English. No exacting promises of what I would do if He would do His part. No deal making - no "fine print" - no "this will be final, contingent upon the following conditions being met"- none of that kind of thing. Just a simple prayer that basically meant "Use me Lord. I'm yours to command." And guess what? Without really knowing it at the time, an epic adventure had begun.

Chapter 4

Wendy

GROWING UP WITH MOM WAS LIKE BEING trapped in a schizophrenic world of randomness. Sometimes mom could be really nice and we'd bake some cookies or some other decadent dessert, if we had a few extra bucks. And during those times something rather wonderful began to take place. I can only describe it as a kind of bonding that made us feel good and maybe a little hopeful. Maybe we really could ride this emotional roller coaster we'd been on all these years and bring it back safely to the launching point. Maybe the next ride will be a little less frenetic. But, as much as we hoped and dreamed, it just never happened. Mom was over-the-top stressed out about work and finances and, of course, relationships. Something had to give somewhere or it wasn't going to end well at all. In spite of our occasional cookie baking fests we just grew further apart. To be perfectly honest I wanted a different life. And above all, though I loved my mother, I didn't want to be like her. I didn't want her life, and I especially didn't want her view of life. I think I was naïve enough to think that mine could be better if I just made some wiser choices that didn't always seem to either implode on themselves, leaving a sense of personal defeat, or explode in a blast that shattered whatever little dream was playing at that moment. I didn't want that. I wanted something better for myself. I would've taken mom along with me on this venture to a new way of viewing life, but I felt that she was trapped in this chaotic world she had made for herself. I also discerned, over time, that she was somehow, as crazy as it sounds, fine with that. At least that's the way it came across to me when I was 15. And maybe I couldn't change my circumstances; maybe I was just as stuck as she was. But I was sure going to give it a try. And so, at the age of 15, I stopped in another small diner by my school and applied for a job. I looked 16 or 17, although I'm not sure the owner cared that much. I didn't want to work at the same diner as mom and this one was just a few blocks in the opposite direction. They couldn't give me many hours but they needed someone for a short, 3-6 shift. Just three hours a day but at minimum wage, plus tips, I felt as rich as Midas. I would keep half for myself to save, as my mom put it, for a rainy day. But the other half went into a pot for household expenses. That relieved the pressure some, but still, just as we seemed to be to be getting a little ahead, something would go wrong. Our toaster would break down and we'd have to buy a new one. Both mom and I practically lived on cheap, white bread toasted and topped with peanut butter. That was breakfast and, in really slim times, that was dinner too. Or, maybe the rent would be jacked up $25 a month. Now that doesn't sound all that bad, but when you're barely scraping by in the first place, $25 can be almost insurmountable. You either have to work more or you have to spend less. And when mom's hours were kept at a steady 30, so that the owner didn't have to pay benefits, you can see where this is going, can't you?

My first relationship with a guy came when I was 15 and waitressing at the diner after school. This guy, who was probably 20 or 21, came in one day and sat in my section. He ordered coffee and a piece of apple pie with a slice of cheese. I still don't get that cheese and pie thing, it just doesn't sound appetizing. Pie and ice cream, on the other hand, I totally get. Anyway, this guy comes in and orders coffee and pie and the first thing I noticed is that he was very good-looking. He was well dressed and had no problem flashing his money around when he opened his wallet. He looked out of place in this part of town, but who was I to question it? When I brought him a refill on his coffee he asked me what my name was. I told him it was Wendy and he said that I had a beautiful name, one that fit me perfectly. And, not having had much experience with guys, I asked him what he meant by that. And he said it was a beautiful name for a beautiful girl. Really? The only one who had ever told me I was beautiful was my mom, but I always figured that moms have to tell their daughters that, it's just the way it's supposed to be. And guys at school were just crude. They'd make comments about me when I passed them in the halls. Maybe in their young, stupid, adolescent minds they were thinking that I would take their comments and be flattered, but believe me, I wasn't. So when this guy told me I was beautiful, I bought it hook, line and sinker. I wanted to believe it so badly, because you see, if I was beautiful, then maybe I had value. I mean, beautiful things are valuable, right? Well he asked me if I'd like to go out with him some time to catch a movie or maybe dinner. And without thinking it through I said yes. We made a date for Friday night. Mom was working a late shift at her all-night diner, leaving me free to venture into this whole new world. Well, let me just say this. It wasn't at all what I was expecting.

He came and picked me up at our tiny apartment just before 7:00 PM. We went to dinner at Luigi's. I suppose most people would have thought the restaurant was all right, nothing too special, but I thought it was downright swanky. There were nice red and white checked tablecloths and a candle in the middle of each table setting. The waitress brought us goblets of water and a little basket of bread-sticks as an appetizer. We were looking at the menu and, for the life of me, I couldn't decide what to order. It's not that the dinners were all so expensive, it's just that when you've never been out to eat they all seemed over-the-top pricey. And being pretty inexperienced with this sort of thing I didn't want to pick anything too cheap and take a chance of insulting him. But neither did I want to order an expensive item and let him think I was a gold-digger. And so, just to play it safe, I ordered something that was in the middle. I ordered spaghetti with meatballs. Well, that was a mistake. When the dinner came I was shocked to see the size of the meatballs. There were three of them, each about the size of my fist. I'd never seen anything like that. The only spaghetti and meatballs I'd ever had was from a can of Chef Boyardee and those meatballs were the size of the tip of my pinky finger. I could've gone bowling with one of Luigi's. The other difficulty was the sauce. It was rich and thick, but halfway through the dinner I looked down at my blouse and it had little splotches of red all down the front. Somehow when I was eating, totally unbeknownst to me, I was splattering myself with the red sauce. I was so embarrassed I thought I would die. What's he going to think of me now? We go to dinner and I walk out looking like my whole chest had hemorrhaged. Real great start on a first date. Finally, the dinner was over and we headed back to my place. We'd been having some nice conversation during dinner and on the ride back. I was excited about being with this guy who seemed light years ahead of me in sophistication. Looking back on it I realize the conversation was just small talk that really didn't amount to much. When I asked him what he did for a living he told me "Oh, a little of this, and a little of that" and then he changed the subject. That should've been a giant red flag for me but again, I was young, what did I know? We got back to my place and he asked me if he could come up for a while and, without thinking it through, I invited him in. Big mistake! As soon as he realized that we were alone he was all over me. Remember, I had zero experience with guys, but I certainly had heard horror stories from some of my other girlfriends at school. Now, the first time he kissed me I thought I was going to die. I had never experienced anything quite like this and believe me, I liked the feelings I was having. They were warm and cozy and felt very intimate. I'm not quite sure how to express it but I felt pretty good. But then he started getting very aggressive and I knew he wanted to go further. I mean even though I was inexperienced, I certainly knew I wasn't ready for this and the harder he tried, the harder I resisted. I know he was trying to wear me down with his persistence. Now, I may be a nice person and I may come across as sweet, but I can also be pretty stubborn and so I kept moving his hands away from places they shouldn't be. But what scared me is how strong he was and it was getting tougher to stop his aggressive behavior toward me. He pushed me down on the couch and tried to climb on top of me, but I rolled off and landed on my stomach, knocking the wind out of me. And as he came at me again I guess the combination of those huge meatballs, along with getting the wind knocked out of me, was just a little too much. When he came at me, my stomach suddenly lurched and I threw up all over his shirt. I don't know if that was his favorite shirt or what, but he got instantly furious. And he began to call me names, some I'd never even heard of before. I was sitting down with spaghetti and meatballs all down the front. I was feeling sick to my stomach. That was bad enough. But I was also feeling sick emotionally. I was all mixed up and had a hundred random thoughts running through my mind simultaneously. What had I done to bring on this kind of first-date experience? Why did he seem so nice at dinner, but change so drastically once I invited him into the apartment? Had I missed out on some kind of cue I should just naturally have known? Did I not act like you're supposed to act with the guy? In other words, what he was wanting to do, was that just all part of the dating game and I hadn't played by the rules? I was pretty confused and really needed time to think, yet he was still there. But he stood up and said, "How could I have ever thought you were beautiful? You're nothing but a piece of trash. You look like something that got dragged in off the street and I wouldn't touch you now even if you begged me. But let me tell you something, slut. You've only got one thing guys want and that's your body. That's all you've got going for you, otherwise, you're pretty much worthless. Grow up and put out! If you don't, you'll never get out of this dump you call home. Remember, you're nothing but a piece of trash and that's all you'll ever be." And with that he spit in my face and walked out the door.

I was crying hard by this time, but as soon as the door slammed, I got up and locked it. I then went into the bathroom and got sick again. I slowly got up from the bathroom floor, turned on the water and took a long, hot shower. I must've been in there for 20 minutes because the water was beginning to get cold. But no matter how long I stayed in the shower, and how hard I scrubbed, I just couldn't get feeling clean again. I finally turned the shower off, dried myself with a towel and got into bed. Mom wouldn't be home for another couple of hours but I didn't want to be up when she arrived. I couldn't bear the thought of discussing what had happened with her. First of all, she didn't even know I had gone out. I never asked her permission because I knew exactly what she'd say. She'd say "no," and I didn't want to hear that. I wanted to go out with him and find out what all the fuss was about. So I got into bed, wanting to just go to sleep and wake up realizing that the whole evening had been a terrible nightmare. I lay there a long time just running through the events of the evening. I finally began to drift off to sleep and that was good. I welcomed the sleep, because I was exhausted in my mind, body and spirit. The night with the guy from the diner was over. I knew I'd never see him again and that was just fine with me. I determined to go on and not look back. I decided that the night was just a very hard, very uncomfortable lesson about life and I needed to pick myself up and learn from it. That's what I decided to do when I found myself drifting off to sleep. The only problem was, I couldn't get those words out of my mind. I couldn't stop thinking about his angry, hateful words when he looked at me with such venom and disgust. I shuddered and recalled, with sickening dismay, his words of prophecy over me: "You've only got one thing guys want and that's your body. That's all you've got going for you, otherwise, you're pretty much worthless. Remember this: You're nothing but a piece of trash and that's all you'll ever be." With these words ringing in my ears, like church bells gone mad, I fell into a troubled sleep, wondering if they were really true.

Chapter 5

John

I WOKE UP THE NEXT MORNING, AFTER MY NIGHT OF commitment, expecting something dramatic like rose petals magically appearing on my bed covers, a sign that God had heard my prayer and was quite pleased. Or maybe I'd look outside and see a bright, sunny day when the forecast had been for a cloudy and gray depressing drizzle. But sure enough, no rose petals, no sunshine, no blue sky, nothing but gray. Now that was kind of a letdown because I thought for sure that something amazing was going to happen almost immediately after I laid myself bare before the God of the universe. A miraculous sign would have been nice to kind of seal the deal. Nothing too fancy, nothing too extravagant, but at least a little something. Maybe God would let my mom know that today was special and so she'd make Belgian waffles with strawberries and whipped cream for breakfast. She always did that on special occasions. But when I walked downstairs there was a box of Cheerios and a carton of milk on the table. I like Cheerios, but they're not usually my choice for a special occasion. Maybe I could have had frosted Cheerios at least. Oh well, the prayer still stands, frosted Cheerios or not.

Working at "Gunner's Mighty Fine Junk" was all right for now, but it certainly wasn't going to be any kind of a career for me. I mean Gunner might have been doing great financially, but the rest of us were making minimum wage and trying to figure out how to get our next tank of gas. So here I am, working away all day in Gunners establishment, just stocking shelves with all kinds of odds and ends that were one-of-a-kind items. Sometimes we actually sold these little knick-knacks and do-dads by the bag. We'd take a bunch of these off-the-wall, unusual items that would never sell in a million years, and just dump a bunch of them in brightly colored sacks that were printed with the words "Grab Bag." And wouldn't you know it, they sold like hot cakes. People couldn't resist the thrill of knowing they were going to get all kinds of surprises in this bag for a measly buck. What a deal. Who knew what incredibly rare items and hidden treasures could be lurking in that bag, just waiting to be discovered? People loved it, and believe it or not, we never had any complaints.

I actually rather enjoyed working at "Gunner's Mighty Fine Junk." In fact, I had spent most of my high school days working there after school. My buddy Ken got me the job and so we worked together for all three years, once we turned 16. I always worked in the store and Ken always worked in the auto yard. He was mechanically inclined whereas I was an idiot when it came to anything even remotely mechanical. Now, Gunner had discovered pretty quickly that Ken was quite handy and loved working with the cars. So he'd send Ken down to extract a certain part from a wrecked 65 Chevy and he'd be back with the part in record time. The only time Gunner got seriously ticked off at Ken and probably thought about firing him, was when he was supposed to go down to this one Buick and cut out a certain part. So Ken goes down with one of those torches that ate through metal and he starts burning. Well, Ken's mind was elsewhere that day, probably thinking about his girlfriend Sharon, and he got a little careless. He looked away for a few seconds and, by the time he looked back, he realized that some oil drippings had caught on fire. It took him less than a second to see that the oil drippings were heading right toward the gas tank and this wasn't going to end well at all. So Ken goes tearing out of there just in time and dove behind a huge metal barrel. A half second later an explosion rocked the entire yard and that car went flying 15 feet into the air, flipped over, and landed on its top. Gunner comes running out of the little trailer he had parked there to use as an office and he's absolutely white as a ghost. He doesn't see Ken behind the barrel and he's got visions of having to pick up pieces of his favorite yard boy. When Ken finally comes out from behind the barrel, looking very sheepish, Gunner goes from sheer panic to over-the-top boiling. His face turns red as a beet and he slips into a kind of broken Swedish dialect that I didn't understand but I'm sure was laced with all kinds of abusive, character-bashing phrases that would make anyone else flee in sheer terror. But Ken just stands there and takes it for the whole seven minute tirade. And then Gunner finally runs out of steam and he looks at Ken and says, "Ya stupid kid, whaddaya gottta say for yourself?" And Ken looks at him and says, "Well, I never did like that model of Buick". And Gunner just stares at Ken, with a blank look on his face and I say to myself, "Oh boy Ken, wrong answer. This isn't the time to be wise-cracking." Gunner stares at Ken and pretty soon a smile begins to play at the corners of his mouth. The smile gets a little bigger, and a little bigger, until Gunner is laughing his head off. And pretty soon we're all rolling on the ground laughing our heads off too. I'm not sure exactly what it was we were laughing at, but when the boss laughs, you just join right in. I think all of us were so thankful that nobody had gotten hurt. Even Ken walked away with just a little ringing in his ears. But I can tell you this. Gunner never gave Ken the torch again. He wasn't about to test his luck a second time. Stupid kid!

I may have joined in all the laughter that day and gave my buddy Ken a bad time about it, but for the next few days I continued to think about that explosion. I was so thankful that no one got hurt and that everything turned out fine. But I also realized how precious life really is. And when you're young you think you're invincible and you're going to live forever. Well, after something like that, you're not so sure. One or two seconds more working under that car and Ken would have been a goner and we'd still be looking for body parts. Not a pleas-ant thought.

I think that's what made me decide to go to school, not because I didn't like working at "Gunner's," but because I felt life could be rather fleeting and I needed to get going on a career. I needed to keep my promise to the Lord in mind. I wanted to serve Him for the rest of my life. And so, once again, I spent time in prayer asking the Lord what I should do. I was pretty sure I needed to go to school for some kind of further education and training, but I wasn't entirely sure what that would be. There are all kinds of ways to serve the Lord, in all kinds of careers. The most obvious choice for me would seem to be something in the arts. I had always drifted to drama and music since I had zero talent mechanically. I'd been in plays at school since I was in Junior High and was pretty comfortable being up in front of people. I liked writing speeches and short stories and always seemed to get good grades and lots of compliments from my friends when I gave the speech or read the story. I also enjoyed singing in choirs and various small ensembles both at school and at church. I even sang a solo once in a while and people were very kind and encouraging. As I'm thinking about all of that, it's like the Lord brings it all together for me as I'm driving to pick up a pepperoni pizza for the family dinner. I was thinking of all the things I like doing, and the fact that after working at Gunners store I began to be energized by helping people. I had truly enjoyed participating in a summer mission trip to Mexico that last summer. Our youth pastor had lined up for us to go down to a little coastal border town and help construct houses for people who were homeless after a huge storm had flattened a good portion of their city. All of those thoughts were beginning to gel together and, as I'm trying to make sense of it, the Lord once again speaks to me in my thoughts. It's like God was saying: "John, if you want to serve me, then use the gifts I've given you because they've always brought you great pleasure and fulfillment. I want you to be a pastor and share my gospel using what I've given you to shepherd my flock. John, feed my sheep and take care of my precious lambs. Each one is vastly important to me. Go back to school and train to become a good shepherd who can lead his flock with kindness and compassion, as well as strength and honor. Use your gifts and love people in my name." And that was it. By the time I had picked up our pepperoni pizza, and was heading home, I knew what my future looked like. I was going to go to one of several Christian colleges in the area and get my four year degree. And then I'd go on to seminary and train for the ministry. It was kind of daunting actually. The idea of spending the next seven years in school wasn't a very pleasant thought, to tell you the truth. And yet, if I was going to serve the Lord then I needed to do it in the right way, and that meant years of training. I had been involved in my church for years, everything from singing in the choir, to teaching a Sunday school class for sixth grade boys, to working with Junior Higher's as one of their leaders. Actually, after working with the Junior Higher's and trying to help them through the various dramas unfolding in their lives, the idea of pastoring a church didn't seem quite so intimidating. I always figured if you could handle 30 hormone-driven 12-15-year-olds and still come away with at least some semblance of sanity, pastoring a church would be a piece of cake.

That next September I enrolled in Bethel College, the school sponsored by my denomination. I took all the prerequisites for the first two years and then decided to double major in speech and choral music. Now, my last year there as a senior was pretty nerve-racking. All my classes that year were performance classes, meaning I had to be up in front of people several times a week. I had speeches to prepare and present to my fellow students. I had choir concerts as well as various solo recitals to prepare. The concerts were always good, although the preparation was a bear. The vocal solo recitals were a little more challenging. I mean it's not like I could get up and sing my favorite gospel songs or some of the new Scripture choruses that were coming out of the Jesus People Movement. We had to choose classical numbers that would really exhibit our vocal range and technique. It was very difficult, and yet looking back it was exactly the kind of training I needed because it wasn't just about learning how to write speeches and singing in solo and ensemble recitals. It taught me something else so very valuable. It taught me the discipline I needed to always work ahead and be prepared for any unforeseen event that may come up. I didn't realize how often I would need to call on that discipline when I became a pastor. In fact, pastoring a church, I came to discover, wasn't a 40-hour work week where you punch the time clock. Your days didn't always turn out exactly the way you had planned on your calendar. And yet, no matter who got sick, or what marriage crisis you were helping to manage, or how bad the roof in the sanctuary was leaking, you still had to have that sermon by 11 o'clock every Sunday morning, no matter what. Thank God that he taught me the discipline of always being prepared in advance. I think that saved my bacon on several different occasions.

Chapter 6

Wendy

IT'S SCARY TO THINK THAT ONE COMBINATION OF words that you use in everyday language, when placed in a specific order, can impact your life forever. If you took all the words and used them in sentences with a different context, they'd be no big deal, right? "This handful of coupons I've been saving have all expired, they're worthless." "I better take the trash out, it's really building up." "Isn't God something? The human body is such a beautiful, marvelous creation." But words placed in certain combinations, within a specific context of anger and a desire to inflict pain can be devastating. They can effectively ruin your life and set your feet on a path to destruction. Maybe you've never thought about this before, but I have. I haven't only thought about it, I've lived it every day of my life.

When diner-guy told me things like I'm a worthless piece of trash and that the only thing I've got going for me is my body, you would think I'd get angry and fight back. Not with him necessarily, but with myself. You see, looking back on it, I should have kicked him out of my apartment and gone on a personal campaign to prove him overwhelmingly wrong. I should have picked myself up, looked in the mirror and said "Well, we'll just see about that." And then I should have started making a plan that would take me to the highest levels possible in terms of achievement. Worthless, huh? A piece of trash that's only got one thing going for her? I should have stood up, stiffened my back and said to myself, "I'm not going to let this man determine the course of my life. Watch me, because I'm going to shine." That's what I should have said. That should have been the launching point of a life of accomplishment, a life full of new and exciting experiences that enriched not only me, but those around me. But that's not what happened, not even close.

It seemed as though no matter what I did, or how many years had gone by, that horrible night just stuck to me like glue. No matter what I did I couldn't get the ringing of those destructive words out of my head. When I'd mess up on something at school, or on the job, it would just serve to strengthen my own pathetic self-talk. I had an image of myself that was going to be with me, I imagined, for my entire life. This is what I am and this is what I'll always be. End of story. I might as well get used to it and just survive.

So, over the next several years of high school I became quite popular with the guys. The girls all hated me, but I didn't really care about them. I didn't need their attention, but I definitely needed the attention of the guys.

I was fairly pretty and always enjoyed watching guys look at me when I walked by. It was almost funny, the way guys would stare at me, and follow me around with puppy- dog eyes filled with longing. It didn't take me too long to discover that I had a certain power over the male species. When I was feeling the need of a little more attention, I would just use my charms and they'd be putty in my hands. I loved that feeling of control. I never wanted to be in a place of fear and submission again, not ever! But here's what I couldn't figure out. I mean, I had no problem getting guys to look at me. I had no problem getting dates or getting a guy to give me his class ring as a sign of going together. We were a couple and everybody knew it. It made me feel proud. It boosted my ego and made me feel loved. But here's the thing I could never figure out. These marvelous, earth-shattering declarations of love and devotion never lasted more than a few months. More often than not, they would begin noticing someone else and were off to greener pastures. I didn't really worry all that much because I went to a big school and there were plenty of guys to go around, but what bothered me was that I'd really given everything to that relationship, and I mean everything. When I'd get together with the guy, I'd use everything I had to draw him to me and make him stick. I would let the relationship get pretty physical after the first date or two, thinking that he would recognize how much he loved me and wanted to spend his life making the woman of his dreams happy and fulfilled. I didn't realize it, but I was more like my mother than I ever wanted to admit. The knight-in-shining-armor fantasy was alive and well in me also, just like in my mom. The result was the same too. The fantasy of an exciting and beautiful rescue, leading to lifelong romance and devotion, would soon evaporate and I'd be back to my ordinary life once again. It wasn't until years later, after much self-discovery, that I realized that physical attributes and a willingness to be physically intimate certainly had the power to attract a guy. But there has to be more than that to make a relationship work; there also has to be genuine love and respect. And when there's no respect, it's pretty difficult to experience genuine love. What I came to figure out later on is that not only did this endless stream of guys not respect me, I didn't even respect myself. But here's the crazy thing. Even when I came to see that valuable truth, that priceless piece of wisdom, nothing changed. I was stuck in a self-destructive cycle and couldn't break it. It was that merry-go-round thing again. I saw it, I hated it and I wanted it to stop, but no matter how hard I tried, I just couldn't jump off. The merry-go-round music kept playing over and over again until it sounded warped, like music in a psychological thriller at the theater. When you're at the movies and you hear that kind of warped, freakish, distorted music, you know something bad is going to happen. That's how I felt, but I was powerless to stop it.

I finally graduated from high school and did pretty well, even with all the drama of broken relationships in my life. Now, if life had been a little less crazy, I could have done much better but, as it was, I still pulled a solid B plus average. That should've said something to me. That should've been the proof I needed that I wasn't a worthless piece of trash. I actually was pretty smart in terms of academics and when I could find the time to study and apply myself, I found that I really enjoyed the learning process. But as smart as I was, I couldn't seem to put two and two together and come up with the right answer. I should have seriously considered my future a little more. Maybe I could go to college and discover what I wanted to do in life. I could finally get out of the diner and actually get into a more positive and challenging career, something that made use of my gifts and made me feel good about myself. I should have listened to my head, instead of what I thought was my heart. I still longed for romance. I still wanted to be swept up in someone's arms, forever loved and protected from the raging flood of pollution around me that was threatening to sweep me away in its current.

At one point, after high school graduation, I was feeling so lonely and angry, that I began a several week campaign of dating as many guys as I possibly could from the diner. I think I went out with eight different guys in one month, desperately looking for the one guy who would take me out of this mess that was my life. Well, as you know, trying to fix one mess with another mess just isn't going to work. I went out with eight guys, wishing and hoping that one of them would turn out to be Mr. Right. He would be my hero, my rescuer. But that's not what happened at all. After a month of almost non-stop desperation dating, something happened that I never even considered a possibility. And when I discovered the truth of the situation, I knew it was going to quite literally change my life forever. You see, after a month of non-stop guys coming in and out of my life, I found out that I was pregnant. And the really disturbing thing, the thought that kept me awake at night? I had absolutely no idea who the father was. Seriously. I'm ashamed to admit it, but it could have been any one of those eight guys in that month- long dating spree. And now my life had just gotten over-the-top complicated. How was I going to take care of myself, let alone a kid?

Over the next nine months I went to my doctor faithfully. The diner's business had picked up significantly when a new cook came on the scene and they were able to take me on full time. I even had medical benefits and so my doctor bills were almost totally covered. And my doctor, who was a very kind, gentle, grandpa type, knew my situation, and simply wrote off the amount not covered by insurance. When I told him that was very nice of him, but he didn't have to do that, he just looked at me and said, "Wendy, you're going to need all the money you can get. It's not easy or inexpensive raising a child as a single mother. Let me do this for you. Let me bless you in this small way and let it be an encouragement to you." I was absolutely overwhelmed by his kindness and generosity toward me. I really wasn't used to that kind of behavior on somebody's part. Most of the people I had known over my life just looked out for themselves in an effort to survive. But Dr. Brown was different. He seemed to really care about me and the baby growing inside of my body. That day he offered to take what the insurance paid was very special to me and his offer made me feel genuinely loved, for the first time in several years. I wondered what the source of that love really was. It was when I was walking out of his office that I noticed a little sign on the door leading out. It simply said, "God is Love." I stopped in my tracks, looked carefully at the sign, and thought to myself, "I wonder if that's really true?" Those words were destined to put me on another path, at least for a while.

I went through my nine months of pregnancy and everything was normal and progressing as it should. I had already decided on the name Travis, if it was a boy, and Robin, if it was a girl. I don't know why I chose those names exactly, I just liked the way they sounded. Travis had a strong ring to it and Robin made me think of spring and the new life it brings. I think I was looking for strength and solidity in my new life of single parenthood. My mom and I had come to an agreement about caring for the baby. She was going to work nights at her 24-hour restaurant and I was going to switch to the day shift. And for the few hours a day when our shifts would cross over, Mrs. York, from down the hall, was happy to care for the baby. She was a very loving grandma of three pretty rambunctious kids and we had watched her in action many times. She could use a little extra money and we both knew that she'd be very conscientious in her care of our soon-to-be-arriving Travis. I had already begun to feel that this baby was going to be a boy, so I started calling him Travis before he was even born. And sure enough, on that beautiful summer night in August, little Travis made his grand entrance into this world and into our lives. And he didn't come quietly, believe me. He let out a cry when the doctor slapped him on his behind that could have raised the dead. He had a set of lungs on him that either was going to make him a drill sergeant or an opera singer. I was hoping for the latter because I've always loved music and anything military scared me. I had already heard of some of the guys from high school who had died in Vietnam and the thought of my son being in a war scared me to death, so I was rooting for the opera singer. But I had a long time before I had to worry about that. For now, I was just thankful for a healthy, bouncing, baby boy of 8 pounds and 3 ounces. I didn't think it was possible, but I realized you really can fall in love at first sight. From the moment I laid eyes on my little boy, I think I knew I was in love. And I thanked a God I wasn't even sure existed, for the gift of Travis. If there really was a God, I've got to tell you, He outdid himself on this one.

Chapter 7

John

WHEN I FIRST HEARD THE VOICE OF GOD telling me to go to school and train for the pastorate, I was very excited because, after all, I was going to make my living doing what I love to do. I always enjoyed music and public speaking and, as an added bonus, I genuinely enjoyed people, even some who were a little odd or a bit cranky. I ran into all kinds of quirky folks when I was working at Gunner's. And when some rather colorful character was giving me heartburn at the store, I made it my mission to win them over with my pleasing personality and winning smile. Most of the time, it worked. A customer might come in and look around the store and start grumbling about the high prices and I'd agree with him. Take this bicycle for example. The paint's chipping off and one of the rubber grips on the handlebars is missing. The bike has this overall, tired look about it. I'm just not sure it's worth the $10 Gunner's charging, I'd say. And then I'd whisper that I saw the same bike, only brand-new, at Sears and Roebuck the other day. It was the same exact bike, but it didn't have the paint chips and it wasn't missing a handlebar grip. It was $99.99 and well worth every penny of it, because it was one of the best bikes made. And I would agree with them that $10 was outrageous for a used bike, when he could pick up a brand-new model for about $100. I mean, after all, what's the price matter when he can have a bike that's brand-spanking new to ride back and forth to the store for a little exercise? Well, it didn't take long for the guy do the math and come to the conclusion that this "junk bike" was actually a steal. Who cares about a little paint chip here and there, it gives the bike some character. And the missing handlebar grip? He could just pick one up at the bike store for about three bucks. Then I'd tell him I'm not sure I should really sell him the bike, because I really want him to be a satisfied customer and obviously he just wasn't happy with the bike and its many flaws. Maybe he'd be a lot happier if he just drove across town to Sears and bought the bright, shiny new one. Well, pretty soon, he starts trying to sell me on the good qualities of this bike that he could purchase for $10 rather than the $100 at Sears. And after a few minutes of this kind of back-and-forth banter, the sides now reversed, I agreed to sell him the $10 bike, with the stipulation that he should bring it back if he's not totally satisfied. So, he'd fork over the $10 and take his used bike out of the shop, realizing what a sweet deal he had received.

You know sometimes people just need to see what's right in front of them to understand the best course of action. In this guy's case he came to realize that he'd save about $87 if he bought the slightly used one, instead of the new bike which was shiny and flashy, but lacked character and experience. Often times something that's been around a while winds up being the thing that's most satisfying. When I could get a customer to see that new and improved doesn't always mean a greater level of satisfaction, they would purchase the item that's been around for a while, but had proven itself, time and time again. It was always fun to see people discover that bit of wisdom on their own. I had participated in that kind of exchange with customers many times, and not once did they return an item they purchased when they truly realized its real value.

I was thinking about that one day when I was musing on my future career as a pastor. I was thinking how the Gospel's been around for a long time. Like the old hymn says, "Tell Me the Old, Old Story." It's been around a while, but it just keeps growing in value, like the used bike my customer bought. If he hangs onto that bike, in a few years, it'll be considered a classic and its value will go up even more. "Tell Me the Old, Old Story." Yeah, the story's been around a while, but in a world that's becoming more and more secular, its value just keeps increasing. It's not that the gospel hasn't always been valuable with the power to save and set people free, it's just that bright, shiny, new messages and movements pop up all the time and can lure people away from what's truly valuable, and has a track record to prove it. People are drawn to an innovative approach to life by this new group who has suddenly appeared on the scene with promises to give life meaning and fulfillment. Or they're swept up into the latest group that purports to be the "True Church." Their group of 45 people is the only one, in all 2000 years since Jesus walked this earth, to receive the genuine truth. And some people will fall for that hogwash simply because they want to be "in the know". They want to be part of the spiritually elite who know hidden secrets of the gospel that only a few people, in all of history, are privileged to discover. I've never understood how people, in some of these whacked out cults and new movements, can't understand that if God can only reach a few people in all of history with the genuine truth, what kind of God is He? He sounds pretty impotent to me. That just doesn't sound like the God I've loved and served and followed all of my life. It sounds more like the all-powerful Oz who was really just about smoke and mirrors. I was a young, 22-year-old, but I knew, even then, that I wasn't interested in the shiny, new and improved model of the so-called gospel, because that was just the same old model of deception that's been around since the Garden of Eden, it's just got a different wrapper on it. No, I wanted the used gospel. I wanted the gospel that's been around the block a few times and had a few paint chips from the battle it's been in. I wanted the gospel that was missing the handle grip, because to me, it represented those martyrs over the centuries that went missing on earth because of their faith in Jesus. I wanted the used gospel. I wanted the old, old story and I'd share it for the rest of my life.

I entered into seminary for the three-year adventure of getting my master of divinity degree. It was during that three-year period of study and skill development that I would also have the opportunity to be an intern in a church located a few blocks from the seminary. That was quite an adventure. It's one thing to be in seminary learning all about church history and theology and the art of hermeneutics and the different approaches to eschatology and so on. It's a pretty safe environment where I'm surrounded by other guys who are trying to figure out the secret to learning Greek, just like I am. But doing the required internship, and actually trying to use the stuff I've been learning was somewhat more daunting. I mean, these were real people I was going to be working with. These weren't just case studies in some of my books. These were people whom God has entrusted to my care. Their eternal destinies were right there in the palm of my hand. One little slip up on my part and they'd be lost forever. I'm their only hope for the future. I'm the one who's been assigned to lead them on the right path, to a life of service and devotion. I'm the one who's been given the awesome job of getting them prepared for their life here on earth and eternity in heaven. It all hinged on me. I was the one who ultimately determined their eternal destiny.

Oh yeah, that's right. There's that little matter of the Godhead, specifically the third person of the Trinity. There's the Holy Spirit. I guess maybe He plays a rather important role in their lives also. Huh? Imagine that. It's not really up to me, is it? Their eternal destiny isn't really in the palm of my hand. God just gives me the joy and privilege of playing a small role in the eternal drama of a person's life. Oh, the arrogance we have at times, trying to somehow be the Holy Spirit to people God brings across our path. It's a lesson that thankfully, I learned early on in my internship. God has simply allowed me the privilege to work in partnership with Him in helping to change my little corner of the world. And guess what? I'm not the Savior of the world-Jesus is. And guess what else? I'm not the Holy Spirit. In fact, the job's not even open, praise the Lord!

You want to know some of the tricks God uses to slap the arrogance out of a young seminary student? One of his most effective tricks is to take them to a church where he's given the title "Youth Intern". Yeah, that's right. Instead of preaching to great congregations of thousands of saints, all hanging on your every word, you're called instead to put all of your seminary training to good use and to help the youth group construct a 30-foot banana split in a rain gutter. I'm not kidding you. That was my first ministry assignment as a youth intern. My job was to go down to the hardware store, pick up 30 feet of rain gutter, get several rolls of aluminum foil with which to line the gutter, and pick up all the ice cream and toppings for a huge banana split.

Now, I have to admit, my attitude wasn't very good. How am I supposed to put my knowledge of Greek to good use when the kids have their faces buried in what looks like a pig trough? I wasn't going to seminary for this. I was going to become a serious student of Scripture and present God's word in such a way that people would leave each service profoundly touched by the Spirit of God. The only thing these kids are going to leave with are messy faces and clothes stained with hot fudge. It's hard to see Jesus and the disciples hunched over a rain gutter, scarfing down their version of a decadent dessert. Where's the dignity? Where's the passion for souls? Where's the heart to touch these kids in a genuine way, a life-changing way? This is going to be a very long year of internship and I'm going to gain 50 pounds if we keep doing this kind of thing.

So, I did the only thing I could think of just to get through the whole night as quickly as possible. While most of the kids were playing ping-pong or foosball or just sitting around chewing the fat and goofing off, I picked out about six kids that didn't seem to be participating in all the other stuff. I didn't know them and they didn't know me. In fact, it didn't appear that they knew anybody at all. Maybe their parents made them come, because they sure looked uncomfortable, just standing there watching everybody else. I think they would have rather been home watching grass grow, than to be here at youth group, being ignored. It was probably a little too much like the lunch room at school. So, I walked up to each one of them individually and said, "Hey, can you help me with something?" And sure enough, after about 45 seconds, I had a team of six guys and gals who looked like the poster kids for wallflowers. I said, "Guys, we've got a mission to do. It's going to be up to us to build the world's largest banana split. We're even going to take pictures with my Instamatic camera and see if this qualifies for "The Guinness Book of World Records."

I've never seen so many ears perk up so fast in all my life. Their energy level just shot up. Suddenly, they had a challenge, a mission that nobody else could accomplish but them. We took two of the team and had them man the scoops. Two others set about slicing a huge bunch of bananas. One kid was assigned the task of pouring hot fudge and the other kid pouring caramel sauce. We had to work very fast. The youth center wasn't air-conditioned and the September temperatures were still pretty warm. We worked fast and efficiently and got all the ingredients down in record time. I then gave each kid a can of Redi- Whip and said, "Cover the whole thing; I don't want to see any ice cream or sauce peeking out. On your marks, get set, go!" And they tore off in a whipped cream frenzy. Everything was going fine and orderly until I decided to change it up a bit and invite them to break out of their shell. Just as we got near the last foot of this colossal banana split, I "accidentally" sprayed one of the kids on the nose with some of the whipped cream. Everything ground to a stop. Dead silence. I just stared at the kid and he stared back at me, a smile barely making its way to my mouth. He wiped the whipped cream off with his finger, put it in his mouth, and calmly lifted the can up with his right hand as if he was going to put it on the table. But just as the can reached table height he brought it up with lightning speed, in one fluid motion, so that it was even with my face and he let the whipped cream fly. Seriously, it was like a gunfight at the O.K. Corral. He got me right between the eyes and I shot back and got him in the ear. And with that, the fight was on. Whipped cream was flying everywhere and all six kids just let go and went after each other. And within 30 seconds, they had their sites aimed at me. What a night of mayhem. What an evening of unbridled passion and fearlessness. What a mess! I'm still finding whipped cream in my ears and nose and it's been over a year.

The other kids had drifted over to watch the fight and everyone was cheering for their favorite "whipped cream warrior." Finally, with the cream exhausted and the cans dispatched to the garbage sack nearby, we all dug in to the giant colossal banana split. And as I was chowing down with everybody else, a thought briefly crossed my mind. We forgot to pray for the food. What kind of a pastor forgets to pray for the food? But then I got real and just figured God probably would never have heard the prayer anyway. He was too busy laughing.

Chapter 8

Wendy

THE SOUND OF A BABY CRYING HAS NEVER PAR-
ticularly bothered me before. What I mean by that is, it's
something you just expect when you see a mom and her
kids. Babies cry for any number of reasons and when you feed them
or give them their binky or change their diaper or rock them back and
forth they'll usually stop crying and be content for a while. Crying
babies are just something to be expected, it's a fact of nature. But when
the crying happens every morning about 2:30 AM it presents some
unique challenges. Number one, it really starts adding up to many

hours of missed sleep. Number two, when it first happens and you're in a deep sleep because you're exhausted, and you hear a crying baby, you think, "Why doesn't that mother do something about that?" And then you remember that *you* are the mother. Nobody's going to get that baby to settle down, but you. Maybe your husband will get up and give him a bottle this time. Oh, that's right, you don't have a husband. You're it. You're going this alone. And so, you drag yourself out of bed and tenderly lift this very loud but precious baby to your breast. Little Travis sucks away contentedly as you gently rock him, holding him very close. And after he's had enough, you go to put him down and realize that his eyes are wide open and he's looking all around. You're ready to fall asleep standing up and he's wide awake and alert. He doesn't want to miss out on anything. And so, even though you're tired and just want to go back to bed so that you can get up and get to work, you continue the rock and talk. You speak soothing phrases and quiet words of love that not only serve to relax him but also hopefully make him feel loved and cared for, confident that he's safe and secure in his mother's arms. You also speak words to this little guy that you hope will turn out to be prophetic. You tell him that you love him, something you've said many times a day since he first came into your life. You tell him what a handsome little boy he is and you know he's going to be brilliant and do wonderful things in this life. He's going to grow up to be a fine young boy and then transition to be a strong, solid, successful adult who will have tremendous impact in this world. You speak over him all the things you wished had been spoken over you. And you realize that what you're saying, the dreams and the hopes about his future, are really sincere; they're not just words that are meant to trick him and make him settle down so that you both can get back to sleep. When you share these words of tender love and devotion, along with a confident anticipation for a bright future, you're speaking truth. These words are as real to you as anything you've ever believed. You still can't get over how much you love this tiny person that's lying in your arms, having no idea that he's changed your life so dramatically. You wouldn't trade this for a million dollars. You wouldn't mind getting a little more sleep, sure, but the joy of holding little Travis is worth it. Holding him close and whispering words of love in some ways feels like your greatest calling in life. And though you haven't always been the most confident person in the world, and even though you've messed things up in your 19 years on earth, you know, beyond a shadow of a doubt, that you're going to be successful in this, your most important endeavor. You're going to be a wonderful mom who watches over your son with great care and consistent, unconditional love. You'll watch Travis growing up knowing that you're in his corner all the way, no matter the situation, good or bad. And one night you breathe what will turn out to be a regular, ongoing prayer. You're not sure when it happened, but somehow, you've come to believe that there really is a God out there who cares about you and Travis. Now, if someone asked you questions about God you're not sure you would have any answers. And whatever answers you might come up with are not exactly going to fill theological volumes, but they're enough for you at this point in your life.

All these thoughts have been running through my head in these first few months of motherhood. I've probably had more conversations with myself and have analyzed this whole mother gig more than any other subject I've ever been confronted with. And I didn't have to be a genius to know that I'm just flying by the seat of my pants. At various points along the way I had expressed my frustration at some particularly troublesome episode in child-rearing and wondered why being a parent was so hard. And why didn't Travis come with some kind of an owner's manual or guidebook? We have manuals for everything else, right? I mean, if I buy a new toaster, I get a little booklet with it telling me how to operate the toaster and how to set it on the perfect level for toasting. It'll even give me hints for troubleshooting if something goes wrong. And all of that is for a toaster. I'm talking a little person here, so much more important than a toaster and yet nothing. No booklet. No instructions on how to operate it. No guide to troubleshooting. Strange, isn't it? I think if I was God I would've done something about that. But, oh well, Travis and I seem to be making it anyway. I'm kind of stumbling and bumbling my way through this new adventure of being a single mom. Fortunately, Travis is blissfully unaware of my total ignorance. Maybe genuine love goes a long way in covering up some of my mistakes and miscues. Well, however it all works, Travis seems pretty happy for the most part. He's developing his little personality already. I can see it. Maybe no one else can, but I see it growing every day and believe me, it's fun and it's exciting.

The weeks turn into months and the months turn into years and before I know it, Travis is in elementary school. Together he and I made it through the sleepless nights of those first months. I don't know who first thought of that "terrible twos" idea but they definitely had some insight there. I guess I wouldn't call it that necessarily because I really did enjoy the various phases of Travis's life but I will admit, those years were definitely more challenging. But, as with everything, we got through it fairly unscathed and sooner than I would have liked he was heading off to kindergarten. Now that was a tough one. He had already been to the preschool run by the church just down the street from me and he seemed to enjoy his time there. He was really becoming quite social for a little kid of his age. He went to preschool for two years and was learning some very good ideas and concepts that would serve as a foundation for his life. I mean most of it was just really fun, with lots of times for organized play and games and crafts and so on. But sometimes we'd have our conversations about his day and I was kind of amazed at what he had learned. He learned some of the letters of the alphabet. He learned how to count to 10 and how that corresponded to the 10 fingers on his hands or the 10 items the teacher had placed in front of them. He even learned the Bible verse "God is love." I know it's short, and not all that hard to remember, but by this time I was really glad that he was getting some kind of a God-concept. It may not have been much, but at least it was something and I really felt good about that.

But the day came when he went off to kindergarten. He graduated from preschool the previous May, with a little celebration for parents and kids. They even made these little square hats out of blue construction paper with a little piece of yarn hanging down for the tassel. It was beyond cute when they all walked in with "Pomp and Circumstance" playing on the cassette recorder in the background. I know it sounds kind of sappy, but I found myself tearing up when he walked in looking so proper and proud. I had visions of Travis graduating from Harvard Law School or some elite Ivy League college. But when the kid in front of Travis stopped abruptly, for no apparent reason, that started a chain of events that you'd see on a Three Stooges episode. The kid stopped dead in his tracks. No warning, no signal, he just stopped. Now Travis, who is right behind him, is watching me with a big smile on his face and doesn't notice that traffic's come to a standstill. Before anyone can stop him, Travis collides with the kid who stopped. And then the kid in back of Travis collides with him and you get the picture. Larry, Moe and Curly couldn't have timed it any better. Within a second or two everybody had bashed into the person in front of them and by now they were all on the ground laughing and rolling around, their hats in total disarray, if not completely destroyed. We parents were a little worried, but when we saw that everything was all right and that nobody was hurt, we all started laughing too. It really was something straight out of a slapstick movie and provided many hours of laughing over the next several months when I would say, "Travis, do you remember graduation? Tell Mrs. York about what happened." And Travis, always the ham, would tell the story and start laughing almost immediately and that would get the person on the receiving end laughing too. I also noticed that whenever Travis would tell the story he'd add a little detail here or there as an embellishment. He was really quite good for a child his age. Now I know I sound just like any proud parent, but I wondered if maybe my son was just a little more advanced and talented than most kids his age. I'm sure no parent has ever thought that about their kid before, right? But in my case, it was all true. It really was!

I continued to work at the diner, barely eking out a living. But even with very little money we were happy. In fact, I could say with all honesty, that I was happier than I'd ever been. I still dated once in a while, but to the tell you the truth, my taste in men had changed. Like I told you before, I was kind of loose and wild, all in an effort to find someone who would truly love me. The only thing I can say is that when Travis came along, my focus shifted to him completely. If I did go out, it didn't take me long to start talking about Travis and that pretty much squelched the deal with most guys. They didn't want to get involved with someone who had a kid. And that was fine with me. If they weren't interested in my son, I wasn't interested in them and nothing was going to change that. If it was just Travis and me for the next decade of life, I was totally cool with that. Being a single mom was challenging enough without adding some narcissistic guy who thinks he's doing me a favor by dating me. Who needs that? Not me, that's for sure.

So, Travis and I walked through life together, hand in hand. I couldn't believe how much I loved him and yes, before you think that everything was perfect, let me assure you that it was not. Travis had a lot of energy, so much energy in fact, I wondered if that was normal. I'd watch him play with some of the other boys from around the neighborhood and it would scare me to death. Here he is in fourth grade, still my little boy, and I look out the window just in time to see him fighting with a couple of other boys. And just as I'm getting ready to run outside and defend him, Travis and the other little boys picked themselves up off the ground and they're all laughing. I guess they're not hurt. Maybe they weren't really fighting, maybe they were just playing. Just then one of the kids takes Travis by the arm, bends over, and throws him over his shoulder to the ground. Travis starts laughing and then wraps his legs around the other guy's legs, does a quick roll to his left, and brings the kid down to the ground. I thought to myself, "What in the world are they doing?" They're going to get killed. But as I stood and watched, I realized they were doing what little boys have been doing since time began. They were wrestling around, rough-housing, playing all out, going for broke, whatever you want to call it. And they didn't seem to be concerned about getting hurt. Although it looked rough to my mother's eyes, I didn't see any indication that this activity was harming them. Maybe I should just leave them alone and let them imitate the "Big Time Wrestlers" that were their current heroes. No bones have been broken yet.

I opened the window so that I could actually hear what was going on. I enjoyed their yelling and their rambunctious activity. It actually brought joy to my heart to hear their sweet, innocent voices being raised in their exuberant play. Oh, the innocence of the young, I thought. They knew nothing of the war in Vietnam or the scandal of Watergate. They were just innocent little boys and all was right with the world. That was the moment that I snapped out of my blissful reverie over the innocence of youth and heard one of the boys let out with a string of cuss words I didn't think any kid his age would know. The words just about turned my hair blue. But as shocked as I was, it occurred to me that neither Travis nor his friends were bothered by the language coming out of the other boy's mouth. In fact, they didn't bat an eye. I knew right then and there that I needed to take some action. Travis needed to learn some things about what's right and wrong. But he needed a lot more than I could give him. I needed to get him into church fast. It was, at the same time, the best decision I ever made and the worst decision I ever made. It didn't turn out the way I was expecting at all.

Chapter 9

John

I 'M LYING IN BED THAT NIGHT AFTER HOSTING THE Super Colossal Banana Split Extravaganza, as it came to be known, realizing that it had been a major hit and yet my attitude hadn't been very good. I was incensed that my valuable insight and training was going to waste that night. As I was out looking for supplies I knew that when I started calling the shots we'd do things a lot differently. I'm a pastor-in-training; I'm not a clown from the Ringling Brothers Circus. Where's the dignity of the pastoral office for heaven's sake? How are kids going to look up to me as a role model and spiritual mentor if they perceive me as the fourth Stooge? Why didn't the church just hire Jerry Lewis if they wanted someone crazy and zany? That's what I was thinking going into this stupid event that was sure to be a disaster.

But let me tell you how I felt when the event was over and my six-member team of wallflower, "whipped cream warriors" was still together helping me clean up. You can't believe the mess that's left over from a 30-foot banana split. In fact, as I'm scarfing down the banana split, right along with everybody else, I'm just hoping that nobody's got some kind of rare communicable disease, because in all honesty, this is a public health nightmare. We're all basically eating out of each other's bowl and I know there's got to be a lot of cross-contamination taking place. If I thought about it for too long the phrase "super gross" came to mind. But as I'm lying in bed that night, trying to shut my mind off, I can't quit smiling to myself. I really wasn't thinking about the gross part of the event. I was thinking instead about what I had learned.

After we had totally demolished the banana split and taken time to hit the bathrooms and clean ourselves up, we all came back into the room and sat in a circle on the floor. I had planned to end the evening with a little devotional about how the Bible had come to be written over a period of 1600 years by over 40 different authors. Riveting, right? But I changed my direction at the last minute. I didn't talk for long, but I just pointed out that we couldn't have done this crazy event without teamwork. I said something to the effect that when it comes to being a youth group, and being all that God wants us to be, the first thing we need to learn is that we need each other. My fearless team of "whipped cream warriors" was pleased when I acknowledged their efforts and the other kids broke out in spontaneous applause for the team's work. I finished off by saying that I was excited about the coming year, and in the words of some showbiz star, whose name I can't recall, "You ain't seen nothin' yet!" Then I prayed, thanking God for the evening and the food. Hey, better late than never, right? And then the kids started leaving and pretty soon it was just my team of former wallflowers helping me to clean up. After we were done and they were also leaving, their parents being kind enough to wait the extra 15 minutes for cleanup, I said goodbye and thanks again. But just as the last kid was walking out the door he turned to me and said, "Hey John, could I talk to you sometime?" And I said, "Sure Matt, what are you doing after school tomorrow?" He was free and so after checking with his mom who had come to get him, we agreed that I'd pick Matt up from school and we'd grab a burger at McDonald's and just spend a little time together. The next day we had a bite to eat and as we sat there I wondered what horrible problem Matt was dealing with that I could help him through. But that wasn't it at all. Basically, I think Matt just wanted a guy to talk to. He was from a single-parent home and really didn't have many other guys in his life. So, we just sat there for an hour and a half talking about school, and home, and girls, and how tough it was sometimes being a kid. And then he said something that blew me away and brought tears to my eyes. I'm kind of emotional and it's embarrassing. I think I got it from my mom who is an All-Star weeper. Anyway, Matt looked up at me and said that last night the "Banana Split Extravaganza" was the best night of his life. I was shocked and hoping that it wasn't really true. The best night of your life? Matt saw my skeptical raised eyebrow and said, "No, it's true John. It was the best night of my life because it's the first time anybody's ever noticed me. I've never had anybody clap for me, for anything, and it was great." That was it, that was destined to chart the course of my ministry in the coming year, and I suspected, the coming decades.

You see, I realized that day at McDonald's that maybe everybody's got a little Matt in them. Even people who come across confident and self-assured have those areas where they feel insecure, maybe even insignificant. Maybe everybody's got this inner need to be noticed and cared for, truly accepted for who they are. Now, I know how selfish and absorbed we can be, even as Christians, but what if we could break that down? What if we could take this youth group to a whole new level of caring and thinking of others, besides themselves? Knowing the teenage mind like I do, I knew that would be a challenge, but what if it could work? What if every kid got to the point that when they came to youth group they felt like they were at home with a loving family? Their family. That little conversation with Matt started me on a quest to do just that.

The first thing I did was look at the congregation to see who might want to join me in this endeavor. I began to get to know some other single adults my age that were in the church, but were just sort of hanging around. Churches have a tendency to emphasize families and so those of us who are single feel a little out of place, sometimes not quite sure where we belong. I began to get to know some of them by grabbing a Coke or coffee with them after the evening service and hearing about their heart for the Lord. And when I felt the urging of the Holy Spirit, I would describe the kind of person I was looking for to join me in changing kids' lives. I also told them that they had the kind of gifting needed to do just that. And then I asked them to come on board and let's change lives together. And you want to know something amazing? Everyone I asked said yes. Every single one! So within about three weeks of coming to First Baptist Church to be the youth intern, I had a team of six leaders, all of them willing and able to give their time to helping kids become all that God wanted them to be. Each of the single adults on the team had different gifting's and that was a purposeful, strategic move on the part of the Holy Spirit. A couple of them had some real musical talent and were in charge of leading the singing. I asked them to look at the newer songs and choruses that were coming out of the Jesus People Movement. And so, each week at group they'd have their guitars and lead us in "Seek Ye First" and "Pass It On" and other popular songs of the day. Others on the team had some pretty amazing creativity and would come up with crazy events that could outshine the "Super Colossal Banana Split Extravaganza." And a lot of these events included food. Giant food! Have you ever had a 30-foot hoagie sandwich before? We did! Have you ever had a giant taco salad made in a kids' wading pool? We did! Have you ever had a giant chocolate milkshake made in a plastic garbage can? We did! It was a *new* garbage can, by the way. And every time we did these crazy events the kids would bring their friends, and pretty soon their friends would be coming to the group on a regular basis. There were a lot of different gifts and talents on that team of youth leaders, but the one thing they all had in common was the desire to touch a kid's life and help them in their walk of faith.

The other thing I stressed with this team of youth leaders is that when you're getting supplies for a youth event, or setting up the area ahead of time, or checking out a new site for our next retreat, take a couple of kids with you and use that time to build relationships. That's what we all did, whenever possible. We built relationships. I came to discover early on that as much as I needed to spend time preparing my little devotional for each week, the interesting thing, and might I say the humbling thing, is that kids were going to forget the major portion of what I said when they walked out of youth group. It sounds like that could get a little discouraging and it did at times, to be perfectly honest. But I always figured that kids were no different than adults. When I preached at the morning service on occasion, I always felt that if a person would take home just one thought and chew on that for the week, the sermon was successful. I always felt good when a kid or an adult would begin a conversation with, "I was thinking about what you said last week," and then go on to tell me how they'd been processing that thought for days. That felt pretty good. Because as much as I wanted to build the numbers through all kinds of wild and crazy events, the fact is, I was really concerned for their spiritual growth first and foremost. The memory of an event will fade over time, but the impact of the gospel is forever. So, while we were together for that year of internship I was determined that this youth group would build lasting memories of loving, laughing, and growing together. It didn't happen all the time and with every kid, but it happened often enough that we knew God was pleased and smiling down on us. Even when we spilled that giant milkshake on the new carpet in the youth room. Yikes! The trustees weren't too happy about that one!

As I got toward the end of my seminary training and my one-year internship, I felt a little anxious. I was happy to be through with school and was looking forward to walking across that stage and receiving my Masters of Divinity Degree. I was also looking forward to the service of ordination that would come later that evening. That's when the denominational leaders would gather around this new batch of freshly graduated seminary students, lay hands on them in an activity that's been practiced since the time of the Apostles, and ordain them to lifelong ministry. It was a very touching service and I somehow felt a great responsibility to serve the Lord more fervently than ever before. It was an awesome privilege and responsibility to be the hands and the feet and the voice of God here on earth. I always knew that, but that night at the ordination service just brought that sobering truth home to me more clearly than ever before. That feeling has really never left and I hope it never will.

First Baptist asked me to stay on full-time, after graduation, as their permanent youth pastor. I looked at what had been accomplished over the last year and the kids that were in my youth group and I accepted gratefully. I didn't want to leave these kids that I had grown to love. I thought of Matt and my other wallflower kids who were so involved now ever since that first night when the "Whipped Cream Warriors" had come together, bonded forever by cans of Redi-Whip. I knew they were happy about my decision to stay when I was officially installed a couple of Sundays later in the morning service. I looked out over our congregation that morning and spotted all six of my wall-flowers sitting together in the front row, each of them smiling and holding a can of Redi-Whip high, so that I'd be sure to see them. I knew some great years of ministry were ahead and I was excitedly looking forward to them. I really wondered if God was going to keep me in youth ministry for my entire career. I didn't see youth ministry as a steppingstone to the Senior Pastorate. I saw it as a ministry that I could easily spend my entire life doing. In fact, I knew one youth pastor from another church who was approaching his 65th birthday and had spent his entire ministry of 45 years working with youth.

At that moment, I wanted to beat my friend's record. I wanted to stay there forever. And I think I would have as the next two years just continued to get better and better. I think I could have stayed there forever, if it hadn't been for the split.

Chapter 10

Wendy

WHEN I WAS GROWING UP I LOVED TO
watch TV shows about families. I think I was trying
to get some idea of what real families looked like. As I
got older, and got a glimpse of reality, I came to understand the difference between a television family and a modern family of the 70s. When
I would watch "Father Knows Best" or "Leave it to Beaver" or maybe
the "Andy Griffith Show", as a little girl, I was always so impressed
with how stable those families were. There almost always was a mom
and dad and two or three kids. Now Andy Griffith was the exception.

Sheriff Andy Taylor lived in the little town of Mayberry. But Andy Taylor, being a single father, didn't come from divorce because he was out sleeping around with the loose women of Mayberry. In fact, I'm not sure there *were* any loose women in those shows. That would've taken away from the innocent nature of life portrayed in those 30 minutes each week.

I liked the fact that in all of these shows, I actually got to live the life I'd always wanted. "Father Knows Best" and "Leave It to Beaver" both had the families I had never experienced. Mom was always dreaming of being rescued from her miserable existence. The thing that used to bother me was the thought that I played a huge role in that miserable existence. Now, she never said that, but she didn't have to. Even as a kid I just figured that her being miserable was somehow my fault. In my young, innocent mind, I felt that somehow I was holding her back. And you know something? When you feel like that as a kid, feelings of safety and security are just about non-existent. You grow up feeling that if things get too hard, or complicated, or boring, or chaotic, or financially difficult, and so on, that whatever world you've come to accept as your own is going to come tumbling down like Humpty Dumpty. And you're not sure what all the pieces look like, but you're pretty sure that just like in the nursery rhyme, nobody's going to be able to put it back together again. And so, one way you help yourself feel a little more safe and secure is to imagine your life like Kathy on "Father Knows Best." Or you see yourself as the female version of Theodore Cleaver, the Beav. Or you dream of being Opie's non-existent sister whose father is the sheriff and whose Aunt Bee is the perfectly plump and pleasing substitute mom, always loving and always wise, in a nice, down-home country way. Not only that, she's an amazing cook and baker and always whips up simple, but absolutely scrumptious meals, including breakfast and dinner. And when you went off to school, she'd pack you a lunch that was the envy of every kid in the lunch room.

I used to wonder what it would be like to live in that kind of a family. I mean, sure, there were always some tensions in the show. One of the kids would mess up big time;well, big time for their mythical little world. But, lo and behold, whatever tension there might have been was completely resolved in 30 minutes. Imagine that? In 30 short minutes, 22 if you cut out the commercials, all your problems are solved and your world is wonderful again. And over the years I was growing up, that was the life I always wanted. Of course, as an adult having experienced the challenge of being a single mom in a world that is so far removed from Mayberry, I've come to accept that life isn't like that anymore, if it ever was in the first place. But as I'd think back on those shows, and get past all the perfect scenarios, for the perfect life, another thought would grab me. Although you didn't see it acted out all the time on the screen, you saw it or heard it referenced enough that you knew those TV families went to Sunday school and church. It was just a given;that's what families in the 50s did, I guess. And even though most of those shows were pretty far from what I was experiencing in this bizarre decade of the 70s, the idea of church intrigued me. This may not be Mayberry, with a little country church that everybody attended, but even in Chicago we had churches. Barney Fife may not be singing in the choir with that shaky tenor voice of his, but I'm sure I could have found someone with the Barney-voice in some of the churches down the street. And after the string of cuss words that came out of Ryan, Travis's wrestling friend, didn't seem to surprise or shock

Travis, I knew I had to get him into church. Whatever he needed spiritually, he certainly wasn't getting it from me. Maybe going to church would help train Travis to grow up in this world with a desire to live a decent and moral life. Although since having Travis I'd calmed down significantly, I knew I wasn't going to be able to give him the kind of moral training he needed. And it wasn't just moral, it actually was beyond that. I'd begun thinking that maybe there really was a God out there who cared about me and my son. And if God existed, maybe I should pay a little more attention to Him. I mean, what do I have to lose, right? I found myself almost unconsciously sending up quick prayers here and there when things got tough. I even found myself thanking God when things were going well. Kind of weird, isn't it? Thanking a God you're not positively sure even exists, and yet, it somehow seems almost natural to talk to Him. Well, I can't figure it all out; at least I haven't so far. But I do know one thing for sure. I need to get us to church. I can't just send Travis. I need to go with him.

Now, here's the deal. I'd never been to a church in my life and I didn't know Baptist from Lutheran. I didn't know Methodist from Presbyterian. If I walked into a church I wouldn't have been able to tell if I was in a Jewish synagogue or a Mormon ward. In other words, as my mom would say, "I don't know nothin'." And so, I decided the best thing to do would be to check it out first and see if it would be good for Travis and me. Mom was off the Sunday I went out looking. When she asked me where I was going and why I couldn't take Travis, I hesitated to tell her. But I figured that maybe lying about going to church might be a major sin and start me off on the wrong foot with God. And when I told her that I was going to look for a church she surprised me. I was afraid she'd make fun of me but she didn't. In fact, she said, "I think that would be real nice." I watched her closely for a second or two to see if she was being sarcastic, but she wasn't. Mom was absolutely sincere in her comments and that made me wonder if she had some regrets about the way she raised me. I had received zero spiritual input in all my growing up years. That might be an interesting topic of conversation sometime.

That next Sunday morning I got up, showered, fixed Travis some breakfast and went in to get ready. But as I was looking for something to wear, it suddenly dawned on me that I had no idea what was appropriate. Do I wear my bell bottom jeans with the super-wide cuffs? Do I wear the dress that I bought for my last date that turned out to be a waste because the date was a disaster? Do I wear the new jumpsuit that I purchased recently at a discount store? It looked kind of cool but it was a pain-in-the-neck if you had to go to the bathroom. They should make jumpsuits with little flaps in the back for taking care of any business, if you know what I mean. I'm trying to be delicate here, you understand.

I figured you couldn't go wrong with a simple skirt and blouse. It was a beautiful, sunny day anyway so I thought I'd just dress in something light and airy. I chose my powder blue mini-skirt with my sunny yellow and blue paisley, short-sleeved blouse. I put them on, said goodbye to Travis and mom, and walked to the Redeemer Community Church, three blocks down and two blocks over. Their service began at 11:00 AM and I got there about 10 minutes early. I suddenly got very nervous. I thought to myself: Oh boy, what am I doing here? It's not like I've lived my life like a saint. Maybe God doesn't want me here and the roof is going to come crashing down. But I just swallowed hard and made my way up the stairs leading to the church. When I walked in it took my eyes a little time to adjust to the dimness of the foyer. But pretty soon I could see well enough to notice that people were kind of staring at me. When I'd catch their eye, hoping for a smile or a nod, they'd just quickly turn their face and pretend to be engaged elsewhere. I thought that was kind of odd, but maybe they're not used to visitors, so I gave those first few minutes a pass. I mean everybody's uncomfortable in new situations, right? And I guess I'm the new situation.

I walked into this large room with all these long benches that I came to find out later were called pews. I sat down on one of the benches and just looked around, not knowing what else to do. I noticed that people would glance at me and then quickly look down, suddenly becoming absorbed in the program the usher handed us at the door. I was amazed at how shy these people were. And that was fine with me, because even though I'm perky and outgoing at the diner, I wasn't sure if these were the same personality traits that were usually desired at church. Well, evidently, they weren't, at least not at this church.

Pretty soon this group of folks dressed in black robes came in and sat in a special section up on the stage. Then a couple of other guys walked in and sat in some chairs right behind the big wooden podium. A piano started to play and I realized that the group up in front is a choir and they're getting ready to sing. They began to sing a very slow song telling us to be quiet because, "God Was in His Holy Temple." Then one of the guys in the chair gets up to pray for a minute or two. After he's done praying he tells us to take the hymnal and turn to page 143. The first thing that flashed through my mind was "what's a hymnal?" But as I watched the other people I realized that the hymnal was a book in the rack in front of me, and it was full of hymns. Obvious I know. But remember, this is all new to me.

We sang three hymns, all of them pretty slow, but the words were amazing. I'd never heard these songs before and I was surprised at how moved I was just to understand what the words were saying. After the three hymns, we were instructed to be seated and the same guy who directed the hymns jumped right into the commercial. He told us about different things that were happening in the church that week and welcomed any visitors who were there for the first time. I was glad he didn't point me out because it felt like everybody knew I was a visitor anyway, the way they were stealing little glances at me. But after he welcomed the visitors, he asked the ushers to come forward for the morning offering. Well, when he started to pray I panicked because I didn't have any change on me. I had a $20 bill, but I couldn't put that in the plate, that was money for groceries. So, I reached into my purse and found two quarters, a nickel and a button. I took the change and the button and put it in the offering plate when it passed by. I don't know why I gave the button; I guess I thought it would look like I was giving a little more if anybody was watching me. Anyway, I got through the offering episode, but it made me so nervous I was beginning to sweat.

After the offering, another man stood up at the podium and began to read a few words out of the Bible and then talk about them. He wasn't a particularly great speaker, but I could tell that he was sincere and really believed the words he was saying about the importance of loving each other. I remember thinking to myself, "That's pretty good; we all need to have more love." And then, after he had talked for about 25 minutes, he prayed another prayer. Then the other guy got up and led in another song called, "We've Story to Tell to the Nations." It was kind of peppy and had the basic idea of telling everybody, everywhere, about God. That's a good thing, I thought. Maybe everybody all over the world needed to hear this stuff.

After we sang the hymn I realized the service was over because people started to leave. As I walked out into the foyer I noticed again that people would look at me, but wouldn't say anything. And, once again, I was amazed at how shy they were. So, I thought maybe it just takes them a little while to get used to visitors. Anyway, as I'm making it out of the foyer and onto the front steps, I noticed that everybody else was heading down the hall into another room. I saw a sign that said Coffee Hour, with an arrow pointing down the hallway where everyone was going. I thought about going back into the foyer and down to the coffee hour in hopes of meeting a few folks. But just as I'm thinking about it, I see a lady walking toward me. She was fairly tall and thin, and had what looked like a scowl on her face. I just figured that her shoes were pinching her feet and she was anxious to get home and take them off. She's heading towards me and I figured she was going to invite me to the coffee hour. I thought that going in with someone who invited me would be a whole lot more comfortable than going by myself, so I was excited about meeting this woman. But when she opened her mouth and spoke, I wasn't so excited anymore. These were her exact words: "Young lady, I feel it's my duty as a good Christian to let you know that the skirt you're wearing is an abomination to the Lord. It is so short that it leaves nothing to the imagination. You need to dress modestly when you come to our church. This is God's house and we won't let it be dishonored by this mode of apparel." And with that she turned around and walked away, leaving me alone on the church steps. I was so shocked and hurt that I started to cry. But just as the tears began to flow I heard someone say, "Don't waste your tears, it's not worth it." I looked up and saw a long-haired, bearded hippie, in a tie-dyed shirt, standing on the sidewalk below me. He looked up at me with what I can only describe as love and kindness and he said, "Hey, they kicked me out too. Evidently, they don't do long hair and beards in this church. It makes me wonder how a church can so completely miss the heart of the Jesus they claim to follow. Hey, I'm Kevin-would you like to go to lunch?"

Chapter 11

John

WHEN I WAS IN SEMINARY I KNEW THAT THE whole three years of writing papers, endless lectures, stimulating class discussions, informal theological debates with other guys over lunch, a year internship, and so on, were all supposed to prepare me for ministry. The idea was that by the time I finished I'd be ready to take on whatever church God led me to.

When I saw how some of the crazy things we did impacted Matt and my other wallflower kids, I was hooked from that point on. I thought that this was the greatest gig in the world. I couldn't believe that they were actually paying me to do this. Now granted, as an intern the pay wasn't very much, but hey, some of the guys I knew had internships that didn't pay anything, so I felt very blessed. The year was a good one, and when they offered me the position of youth pastor full-time after graduation, I took it without hesitation. Just think about it: I was actually going to make my living doing what I love to do. How many people are fortunate enough to be able to say that?

By this time, I was 26 years old, single and making about $13,000 a year full time. I know it wasn't a great salary but it was certainly more than I'd made at Gunners and for a young single guy that didn't have a lot of bills it was certainly adequate. I'm not sure how I would have made it financially if I had a wife and a couple of kids, but that seemed pretty far off and so I'd just handle that if and when it came along. Besides, I really believed that if I was faithful to my calling, gave a tithe of 10% of my income back to the Lord, and just followed His will, all would be fine. In fact, interestingly enough, I had also seen what I called "God's Miracle Math" in action plenty of times. I would suddenly get hit with an unexpected bill like a car repair, or maybe an extra high heating bill because it was so cold that month, and living on a pretty tight budget I wondered how I was going to pay for it. But then, just in time, the Lord would bring a little extra money my way. One of the church members was getting married and asked me to sing at her wedding. And so, I'd sing and get paid an honorarium that was just enough to cover the extra that was needed that month. I saw that kind of thing happen on several different occasions during my first couple of years at First Baptist. The thing that always amazed me though is that God would bless me with the amount I needed, and yet I never charged anything. If I did a wedding, or a funeral, or anything of that nature, I never had a set fee like some pastors did. When people would ask me what I charged, I'd just tell them that they're welcome to give an honorarium if they'd like to, but it's entirely up to them. There were a few times I didn't receive anything, but for the most part people were pretty careful about giving me something for my extra time and service.

That first year as full-time youth pastor was challenging, but in a good way. I had regular midweek weekly youth group meetings, a pretty lively Sunday school class, monthly outreach events encouraging kids to invite their friends; all the typical youth group stuff. And having been a choral music major in college I was able to put together a pretty good youth choir that sang some of the best contemporary Christian music that was popular at that time with young people. We even went out on a limb and used a few other instruments as backup. Of course, we always had a piano, but one time I added a bass guitar and drums. And the only thing I can say is that drums in a Baptist church was a bit of a stretch, it just wasn't done. I knew I was getting into sticky territory, but I was hoping that the folks at First Baptist, who I had really grown to love, would look upon the youth music with grace and joyful acceptance. I knew the music wasn't their favorite style necessarily, but I was praying that they'd look past the foreign sound and realize that these kids were praising God in a way that made sense to them. I also prayed that the congregation would feel thankful that these kids were in church, singing in a choir that's praising the Lord, instead of being at one of a hundred other places they could be that weren't nearly as healthy or uplifting. You catch my drift, don't you? There was a lot out there that was trying to grab our kids' attention, and most of it wasn't good. Every time I saw my kids in church,

I was just thankful they were there, instead of being involved in activities that could literally destroy their lives.

So, the first time we added backup bass guitar and drums, I was pretty nervous. But the most amazing thing happened. Most of the people responded the way I was praying that they would. A lot of them came up afterwards and said that it was so good to see and hear kids in church and that they were thankful for the youth ministry we had at First Baptist. I was greatly relieved on two counts. Number one: I still had a job and evidently my initial foray into the contemporary music scene wasn't going to end with my public disgrace and subsequent dismissal. And number two: I was thankful that the good people of First Baptist were as gracious and loving as I had always perceived them to be. And sure enough, after that initial introduction, the "young people's music" as it came to be called, was always well received. In fact, some of the older folks would say, "Pastor John, when I first heard that kind of music I didn't like it. I didn't really want that rock 'n roll stuff in my church. But when I looked at the faces on those kids I saw a lot of joy and excitement. And to tell you the truth, we need that kind of joy here at church. Some of us older ones get set in our ways and our faith can become old hat and routine. The young people bring a freshness, a vitality to the faith that we haven't always had. Thanks for what you're doing John."

Those were the kind of folks that I served at First Baptist. Now, not everyone was as positive as most of the others. Some people were a little cranky about the new music and you could see it on their faces at first. But when a kid would stand up and give a testimony about where they'd been and what they were doing before they came to church, even the hardest, crankiest heart would melt and some of those scowlers would become our greatest supporters over that year. It truly was a very gracious and loving congregation.

I think that much of that love and graciousness was due in large part to our senior pastor. Pastor Tim was a really great guy on many different levels. As a young pastor I couldn't have asked for a more positive, supportive, and godly role model than Tim. He had been in ministry for over 20 years, which to a young kid just starting out, seemed like a lifetime. As I got to know Tim as boss, as pastor, and as friend, I saw something that one of my seminary profs told us. He said something to the effect that, "A church will take on the personality of its pastor over the years." I think First Baptist was gracious and loving because that's what Pastor Tim was like. Pastor Tim had been with the congregation for about 14 years, which was about 10 years longer than the average pastor stayed in a church. And so, when we received Tim's letter of resignation to accept a call to another church out in Southern California, we were shocked and saddened. And yet we also knew that that's the way things often played out in churches. The pastor would sense God leading him to go elsewhere. Now the real work would begin; the church had to find another pastor.

Pastor Tim had given our church two months' notice and within a couple of days the church board had established a search committee. They collected resumes and conducted interviews of various potential pastors. During the search process, which they determined would be as short and efficient as possible, I did most of the preaching. They asked me if I was interested in "throwing my hat into the ring" but I told them no, and that I thought I was still called to the young people. They accepted that and continued to search, determined to find someone quickly. I appreciated the opportunity to hone my preaching skills and actually learned a lot during those months of searching.

Finally, after four months of searching, the committee had a candidate. They shared his resume with the congregation and brought him in for a weekend of candidating during which we would hear about his call to ministry, his experience level with other churches, and his vision for our church. We met his wife and kids and they seemed very nice, although I thought his wife was a little subdued, but I just chalked that up to being shy in these new surroundings. Nothing to be too concerned about, really. And yet, it bothered me a bit.

To make a long story short, the interviews went pretty well and when we got to the Sunday service his preaching was absolutely outstanding. This guy could preach. I felt like I was sitting in a seminary class, his command of the Scriptures was so strong. His delivery was excellent and his points very practical, very useful for growing in our Christian faith. Later that night the congregation came together to vote about extending Pastor Charles the call to come and be the senior pastor at First Baptist. The vote was 232 *yes* and 3 *no*. With numbers like that the folks were confident that we had God's man for this season in our church.

How do I say this graciously and discreetly? I would never tell anyone else this, but I was one of the three *no* votes. But when the *yes* votes were overwhelming, I just figured that maybe, subconsciously, I didn't want to give up preaching, or maybe I really did want to be the senior pastor after all, and I was just now figuring that out. I didn't know exactly what I was feeling, I just knew that I wasn't feeling comfortable with the decision, but I needed to let that go. It's just that when Pastor Charles and I met alone to talk about the potential of working together, I noticed how different he was compared to Tim. Pastor Tim was always warm and welcoming, and never gave any indication that you were taking up his valuable time. But the initial feeling I got from Charles is that he was indeed very much the professional, which is a great thing on many levels. You certainly don't want a guy standing up in the pulpit every Sunday who lacks the professionalism of the pastoral office. That could make people feel very uncomfortable wondering what their pastor was going to say that would be embarrassing, or just plain wrong. So, Charles was definitely professional. But what I didn't get from him was a sense of warmth and genuine caring. I didn't get the sense that I was in the presence of a true shepherd. I knew that Pastor Charles could lead with a strong and firm hand, but I just wasn't sure he could shepherd the flock. I knew he could drive his flock to achieve, but I wasn't sure I could see him leading his flock to green pastures and quiet waters. And that, quite frankly, concerned me greatly.

Over the next year and a half, the atmosphere at First Baptist slowly began to change. The sermons were good, and the various programs were stronger than ever before. There was even some growth as people who were out church shopping came to hear the "new guy in town." On the surface things seem to be going pretty good. But something was happening underneath it all that was very concerning. The love and the grace were slowly eroding over time. People were discovering that if a person messed up in some area of their service and ministry to the church, Pastor Charles would be all over that. He wouldn't tolerate what he thought were lame excuses for failure. He didn't want excuses, he wanted excellence. If you couldn't do your ministry, whatever it was, with excellence, you'd be out and he'd recruit somebody else who could. He was a professional, yes, but in all honesty, he was cold as ice. I saw many folks who had once been joy-filled servants of God that taught their Sunday school class of fifth grade girls, or sang in the choir, or helped on the kitchen crew, or visited the shut-ins - I saw many of those folks shrivel up under his cold and harsh demands to do their ministry better and with excellence. Frankly, I grew to hate the word excellence. I always wanted to do a good job with the youth. I always wanted to give back to the Lord the best we had to offer. After all, He gave His best for us, why wouldn't we want to do the same for Him, right? As the next year went on I began to hear rumblings under the surface. Pastor Charles had offended many of the dear saints at First Baptist. I'm not sure "offended" is the appropriate word; "hurt" would be more accurate. Many people felt hurt by their pastor, the very one who's supposed to lead them to the safety of the sheep pen. The atmosphere of love and grace had disappeared and a rather cold, judgmental spirit was beginning to take over. Over time the young people and their music began to be a topic of harsh criticism. The long hair on the guys suddenly became of great concern because it was "un-natural." People who struggled with some of the various vices that can be found in any group of folks were beginning to feel judged, and looked down upon because they hadn't experienced the "victory" yet.

The rumblings became stronger and stronger over time. The tension was so thick that you could literally feel it in the worship services. I was out for lunch with a friend after church one Sunday and I heard a couple in the booth in back of me. They were discussing the new church they had visited that day in their search for a place to land. And as they talked I heard the wife say that she just felt weird at the service. And he agreed, he felt the same way. He couldn't put his finger on it, but something wasn't right there. And then she said, "Well honey, I guess we can cross First Baptist off our list." And you know the really sad thing about that? I had to agree with them. There was something weird about the church and the atmosphere it presented. I knew that if a friend of mine just moved to the city and was looking for a church, I couldn't invite him to ours, it just wasn't healthy. It no longer built people up, it just slowly, over time, robbed them of the joy that they should have had in their faith.

I don't want to go into all the gory details of what happened in that year and a half, particularly the last month or two. It's too painful, even to this day. Suffice it to say that First Baptist didn't survive. More and more people just kept drifting away. And finally, when the church had gotten down to half its original size, a vote was taken to oust Pastor Charles. He was let go and he and his family packed up and left for another call. I realized a couple of things. Oftentimes a church that wants to get a new pastor very soon instead of having a long search process will look at the great resume in front of them and never thoroughly follow up on the references. And secondly, I realized that the look I originally saw on Pastor Charles' wife, Diane, was one of defeat, before this new work even started. She had been through this several times before. She knew her husband and she knew that nothing had changed. And so here they were again, doing it all over.

People at First Baptist who had at one time been so loving and caring now had chosen up sides. And when the vote was taken and Pastor Charles sent packing, the half of the congregation that remained wound up splitting, not in two, but in a dozen different ways. People took off for other churches, while some never did go anywhere else.

My youth group, composed of kids from the various families of the church, was also greatly impacted as they heard their parents talking about church business at home. My youth group also began to disintegrate, taking up sides, just like their parents. When I realized what was happening, and that I was powerless to stop the momentum, I slipped into what I could only describe as depression. If you know me well, you know that's just not me. I'm always positive, and up, and looking for the next challenge God may bring our way. Well, this was a challenge all right, but God didn't bring it - the enemy did.

Finally, after a period of time, I went home one day absolutely broken. I was crying, my pillowcase soaked with tears. The thing that hurt me most was when Matt, my original wallflower, looked at me and said, "John, I thought Christians were supposed to be different. I don't believe that anymore." Matt walked away and I've never seen him since. My heart was broken and my spirit was crushed.

Chapter 12

Wendy

HAVE YOU EVER HAD AN EXPERIENCE WHERE you were confronted with a choice that you needed to make on the spot? Absolutely zero knowledge of it. No time to think it through. No chance to process the good and bad points. No idea what the eventual outcome would be of whatever choice you made. All you knew is that you needed to make a decision. But inside you're feeling that this is a really important moment in time and how you choose to respond could have a lasting effect on your life. That's how I felt when Kevin, this guy I met on the front steps of the church that had just kicked me out, asked me to lunch.

What I need you to know, to give you some perspective, is that Chicago is no different than any other large city. We have a ton of truly wonderful people who just want to live their lives and raise their families and get the most out of life possible. But, in the midst of all those nice folks, live a few creeps, and I swear I've dated at least half of them. I don't know if I've got a sign on me that says, "Creeps Welcome," or if I just give off a social-worker vibe, but I always have this ability to attract some real weirdos, beginning with diner-guy. So, over the years I've developed some pretty accurate radar when it comes to potential dating partners.

Now having said that, don't start thinking that I've got my act together when it comes to relationships. Like I said before I've dated some real weirdos and within the first few minutes I could tell that this was going nowhere but downhill fast. Sometimes I'd fake being sick and needing to go home. And when they'd call again, I'd just keep making excuses about why I couldn't go out with them, until finally they'd get the hint and quit calling. But every time I did that I'd kick myself and say, "You dummy. You're doing the same thing you always do. Get some discernment, get a little pickier, and start making smart choices. Otherwise someday, you're not going to be able to shake this creep so easily and you're going to be in some major trouble."

So, all of my dating history, and the chaotic way I've run my life in the past, flashes through my mind as I'm standing on the steps of Redeemer Community Church. This good-looking, long-haired, bearded hippie named Kevin has just asked me out to lunch. I met him about 30 seconds ago and now I've got to make a decision. Is he a creep or is he at least somewhat normal? Is he a weirdo or is he just kind of quirky? Is the invitation something I need to decline because inside I know he's a serial killer? Or is the invitation something that might change my life in a grand and glorious burst of romance and adventure?

I didn't know for sure, because after all, it's not like I've got a great track record on this sort of thing. But this guy made me feel safe. In the first 10 seconds I met him and heard his words encouraging me not feel bad about being given the boot by the church lady, I'd felt a measure of love and kindness I'm not sure I'd ever run into before. So, his love and kindness vibe got to me and I said *yes* to his offer of lunch. But just to be on the safe side I invited him to go the few blocks to the restaurant where my mom worked. I knew she was at home with Travis and that I would never run into her and have to make awkward introductions. I also knew that very few, if any of the folks on the Sunday shift would know me, so there'd be no finger pointing and behind the door gossiping about my new boyfriend. I didn't need that in my life right now. Life is complicated enough being a single mom without a bunch of storytellers getting all caught up in my business.

We walked the few blocks to the restaurant and by the time we got there I swear I was having heart palpitations. This guy was so gentle, so kind, it kind of blew me away. I mean to be perfectly blunt, we Chicago folks can be a little outspoken and abrasive at times, but Kevin was the exact opposite of that. I wasn't sure if I'd ever met anyone like him before and the couple hours we were together were quite delightful. I knew I hadn't fallen in love at first sight, but I wondered if I was close. There was just something about the way he talked that was very intriguing, in a wholesome, healthy way. But what I noticed most wasn't his talking, it was his listening. Kevin had this ability to get me to open up about myself. I heard myself telling him details about my history that I really hadn't shared with anybody. Maybe he was a professional counselor or he was just really good at getting people to open up to him. Or maybe it was just the fact that we shared a bond together of both being kicked out of the same church for the same reason - appearance. Now there's a good reason to risk a person's eternal soul, right?

As we sat there and talked, sharing details of our lives together, I realized what it was that made Kevin so different. Kevin was what I would have termed a "Jesus Freak." In years past I'd see people running around with their index finger pointed into the air and came to find out that that meant "One Way." In other words, that was the Jesus Freak way of letting people know that there was only one way to God and that was through, you guessed it, Jesus. I never really paid that much attention to all that stuff because I'd never really known a Jesus person before. But sitting with Kevin, the Jesus Freak, and eating turkey sandwiches, gave me a whole different perspective that I found surprisingly winsome. This whole vibe Kevin gave off wasn't something he had to try hard to manufacture; it was just there, naturally. I came to find out later that it was something the Bible called the "fragrance of Christ" and when I first heard that phrase I just knew I had experienced it in Kevin. If I had to conjure up a picture of Jesus in my mind, all I'd needed to do was think about Kevin. Not only did he look like what I always imagined Jesus to look like with the long hair and beard, he also felt like what I imagined Jesus to feel like. I never knew much about Jesus, but once in a while I'd see a picture of Him holding a little lamb in His arms. And it would hit me that that was who Jesus was. He was a gentle and kind loving shepherd who was there to embrace us and care for us. That kind of image always gave me goosebumps because I wanted to feel that so desperately.

Sometimes, in my most private moments, I would imagine myself to be that little lamb that was being carried in the loving arms of Jesus. I didn't really know who Jesus was; I just knew that I desperately longed to be carried, tucked away in the safe and secure arms of the Jesus in the picture. I wanted to be a little lamb.

Kevin and I talked for two hours and it was wonderful. He told me not to give up on my search for faith. And when I told him how it was my son Travis that prompted me to seek some kind of church experience, he didn't blink an eye. The guys I dated before would suddenly grow quiet and fidgety when I mentioned that I had a son. But not Kevin. I could tell that he really liked children and could imagine he and Travis wrestling around on the ground, trying out different holds. When I caught myself daydreaming like this, I told myself to hold on for heaven's sake, it's just a turkey sandwich at a so-so restaurant. It's not like there's wedding bells ringing here. Calm it down girl!

When it was time to go, Kevin walked me home. It was a beautiful day and the sun felt warm on my skin. I realized that I hadn't felt this good in a long time and that nobody else made me feel this happy except Travis. But now Kevin was giving me those same feelings of happiness just being with him. I didn't know what all this meant, but I was hoping like crazy this wasn't a one-time deal; one solitary afternoon of honest talk. I desperately wanted more. The words that kept coming to me were either a personal plea, or perhaps a prayer. I didn't know which. All I knew is that the words, "Ask for my number, ask for my number, ask for my number," kept running through my head. When we got to the door Kevin said that he really enjoyed our time together and thanked me for taking a chance and having lunch with him. I told him that it was wonderful to meet him and thanked him for helping me sort through my feelings of rejection from the church. He, in turn, said that he was glad he was there. So here we had all these nice thank you's and words of encouragement going between us, but still no mention of a number. Kevin told me that he had better get going and turned to walk away. My heart sank. Chicago's a big town; it's not likely that we're just going to run into each other again, especially not at that church. My heart was already sinking in the waters of despair. Just as I feel I'm on the verge of drowning, suddenly Kevin turns around and faces me. He looks into my eyes and says, "Wendy, I don't want to be too forward or presumptuous, but I was wondering if I could have your phone number?" I felt like saying, "Too forward, too presumptuous? You idiot, I'll tattoo it on your forehead, if you want me to. Of course, you can have my number!" That's what I felt like saying, but I restrained myself and said a simple, "Sure." But then, just to add a little encouragement, I said, "I hope you'll call soon. I really enjoyed our time together." Kevin reached out and briefly touched my shoulder. "So did I, Wendy, so did I." And then he turned around and began to walk away. And maybe I'm mistaken, or just overly emotional, or a hopeless romantic, but he seemed to have a vitality to his step, like he was walking on air. Maybe I imagined it, but I don't think so.

I wondered how long it would be before I heard from Kevin, but thankfully he called the next day as I was getting ready for work and wondered if I'd like to go to a movie with him, and of course I accepted. I called Mrs. York and asked if she could babysit the next night and she said she'd be glad to. Kevin picked me up in his small Volkswagen bug that had a bumper sticker that said, "Jesus is the

Bridge Over Troubled Waters." I wondered if Simon and Garfunkel new that they were evangelists of sorts. We went to the movie and saw "The Gospel Road" with Johnny Cash. It was about the life and ministry of Jesus. Now, I have to say, it was a little bit cheesy. I think Jesus was blonde and Mary spoke with a southern accent. And even though I didn't know very much about the middle-Eastern culture, I was pretty sure that it wasn't like that. But nevertheless, I enjoyed the movie and it certainly gave me a greater appreciation for Jesus.

When we left the movie theater we got into his Bug and then stopped to have a bite to eat. As we were sitting there, finishing up our late-night snack, Kevin asked if I'd like to go to church with him on Friday night. I told him that right now the idea of church made me nervous, but he assured me that it wouldn't be like my last experience. So, I said sure. I would have gone to watch cars rust if he asked me; I just wanted to be with him. So that Friday night he picked me up and we went to this huge house which was about 10 miles from my place. My first thought was that this didn't look like a church, but when we walked in I knew right away that it was. And yet, it wasn't at all what I expected. There was no stage, no choir, and no men sitting up in front. It was just a big living room full of people. One guy was up in front with a guitar and was leading the group in a song called "Pass It On." I didn't know it but joined in as best I could. After a few more songs the guy up in front opened it up for what he called "sharing." People just began to stand up and talk about what God was doing in their lives. Some were having wonderful seasons of blessing and were praising God for His goodness to them. Others shared about struggles they were going through at the present time. I felt badly for them and hoped that things would get better. But I witnessed something I'd never seen before. When someone would share a need, the others would get up out of their seats, go to the person who had just shared, and place their hand on his head or shoulder or knee. And then they prayed. Boy, did they ever pray. I always thought prayers had to be written out and had to use the old English, like Shakespeare or something. But these folks prayed to Jesus like he was right there in the room. It was like they were on a first name basis with Him. I wasn't even sure if God knew who I was, let alone be on a first name basis with Him. It was all very strange, but in a good way. I remember thinking: I really want this for Travis and me.

Over the next few months Kevin and I spent more time together. Kevin, I came to find out pretty early on, was indeed a counselor. He worked with kids at a public school across town and saw it as a way to help kids who were struggling. And although he couldn't talk about faith very much, if the kid brought it up, providing the opening, Kevin was free to help him process his questions. Kevin saw it as a ministry that he did for the Lord and the state paid for. Just being able to help a kid, no matter what they were going through, brought joy to Kevin's heart.

By this time, of course, I had introduced Kevin to Travis. Travis was a bit nervous at first because although I'd try to protect him, Travis had seen some of the losers I dated and was a little scared for me. But it didn't take long before Travis and Kevin had a pretty good relationship going. They'd throw the football around, or try out different wrestling holds, or see who could eat the hottest sauce on a taco. Once I found that the taco challenge wasn't going to kill him, I relaxed a bit and let Travis and Kevin have their little contests. Boys will be boys, I guess.

I was falling deeply in love with Kevin and I knew he was falling for me. We saw each other most days, although sometimes I needed to fill in for a night shift or Kevin had some school function he had to attend. But otherwise, we were together pretty much every day and I could tell that our love was growing. With Kevin I didn't have to wonder because he told me frequently and with great feeling. I was getting the idea that he was going to ask me to marry him and my answer would be a heartfelt *yes*, in caps, for all the world to see. Kevin was mine. God gave him to me and I wanted to shout it from the rooftops.

I had asked Jesus to come into my life as my personal Savior and Lord. That Friday night church we attended, along with Kevin's constant witness for Jesus helped me to see my need of Christ. I came to believe that God really did have wonderful plans and goals for my life. I began to feel like that little lamb that was being held safely and securely in the loving embrace of Jesus, just like I had seen several years ago in that Shepherd picture. I didn't really know much about the Bible, and theology, and doctrine, and all that other stuff. I just knew that God loved Travis and me and was watching out for us every step of the way.

Kevin was hinting at marriage but had yet to propose. One day he called me up and asked me out to one of the nicest restaurants in our particular part of town. It's not the kind of restaurant you go to on a school counselor salary. It was small, intimate, romantic, and outrageously expensive. So, when he asked me out for Saturday night and told me where we were going, I knew something was up. We weren't celebrating anything special, so to go to this particular restaurant that was going to put a serious dent in his wallet, meant that he had something up his sleeve. I was excited beyond measure. I wore a brand-new dress I picked up for the occasion. I was listening to Christian music on my cassette recorder and just thanking God for his goodness to Travis and me. Travis was going to have a father who deeply loved him and I was going to have a husband. And not just any husband, but one who loved me unconditionally and had brought me to the Savior. Thank you, God, for loving and protecting us all these years, just for this exact moment in time.

I looked at the clock and saw that Kevin was running late. I began to feel a little uneasy because Kevin was on-the-dot prompt, always. I could set my watch to Kevin's sense of time. Pretty soon 10 minutes became 15 and I started to really feel queasy. Something was wrong. I could feel it. It was at that moment that I heard sirens coming toward us, and somehow, I just knew they involved Kevin. There had been an accident between a small Volkswagen bug and a city bus whose driver had a heart attack. When I talked to the police officer later, I learned that Kevin had a little box in his jacket pocket. When he found out who I was, he put two and two together and showed me the box. I looked inside and saw a beautiful diamond ring. Nothing big, nothing fancy, but it was meant for me. And now the dream was gone.

Kevin died in that crash and with him died my life and my future. But something else died that night. My new faith. And from that point on my life spiraled down into the depths of despair and darkness. And you know what? I didn't even care.

Chapter 13

John

I T WAS MONDAY MORNING, THE DAY AFTER THE church officially closed up shop. After Pastor Charles was forced to leave, the leaders at First Baptist tried to breathe new life into the already dead church, but it was pretty hopeless. People that left were definitely not coming back. And those who had stayed had little hope for the future of the church. Barring a miracle on the order of Lazarus' resurrection, the church was destined to stay in the tomb it was already inhabiting.

I tried to hold it together, as best I could, but my heart wasn't in it. I didn't know what I was doing, what I should be preaching, how I should be leading. I was totally lost and was very relieved when the leaders suggested we have a special business meeting to decide what to do. I had already made a personal decision concerning my ministry there, but I was interested to see what would happen at the meeting.

The night of the meeting came and different people stood up to say their piece. Some people were crying out of deep grief for their beloved church family. They'd come to know the Lord at the little altar in the front of the sanctuary. They'd been married at that same altar and had dedicated their kids to the Lord there. Several memorial services for various friends and loved ones were held in the church, and the memories of those services, as well as the almost sure closure of the church, brought many to tears. Other folks weren't quite so tearful, they were just flat out angry. How could this happen? Whose fault is this anyway? This is the work of the devil! We can't let Satan win, we've gotta fight! Still, others weren't so much sad or angry as they were philosophically resigned. Churches come and go, just like any other organization. We've done a good work here for over 50 years, we can be thankful for that. Maybe it's just time to let it go and pass the building on to that up-and-coming church renting the school down the street. That way, in a sense, we're passing the mantle on to them. And slowly, but surely, I think everybody gathered there began to see the wisdom in that kind of thinking. It might not have been the perfect scenario, but it was pretty clear that it was probably the only scenario that made any sense and would at least salvage some of what had been a thriving house of worship.

After two hours of talking back-and-forth, as well as several people standing to pray for God's will to be done, ballots were passed out and the people were asked to vote by the Spirit's leading. And when the ballots were collected and counted, the vote was unanimous to suspend operations and begin the process of disbanding immediately. Next Sunday was to be our last service. We contacted the pastor of the church that was meeting at the school and made them an offer they couldn't refuse. In an effort to ensure that an effective witness for Christ would still continue in this area, we offered to sell them the building for one dollar. Like I said: An offer they couldn't refuse.

So, that last Sunday came and the service was quite inspiring. I invited Pastor Bob from the Lester Park Community Church to bring his congregation and worship with us in their soon-to-be new facility. We joined our two choirs together and did a rendition of "How Great How Art" that was grand and glorious and brought tears of sorrow for what could have been, as well as tears of joy for what the future would bring. These were dear brothers and sisters in Christ, and we knew that the light of the gospel would shine forth for years to come.

I preached for 15 minutes on the healing benefits of remembering all that God had done in the past through First Baptist Church. I also encouraged all of us to ask forgiveness for whatever sins had been committed as we navigated the split, at times, not too graciously. I'm convinced that very few, if any, people can go through a split without sinning. And we needed to ask God's forgiveness for our part in it. I also encouraged people to release forgiveness to those who had hurt them during the rough months leading up to this juncture. Forgive those who said or did things that weren't right and they hurt you. Jesus tells us to forgive, not so much for the benefit of the one who sinned against you, but rather for your benefit. Take that load of unforgiveness and dump it at the foot of the cross. Take the monkey off your back and walk in the freedom that forgiving others brings. And as I'm preaching these wonderful, thoughtful, biblical words, inside I'm wondering if I'm actually going to be able to practice what I'm telling others to do. I'm not there yet, but I hope I will be soon.

When I was done, Pastor Bob stood up and preached about the future and the glorious plans and goals that God had for the Lester Park Community Church. "I know the plans I have for you," declares the Lord and so on and so forth. It's a wonderful passage from Jeremiah 29:11-13 and I sincerely believed every word of that marvelous text of Scripture. But I'm not sure I believed it for me personally, because inside I was really struggling. The church's move to suspend operations was the right decision, but it also clearly reaffirmed the personal decision I had already made for myself. Before I went to the business meeting, I had written my letter of resignation, put it in an envelope addressed to the church chairman and stuck it in the inside pocket of my sports jacket. Whatever the vote, I was convinced that my time was over. So, when the vote came, it's not like I was surprised, it's just that it became very clear to me that in one week's time I was going to be unemployed. My phone had been absolutely silent; no calls, no inquiries from other churches, not even a request to do a wedding or a service at the local funeral home. Nothing! Zip! Nada!

So, I went home after the service, having stopped at Kentucky Fried Chicken for their five-piece meal, brought it home and proceeded to eat all five pieces, plus all the sides, plus everything else in my refrigerator, all in one sitting. It's a good thing I don't drink, that could have been disastrous. But there's nothing like five greasy pieces of fried chicken to get you over the depressive slump and back on the road to a positive future. Actually, I felt kind of sick and so I just laid around that afternoon and watched baseball on TV. I tried to read after the game, but I couldn't really concentrate. I think I must've read the same page 20 times and I still didn't know what it said. My mind was shot, it needed a break. Tomorrow I would get up and start problem-solving. Where do I go from here? Where do you want me Lord? How are you going to revive my crushed spirit? It's got to be you Lord, because I'm totally clueless right now. So finally, after wallowing in despair for the remainder of the evening, I decided to go to bed and trust in the old saying, "Things always look better in the morning." I wasn't sure if that was going to be true in my case, but hey, what else am I going to do? It's not like I had a lot of options.

I slept fitfully through the night and after eight hours still didn't feel rested, but I got up anyway and decided that taking a shower might revive me. I washed my hair and got out of the shower and dried off. I brushed my teeth, sprayed a good dose of Right Guard, combed my hair and beard, and went down to have a bowl of Fruit Loops for breakfast. Not exactly healthy, but it's my only vice and Fruit Loops bring a little pleasure to my dark and depressed world. Besides Fruit Loops, the only other breakfast I usually have is chili and corn chips. I know that's weird, but I'm just not an eggs person and chili has been on all-time favorite of mine since I was six. Very strange for a Swedish kid, but sometimes you just need a little spice to kick things up a bit.

I finished my Fruit Loops and was taking the bowl to the sink, wondering how many other breakfasts I was going to have in this place. After all, it's a parsonage, and I'm pretty sure that I'm going to have to vacate it fairly quickly as things get moving from the financial and business angle of the church shutdown. Just as I put my bowl in the sink and started to run the water, the phone rang. I pick it up and say "hello" and a deep, booming voice on the other end of the line says, "Hey buddy, I'm trying to reach Pastor John Larson." Now, I'm wondering who this is and how I got to be his buddy, but I refrain from making any funny remarks and I say, "This is John." Well, that started a conversation that lasted for about 30 minutes. After that conversation with Max Sherman, who turned out to be a very friendly and likable guy, I actually did feel like his buddy. And as he explained to me the nature of his call I just looked up at God and silently mouthed the words, "Thank You."

Max was calling me because he had been talking with a childhood friend of his, a guy who we both knew. I asked him who the mutual friend was and he told me it was David Wilson. I said, "Who's David Wilson?" And Max went on to tell me that David Wilson was an instructor at my seminary. Then it all made sense. Max was a childhood friend of Prof Wilson, the toughest instructor to ever teach at my school. I didn't mind the fact that he was tough; it's just that he gave no indication at all as to your competency. You couldn't tell if he thought you were going to be the next Billy Graham and take the world by storm, or if you were going to crash and burn right out of the gate at your first church.

As we continued our conversation I discovered that Max was the chairman of the pastoral search committee at the Pleasant Pastures Community Church in eastern Washington. They weren't quite sure where to start searching for a replacement for their pastor who had retired after being there for 18 years. Max just thought he'd give Dave a call and see if he had any suggestions. Well, believe it or not, Prof

Wilson brought up my name. He told Max that he had heard through the grapevine that the church I was with wound up splitting and I would be available immediately. So, I'm thinking, "Thanks for the vote of confidence Prof, but did you have to tell him about the split? No church is going to want to touch me with a 10-foot pole." But Max surprised me and addressed the split situation. He said that Prof Wilson also told him that I did an outstanding job in the midst of a very difficult and unhealthy situation, when most associate pastors would have gone on to their next call. He told Max that I showed a lot of strength and maturity in what could have only been a very stressful atmosphere. It's a good thing that Prof didn't see me crying in my pillow like a little baby; I'm not sure his assessment would have been quite the same.

Anyway, after about 30 minutes of telling me what they were looking for in a pastor and the kind of church Pleasant Pastures was, and the makeup of the congregation demographically, and all that other stuff that search committees pull out—after all that— he asked if I'd like to come and try it out. I said, "But you haven't even seen my resume yet." And Max told me that if his friend David recommended me, that was good enough for him. I asked him when he was going to share our conversation with the rest of the search committee. And he said, "Oh, don't worry about that, I *am* the committee. The church just said go find someone good, so that's what I'm doing. You want to come for a visit and see if you like us and we like you?" I asked him if he had any particular dates in mind and he said that he thought this Sunday would be great. "This Sunday? You want me there this Sunday?" Max gently reminded me, that unless he wasn't getting the whole picture, I didn't have any place else to be. And you know what? He was right. I was as free as a bird, so I made the decision to come, as Max put it, for a visit. He told me they would fly me out and pick me up at the airport. I told him that was fine and that I was looking forward to coming. But then a thought struck me. Why don't I just drive out? I live in a parsonage, so everything I own can fit in my car in about three suitcases. I've never been west before and I'd always wanted to see the Space Needle in Seattle and the Pacific Ocean and maybe even Victoria, BC. I'll just drive out and if it works out, great, I'm already there, ready to go. If it doesn't, I'll just keep going on my little vacation to the Northwest and figure out where to go and what to do from there. So, I told Max I'd leave the next morning and plan to see him late afternoon on Thursday. We said goodbye and hung up the phone.

I stood there for a minute, processing what had just happened, and then I let out a holler of delight and went running around the house, completely energized for the first time in several months. I had a purpose! I had a plan! I wasn't sure where that plan would take me exactly, but I knew that at least I'd be out of here and on my way to a new adventure.

Chapter 14

Wendy

FTER KEVIN'S DEATH I FELT A THICK SHROUD of black fog around me constantly and I couldn't shake it. I'd go to bed at night, hoping and praying that I wouldn't wake up. The days were just unbearable, and I honestly didn't want to be here. I loved Travis with all my heart and wanted nothing but the best for him, but the way I felt now, with the darkness that had invaded my life so suddenly, made me consider that he might actually be better off without me. Honestly, I'm not even sure I made him breakfast some mornings, or packed his lunch for school. When I look back on that period of time, these months later, I'm actually surprised that I didn't try to just end it all. I felt like it. I thought about it. I started to make a plan how to do it, while trying to convince myself that it would actually be a loving act of sacrifice on behalf of Travis. He would be better off without me, because after all, I'm probably doing more damage to him by being in this unending state of agony and despair. I wanted to end it for the sake of my son, and I would have, I think, if it hadn't been for this nagging thought deep inside. I couldn't get past the idea that if I'm grieving so deeply because I lost Kevin, who was my boyfriend for a few months, how's Travis going to cope losing his mother who's been with him for the entire seven years of his life? Not only that, but moms are supposed to be there a good portion of his adult life too. Mothers and sons are supposed to have 50 or 60 years together, not a measly seven.

I somehow was able to make the decision to go on living, if you could call my bleak existence living. Sometimes I felt that I was dead, my body just barely hanging on with some kind of life support that was keeping me breathing. I'd like to be able to say that I was a brave person, that I just picked myself up by the bootstraps and by sheer determination of will and strength of character, I overcame the darkness. I'd like to be able to say that, but that would be a lie. I'd also like to tell you a wonderful testimony of how my escape from this hell on earth came from my new-found faith, but that would be a lie also. My new-found faith was missing in action. It died along with Kevin that night.

I somehow got up and went for my shift at the diner most days, but my head wasn't really in the game. After taking a week off to sit home and cry and mourn and question everything that had happened,

I knew one thing for sure; the bills weren't going to pay themselves. And even though mom still had her job at the restaurant, her salary wouldn't cover all the household bills we had coming in relentlessly each month. I knew both of us were living paycheck to paycheck and there was very little wiggle room. So, I slowly pulled myself out of bed that first morning I was due back, made a feeble attempt to make myself presentable, and headed for the diner, not really knowing quite what to expect.

I got to the diner and everybody greeted me with expressions of sorrow for my loss and for the pain I was in. I mumbled a quiet thanks and then tried to do my best. But it was a disaster. I couldn't keep myself from breaking down when I'd catch a glimpse of a long-haired, bearded, hippie-type walking by outside, or coming in for coffee and a piece of pie. They all reminded me of Kevin. I couldn't keep even the most basic orders straight and wound up getting a lot of complaints from people who felt that I just didn't care, and they let my superior know it. I thought it would get better, but it never did. The challenge with waitressing is that your head has to be on straight every minute you're there, because it's all about details. Sometimes you've got so many orders going, with so many specific little requests, that you can hardly keep them straight on a good day. "Please hold the mustard on this burger." "Please put the salad dressing on the side." "I want a Coke with very little ice." "Could I have a refill on my iced tea?" The list of personal preferences and adjustments to the way the menu was prepared was endless. In the past, it wouldn't have been a problem. I could keep it all straight in my head and never even had to look at my order pad to see who ordered what when the food came. But that skill was gone. It had just evaporated and slowly, over the next month, so did my boss's patience. And finally, after a particularly bad day that had followed multiple warnings, each growing more serious and threatening, my boss finally told me he had no choice but to let me go. He advised me to get help and maybe find some kind of work that I could do that didn't require such concentration.

So, that was it. I'd be done by the end of the week. He let me stay on until Friday, which at least gave me time to think about what I was going to do next. For the next couple of days, I tried my best, but to no avail, his mind was made up. I didn't have the slightest notion what I was going to do for work. I certainly couldn't go to another diner; I'd be a mess from the very start. I thought about getting some factory job, but chances are I'd have to start on a late shift and that wouldn't work out for child care for Travis. Even though I had a car, I didn't want to have to drive into the industrial center of town every day, adding to my anxiety. So here I am, on my last day of work, still having zero options. But then Nick walked in.

Nick was a guy I had seen at the diner a few times before. He was obviously Italian. Nicholas Salerno. You can't get much more Italian than that. He was also very good looking, in that dark Italian way. Thick, wavy black hair and beautiful white teeth that enhanced a very charming smile. And though I was still in mourning, I wasn't so depressed that I didn't notice him. I wasn't interested, but it would be difficult not to notice a good-looking man, who was dripping with charm and charisma. Oh, did I also mention that he gave me three tips that were my best ever? I had waited on Nick three times, and every time he gave me a 25% tip. I'd never had that kind of thing happen to me before, so when somebody does that you have a tendency to pay a little more attention to them.

As I waited on Nick that last day, it was kind of slow and so Nick engaged me in conversation. He told me that he had noticed that I was looking a little down, particularly the last several weeks. I don't know why I did this but, like I said, it was slow and so I just told him what had happened, and how because of that, today was my last shift. They had to let me go, and I couldn't blame them. I was having a very difficult time keeping all the details straight, and in waitressing, details are crucial.

After I had disclosed all of this to Nick, a guy I didn't really know, he asked me a question that seemed to come right out of the blue. He asked me if I liked music and did I like to dance. I thought that was kind of odd and I was wondering if he was going to ask me out for a night of dancing at some club. I would have turned him down, but the question intrigued me. So, I said that actually I love music and dancing but I really hadn't had much of it in my life lately. Nick looked at me and said something to the effect that I was very pretty and he enjoyed my company. We hadn't spent much time together at the diner but he assured me that he had enjoyed every minute of it. He said that if I was interested he might have a job for me. And I said, "Well Nick, you know they fired me because I wasn't doing my job well. Why would you offer me a job?" Nick went on to tell me that it was a different kind of job, one that didn't take quite the same kind of concentration. He asked me how I would like to get paid for listening to music and dancing. He told me that he owned a couple of nightclubs in town and that he always had go-go dancers for the entertainment of his guests. The dancers would lend a party atmosphere to the place, which kept people there drinking a little longer than they intended. He assured me that the dancing attire wasn't anything different than what you'd see at the beach. It was just skimpy enough to keep the guys' attention, but would still keep the girls appropriately covered. I wasn't sure how to answer him about his offer until he told me what the pay was. The hourly rate was four times the rate I was making at the diner. He also told me what the average dancer in his clubs got in tips each night, and the figure absolutely blew me away. I could make in one night what I made for the entire week in the diner. But the best part of the offer was when he told me that I could let my mind wander and just groove to the music. That was it, that was the job. Just listen to the music, tune out the outside world, and move my body to the rhythm. Well, like I said before, I've always liked music and dancing, but I never considered being able to make money doing it. When I said that it sounded interesting , he told me to come by for an audition that night. I made arrangements for Travis, danced for the head lady and wound up getting the job, starting that next week.

The thought of making that kind of money for listening to music and just moving my body to the rhythm sounded great to me. I even thought it might help me to get out of this dark, depressing funk I'd been in. I was more excited about that job than I'd been about anything since that awful night. But something bothered me. Every time I went to bed from that point on, I kept having the same dream. In the dream I was walking down a long, dark tunnel towards a light. In my dream I perceived that the light was kind and benevolent, but when I got close enough I discovered that the light was from the devil's eyes, shining with glee in the darkness. I didn't know what that meant exactly but it left me feeling very uneasy.

Chapter 15

John

THAT LAST YEAR AND A HALF THAT PASTOR Charles was at the church was absolutely awful. I'm not saying that nothing good ever took place or that there wasn't any kind of ministry happening. I still had kids coming to youth group and Sunday school and they were glad to be there. And we still had people who grew in their faith as they came to church and entered into worship and listened to Pastor Charles speak. Like I said before, he was a great preacher, truly gifted. What he wasn't however was a people person. He just didn't know how to do genuine empathy or personal relationships of any kind, which is imperative for a pastor. Some pastors recognize that relationships are just not their strong suit, and so they make sure to surround themselves with staff and lay workers who love people and are anxious to help meet whatever needs they might have, in a loving and caring way. And that usually works because people recognize that not every pastor is warm and fuzzy and anxious to sit around holding hands singing "We Are One in the Bond of Love." You see, that's one thing that people can understand that makes sense to them. Some people, including pastors, are just more reserved and they get very nervous in situations where they're expected to come out of their protective shell, their halt-hand approach to personal contact, and suddenly be warm and fuzzy. So, people get that one, for the most part. But in Pastor Charles' case it wasn't a matter of just being a little reserved, he was just plain harsh with people. His desire for excellence was certainly admirable because we always want to do our best for the Lord, right? But his wasn't just a matter of desire; his was a matter of harshness. I can't sugar-coat and make it more palatable or less offensive. And here's the deal; you can hide that kind of an attitude for a while, particularly if that harshness only comes out with your staff or your top leaders. But, if that's going to be the general mode of operation, pretty soon the atmosphere is going to be poisoned and once that happens it's very difficult to go back and be something different.

The reason I was so excited about hitting the road to Eastern Washington for a little visit with the folks at Pleasant Pastures Community Church was simply because it was the only time in the last year that I felt any hope whatsoever. What Max Sherman's call to consider becoming their pastor said to me, loud and clear, is that God wasn't finished with me yet. And for a guy who really felt he had a genuine, life-long call to ministry, this new opportunity was huge. Even if it didn't work out at Pleasant Pastures, I still knew that God would have something else for me.

The second reason I was so excited was that, as terrible as this might sound, I wanted to get as far away from First Baptist as possible. Number one: The church didn't exist anymore and it began to die a slow death while I was part of the pastoral team. I can't adequately explain how that feels; just know that words like agony, defeat, failure and so on, figure in there quite regularly. And number two: The church split didn't happen on the night when we took the vote to suspend operations. No, it died a slow death throughout the past 6-18 months. It felt like being skinned alive, one inch at a time. Although there were many conflicting thoughts and emotions and it was going to take me a while to work through them, the pain of watching something beautiful disintegrate a little at a time, was finally over. As badly as I felt for the people I was leaving behind who were going to have to deal with it also, right now I was in survival mode, and the call to come and check out Pleasant Pastures was helping immensely. Besides, the radio in my car was broken, so I would be alone with my thoughts for the next 2 ½ days as I made my way out west. I've always held to the belief that road trips can have a tremendous healing effect, provided the person will embrace the hours of solitude and let the peace and quiet of each mile traveled wash over and through them.

I packed up all I owned in my three suitcases on Monday night. I went to bed early and planned to take off at 7 AM the next morning. By 4 AM I was wide awake and lying in my bed thinking that this was kind of dumb; why didn't I just get up and hit the road? So, after a quick shower and a breakfast of two Pop-Tarts from the toaster I'd never see again, I walked out of the parsonage at 4:30 AM. I turned around and faced the parsonage and the church a few yards to the right, and began to pray, "Lord, thank you for bringing me to First Baptist a few years ago. We had some great years together, didn't we? And although it didn't end well, we still can't discount the lives that were changed during the good years. Thanks for letting me be a part of it. Thanks for the privilege of seeing my youth group come alive in their faith and in their personal walk with Christ. I pray for my kids, wherever they are right now, but I especially pray for Matt. I know he's discouraged, but allow him to process this in your way and in your time. Help him to sense your presence, even in the midst of his anger and disillusionment. Help him to also understand that what we did in bringing about the agony of the split in no way should reflect on your character and your nature. You've been weeping with us this past year. Your heart has been breaking also as you've watched your children fighting among themselves. Forgive me Lord, for whatever part I played in this and lead me to a church home that is healthy, vibrant and alive. Oh, and one more thing Lord. Help me to be a pastor who operates in grace and brings encouragement and healing to those you've entrusted to my care. I ask all of this in the name of Jesus. Amen." And with that prayer, I got in my car, started it up and hit the road.

The trip out west was pretty much what I thought it would be. The scenery was absolutely beautiful in some places and a little boring in others. But to be honest, I even enjoyed the so-called boring stretches, even finding beauty in those. And sure enough, the long miles of endless highway began to wash away some of the lingering anxiety from the past year. I knew I would still be processing what had happened for years to come, but that little road trip helped me to realize that though

I would always remember First Baptist, it certainly wasn't going to define me or my ministry. The miles of road were helping wash away months of lying awake second-guessing my call to the ministry, and the irrational fear that nothing good had been accomplished there at all. The hours of solitude helped me to come to grips with some issues that were necessary to face head on if I had any hope of recovery from the trauma. It was truly a marvelous time of prayer and soul-searching. I often wondered what people thought when they'd pull alongside me on the highway and look over at the crazy guy in the next car who was talking to himself. My lips would be moving a mile a minute as I was praying out loud, or reliving conversations I'd had with angry church members, or arguing with myself about what I could have done or said that would have brought a different outcome. When I'd notice them watching me, I'd just look straight ahead and began fiddling with the radio knob, hoping they'd just think I was singing to the radio. I'd nod my head to the imaginary music and do what I felt was a pretty good imitation of a man grooving to the sounds of The Beach Boys. For all they knew I could be heading to California to join the surf scene. Pretty soon they'd pull on ahead or pull off at the next exit. Oh well, if they think I'm crazy, so what. I'll never see them again anyway.

After 2 ½ days of luxurious freedom I was nearing Washington State. I stayed in motels the two nights on my way over and although they weren't expensive, they were clean and the bed was good. I slept pretty soundly because driving 10 or 11 hours a day, as enjoyable as it is, does have a tendency to sap your strength. I also ate nothing but fast food on my trip out. I didn't want to waste time going into restaurants and so I just hit McDonald's for a Big Mac and Fries or maybe Taco Bell for a couple of burritos and those little potato balls that were basically Tater-Tots with a different name. Actually, I've always loved fast food, even though nutritionists say it's not all that healthy. But I figured a couple of days of it wasn't going to kill me, so I just grabbed what I could and got back on the road.

I pulled into Washington State somewhere around noon on Thursday and kept driving following the highway signs and consulting the roadmap I'd picked up at a gas station along the way. When I saw signs for Wenatchee and Leavenworth, I knew I was getting close. I followed the specific instructions that Max had given me over the phone and they were spot on. I rounded the bend of the highway and saw a little sign that said Pleasant Pastures and pointed right. I took the right turn and continued on for about 5 or 6 miles, all the while thinking that all I'm seeing is some beautiful country, but there's no city in sight. I hoped I got his instructions right.

I continued down the road, wondering if maybe I should turn around and find a gas station and ask for directions. Pleasant Pastures wasn't on the two roadmaps I picked up and so, other than the general directions Max gave me, I was driving blind.

I came up over a little hill and looked down into a beautiful valley with acres and acres of green pastures, fruit trees of every variety, and livestock grazing in the dry grasses that were on the perimeter. In the middle of all of this breathtaking beauty, I saw a little town. There were the same shops and businesses that any small town would have and I took note of them as I began to drive down what must have been the main street. In fact, sure enough, I looked at the sign and it was indeed called Main Street. Not too original, but at least you know that this is the street where it all happens - whatever *it* is.

I was quickly impressed with how clean everything was. My mom would have said that it was tidy. The buildings were maintained with great care, the paint looked fresh and the buildings colorful. The streets were free of litter and looked like they had just been swept. It was a lovely little town that probably didn't see too much action, even on a Friday night and that was great with me; I've never been what you would call a real party animal, a man of action. I'm more of the "get together with a few friends" kind of a guy. A big night for me is sitting around talking and eating pizza and just enjoying each other's company. As I'm driving through town, which only takes about six minutes by the way, I'm trying to picture myself living here. It's quiet and looks to be pretty slow-paced. The people on the street are greeting each other with a friendly wave, some of them stopping to chat or maybe just a quick inquiry about how the kids are doing. Pleasant Pastures just has this great sense of small-town-ness and I'm really buying into it by the minute. After the past year and a half of sleepless, anxiety-ridden nights, I'm ready to embrace my own personal Mayberry.

As I come to the end of Main Street I see a little white church with a tall steeple right at the end of the block. It's a beautiful little building with colorful flowers in the bed surrounding it. The church itself, being on the edge of town, is centered in probably an acre of the greenest grass I think I've ever seen. I have a feeling that the water bill must be fairly high to keep it looking like that, but it's worth it. There's even a little brook that runs through the property as it winds its way to the Wenatchee River a few miles away. If I wanted to paint a picture of peace and serenity, I couldn't find a more fitting scene. Pleasant Pastures Community Church exuded a calm atmosphere and just looked like a place of encouragement and healing. It was a place that reminded me of the descriptive biblical phrase, "Green pastures and quiet, still waters."

I looked at this little church, in this lovely setting and it reached out and grabbed my heart at that moment. I pictured spending my life here, as the pastor of this flock. And as I'm enjoying this moment of blissful reverie, I hear a booming voice say, "Hey Pastor John, you finally made it. Welcome to Pleasant Pastures buddy!"

Chapter 16

Wendy

WHEN I WAS DATING A LOT, SOMETIMES THE guy would wind up taking me to the newest and grooviest night spot in town. They'd have a band that was so loud that you couldn't possibly carry on a conversation without shouting the whole evening. I didn't mind that most of the time because the guys I dated weren't always the best conversationalists. They just spent the night talking about themselves, their new car, or how their favorite team was doing, or how successful they were, or how much money they made, and on and on and on. Big Yawn!

But every once in a while, I'd run into a guy who was kind of interesting, and seemed to desire a two-way conversation where I would actually be asked about my thoughts, or opinions, or personal experiences. The few times I'd meet a guy like that, and he'd suggest that we go to the favorite nightspot of the moment, I might suggest an alternative. I would tell him that I'd rather go to a lounge where they have quiet music in the background, so that we could have a normal conversation. And he would usually agree, because he didn't like the super loud places any more than I did, but wanted to look like he really knew how to party for his new date.

Anyway, we'd go to a lounge, or a more laid-back club, and there'd be a piano player or maybe a combo of piano, bass and drums providing some easy-listening background music. They'd also have a vocalist oftentimes that was either the pianist, who sang with a boom mic, or maybe someone who didn't play, but just sang a good portion of the songs. I don't know, maybe it's just me, but talking during background music by the instrumentalist seemed fine, but talking while someone was singing seemed rude to me. It felt like when we were kids in school and used to whisper when the teacher was talking. I wasn't the greatest student in school but I never wanted to be rude to the person talking up in front. Sounds a little out of character for me, I know, but like I said before, I was always pretty nice, and never wanted people to feel bad.

The reason I bring this up is that this dancing job was kind of like background music at a club or a lounge. And what I mean by that is that nobody really paid much attention. I don't know what I was thinking exactly, but I guess I thought that making my living dancing, meant that the audience would be paying attention. I don't want to brag, but I'm a pretty good dancer, and I put a lot of myself into the music and the rhythm. Now, at the same time, I was kind of nervous about dancing in front of a room full of people in a bikini, like Goldie Hawn on "Laugh In," but like Nick said, it's nothing they won't see at the beach, so what's the big deal? So, I get up in my little, clear plastic cage, suspended from the ceiling, and just dance the night away, recognizing that for the most part, after a few minutes in the club, most people are just oblivious to what I'm doing. It was a little insulting in some ways, but on the other hand, it allowed me to tune out everything. For those few hours each night, I was just lost in the music and able to forget the tragic turn my life had taken.

Now once in a while, I'd get a little bit nervous because some guy would be staring at me, a little too long, or way too intensely. It gave me the creeps when the guys would do that, because it brought back what diner-guy had said to me all those years ago, about the only thing I had going for me was my body. I've never been able to shake that thought, even after all these years. The one exception to that were the few months I spent with Kevin. He treated me with such respect that at first, I thought he just wasn't interested in me in a physical way. But I came to understand that it wasn't a matter of not being interested, in fact, I could tell he was battling this strong, physical chemistry that was obviously between us. I asked him one time why he never did anything but kiss me, and he told me that he loved me for who I am and not just for what I looked like. He also said that I was beautiful, and was very attractive to him, probably more than I could ever possibly imagine. But he believed that God's best was that we would wait for marriage before engaging in physical intimacy. I don't know, maybe that's why he had a ring in his pocket that night, after only a few months of dating. Maybe he was finding it tougher to hold onto his Christian morals and values, and just figured that we'd better get married before he blows it. I know that's a pretty old fashion way of looking at this, especially with the whole "free-love" hippie mantra that shocked the culture a few years ago, but that was Kevin's belief, and he was doing everything he could to live by it.

So, when guys would stare a little too long, with a look that went from mildly interested, to outright leering, it gave me the creeps and made me feel like I wanted to go home and take a shower. I talked to Nick about that one night after my shift and he told me not to worry about it. He always had armed security guards walk the dancers to our cars when we closed up for the night. Nothing really ever happened, but I still couldn't shake the feeling that this was a dark kind of underworld I'd crawled into. I know it was only dancing but it still felt wrong somehow. I wasn't really sure if the hours of tuning out the world, and just moving to the rhythm of the music was helping me escape my despair, or actually adding to it.

During one particularly bad night, when I was dancing and flashing back to diner-guy's assessment of me, I was so angry that I tried a little experiment. This one guy was staring at me a little too intensely, and so I began to stare back at him, in a sultry, provocative way. I made it seem that I was dancing for him alone, and that the rest of the audience didn't matter. Pretty soon I could tell that he was responding to me. The look in his eyes got very intense and he was sweating quite profusely. I knew that he was convinced we had something special going on here and that he was going to hang around until the end of my shift, hoping we'd go home together. I'm not kidding; I saw this intense reaction in his eyes and in his body language. It actually scared me and so I gradually turned my attention elsewhere, hoping he would think he was just imagining it. Pretty soon I turned back around and he was gone, evidently having left the club. I was a little nervous after my shift and was thankful for Tom, the security guard, who was walking me back to my car. Thankfully, nothing happened and I never saw that particular customer again, but I learned something that night. I learned that in a very sick way, diner-guy was right. I had my body going for me, and in my dark and depressed, angry state, the thought began to play through my mind, that maybe I ought to use that to my advantage. In other words, if that's all I really have going for me, if that's what I'm really worth, then maybe I need to pay a little more attention to that. Maybe I need to play that up a little and see if I can double my tips, just by a little more flirting, and a few more provocative moves.

That's why when Nick approached us girls about his new idea for the club, I was intrigued with the possibilities. Nick suggested, or more like informed us, that we were going to join the other clubs and go topless. Topless bars were making a killing, ever since becoming popular a few years ago, first in California, and now spreading across the country. The idea of dancing in front of people topless made me stop and think for a bit. It was hard enough to get up there in a bikini, but topless? He assured us that there would be a hefty jump in salary and tips, and that should help us overcome the initial embarrassment pretty quickly. He told us that getting rid of a bikini top, that's barely there anyway, should be worth a thousand or more a month. We'd have the same security watching over us every minute. The only real difference is that we'd be out of the cage and down on the stage, closer to the customers. Nick assured us that leaving the cage would be a great thing for us, because if the customers could connect with us on a more personal basis, and hand the tip to us personally, instead of slipping it into a tip jar, our tips were going to absolutely skyrocket. Well, it didn't take long to convince the other dancers to go along with it. The money would really be a welcome relief to the gals who were working their way through college or were single moms.

I was still hesitant, but didn't want to make my reservations known in front of the other gals. I looked at Nick and he looked at me, obviously picking up on my concern. He thanked the other girls and they took off and began to get ready for the evening crowd. Once they were gone, he asked me to come into his office for a minute. We got in there and he closed the door to give us more privacy. And then he closed his blinds, blocking anyone from seeing inside.

Now, I have to tell you something. Nick can be a charming guy with a huge amount of charisma. He's very good looking and when he smiles that beautiful smile of his, women's hearts begin to flutter. But over the months I've known him, I've discovered something that always throws me back. I've watched Nick turn on the charm, and use that smile to get his way in things, whether that's business or personal. But the thing that I noticed, after these few months, is that his mouth might be smiling, but his eyes are totally dead. The smile never reaches his eyes. It's like looking at a beautifully made up mannequin in exquisite clothing. You see the beauty initially, and are really quite taken with it, but it doesn't take you too long to realize, that underneath all the outward trappings, is nothing but emptiness. There's no life in that mannequin. And that's what I discovered about Nick, in a pretty short period of time. He's handsome and charismatic on the outside, but inside he's dead, no life whatsoever.

When Nick closed the door, I got kind of nervous, wondering what he was going to say or do to me. Don't get me wrong. Nick has never been anything but kind to me the few months I've known him. There was this underground sinister part of him that was always there, but he kept it buried. It was un-nerving, to say the least, but since I'd never been on this side of any threats or actual harm, I just always buried my feelings and let it go. But now I'm in his office, with the door and the blinds closed, and I'm not sure where this is going.

Nick smiles at me, puts his hand on my shoulder, and tells me that I've always been his favorite of all the dancers. He told me that he's watched me, and that I have real talent, and that I had the ability to make men long for more. And that longing keeps these guys coming back, and that's good for business, which in turn, is good for my pocketbook. And then he said something that took me by total surprise. He told me that he asked me into his office, because he wanted to make me a special offer that wasn't for the other girls, and he wanted to keep this just between us. Nick said that he remembered me saying one time that I wished I could send Travis to that private school a few miles away, instead of the public school he had been attending. Travis was a good kid and seemed to get along with everybody, but I was sometimes worried about his safety. I was also concerned that his friends weren't always the best influence on him. Nick looked at me, eyebrows knitted with concern, and offered to pay the tuition for Travis to attend that private school. Well, I've got to tell you, I was shocked and I told Nick so. I told him that I didn't know if he knew this, but the tuition was $1000 a month. Nick assured me that he had already checked it out, and was comfortable giving that to me as a gift, because I deserved it. I was his best dancer and the most beautiful and shapely of all the girls. Of any girl on the team, I would be the one who could really bring in the money. Nick told me that he would love to do this for Travis and me, as long as I could find my way to do something for him. He reiterated his vision to turn his club into a very high-class, and very lucrative, topless venue, but he just couldn't see being able to do that successfully without me. And then he looked at me and pleaded with his eyes for my positive response.

I sat there stunned, on several levels. First of all, he acknowledged my worth by admitting that he couldn't do this without me. Secondly, he tackled my problem of a terrible self-image by telling me how beautiful and desirous I was, and that combined with my amazing talent as a dancer made for a winning combination. Thirdly, he pulled at my heart as a single mom who just wanted to provide the best she could for her son.

My mind was going a million miles a minute as I was processing this amazing offer. And after thinking it through, for maybe 30 seconds, my heart as a mom won over. What kind of a mother would I be if I wasn't willing to suffer a little embarrassment to make sure that my son was safe, and getting the kind of education that would really help him in the future? And so, I told Nick I'd do it, and I thanked him for his generous offer.

But as I walked out of Nick's office with a promise of more money and benefits than I could have ever imagined, I wondered if I had just made a deal with Satan, the devil with the bright, gleeful eyes. The tunnel was there and I had just entered it. But this time, it wasn't a dream.

Chapter 17

John

THE BOOMING VOICE BELONGED TO A MAN who, from a little distance away, looked pretty big. As I walked over to him he just kept getting bigger, until I could only describe him as huge, massive. I got within a few feet of him and realized that I had to look up at him. Now, if you'll remember, I'm 6'2" tall. This guy, who I knew was my "buddy" Max Sherman, was at least 6'6". But it wasn't so much his height that gave Max his massive appearance, it was his bulk. I came to find out later that he weighed 300 pounds. And before you conjure up a picture of a heavyset guy who looked like a reject from a weight watchers program, that's not what I'm talking about. Those 300 pounds were nothing but sheer muscle and you could tell it. It's not like Max had a big beer-belly hanging over his jeans, in fact, it was quite the opposite. I could tell that his broad chest just narrowed down to a slim, but muscled abdomen. His arms and legs were solid, and looked like they could pull a tree right out of the ground. I came to find out a little while later that I wasn't too far off in my tree-pulling assessment. Max, as it turned out, was a logger. He didn't pull trees out of the ground, but he took them down in other ways and wrestled them into position for eventual delivery to sawmills. Max worked long, hard hours, and it showed in the way his well-muscled body moved. He may have been huge, but he moved with purpose and strength; not exactly fast, but definitely with power.

I walked over to him, took his hand and immediately felt like a kid shaking hands with his dad. His massive paw completely enveloped my hand; a hand that I thought was pretty solid from the various sports I participated in. I couldn't do sports that required a lot of running, due to an annoying asthma condition, so I drifted mainly to weightlifting, wrestling and boxing. I even went to college on a partial boxing scholarship. It wasn't a full-ride, but it certainly helped my folks out with tuition costs.

After he had vigorously shaken my hand and left me feeling like a ragdoll in the jaws of an energetic dog, we began to introduce ourselves properly. It was indeed Max Sherman I was talking to, my buddy from the phone call a few nights ago. He told me that though his name was Max, his friends called him Tank. Well, it didn't take me too long to understand the reason for that nickname. The name fit him like a glove. Max Sherman was indeed the closest a human being could come to being a tank. A Sherman Tank is known for its power and size, its ability to mow down everything in its path. That was Max. Of course, as I got to know Tank better, I realized that he was actually a pretty gentle guy.

Now, Max hadn't always been quite so gentle. In his B. C. days, before Christ days, he was an angry, brawling, bar-fighter who would never back down. That had landed him in jail so many times he'd lost count. Max was a Vietnam vet who had served two tours of duty with the 101st Airborne Division stationed up in the Hue and Phu Bai areas of the country. He had survived the 1968 Tet Offensive and distinguished himself in battle winning the Bronze Star with an oak leaf cluster. He was a great soldier, the "original lean, mean, fighting machine." But his two tours of duty took their toll on Max and he came home a different guy. It's not that Max had exactly been gentle before Vietnam, he certainly had his share of fights through his high school days, but there was a difference. Max came home with a temper that could only be described as having a hair trigger. It didn't take much to get him riled up and when he got in that agitated, angry state, watch out, because Max, the Tank, would mow down anybody or anything that stood in his path. When he was on a mission to search and destroy, you didn't want to be anywhere near him.

Tank told me his story as we sat on the church steps, a story that actually was quite familiar to me. Familiar, not so much with the Vietnam angle, but familiar concerning the change that came about in him over a period of time. Max told me how he was at home one night watching TV by himself, and as he was turning the channels, he came across Johnny Cash singing on some show. He'd always liked "The Man in Black," and so he kept it on that station. Pretty soon another guy got up and began to speak, thanking Johnny Cash for appearing on the program. The guy started speaking and something came over Max that he couldn't explain. Normally, he would have just gotten up and changed the channel when Johnny was done singing. But what this guy was saying really grabbed a hold of him and he was pretty much spellbound. He was talking about how anger can destroy our lives and the lives of others that we love and care about. Max thought about how his anger had brought an eventual separation between him and his mom and dad. He felt badly about that, but didn't know how to stop it. But it wasn't the rift between him and his folks that bothered him so much, it was the separation between him, and his younger brother, Ryan. His little brother had always looked up to him and was proud of Max for his service. But that hero-worship faded when his brother recognized that there was no way he was going to break through that tough shell and find the Max he had always known, but now was lost to him. Max seemed to be someplace else entirely, and he wasn't about to let anybody break through and enter that private world he had set up for his own protection.

As Max continued to listen, the man on the TV said that he could be free of the anger and the rage, but it would mean taking the biggest step he'd ever taken in his life. TV guy started to talk about how Jesus of Nazareth died on the cross 2000 years ago, to take away our sin and shame. He told Max how God sent his Son to pay the penalty for our sins, and how the gift he offered was free; all he had to do was to receive it. All he had to do was acknowledge his sin, acknowledge the fact that he was missing the mark all over the place. He needed to give his life to Jesus, to do with as He desired. And as the TV guy invited people in the stadium to come down to the front and give their lives to this Jesus who died for them, Max watched in amazement as thousands began to pour down the stadium steps and come to stand at the front. TV guy was actually Billy Graham, a guy Max had certainly heard of, but had never paid much attention to. In fact, these Jesus Freaks used to make Max angry with their street-corner preaching and their long-haired, hippie looks. But that night something was different. Max said the same prayer as others in that stadium, and gave whatever was left of his angry, miserable existence to God. If God wanted his pathetic life He could have it, and Max meant it sincerely.

Since that night, although everything wasn't perfect, Max could see the changes that had come, some subtle, and others as dramatic as anything he had ever seen. And other people noticed it too. They didn't dare say anything to this huge, hot-headed angry man because they had heard a long time ago to give him a pretty wide berth for their own safety, but now things seem to be changing; little things really. Max could be standing at the grocery store, watching a little old lady hold up the line as she slowly filled out her check, making the appropriate mathematical deductions, before handing the check to the clerk. It was driving everybody nuts. But not Max. He just stood there patiently, seemingly enjoying the opportunity to slow down for a bit. Or, the time several people observed Max standing in line at the post office, just a few days before Christmas, needing to pick up a roll of stamps. The lady in front of him didn't have enough money on her to send a Christmas present she had purchased for her grandson and had to mail all the way to California. She was short by two dollars and would have to trudge to the bank, get some more cash, come back, and navigate the holiday post office lines again. And as she turned away to go, disappointed, but determined to mail the package that day, Max reached into his wallet, pulled out a couple of dollar bills, and handed them to the postal worker behind the counter. He told the shocked lady that it was important that her grandson got his present on time, and he was happy to be able to help out. He wished her a Merry Christmas and then awkwardly received the hug she spontaneously gave him, despite knowing who he was and his reputation for a red-hot temper. He gave her a tentative, but tender hug back, and then she went on her way and he got his roll of stamps and left.

Well, when that little episode took place at the Post Office, two things happened almost immediately. The first thing that happened was that people started talking. That story of Tank and the lady took off like a shot, and pretty soon people began to talk about the change that had come over him. A person can't change that drastically and not be the topic of conversations around the water coolers and dinner tables all over town. The second thing that happened took place in Tank himself. He had begun to notice the difference also, not all at once necessarily, but gradually over time. What used to set him off and make him go down a path of rage that wasn't going to end well for the person of the other end, now didn't affect him quite so much. In fact, Max began to see the world differently. He came to realize that being able to walk around with a sense of peace, not looking for trouble at every turn was in reality, quite enjoyable. For the first time since coming home from "Nam," Max was happy and content. His work as a logger felt different also. There he was with a bunch of guys, many of whom were crude and angry and a little mean in spirit, but Max wasn't feeling that way anymore. The only word he could find to describe the change was "peace". He had seen a bumper sticker on a car that said, "Jesus gives real peace." And Max knew that it was true.

Over the next several months, Max continued to grow in his faith, and then one day he got an idea. He thought that this change in him should bring about another change also. He'd been trying to live his life as Jesus would and that had been working out pretty good. Max had read the story of Jesus feeding the 5000 and was captivated by that miracle. Now he knew he couldn't do that, but maybe he could do something like it. So, Max volunteered to work at the local food bank, run by the people at Pleasant Pastures Community Church. The folks at the food bank were overjoyed to have Max on board. They really put his strong body to use hauling in boxes of canned goods and other nonperishable items. And Max not only enjoyed working with the crew one day a week, he also enjoyed those who came by to take advantage of the bank. He found himself talking with them, and even praying for them, on occasion. Max felt that he had found his true purpose in life. His purpose wasn't the food bank necessarily; it was just anything that allowed him to do the work of the Lord. It didn't matter what it was, if God was in it and wanted Max to join Him, Max was all in, no questions asked.

I guess that's how Max became the head deacon at Pleasant Pastures, John thought. He was kind of young in the Lord to be the head deacon, but with his tender heart, and a desire to serve the One who had changed him, I can see where the people would trust him. And to be the head of the Pastoral Search Committee was another surprise. But people had recognized not only a willing heart, but also some genuine organizational gifts that you wouldn't necessarily find in the typical guy who does logging for a living. Max was discovering all kinds of gifts he never really knew he had.

As we sat and talked, I began to really enjoy this guy, and I could see us working together in this church he so obviously loved. We sat and chatted a little more about what they were looking for in a pastor. And when I told him that I really wanted to help develop an atmosphere of encouragement and grace, Max looked at me and told me that there was already a good start to that. He said that the church needed to grow in that area, but he knew that I could help them along in that journey of grace. We talked a little more, and the longer we talked, the more convinced I became that I had landed at the place God wanted for me. I still had some more people to meet obviously, and they still had questions for me, just as I had questions for them. But I had this inner sense that God was leading pretty clearly. And to meet this massive man, with a huge heart, was something that had reached out and captured me. Sometimes people see church just for grandmas and grandkids, but Max busted that preconception all to pieces. If someone like Max could have his heart tenderized by Jesus, anybody could. This town may be small, just a few thousand people, but who knows how many Max Sherman's could be living out their angry existence in the hills and valleys of Eastern Washington. And as I thought about this, I pictured Pleasant Pastures Community Church being a vehicle of God's love and forgiveness and grace to anyone and everyone who needed it. No matter what their story and no matter what they've done, there's always grace and forgiveness at the foot of the cross.

I didn't realize at the time just how accurate that vision would turn out to be.

Chapter 18

Wendy

I T'S VERY HARD TO DESCRIBE WHAT I WAS FEELING, once I'd made the decision to be a topless dancer in Nick's club. I knew that Nick would keep his promise about paying Travis' tuition to that private school and that excited me greatly. Travis was able to begin almost immediately in January, the beginning of the second semester, which was just a few weeks away. I wasn't sure how I was going to get him in at such a late date, but I hurriedly applied and waited anxiously for a letter of acceptance. And believe it or not, it came within a few days. Travis was in, and both of us were very excited about what this could mean for his future. I was still amazed that they let him in mid-term, because they originally told me that students wouldn't normally be accepted unless they could begin in September with all the rest of the kids. But this was an unusual case, they said in their letter, and they were happy to welcome him into their fine institution of learning. I was kind of puzzled about why this was an unusual case, but certainly wasn't going to question it. I was just glad that Travis could go.

When I told Nick the good news about Travis being accepted in the middle of the school year, and how unusual that was, he got a little smile on his face and told me that he might have spoken to the headmaster. I asked him what that meant exactly, and he told me not to worry about it, just be thankful that they made an exception to their long-standing policy. I thanked him profusely while Nick reiterated that he was glad to do it. Then I said something that I later wished I could take back. I said something to the effect that I owed him one. At that, Nick looked at me, with that charming smile that never quite reached his eyes, and assured me that he'd collect someday, but not to worry about that now. So, I thanked him again and left to get ready for my shift. But as I walked out of the office, I felt a shiver go up and down my spine. The idea of owing Nick anything didn't make me feel very good, smile or no smile. I wondered what that would mean in the future.

Dancing topless is something that I look back upon now and wonder how I could have ever done that. It seems so out of character for me now, but in the early months of the New Year, I just handled it like I did when I first started as a go-go dancer. I zoned out and just moved to the rhythm of the music. But no matter where I went each night in my head, whatever private world I would seek out in my own mind, I still couldn't completely shake the feeling that I had sold myself. Men were paying lots of money to see me and my fellow dancers entertain them, and in our estimation, they got their money's worth. But as much as I enjoyed the jump in salary and the increase in tips, not to mention Travis' delight at being in the private school, it still felt wrong. I still felt like I had destroyed my last shred of dignity, and that I had just come to accept diner-guy's assessment of me all those years ago. It seemed that he might have been right all along. Maybe my body really was the only thing I had going for me. I certainly didn't seem to have success in any other arena of life. And so, I just kept going.

Now Nick was beginning to pay a little more attention to me as the days went on. He would ask me how Travis was doing in school, and when I told him that all was great, better than I could ever imagine, he'd smile and say that was wonderful. And then he'd say that he was glad that his little visit to the headmaster paid off. He'd kind of chuckle, and I'd laugh a little bit, and tell him how persuasive and charming he could be. We'd both smile, and then get on with the duties of the day. But every time we'd have that conversation, I couldn't help but feel that he was simply using it as a reminder that I owed him, and though he never came right out and said it, the clear impression I got was that someday he was going to collect on that little favor.

I wrestled back and forth about whether Nick was just doing me a favor concerning the private school, or if he did it because he liked me. I wondered if, in Nick's mind, our relationship was more than boss to employee. I tried to imagine having a boyfriend/girlfriend kind of thing going with him, but I could never really quite picture it in my mind. And though he was good looking and charming, not to mention very wealthy, I just couldn't see it progressing to a love relationship. The problem came down to comparing anything that I could ever hope to have with what I'd had with Kevin. That love was so beautiful, and pure that I was pretty well convinced that it was once in a lifetime. Just thinking about it made for some very bittersweet memories, and when I found myself dwelling on them, I quickly switched gears to something else, it was still so painful.

As the first few months of the New Year came and went, I got used to my job. It was just another form of entertainment that the laws of my country and state deemed acceptable and was obviously very much in demand. I'd still get creeped out by the catcalls and rude comments some of the guys would make, but that's what they were paying good money for, and so I just put up with it. I also discovered that if I'd pay a little more attention to some of the regular customers, it paid off in tips. If I'd dance a little closer, never letting them touch me, but close enough to imply a new level of intimacy, I was always rewarded with cash. And as a single mom, cash always seemed to be in short supply.

As we started moving from the harsh Chicago winter into the beautiful spring, when everything was fresh and new and alive, I sensed that a change might be coming. Nick was paying more attention to me and telling me what a good job I was doing. He would tell me how proud he was for stepping up to the plate and helping his club become one of the most popular in all of Chicago. He assured me that the club's popularity was due, in large part, to me. Guys wanted to come and see this beautiful, blonde dancer, with the winning smile, and the girl-next-door looks. And that, combined with some of Nick's other promotional ideas, made the club a sure-fire hit. Nick would complement me and tell me how wonderful I was, how successful I was, and how much I meant to him. Now, I was pretty confused about that because it sounded like something a guy might say to his girl, but Nick never made those kinds of moves on me. And yet, the idea that I was his exclusively was pretty strong in the way he talked to me. So, I was confused, not really knowing where our relationship stood.

Things went on this way as we left spring and drifted into the heat of the approaching summer. June was beautiful and sunny, with higher temperatures than normal, and after a cold winter and a cooler than normal spring, I was ready for a change. Travis was just out of school for the year, having had a wonderful time socially, and much success academically. He was a smart kid, one of the top students in his class. I may not have been very proud of the way I was putting food on the table, but I was sure proud of him. He was the light of my life.

Everything seemed to be going along, business as usual, but again, as I said before, I was sensing that a change was coming. I'm usually pretty intuitive about things like that. I could just feel when something was going to happen that would impact my life. Maybe it came from developing a kind of radar in my wilder years, radar that helped me protect myself from situations that could have been very bad indeed. I didn't know what was coming but something was up, I was sure of it.

One day, Nick called me into his office for a little chat. He closed the door and shut the blinds; reminiscent of that first little chat we had months ago when he offered to pay school tuition for Travis, if I'd agreed to dance topless. I agreed and Nick absolutely kept his word. But as we sat down in his office, I wondered what kind of a deal Nick had for me this time. This seemed to be his deal-making mode of operation, and so I waited, rather anxious about what he was going to say.

Nick started out his proposal, once again, telling me how much he liked me and valued our relationship. I wasn't quite sure what that relationship was, but Nick seemed to know, so I just went with it. He spent time flattering me, telling me things that for a gal who had serious rejection issues from the past, were very nice to hear. He told me how many men would come up to him, after an evening of entertainment, and tell him how impressed they were, especially with that beautiful, blonde dancer, meaning me. Nick said he was so proud of me for the gift I had to attract their attention that way. It was truly amazing that I had that kind of charisma, that kind of natural beauty that just made a guy feel that he and I were alone in the room, just him and me. I had never thought about that kind of thing much, other than to play that little game for bigger tips. It never dawned on me that any normal guy would really believe that. It was just entertainment, a form of sales, really.

Nick mentioned some of our regular customers who were very powerful and wealthy in the community, had mentioned me specifically. I was flattered because these men were top in their fields of business, while others were well-known political figures. Nick told me how several of them had expressed the desire to spend a little extra time with me, alone, and they were willing to pay big bucks for that privilege. Nick assured me that if I would agree to spend some time alone with them, after a shift, or maybe in my free time, it would be very lucrative indeed, for both me and the club.

I was beginning to get extremely nervous at what Nick was hinting at, in a somewhat non-direct manner. And so, I just asked him.

I said something to the effect that what he was really saying was that he wanted me to sleep with these high-powered customers. That was it, right? That was his proposal - a proposal that he felt would benefit both of us immensely. Nick looked at me and calmly answered, "Yes." And then he said that this could do more for me and Travis than I could ever possibly imagine. Just think what I could do for Travis if I had all that extra money. Because what he was suggesting wouldn't come cheap. The price tag for a night spent with me would be $1000. That's the offer, take it or leave it. And the customers he's referring to wouldn't bat an eye at that price. Nick promised that he would take care of me always. He'd never consider setting something up with a customer, unless he knew beyond a shadow of a doubt that the customer was a stellar guy, a real high-class man of means and integrity. Only the best for me. Nick smiled that smile and waited for my acceptance of his offer.

But I think I surprised him when I said a strong, loud, absolute, no-room for debate, "No!" I wouldn't do it. This is way over the line. I'm not going to prostitute myself just for more money; I don't care how much it is. I still have some shred of dignity and self-respect. It's never going to happen."

Nick listened to me rant and rave, and lay down my final answer. The answer was "No," and would always be No! He calmly smiled at me, walked up slowly, placed his hands on my shoulders, looked me in the eyes, and said softly, "Wendy, you owe me. If you don't do this, I'll kill you!" And the evil look that I saw in his eyes at that moment left no doubt in my mind. If I didn't do what Nick said, he would follow through on his threat, of that I could be sure.

Chapter 19

John

WHEN A PASTOR GOES TO A CHURCH TO candidate for a pastoral position, it can be pretty intimidating. Although I'd really enjoyed my time at First Baptist Church, I had to admit there could be some very interesting characters, to put it mildly. And when I say interesting I'm not just talking quirky or odd, some of them were just down right cranky. We Baptists used to joke about people who had a sour disposition as having been baptized in pickle juice, by full immersion.

I remember the one guy who would always stand up in a quarterly business meeting and speak against any new proposal the pastor or the church board wanted to offer. It really didn't matter what it was, he was against it. He just didn't like change of any kind, didn't see the need for it. Now, he usually got voted down by the majority who wanted to be a little more progressive, but his constant anti-whatever thing got old and tiresome after a while. It also extended the length of the meetings because the chairman would have to allow time for discussion. When you get a bunch of Baptists together discussing some new, radical program, watch out, it could take hours. And that's the other thing about Baptists and the way we govern ourselves. Nobody has any real decision-making power. The congregation has to vote on everything, from what color to paint the bathroom, to whether or not to buy a second Sunday school bus. There were always people for it, and always people against it. You could make a motion to give away free ice cream and somebody would be against it. For heaven's sake, who wouldn't like free ice cream?

Anyway, with these kinds of experiences under my belt, you would think that candidating for the position of pastor could be a little intimidating, but actually I was very pleasantly surprised. Tank set up appointments with him and me to meet with various committees to let them hear my thoughts on missions, Christian education, children and youth ministries, Vacation Bible School and so on. I was fine with all of those meetings, and I really wasn't too worried about saying something about any one of those areas that could be construed as controversial. The only group that ever scared me was the music committee. I don't know what it is about music in the church, but I'll tell you what I discovered. Here it is, the big revelation, the giant headline:

everybody's got an opinion. And I mean everybody, young and old alike. I saw people at First Baptist have a conniption fit when we first brought guitars into the sanctuary. Now, eventually, the young people won them over with the testimonies that went along with their new Jesus music, but it always was a bone of contention. We got through it every time, but sometimes just barely.

The last group I was scheduled to meet with was the music committee. Honestly, that was the meeting that had me a little nervous because I wasn't sure where they stood on the question of hymns versus choruses. You see some people only wanted to sing hymns in church. If it wasn't at least a hundred years old, it didn't count as real music. These new Jesus People choruses were too simple and trite. Of course, people would get a little upset when I'd point out that many of the choruses were "Scripture songs," meaning they were straight Scripture set to music. Well, that kind of stopped the trite lyrics argument head on.

And then there were those who only wanted to sing choruses, the newer songs that were being written today, because, after all, if it's new, it's fresh and alive. You had all kinds of people, with all kinds of thoughts and ideas and personal preferences concerning what kind of music they wanted to sing. We used to call the somewhat loud and vocal wrangling about music, "The Worship Wars," and that term described it quite well. I often wondered if, when we all got to heaven, there was suddenly going to be peace about the music there. I mean when you have, "People from every tribe, tongue and nation," there's bound to be music that's new, at least to you. So how are we going to handle that then? Well, I guess I won't have to worry about that, that'll be God's job, let Him take the heat. But while we're still on earth, it pretty much falls to the pastor to set the direction. And to tell you the truth, having been a choral music major, I could enjoy it all, from the strong foundation and theological depth and beauty of a 200-year old hymn, to the simple chorus that honored Jesus and was written by a long-haired Jesus Freak. If it honored the Lord and brought joy to His heart, I was cool with it, and I hoped and prayed the music committee at Pleasant Pastures was also. And you know what? They were. They were really amazingly open to new forms of music, both instrumentally and vocally. I was overjoyed to realize that not only were they open to guitars in the sanctuary, they already had them on occasion. That's half the battle right there.

All in all, the meetings with the various groups went better than I had expected. The people were friendly and thoughtful. They were anxious to hear my thoughts and opinions on certain theological issues, but being a community church, they were quite a bit more open to different interpretations of Scripture and the theological position derived from those scriptures. But evidently, nothing I said, or theological ideas that I explained, sometimes in more depth than necessary, gave them cause for concern. They were just a wonderful group of people who loved Jesus and wanted their church to be a light in the community.

The next day was Sunday and I was scheduled to preach. When I got up into the pulpit, I got the distinct impression that this was going to be the first of a whole slew of Sundays in the coming years, maybe even decades. I preached from favorite passages of mine that talked about taking care of those around us who are sick and dying, are hungry and cold, and naked and lonely. In other words, I wanted them to understand that my heart for the church I pastor would be one of grace and encouragement to all those who were in need of a touch from Jesus. And the last time I checked, that included every one of us.

I preached my heart out, with passion and enthusiasm, and laid myself bear before this congregation that needed to know who I really was. This was not the time to try and put on a good show. This was the time to be very honest and transparent concerning what I felt was truly important. To do otherwise could wind up being disastrous for everyone concerned.

After the service we had a potluck dinner in the fellowship hall and it was like every other church potluck I ever attended, with one exception. The bounty of fresh fruit that was available was truly amazing. Eastern Washington fruit is some of the best in the world and the bowls of peaches, cherries, apples, nectarines, and so on were plentiful and deliciously ripe. I had to pace myself on the fruit a little bit, but all those salt-laden, fast-food meals I consumed on the trip out here had caught up with me and I was craving something fresh. All in all, it truly was a wonderful dinner. And the fruit pies were in abundance, which was like dying and going to heaven for me. I've always had a sweet tooth, but particularly for pie. I've never met a pie I didn't like with the exception of mincemeat, which I don't consider true pie anyway.

After the potluck we had a final "get to know Pastor John" question and answer time. Because I'd met with so many groups before the time, most of the questions weren't new. The only time I got a little nervous was when they brought up the topic of music, and I thought to myself, "Oh boy, here we go." But it wasn't that way at all. It was really quite a pleasant exchange and let all of us know, pretty clearly, what our services would be like if I became their pastor.

I told them that I appreciated all forms of Christian music from the hymns of Fannie J. Crosby, to the gospel music of the Gaither's, to the Jesus music coming out of Calvary Chapel in southern California. If it honored the Lord Jesus, it was good in my book. A very touching moment occurred when a gentleman stood up and just made a statement. I came to find out later that he had been a church choir director for much of his life, but he had retired. He still loved church music but especially the hymns. To this gentleman, Harold, hymns were full of depth and meaning, and musically, very solid and sure. He just didn't understand the fascination with these new songs that seemed kind of lightweight and didn't carry the depth and theological soundness of the great hymns of the church. I was going to give what I hoped was a good, articulate response to his concern, when a 14-year-old girl raised her hand and said, "Can I say something?" I called on her and found out that her name was Heather. I said, "Heather, tell us what you think." And Heather said something that stopped everybody in their tracks. In essence she said, "When I sing the hymns, there are a lot of words, and the words are great, don't get me wrong. But when I sing some of the new choruses, the words are simple and they just let me concentrate on Jesus, and how I can love Him more." Well, who can argue with that? That brought a tear to my eye and to a few other folks too. Harold stood up and said, "Heather, thank you for sharing that. I think you helped me to understand a little bit more. That was beautiful." And then he sat down and I watched as a tear rolled down his face. I think he realized that there was a whole new generation of young folks who were coming up who loved the Lord, every bit as much as he always had. And that was wonderful, that meant the church would go on. And the fact that the new music was being written, meant that the Holy Spirit was raising up others to share the gospel for their generation. Harold may not have understood the music exactly, but he sure understood the love behind it. And over the years, Harold became a great champion for the young people. He was every kid's grandfather and they loved him.

The dinner and question and answer time came to a close, and they dismissed me while they took a vote. I went back to my little motel room that was up the road, just on the outskirts of Leavenworth. It was a beautiful, sunny day and so I walked into the quaint little Bavarian-esque town and got an ice cream cone. I walked along enjoying all the little shops and interesting folks I'd see on the street. It was getting to be quite the tourist attraction, and it was fun to see families enjoying the day together. I wondered if maybe someday God would bless me with a family. As I walked along I just prayed silently for God to direct my future in all things. "Lord, I want what you want, nothing more and nothing less."

It was getting to be about 4 o'clock in the afternoon, the time that Tank said he'd call me with news of the vote. I went back to my motel, and breathed a sigh of relief, as soon as I felt the coolness of the air-conditioned room. You've got to remember, I'm from Duluth and anything over 70° is a heat wave so the 80+ degree weather kind of took the sap right out of me.

At 4 o'clock on the dot, Tank called me. I found myself getting a little nervous when the phone rang. I thought I knew what God was telling me, but I've been wrong before. Sometimes my own dreams and ideas get in the way and make it difficult to hear God's voice. But on this occasion, as momentous as it was, I needed to hear Him very definitively. Tank told me that the meeting had gone well. I wasn't entirely sure what that meant. Did he just mean it was short? I always like short meetings. Did he just mean no fistfights broke out? That was always a good thing. But Tank got kind of quiet and he said softly, "Pastor John, we would be honored if you would accept the invitation to become our new pastor." And I said, "Tank, it would be my privilege to pastor this wonderful church. Thank you for your confidence in me. Let's do some marvelous work for the Lord together. What do you say?" And Tank replied, "It's going to be a blast, I know that for sure." And sure enough, Tank was right. I could hardly believe it. I was now the new pastor of Pleasant Pastures Community Church.

Chapter 20

Wendy

I'D NEVER BEEN SO SCARED IN MY LIFE. I LIVED A pretty wild and chaotic life, especially before I had Travis. Some of the situations I got myself into from making very foolish choices were flat-out dangerous. But I had always been able to talk my way out of those rough spots, for the most part. Or, I would deal my way out by making an agreement of some kind, just to get the person to leave me alone. Believe me, I've been in some pretty tough situations that could have ended very badly.

But the predicament I was in now was the scariest ever, and I walked away from Nick's threat shaken to the core. Just the thought of doing what Nick said made me nauseated. I wasn't proud of what I had done over the years, the way I'd lived my life, the choices I'd made. Let's just say that if I could have a giant do-over, I'd snatch it up in a minute. It was a lifetime of poor choices on my part, as well as selfish choices on other people's parts that greatly affected me negatively. I'd always somehow been able to turn those bad choices and the corresponding consequences around, to some extent, so that I didn't lose everything and just try to off myself. But don't think for a moment that I didn't seriously think about taking a whopping dose of sleeping pills. The only thing that ever stopped me was fear of death. What if death was worse than the life I was living? Where would I be then?

Of course, when Travis came along, that changed my entire outlook on life. Even though Travis was born out of my crazy, eight-guys-in-a-month, anger fest, and even though I had no idea who his father was, nevertheless, Travis turned out to be the best thing that ever happened to me. I'm not saying that living a promiscuous lifestyle was good and wise. And neither am I saying that being a single mom was a walk-in-the-park, because it wasn't, not by any stretch of the imagination. I'm just saying that somehow, having Travis, gave me a whole new outlook on life. Though it sounds crazy now, Travis was my reason for beginning to dance at Nick's club. I could make more money, which meant I could give Travis a better life, certainly better than I'd ever had.

Nick coming to me and the rest of the gals, telling us we were going to turn into a topless venue, made me hesitate for a minute. I wondered what Travis would think of his mother when he eventually found out what I did for a living. But when Nick sweetened the deal with a promise to send Travis to that fancy, private school, I just figured that as a good mom, I had no other choice. I had to make this embarrassing sacrifice for Travis; what mother wouldn't? And so, I began to dance topless and got used to it fairly quickly. The tips that came in certainly helped lessen the embarrassment of my new career.

Okay, so here's the deal. Dancing topless was extremely difficult for me, particularly at first, and it robbed me of any self-esteem I might have had. But, like I said before, I got used to it and really appreciated the huge jump in my income. I felt dirty and used and just kept thinking that diner-guy was right. All I had that was worth anything at all was my body. And I guess I pretty much came to grips with that. That's just the way it was for me, and there's nothing I could do to change that.

The thing that really puzzled me, however, was the few months I was with Kevin. He had the ability to make me feel beautiful for who I was on the inside. And even though he was obviously attracted to me, he wanted to show respect for me, and for the faith he tried very hard to live by. I felt totally different when I was with him. I felt clean and smart and hopeful and valuable and loved, not just by Kevin, but by God also. I thought that God really cared about me, and that's why He gave me Kevin. It's like I could imagine God sitting up in heaven thinking that Wendy Baker had had enough trauma in her life. She's had one disappointment after another. So, He decides to change that. He decides to send Kevin her way. And that's how I thought this had all happened. But then came the worst nightmare of my life, and Kevin was gone in a split second. I was alone. Utterly, alone. No Kevin and no God. If there was a God, what kind of a sadistic ogre would He have to be to get my hopes up, let me fall in love with a wonderful man, and then snatch him away from me? It had to be God, right? Isn't He the one who controls everything? Well, if He controls everything, then I guess He's to blame. Makes sense, doesn't it? And if He set this up, why would I want Him in my life, if He even exists in the first place? And that's a big if, as far as I was concerned.

So, I had all these thoughts running through my mind the last year since Kevin's death. My anger had dissipated some, and I was able to do my job without reflecting the anger that was left. But if you were somehow able to delve deep inside the unreachable world of my mind and emotions, you would see it there. You would see the ugliness of my anger and hatred; hatred for God, yes, but the hatred toward myself was much more pronounced and dramatic. I'm not sure I would've been able to recognize that back then, but it's so clearly apparent now.

When Nick approached me about spending time alone with some of our best customers, I knew exactly what he meant. It's not like they were willing to pay $1000 to sit and play Scrabble with me. Nick was telling me that he wanted me to sleep with these guys for money. He wanted me to prostitute myself and he, in essence, would be my pimp and set up the appointments. I'd, and set up the appointments. make a bundle of money, and he, of course, would get his fair share, which I knew meant that he'd take the majority of it. It became very apparent in that two or three-minute conversation, that any thoughts I had about Nick liking me in the boyfriend/girlfriend way were absolutely false. What kind of a boyfriend pimps out the woman he loves, just to make money?

It hit me pretty hard just how evil and demented Nick really was. And when he threatened to kill me if I didn't go along with this new angle to the business, I knew I was in way over my head. And so, I did the only thing I could do. I spoke slowly and calmly, trying to defuse his anger. I had said an emphatic no, and all that did was to earn me a death threat, and so I took a different approach. I told him that I wanted to do the best I could for Travis, but that he needs to understand what a monumental change this will be for me. I needed a few days to wrap my head around this new approach to my career. I just needed a day or two to get used to the idea, just like I needed time to come to grips with the new, topless dancing policy.

Nick looked at me and smiled, in that charming but fake way of his, and said, "Of course Wendy. You need a little time to get used to the idea and understand how good this will be for you and Travis. You'll be able to give him everything he could ever possibly want. I know that's who you are Wendy. You're a good mother who wants nothing but the best for your son. Take a couple of days, and I know you'll begin to see the financial wisdom of this opportunity I'm giving you. I'm not doing this for all the girls; you're the only one. You're the one who's in demand by so many. You should feel very proud that you stand out from all the rest. That's why you've always been my favorite."

Nick reached into the inside pocket of his suit coat and pulled out a slip of paper. On the slip of paper was the name of one of our best customers. He was very wealthy and owned a chain of furniture stores in Chicago and all up and down the East Coast. I asked Nick what this was and he told me that it was my first step to a new and glamorous life of dreams and adventures being realized for Travis and me. The man I was going to spend time with was very influential, and could do a lot for my new career. Nick told me that the details were all on the paper. Just show up on time at the Presidential Suite of the Mayflower Hotel and you'll be on your way to more money than you ever dreamed possible. And above all, come dressed for your premier. Wear your best outfit, nothing cheap, and nothing too sexy. You've got to ooze class when you walk into that lobby. Nick thought for a minute and then reached into his wallet and took out 10-$100 bills. He told me to go to a certain exclusive woman's clothing store in Chicago and get myself a new outfit, top-of-the-line. He told me that the investment was worth it. He also told me to enjoy my two days off, but that he was excited to hear a full report the day after. He said goodbye, turned around and walked away, leaving me stunned, but determined to work this through in my head.

Over the next 48 hours I wrestled back-and-forth with my decision. A huge part of me still said absolutely no way. This crosses a very major line here and I'm just not going to do it. But I'd start thinking about the money, and the kind of life I could give Travis, and I'd drift to the other side. Then I'd reverse it and think about how bad I'd feel if Travis found out what his mother did for a living. I'd be a "call girl" for heaven's sake. Then I'd do an about face and think about having enough money saved up for Travis to go to a great college, maybe even Harvard or Princeton or Yale. He was very smart, maybe even brilliant, and that's not just a mother talking. But once again my mind would flip-flop and I'd be right back to where I started. No way was I going to lower myself to do this kind of work, no matter how lucrative it might be.

I went back and forth like that for 48 hours until I finally made my decision. It really all came down to one major point. I wanted to live. I had no doubt that Nick would follow through on his threat to kill me. I had never seen Nick be violent with me, or anyone else, but it wasn't hard to imagine those cold, steely eyes shining as he choked the life right out of me. Oh, I knew he'd have regrets if he did that, but his word and honor was at stake, as messed up as that sounds. He had a reputation for taking care of business and getting things done, and I guess I was just one more piece of business.

I went to the woman's clothing store that Nick had recommended and I bought a complete outfit, including shoes and purse. I didn't quite know what to say when the sales lady asked me what the occasion was. What am I going to say? "Oh, I'm just starting my new career as a hooker." Obviously, I wasn't going to say that, so I just said that I was having dinner with a new gentleman friend at Francesca's Italian Restaurant in the Mayflower Hotel. I could tell that she was quite impressed and envious of my night out on the town.

I started getting ready two hours before my scheduled appointment with destiny. I showered, washed my hair, blew it dry and put on my makeup. I wanted to use just enough to highlight my eyes and cheekbones, and yet not give any indication to people in the hotel lobby, what my real intentions were. Discretion was obviously required in a meeting such as this. He was a well-known, and supposedly, happily married man, and if the press or gossip chains got a hold of this, they'd have a field day.

When I finished getting ready, I got into my car and drove to the hotel. I was a little early, so I circled the block a few times, trying to steel myself. On the last time around, I was just ready to approach the valet and get the show on the road, when I got the distinct impression that I needed to go around one more time. But as I drove slowly, due to the heavy traffic, I heard a voice speak to me as clearly as anything I've ever heard. I don't know if that voice was in my head, or if it was audible. I don't know if I had had a passenger with me, if they would've heard the voice, but I heard it clear as a bell. The voice said, "Wendy, this isn't who you really are. You need to run now!" I was shocked. Absolutely, totally shocked because the voice was so clear. "Wendy, this isn't who you really are. You need to run now!" I knew, beyond a shadow of a doubt, that was the voice of God. Don't ask me how I knew that, I just did.

I quickly maneuvered around the traffic and headed for home. When I got to my apartment, I went racing in and told Mrs. York that something had come up, and that Travis and I were taking off on a little trip. I threw my new clothes on the bed, and jumped into my comfortable jeans and shirt. I asked Mrs. York to pack a suitcase for Travis with as many of his clothes that she could get in. I took my own large suitcase and packed my stuff in under five minutes. I reached into my dresser drawer and pulled out the little box that was full of scarfs. I reached under the scarves and released the little latch to the secret compartment. The compartment opened and I took out the money I'd been saving for a trip to Disneyland for Travis and me. I took all the bills and shoved them into my wallet. I wasn't sure of the exact amount, but I estimated that it was about $1700. I quickly wrote a note to my mom and left it on my bed. The note just said, "I love you mom, but Travis and I need to get out of town for a while. I'll explain later. Don't worry, this is a good thing." Love, Wendy.

I wrote a second note that said the following: "Nick, I just can't do this. Here are the clothes; I hope you can get your money back. I'm heading somewhere to start a new life." I then took the clothes, and the note, and put them all into a black, plastic sack, tied it shut, and put it with my suitcase. I went and told Mrs. York that we were leaving now.

And when Travis's eyes grew big in amazement, I told him that we were going off on a new adventure, kind of like Huck Finn and Tom Sawyer. Well, Travis being the adventuresome kid he's always been was jumping with excitement.

We loaded up the Skylark and took off; first swinging by Nick's house that I knew would be empty at this hour of the day. We dumped the black, plastic bag, with the note inside, on the front porch, behind the big planter. I jumped back into the car and took off. I had a map of the United States, a tank full of gas, a wallet full of money, and a head full of random thoughts and questions. But what I didn't have was a plan. The only thing I knew for sure was that I was going to head west and figure it out as I went. Oh, I guess I knew one more thing for sure. Travis and I were gettin' out of Dodge and we were never coming back. NEVER!

Chapter 21

John

SOMETIMES WHEN A PASTOR STARTS AT ANOTHER church, he or she has to spend several months preaching on themes that will help a congregation to heal. For example, if the church had been through a rough time, like we'd had at First Baptist, that pastor might preach on what I call the one-another's. There are lots of one-another's in the Bible, such as love one another, serve one another, be kind to one another and so on. You get the idea, right? And the reason you would do a series of that nature is so that your congregation would begin to learn what it means to be a member of

Christ's body, the Church. How do we treat each other? How do we learn to think of our fellow Christians and in turn serve them, even before ourselves?

You see, this idea of being a Christian isn't just about dying someday and going to heaven. Too many of us fall into the trap my grandma used to warn us about. She'd say, "Some Christians are just so heavenly minded, they are of no earthly good." Well, I wasn't sure about that necessarily, but I knew that we spent a little too much time perhaps thinking about "pie in the sky, by and by, when we die!" It's good to know where we're headed, sure, but what can we do now while on earth? That seems to be an important question that has to be addressed. What can we do now?

Anyway, I didn't need to preach a sermon series about healing because the folks at Pleasant Pastures hadn't been wounded from a church split like I had come through. And I didn't need to preach a series on forgiving each other, which is the crucial first step to finding personal healing. I didn't even have to preach on the one-another's, at least not to get the congregation back on track. They were already there. The more I got to know them, the more I realized just how closely knit they were.

I knew when I accepted the position at Pleasant Pastures there was going to have to be time to heal, not for them, but for me. And so I just preached what was on my heart. I wonder if I was preaching sermons that were almost more for me than for the congregation. But you see, that's the great thing about the Bible. It's the word of God and what it has to say is prophetic and relevant to any generation and to every person, no matter what they're going through.

So I would sit in my office each Monday morning and say, "Lord, what do you want to say to us this week? What's on your heart? What do we need to know?" And each time God would direct me to a Scripture, or He would give me a thought, or an idea and the corresponding Scriptural text. And then I'd spend a couple of hours studying the text. What did it say to me personally? What am I getting out of it on my own? And then I'd read what others had said about the same passage of Scripture. I'd take some notes, and then leave it alone for about 24 hours, just kind of letting it percolate inside of me, so that by the next morning, I'd have an outline in my mind and be excited to flesh it out on paper. I'd come into the office early, usually about 5 or 6 AM and just start writing, before the phone started ringing, or people started dropping in. And by 8:00 AM when Kathy, our church secretary came in, I'd be done. I'd give her my notes to type up and by 10 AM Tuesday morning that sermon would be in my box. I'd spend the rest of the week preparing and rehearsing it, so that I could deliver it with the power and punch it deserved.

I always kind of envied those preachers you'd see on television who could speak for 45 minutes and hardly ever use a note. Now if you'll remember, I double majored in music and speech, but I was never the kind of speaker who was so smart and silver-tongued that I could just get up and wing it. I needed to study and I needed to rehearse it almost every day. I had a pretty good memory, but there was no way I could memorize a 30 minute sermon every week, not with board meetings, hospital visits, calls on shut-ins, funerals, weddings, and the countless other duties a pastor has. So I'd go into the pulpit each week with a fully written manuscript. I wished I could do it another way, but I always figured that in a sermon where you're speaking what should be the word of God, it's very important to get it right; every word counts.

If you've got a congregation of 200 folks and you preach a 30 minute sermon, that's 100 hours of people's time. And time is precious. Just ask the person who's dying a slow death from some nasty disease that's right out of the pit of hell. Every second of life spent with their loved-ones is precious, we all know that. Time is so precious, in fact, that I always remind the guys at our monthly Saturday Men's Breakfast to spend time with their families. Working hard at their job is important, yes, but so is spending time with those who are most important to you. I'd encourage them to find the balance between hard work and leisure time spent with their loved ones. And then I'd remind them of something I've observed at the bedside of dying church members, over the last few years of ministry. I think I've sat with maybe 10, perhaps 12, who were just getting ready to meet the Lord. And not once have I ever heard one of them say, "Oh Pastor, I wish I had spent more time working." Never once! They'd always say, "Oh Pastor, I wish I had spent more time with my family."

Anyway, those first few months at Pleasant Pastures had been great. I was inspired and blessed to be preaching every Sunday. I was excited about what God was doing among the people and how they seemed to be responding to my leadership. I was even excited to go to the monthly church board meetings. Now granted, some of the business got a little tedious, always going over budgets and shortfalls, and a roof that had to be fixed, or a furnace that needed repair before winter set in. All of that kind of stuff just left me cold, and yet I knew it was important, so I was very thankful for the group of guys and gals who took on the task of maintaining the church in top working condition.

And they did a great job, to the point that I never really had to worry about it. That was a blessing indeed.

Tank and I were becoming pretty good friends. I had liked Tank since I met him that first day on the steps of the church. One of his jobs at church was head of the Pastoral Search Committee. But since I accepted the call and was now the new "head cheese" his job on that committee was over. He still headed up the deacons and that kept him pretty busy in terms of his church work. The deacons served communion once a month and sometimes went on hospital calls, either with or without me. If we had a need in the body, they'd try to figure out a way to meet that need. They were a very valuable team of guys to have on board. We also had a team of deaconesses, ladies who did essentially the same thing, but centered on the female population of the church, and some of the needs that might be unique to them.

Tank and I spent a lot of time together. We were both single guys and had a real passion to serve the Lord. I'm not sure that I'd ever met a more dedicated young man, particularly with his kind of background. Like I said before, his previous life was pretty rough, and I'm sure there are plenty of local guys walking around with crooked noses that had been broken in a fight with Tank. But all that changed when he met the Lord. Tank was a big man, with an even bigger heart. I remember thinking to myself that if I ever got into trouble, Tank would be a great guy to have around. He looked like a bouncer, not that we'd ever need one at church. I mean after all, everybody's welcome to come, right? At least that's the way it's supposed to be and I've never had an occasion to turn anyone away so far. But, nevertheless, I was still thankful that Tank was in our corner. I'd sure rather have him as a friend, than an enemy.

So, one day I'm asking Tank about his growing up years, and how he'd gotten the notion to go into the service, and make the elite Special Forces. He told me that he just really wanted to serve his country, while at the same time have a legitimate way to work off his aggression. And what better way to do that than to take on the incredibly rigorous training required of the Airborne Rangers?

I could certainly see the wisdom in his thinking, and I told him so. But when I asked him if he had always been angry, he assured me that he had not. In fact, though he was always big, he really hadn't played that to his advantage except on the football field in high school, as well as the varsity wrestling mats. He told me that his whole family was big, even his mom was 5'11" and weighed 235 pounds, most of it pretty solid also. They have the kind of build that made it look like they worked out constantly. But to be honest, it wasn't a matter of purposely exercising; it was simply just the normal work of running a big farm in eastern Washington. You're always busy, always lifting or dragging or carrying something and all the work built up your muscles better than any workout at a local gym ever could.

And then he told me that his little brother was coming to visit in Pleasant Pastures. And, of course, I thought that was great. He was going to work with Tank on the same logging crew and if he worked out, he'd just relocate here and start making a new life for himself. I asked Tank what his brother's name was and he told me it was Ryan, but everybody usually called him by his nickname also. I asked Tank what his brother's nickname was and he smiled and said, "Tank Two. I'm Tank One and he's Tank Two." I asked, "Well, how much bigger are you then your little brother?" And Tank said, "Oh John, you don't understand. He's huge. He's 6'8" tall and 350 pounds. He's got

50 pounds on me. I'm excited for him to come and for you to meet him. He met the Lord shortly after he saw the change in me and now my whole family believes. So I'm looking forward to having my little brother with me, not only in logging, but alongside as my fellow deacon. I mean just think about it. The two of us could really help care for some of the elderly folks in our congregation, or even some of the single moms. There's really not much we can't fix or do or make happen. I think we'd be a pretty good team together."

Three days later Tank Two showed up. And when I saw him I had to look up at him, just like I did his brother, and I realized that there had been no exaggeration. He really was massive and shaking his hand could easily have brought me to my knees. But I think he took it easy on me, and pulled back a little. I remember thinking Lord, I'm so glad these guys are here at Pleasant Pastures Community Church. For all those guys who think church is for sissies, all I've got a do is introduce them to the double Tanks. That ought to give them a different opinion real quick.

The Tanks and I made a pretty good team. We were young, single, strong, and had a heart to serve. It wasn't uncommon to go to some older member's home and help with a project they couldn't handle by themselves, and maybe didn't have the money to pay another person to come in and do it for them. Working together was always great fun and even though the people objected at first to seeing their pastor in his jeans and work shirt, sweating up a storm in the 90+ degrees of the Eastern Washington weather, I assured them that it felt good to get outside once in a while and do some physical work. I can't just sit in my office all day and study, or visit little old ladies in their home and try to balance a tea cup and saucer on my knees. That would drive me nuts. The physical activity was great for me and really helped clear my head of all kinds of theological ponderings that somehow seemed to land there. The Tanks and I would even hit the local gym on occasion. We'd put on the gloves and go a few rounds with each other. I was lighter, and much quicker, so I could almost always prevail in boxing. The secret was in moving fast, dancing around and landing punches when and where I could. I kept dancing because I knew if they ever really landed a good, solid punch, I'd be history, no doubt about it. It was all in good fun anyway, and sometimes I figured that they were just humoring the 6'2" "Shorty" who kept challenging them to a duel of fisticuffs. They challenged me to a wrestling match one time, and so I took Tank One on. I did it once and never again. It wasn't a pretty sight.

So, between the work at church, the extracurricular service at the homes of the older members, and the occasional workout in the gym, I was pretty busy and life was good. Folks in this little city began to hear about the new pastor in town, and they'd come by for a visit. We began to grow and in about a month we had gained about 15 new members, which for our church was great, almost like an honest to goodness revival. Okay, overkill, but exciting nevertheless.

But in the midst of all this ministry and activity and growing friendship, something was eating away at me. I kept getting this nagging feeling inside that change was coming. Now I've had this sense several times before. The last time this occurred, I wound up leaving First Baptist in some not-so-good circumstances. But this was different. It wasn't a feeling of dread or fear. That wasn't the kind of sense I was getting this time. It actually was a feeling that pretty soon I'd be off on a new adventure. Now I have to tell you, I was really praying that it wasn't going to include leaving Pleasant Pastures, because I'd only been there a month or two. Plus, I really felt that the Lord had led me there and I was just flat out enjoying myself. I could see being there for decades to come.

No, it wasn't that. It had more to do with the restlessness I was feeling in terms of my relationships. I'd see these beautiful, young families that were beginning to attend the church, and I'd go home after the service to the emptiness of the parsonage, and just kind of wish that I could have that in my life also. Now, to be sure, quite a few of our older ladies would try to line me up with a granddaughter, or a neighborhood girl, or the checker at the Safeway store in Leavenworth, or the cute girl who pumped gas at the only station in town. But even though I desired to be in a relationship, I didn't take advantage of the offers.

I've always felt that the Lord would have to bring the girl He had for me right to my house, and deposit her on my doorstep. Not literally of course, but bring her to me in such a way that I just knew, from the very beginning, that she was the one. I know that sounds terribly romantic, in a very naïve sort of way, but you need to understand where I'm coming from. I'm the Pastor for heaven's sake. If I start going out with every girl that Lily, or Sarah, or Virginia, or Agnes wanted to set me up with that wouldn't look good, no matter how well intentioned these older ladies were. Nobody wants their pastor to be the Casanova of Pleasant Pastures, breaking hearts wherever he goes. Leaving a string of girls by the side of the road, while I moved on to other unsuspecting females, would do nothing positive for the ministry. But on the other hand, if all of the girls dumped me, which was more likely to be the case, what's that say about their pastor? He must be a major loser if he keeps getting the boot. This was a very tricky situation indeed. I was lonely and really wanted someone to share my life with. But how that was going to happen, I didn't have the slightest clue. I'm just glad that God wasn't as clueless as his thick-headed servant, Pastor John!

Chapter 22

Wendy

THE APPOINTMENT WITH THE "GENTLEMAN" was late afternoon, and after I picked up Travis, I figured I had about eight hours in me for driving, before I needed to get some sleep. I didn't know exactly where I was going; I just knew I was going to head west. I didn't want Nick to have any idea where I was heading and I figured west would be the direction he'd least expect.

I'd often talked about how tired I was of the cold, bleak, windy, winters of Chicago, and how nice it would be to wake up in Key West,

Florida, with the sun streaming in the windows and the warm, tropical waters, just a few steps out my door. So, I figured that Nick would just assume that I took off for a warmer climate, if not in Florida, at least south, in that general direction. I mean, if I'm going to run away for a new start, why would I head toward Minnesota or the Dakotas? All I'd get were even colder temperatures and snow that was a couple of feet deep at times. I was banking on Nick seeing beaches and white sand in my future, and maybe a bad case of sunburn.

So, as much as I would have liked to go south, I felt that the safest option would be to head west, about as far as I could go. Seattle, Washington seemed to be a pretty good destination, despite what I'd heard about the rain. It couldn't possibly rain as much as they said. They'd all have to have webbed feet just to get around. Besides, even if it was wet, at least the temperatures and the snowfall would be a little less severe, so there's something to say for that.

As soon as Travis and I dumped the plastic bag off at Nick's, we headed straight for I-94. I was constantly checking my rearview mirror for any signs of Nick or his big, gold Cadillac. It wouldn't be too long before he'd realize I had ditched the guy at the hotel. Although, as I started to think about it a little bit more, if my customer was smart, he wouldn't make too big a deal out of it. He hadn't paid anything yet, and he certainly didn't need to get caught up in some drama that, by a fluke, could make the evening news. Not a good thing to have to explain to your wife. Now normally, missing an appointment like this wouldn't be that big of a deal for a professional lady-of-the-evening, but with two guys as well-known as Nick and the Furniture King himself, who knows where a story like this could have gone. So, I figured it's entirely possible that he wouldn't find out until the next morning when he tried to reach me for a full report. Well, it didn't really make a difference, because I was going to get as far away as possible, in the shortest time the speed limit allowed.

By 12 o'clock midnight I was passing signs for food, gas, and motels, just outside of Minneapolis, Minnesota. I pulled off at a Motel 6 just outside the city limits, but then I thought better of it. If by some strange turn of events Nick really was following me, just a little behind, this would be the first place that would catch his eye. I would be tired, the Motel 6 would be cheap, and I'd have a very quick and easy access to I-94 in the morning. I really didn't think Nick would follow me, because after all, not even my mother knew where we were heading. I left absolutely no clue as to our destination. Of course, I didn't even know our destination when I left, I just knew we were heading in a westward direction, but that could have taken us to many locations. Nevertheless, I pulled off the main highway and found another motel several blocks away, surrounded by fast food restaurants, and a truck stop, whose parking lot was full of big rigs. It wasn't going to be a great night sleep exactly, but at least the trucks provided a nice cover for my car. You'd have to get pretty close to see my Buick, in the midst of all those huge vehicles.

Travis and I checked in and fell asleep, pretty exhausted. I initially thought that Travis would sleep in the car after about 8 PM, but he didn't. In fact, I didn't even see him nod his head. That kid of mine was so excited about our little adventure, he helped me stay awake just talking my leg off. I told him that our ultimate destination was a surprise, but he'd love it there once we arrived. I was hoping that would be true, but I wasn't sure. I suppose I could just take him to the Space Needle in Seattle, and yell, "surprise," and knowing Travis he'd be happy as a clam. It really wasn't too hard to please him. What a great kid!

We woke up the next morning and got showered and dressed at a leisurely pace. I didn't want to hit the road too early because Nick knew I was always an early riser, and if he was anywhere near, he'd be looking for me to get on the main on-ramp sometime between 5:30 and 6:00 AM. I knew I was being a little paranoid, but honestly, I just didn't trust Nick. He scared me, especially the last few days of our new business venture. So paranoid or not, I wasn't taking any chances. How's that old joke go? "Just because you're paranoid, doesn't mean they're *not* out to get you!" That made pretty good sense to me.

Travis and I shared a little mom and son breakfast at a pancake house just up the street. Travis had a plate of buttermilk pancakes that was listed as the short stack. It was a short stack alright; just three pancakes, but nobody told us the pancakes were the size of a dinner plate. Holy smokes! I could've fed an entire football team with those three pancakes. Travis didn't finish all of it, but he sure got a good start. By the time I looked over, he had eaten about three quarters of it and was looking a little green around the gills.

I had ordered something called Swedish-ers. They were very flat pancakes, kind of like crepes, but a little spongy in texture, I believe. They served them with melted butter and Lingonberry jam. I'm not sure I've ever had a breakfast as good as that one. Those Swedish pancakes were absolutely wonderful and I found myself tempted to order another round. But my good financial sense won out, and I wound up eating the rest of Travis's breakfast which was good, but nothing compared to the Swedish-ers.

We got back on I-94 at about 9:00 AM, and after looking around for Nick's Caddie and not seeing a thing, I just decided to relax and enjoy the trip with my son. We talked for hours, and when he got tired he just zoned out for an hour or two, and then he'd be back in for round two of the Huck Finn/Tom Sawyer River Rafting Adventure, except in a car, with his mom, on the highway. Well, I guess it wasn't exactly like the Mississippi River, but it was fun and exciting nevertheless.

That first full day was a real doozy. We drove all the way up from Minneapolis, Minnesota, through North Dakota, just stopping for a 30-minute lunch in Bismarck, and hit the road again, determined to reach Billings, Montana. I thought I could make it by midnight if I really pushed it. But just as I was starting to get kind of sleepy, I-94 sent me right onto I-90 and guess what? There was no speed limit in Montana. None! Zip! I didn't even see a State Trooper the entire time driving through Montana. There was very little traffic, and I just pushed that eight-cylinder, Buick Skylark, with the plush leather seats and excellent shocks, up to 80 mph and cruised right on into Billings by 11:10 PM. That's got to be some kind of a record. And the exhilaration of keeping at that speed was great. It was very freeing indeed. I remember thinking that maybe I was heading into the Wild West after all, and that was all right with me. It couldn't get any wilder than my last few days with Nick and his pressuring me to take on the new business venture, that's for sure.

We hit the sack at the Holiday Inn and got up the next morning, bound and determined to make it to the Space Needle. That was our ultimate destination. It was going to be another long day of driving, but I was pretty sure we could make it. So, we jumped back onto I-90 and hit the gas. We kept going through Montana and then late afternoon found ourselves in Spokane, Washington. We weren't sure if we were going to make it all the way to Seattle, but we were going to try.

As we were driving on I-90, I saw a sign for Highway 2, and then another sign that said Leavenworth. I had actually heard of Leavenworth and suddenly got the urge to go and visit the little German-style town that had a reputation for being quaint and charming. I just figured that we're not really in that much of a hurry, so why not take some time to stop and smell the roses along the way. I mean, why not? Let's go and see Leavenworth and maybe stay there the night. It was probably as close to a quaint, little town in Germany as I would ever get.

So, we're heading for Leavenworth and I'm telling Travis all about it. Of course, I don't really know all that much, never having been there, but I was making it up as I went along, and he seemed to be enjoying the adventure of it. I was so busy blabbing, and thinking up all sorts of stories to tell him, that I somehow got off Highway 2 and started heading on another small road that seemed to go between two mountains. I was trying to figure out how to turn around on this road, where there didn't seem to be any rest areas or stopping points on the shoulders, but I just couldn't find any place that looked safe. I saw what looked like a possibility, way off in the distance, but I couldn't be sure. I glanced down at my map, just for a second, to see if there was any hint there at all, but when I looked up, a pickup truck was barreling right towards us. He had tried to pass a huge logging truck and had misjudged his distance, and now he had no option left. I looked around in panic for a place to go, or a way to get way over to the side, but it looked like we were all out of luck. But just then, maybe 15 seconds before there was going to be a collision, I spotted a road off to my right. I braked hard, for just a second, to slow myself down and then made a sharp right turn, fishtailing onto the road just in time as the semi-truck and pick up whizzed by, missing Travis and me by maybe 20 feet.

We had made it by the skin of our teeth. I was so shaken up that I felt my heart was going to beat its way out of my chest. The road I was on now was quiet and still. There was no noise, no traffic, and no accident waiting to happen. It was a wonderful feeling to be alive and I began to feel calm and serene. I was still determined to make it to Leavenworth and I wasn't going to let this near-death experience derail me. So, I continued to drive through some absolutely gorgeous country. The pasture lands were lush and green, while the hills were a dry assortment of tans and browns, and yet had their own unique brand of beauty. You sure didn't see this in Chicago. And Travis was as charmed as me, by the beauty all around us.

I was starting up a little hill, and when I got to the top I looked for a spot to turn around and then find our way back. But then we crested the hill and just stared at the beautiful sight right in front of us. I looked down, and in the midst of the lovely, brown shades of the surrounding hillsides, was a little town that looked like it was built on several miles of verdant, green pasture land. The buildings that lined the main street were very picturesque. But the one that caught my eye was a little white church, with a tall steeple reaching into a flawless, blue sky, decorated with fluffy, white clouds. My immediate thought was one of heaven. Could heaven itself be more quiet and peaceful than this? I was from a life of chaos, and so peace and quiet was very precious to me.

I looked at the words on the sign and it said, "Welcome to Pleasant Pastures." Even the name of the town gave me a deep sense of tranquility within my spirit. I half-jokingly said to Travis, "Wow, Travis, how would you like to live here?" And he looked at me, with all seriousness, and said, "I'd love to mom. Can we?" And you know what? I couldn't blame him. After all the chaos of a big city, with all its noise and crime and violence, why wouldn't Travis see this as the perfect place? I was feeling the same draw to the place as he was.

But of course, being the mom, I had to be practical. And so, I told him that as lovely as this little town was, it would be very hard for me to get work here. How would I support him? How would I make enough to find us a place to live, and put food on the table? I assured him that little towns like this just didn't have any job openings. And Travis, very matter-of-factly, looked at me, pointed across the street, in the opposite direction, and said, "There's one." I turned and followed his finger to where he was pointing and I saw a cute, little yellow building, with a red, gingham-patterned sign that read, "Maggie's Country Diner." But the other sign that really caught my attention was in the window. It read, "Waitress Wanted/Apartment Included." I looked at Travis and he looked at me. We both broke out in smiles and I said, "Let's go see about a job."

Chapter 23

John

AS I'VE TOLD YOU BEFORE, LATELY THE IDEA OF finding just the right girl and settling down had been taking up quite a bit of my day-dream time. The odd thing is that thinking this way was kind of new for me. I had always dated, at least somewhat, but once I became a pastor it was a bit harder. For one thing, the demands of the position kept me very busy. And if I found myself with some extra free time, it was no problem filling it with some kind of ministry. There was always something to do, to either help a parishioner, or to launch a new ministry.

You see, that's the thing about ministry. The scope of the ministry, for any pastor, is really only limited by vision and time. I actually had plenty of both. What I came to find out is that a new ministry could begin just because I, or somebody else for that matter, would recognize a need in the congregation, and then devise a way to meet that need. It actually didn't take as much vision, I suppose, as simply having eyes that were just open to seeing what was really there, staring me in the face.

Let me give you an example. As we were going along in that first couple of months, I had noticed that a lot of the normal ministries had shut down for the summer. And if they didn't shut down completely, they at least slowed down. And that's a good thing, as long as it didn't go too far and actually ruin what had been a pretty good program. People needed to rest up a little and then be back to it in September. I can understand that completely. However, I also noticed that people had a lot of extra time on their hands and I wondered if maybe they'd like to try something new. I wasn't trying to take up every minute of their spare time for heaven's sake; they needed that time to re-energize, to slow things down and be ready to go again in the fall when the kids went back to school, and everything at church started up again.

So, with all this free time people had, I wondered if they would like an opportunity to use it in a different way, something that benefited them, while at the same time helping strengthen the church also. Well, one day I'm sitting on my porch at home drinking an ice-cold Coke, and trying to cool off. My mind was wandering while thinking about the folks that I had come to love and appreciate in my short time as their pastor. I was amazed at the group of folks that I had met so far.

Not only were they just plain nice people who had made me feel welcome, but I was thinking about how talented they were.

Take Virginia Crupp for example. She headed up the Martha Circle and did a great job. But, as good as she was with organizing and leading that ministry, she had another special talent. She was, by far, the best pie baker in the church, and maybe in the whole of Pleasant Pastures. I have quite a sweet tooth, and if you were to put a buffet of desserts in front of me and tell me to pick one, I'd go with pie every time. And I'll tell you what. Virginia's was probably some of the best pie I'd ever had. It rivaled my mom's, and that's really saying something. And so, as I'm thinking about her pie, an idea pops into my mind. I wonder if she would be willing to teach others her pie baking secrets. What if she ran a little mini-seminar on pie baking, for anyone who was interested in our church or in the town, for that matter? Huh? Interesting idea.

And then I thought about Harley Logan. I'd heard Harley play his guitar and sing as special music a couple of times since coming to the church. Now I play guitar, after a fashion. When I was a youth pastor, I played the newest Jesus People music and led kids in worshiping the Lord, but my guitar expertise was limited to three or four basic chords. That's all you really needed for some of the new songs that were pretty simplistic musically, and yet very worshipful in content. So, I played guitar to some extent. But Harley was amazing. He didn't just play chords; he played wonderful riffs, and lead lines in the course of the songs. He could make one guitar sound like two, just because he knew how to play with a more sophisticated touch. Once, when I asked him how many years he took lessons, he told me that he was actually self-taught, except for a couple of tapes he had bought that helped him with some key steps to, "playing the guitar like a professional." I said he was amazing, and he told me that anyone, who is musically inclined, could learn to play like that, with a little practice.

And then there was Diane Landers who was quite the artist. I was first made aware of her talent at an evening service when the organist started playing the hymn, "In the Garden." The lights started to dim and I thought, at first, we were having a power failure. But then I saw Diane walk up to the stage area, and sit down at an easel that had been placed there. I just thought that one of our church board members was going to do some kind of financial update in the service and had a couple of charts he was going to use. That happened occasionally, and I was going to have to shut that kind of thing down as soon as I could do it tactfully. That can absolutely ruin a service really quick. But it wasn't an impromptu board presentation after all. The music com-mittee had lined up Diane Landers to do a chalk drawing, while the organist played, "In the Garden." The organ played the hymn slowly, and with much feeling, and I was spellbound, watching this beautiful garden scene begin to appear on the canvas that was lit with a black light. The flowers, the trees, the detail of the setting itself was stunning, and with the music playing in the background, it just transported me to a beautiful garden, where I could spend time with the Lord.

I was thinking about all this talent we had in the church and an idea began to take form. What if we offered classes that highlighted those various talents, for anyone who'd like to come and learn a new skill? And as much fun as it would be, the real benefit to the church would be in the relationships that could form when people would meet others around a common interest. And it wouldn't be for just the church folks. What if it was opened up to the community? What if anybody could come, and in the process of developing a new skill, they would meet the very special folks at Pleasant Pastures Community Church? It was a two-for-one. Not only would the body at church grow closer, it could also expand as people from the surrounding neighborhoods discovered the joy of being part of a community of faith.

To make a long story short, we launched it. It's been going for a few weeks now and seems to be working just fine. The only glitch we had was when Virgie brought all the ingredients for making pies. She was doing great, and everybody was so impressed. They had watched her finish up a beautiful, wild blackberry pie, brush an egg wash on the top crust, and sprinkle some sugar on top before putting it in the church oven. Then they all sat around telling stories, and drinking coffee, while the pie baked. And when the timer went off, they got up, checked the pie, and discovered it was done to perfection. They put it in the freezer for 10 minutes to let it cool, then sliced up the pie, said a little prayer of thanks to the Lord for the gift of food, and then all dug in at the same time. And everyone agreed that it was a perfect pie. With one exception. Virgie had gotten mixed up and sprinkled salt on the crust, instead of sugar. Huge mistake. But they were resourceful, and just carefully took off the upper crust and ate the filling and the bottom crust, which everyone agreed was fabulous. So, two lessons were learned. The first was how to bake a really great pie. And the second was to be sure to clearly label all the ingredients.

All in all, "Summer in the Son," as we had called it, was a great success. Friendships were formed that may never have come about if it hadn't been for discovering the shared interests in the church and in the community.

Being young and single, I found myself developing more programs and opportunities simply because I had the time. And that extra time and energy spent was great for the church. I can understand why the Apostle Paul was a great champion of Christians staying single so that all of their time and energy could go into ministry. After all, when a spouse and kids come on the scene, that's going to change your priorities a little bit. Or at least it had better, if you want that marriage relationship to grow and flourish.

But I have to be honest with you. I'm no Apostle Paul. Although I admired him greatly, and appreciated his amazing spiritual insight and direction for life and ministry as a Christian, as well as his dedication to remain single for the cause of Christ, to be perfectly honest, I knew that the single part just wasn't for me. I loved the Lord with all my heart and wanted to serve Him for the rest of my life. But I also knew that I had a strong desire to meet a beautiful young woman and share my life with her. And as those feelings grew stronger during those first few months at Pleasant Pastures, I realized a couple of things. First, the feelings I was having were perfectly normal, and were placed there by God Himself. He invented marriage for heaven's sake; it was His idea, so who was I to argue with God? And secondly, if this was going to happen, it would have to be in such a way that people would not only understand it, they would stand up and cheer. Like I said before, nobody wants their pastor dating all the single women in the town. Playing the field doesn't seem to be a very good plan of action. Too many rumors could get started, and too many people could get hurt.

What began as just an admission that as much as I loved what I was doing, and as much as I enjoyed the relationship I had with the Tanks, to be perfectly honest, I wasn't feeling complete. I felt that there was a hole in my life that I didn't think any new program, or adventure, was going to take care of. I'd much rather be walking along on a beautiful mountain trail with the woman I loved, than sitting at the local Pizza Hut seeing who could eat the biggest anchovy pizza without throwing up. There really wasn't much up for debate on that one, that's for sure.

But how this all was going to happen was quite a mystery to me. I tried to imagine meeting the girl of my dreams with a variety of scenarios. I would meet her while walking down the street. She'd drop her packages, I would stoop to help her, our eyes would meet, and we'd instantly fall in love. Or, I'd be in the Safeway store up in Leavenworth, and the gal in front of me wouldn't have quite enough money on her. And so, she'd tell the clerk to take off the ice cream. And I'd lean over with five dollars and say something to the effect, " Everybody deserves ice cream, let me take care of it for you." She would blush and say, "Thank you." And then she'd turn and smile at me and say, "Would you like to come over and share it with me sometime, like right now?" I'd accept, and pretty soon we'd be engaged, and a short time later we'd be walking down the aisle.

As you can see, I'm a bit of a hopeless romantic, but that's always the way I just figured God would do it. I also knew, however, that life wasn't usually like that. The song I had sung, when I was in the stage production of South Pacific, was stuck in my head. "Some enchanted evening, you may meet a stranger. You may meet a stranger, across the crowded room." How romantic. How beautiful. And yet, how improbable. I wished I could experience what my character in South Pacific had, but I knew that was just a pipedream. Real life just wasn't like that, or so I thought, until Wendy Baker walked into my life.

Chapter 24

Wendy

THE MINUTE I WALKED INTO MAGGIE'S COUNTRY Diner, I felt like I had come home after a long trip. You know how it feels to be away from home for a couple of weeks and finally walk into all the familiar sights and sounds and smells? If you like your home and it really feels like a part of you, coming home can be one of the great joys of life. Even if you had gone on a dream vacation and thoroughly enjoyed yourself, there's still something about coming home and crawling into your own bed, that's better than anything some fancy hotel can offer. Well, that's how I felt walking into the diner. It felt like the home I had always dreamed of.

I looked around and noticed all the typical diner stuff. There were booths with bright red cushions and yellow Formica tabletops. There was also a row of seats up at the counter for those who were eating alone, or, just liked to have a little more interaction with the diner staff. There were salt and pepper shakers, some bottles of ketchup and hot sauce, a metal container of sugar, and a small dish full of little plastic tubs of cream. And stuck in between all of those items, balanced somewhat precariously, was an 8.5 x 11 menu, covered in washable plastic. I glanced at the menu and noticed that they had all the typical diner-fare. There were several kinds of breakfast options, including my favorite - biscuits and sausage gravy. They also had burgers and fries, Reuben sandwiches, French dips and more. They had clam chowder and chili, as well as the "soup of the day." I think it was chicken noodle. And for the larger appetite they offered chicken-fried steak, fish and chips, and liver and onions, just to name a few. And for dessert, there was a list of several options. There were a couple of different kinds of cake, a cinnamon roll, an ice cream sundae with chocolate or caramel sauce, and a fresh peach cobbler. They also offered several kinds of pie, which looked pretty good, by the way, enclosed in the glass containers at both ends of the counter.

The diner looked clean and well maintained, but the one lone waitress looked very harried and hassled, and it wasn't even the dinner rush yet. I just assumed another couple of waitresses would come in for the evening session and relieve this poor woman. I wondered who this Maggie was who would keep her diner spic and span, but didn't have enough sense, or maybe enough heart, to take care of her staff. I knew from past experience that you could have a great-looking diner, with wonderful tasty food, but if you slack on your kitchen or dining room help, it's going to take its toll. Your business will go downhill very quickly.

The waitress came over and looked at me and Travis, then asked if she could help us. I introduced Travis and myself, and said that we had just come into town and found it to be quite charming. I told her that we were leaving the hectic life of a very big city back east, and I wanted to settle in a smaller town, one that maybe didn't have quite the challenges of the big city. I also told her that both Travis and I were very impressed with the beauty and tranquility of Pleasant Pastures, and were feeling very drawn to this place. I then told her that I would like to apply for the waitress job, and since we had just arrived and had no idea where to stay, we'd also be interested in the apartment mentioned on the sign. She asked me if I had any experience working in a diner, and I told her that I had nine years, from the time I was 15 until I was 24. I also told her that I almost grew up in a diner, with my mom also being in the business. Large parties never threw me off, and I could take care of an eight-top and never miss an order.

I could tell the waitress was quite impressed and she asked me when I could start. "I could start right now, if you want me too. I just need to find a place where I can park Travis and let him read a little bit." She told me that the dinner rush was going to begin in about 45 minutes. She was going to scrounge up a clean uniform and try me out, on the spot. Nothing like jumping in with both feet, sink or swim, that's the name of the game in the diner business. I told her that was great, and when she turned around to find my uniform, I said, "Hey, by the way, I never caught your name." And she looked at me and smiled slyly and said, "I'm Maggie. I own the joint." I liked her immediately.

The evening rush was busy, but to tell you the truth, it was nothing compared to the Chicago diner. Honestly, though Maggie apologized for how hectic it was, I didn't tell her, but this was a piece of cake. I had no problem keeping up with the orders, while offering some pretty good service with a smile, and a friendly banter. It was a good first shift and I hoped Maggie felt the same way.

After the shift was over and as we were nearing closing time, Maggie asked me to sit down. Travis had zonked out in Maggie's little office, after he'd had a burger and fries. I think all the travel had finally caught up with him; he was snoring away and actually sounded like a buzz saw. I think his allergies were acting up a bit, but nothing to really be concerned about. So, we sat there for a minute, just enjoying a cup of coffee and a chance to rest our legs. I was anxious to see what Maggie would say about my debut as a waitress at her diner. I didn't really expect her to be too complementary however, because after all, we were going to have to negotiate my salary. And if she seemed too pleased, or too excited, she knew I might hold out for more. So, I braced myself for a so-so review of my first performance.

Boy, was I ever wrong. Maggie looked at me, and I kid you not, got tears in her eyes and said, "Where have you been all my life? That was the most incredible thing I've ever seen. You didn't know the menu. You didn't know the customers. You didn't know me or what kind of a boss I'd be. You didn't even know the salary. But you jumped right in and took over. You see, I lost my two main waitresses just today. Their parents' house burned down, and the whole family had to head to Oregon today to live with one of their relatives. I felt so sorry for them and I'm praying they'll do fine. But I didn't know how I was going to manage tonight. Thank you so much, Wendy. You're an angel sent from God, and I really hope you and Travis will decide to stay in Pleasant Pastures. You could have a great life here."

I don't think I've ever had those kinds of heartfelt words said about me from anyone, except Kevin. It was like Maggie was the female equivalent of Kevin in terms of a very loving spirit. I swear I got goosebumps when she talked to me that way. And the thing is, I knew it was absolutely sincere. She wasn't just jerking my chain, trying to get me to stay because she was so hard up for help. She genuinely appreciative and, evidently, so were the customers, at least if their tips were any indication. It was a very profitable night and I didn't even have to shed my clothes or my dignity.

As we sat there and chatted, she offered to show me the apartment. I went up the stairs with her, while Travis slept in her office, with Terry, the chief-cook-and-bottle-washer, keeping his eye on him as he finished cleaning up. The apartment was one-bedroom, with a small living room, bathroom and small kitchenette. It was tiny, but very clean, with a fresh coat of paint and new flooring throughout. I could see Travis and me living there while we got on our feet, and then, perhaps, we'd move someplace a little larger.

We went back down into the dining area of the restaurant and begin to crunch the facts and figures. As it turned out, I was pleased as could be. Maggie really valued my experience and hard work ethic, and so she offered me a dollar more an hour then minimum wage, plus the apartment, and any meals I wanted for Travis and me, as long as it was food consumed after my shift and the customers were gone. The only expense I would have would be utilities and phone. I didn't have to be a math genius to know that this was a great deal, and I told Maggie so. I thanked her for giving me that very generous offer.

With all the business stuff out of the way, Maggie asked if we could just talk a while. Of course, I said yes; one, because she's my new boss, but two, after three days on the road, it was nice to have some adult conversation. So, Maggie and I talked for maybe 10 minutes about what Chicago was like and how it was going to be different here in Eastern Washington. But after a little while, Maggie looked at me with a face that I can only describe as emanating pure love. She said, "Wendy, I know you've got a story to tell, and I just want you to know that I'm a pretty good listener. And whatever you're going to tell me, don't think I'll be shocked, because honey, I've either done it or heard it all. You don't have to talk if you don't want too, but if you need too, I'm always here."

Her words touched me deeply. You see, I can tell when someone's pushing for information because they want to use it against me. I'd learned that a long time ago, so I've got a pretty good sense about those things. But Maggie was different. She didn't have a mean bone in her body, and I knew that, just as sure as I knew my own name. And so, before I really knew it, and without even making a conscious decision to do so, I began to open my heart up to Maggie. I don't know if I saw her as the kind of mother I never had, or if I just needed someone to unload on, who I knew wouldn't nail me to the wall with it. Maggie was one of those people who could draw you into a deep conversation, one where you not only share your deepest hurt, but when you're done, you actually walk away feeling as if a huge burden had been lifted off your back. It truly is one of most freeing feelings in the world, and it's exactly what I needed.

So, I went for broke. I told her everything about growing up in chaos, and wondering if I was loved, or even safe. I told her about diner-guy and this horrible self-image I've struggled with ever since he spoke that demonic curse over me. I told her how Travis's dad could be one of eight men I dated, and slept with, in a one-month anger-fest of hate and rebellion. I told her about Kevin, and how happy I was to be with a man who honored God and wanted to serve him, because at one point in my life, it was important to me too. But God had shown His true colors, and as far as I was concerned, He wasn't to be trusted, at least not by me. I told her how I had progressed from go-go dancing, to the topless gig, and how that made me feel. Yeah, the money was great, but my self-esteem was in the toilet. And then I told her about Nick and his proposal to begin pimping me out, and how much money he promised we'd both make. I hung my head when I told her how I was on my way to keep my first appointment, but heard a voice, inside me, telling me that this wasn't really me. This wasn't really who I was. I shared how the voice warned me to run away. And then I looked at Maggie through the tears, both hers and mine, and I said, "Maggie, I know Jesus is supposed to be my Savior, but right now, as far as I'm concerned, you are!"

She and I hugged for a long time until we finally broke apart because the shoulders of our uniforms were sopping wet with tears. And you know what? It felt good to get all of that nasty stuff out. It felt good to cry with someone who I felt really understood and maybe had even been there herself. There was an amazing sense of peace and tranquility when Maggie held me. I don't know how to describe it any better than that. It felt like love that was directly from God's spirit. And to tell you the truth, that shocked me, because I still wasn't sure what

I believed about Him and Jesus. But I'll tell you one thing I know for sure. If Jesus came back to earth in the flesh, and He decided to come back as a woman this time, I think He could delegate the task to the woman standing there, weeping with me. As far as I was concerned, she had this Jesus thing down pat.

Now, where all this is going to go, I don't know. All I know is that three days ago I ran away from a man who had threatened to kill me. And three days ago, I jumped on the freeway with my son determined to never look back. But now I felt that something like a miracle had occurred. I felt better about myself and more hopeful of the future for Travis and me. But I also felt something else. I felt that Someone was looking down on me and saying these exact words: "Welcome back Wendy. I've been missing you."

I didn't know what to think of that. There were times in my life when I truly felt that I'd heard the voice of God. The night of my first, "professional appointment," for example. I knew, beyond a shadow of a doubt, that I'd heard a very distinct voice telling me that what I was about to do just wasn't me. And not only that, it was very dangerous on so many levels. And so that same voice told me to run from the situation. I was to run from the plan I had for the next couple of hours, run from Chicago itself, and most importantly, run from Nick. The whole scene was going to lead to nothing but heartache and loss. And according to the voice, that was not for me. That was not who I really was, and so I ran, and you know the rest of the story.

It seemed like so long ago now, but really it was just three days. But in those three days so much had changed. I wasn't running anymore. I really thought I had found my real home. This quaint little town just reached out and grabbed Travis and me. I could imagine us spending the next several years here and perhaps even longer.

I had met Maggie and secured a job and a place to live, all at the same time. Something like that would never happen in Chicago. People in big cities were hesitant to trust that quickly because sometime, someplace, they'd already been burned by letting their guard down. As I met with Maggie and shared my heart with her, and my rather rough life, she did something I wasn't used too. She accepted me for who I was, warts and all. And there were some mighty big warts.

That voice that welcomed me back and told me that I had been missed, was so clear and yet, at the same time, it was confusing. The few times I'd heard that voice inside, I somehow came to think of it as God's. But since Kevin's death, I wasn't sure I believed in God anymore, and even if I did, I certainly didn't trust Him. But after hearing the voice again, I began to process this whole God thing in my mind, and the conclusion I came to is that when a person goes through some really bad stuff, like all of us do at some point along the way, that person has a choice to make. They can either run from God, or they can run to God. A lot of people just get mad or disappointed and run from Him, as far as they can. And that's what I did. I tried to get away as far as possible. I begin to wonder what would've happened, if instead, I had run to Him. Maybe things would have been different.

But here I was, feeling secure for the first time in my life really, and I'd only been here a few short hours. It didn't make a lot of sense to me, but I determined I was going to go with it and just enjoy it, for as long as it lasted.

So, Travis and I settled into the apartment and I went to work the next day as a full-time waitress. I was wondering what to do about childcare, but Maggie assured me that if he was interested, during the summer months, Travis could hang around the diner. There were always interesting people to meet and talk to, and Travis loved it. He was a very outgoing kid and was always interested in learning new things from the various customers that came in. They would strike up a conversation with this little eight-year-old kid and be quite surprised at his ability to converse back and forth. Travis was very smart and had always enjoyed adult conversation.

When Travis would tire of the dining area, he'd wander back into the kitchen and help Terry and Maggie with little chores, like husking the corn for the "Fried Chicken and Corn-on-the-cob" special. Or, he'd wash the lettuce and carefully pat the pieces dry. Or, in the slow times, he'd refill the various salt and pepper shakers, sugar containers, as well as replace little tubs of cream in the dish and so on. In addition to all of that, Terry or Maggie would also take time to show him some of the basics of actual cooking. And Travis seemed to pick up on that very quickly, thoroughly enjoying watching all the ingredients come together to make one delicious dish after another. So, as I looked at Travis and saw how happy and content he was, I just put the thought of childcare out of my mind. He was happy as could be, and if Travis was happy, I was happy. This was looking like it would be quite a good summer for him.

Travis and I had arrived at Maggie's Country Diner late on a Sunday afternoon and after debuting at the evening dinner shift, I went to work starting that next day. I worked all shifts that first week, just to get the training I needed for the specifics of the menu, the operational philosophy of the diner, and the customer base. It wasn't difficult, but I wanted to jump in feet first and learn as much as I could that first week. After that, I'd let Maggie set the schedule for what shifts I would work and which days. Some days and shifts were much busier than the others, and my help was definitely required.

On Saturday of my first week, Maggie and I sat down together when there was a lull between the lunch and dinner crowd. She asked me if I was interested in getting to know some folks in the town, and I said that I thought that would be a great idea. So, she told me that the best way to do that would be to come to church with her the next day. She attended that little white church with a tall steeple that I had seen the first day driving into town. The church was so beautiful, and was located in such a peaceful setting that it gave the impression of being in a picture postcard.

When she asked me to go, I started getting butterflies in my stomach again. The last time I had gone into a church I was very clearly rejected for the way I looked. It kind of scarred me, if I was to be honest, and I really wasn't too interested in being rejected again. But on the other hand, maybe it would be different here. Maybe the people would all be like Maggie, loving and caring, and most of all, accepting. If I could find more like her, I'd have no problem making friends.

I was nervous and I told her so. I reminded Maggie about what I had shared with her concerning my last visit to a church, and that I wasn't real anxious to repeat that experience again. Maggie looked at me and agreed that experiencing that kind of rejection would be horrible. But it would be especially horrible if it came from people who were supposedly representing Jesus. But she told me that she felt very confident that my experience at her church would be totally different. The people at Pleasant Pastures Community Church were very loving and accepting, and a good portion of them had come from some pretty nasty situations in their past, some in fact that would make mine sound like a Sunday school picnic.

Well, I wasn't really sure I believed all that and Maggie picked up on my skepticism right away, and so she challenged me, so to speak, to prove her wrong. She told me that she had a plan, and if I would agree to the plan, it would prove very clearly if she was right in the assessment of her church. And if it proved that she was wrong, she'd never ask me to go to her church again. Then she added something else that blew me away. She told me that if I was rejected at her church, she wouldn't go back either, and we'd go out looking for a new church that very next Sunday.

I agreed to her plan. Sunday morning, at 10:30, I came walking down the stairs wearing the exact same outfit that I'd worn at the other church. The exact same one. The one that made that cranky old lady think I was disrespecting God and leaving nothing to the imagination. It was a miniskirt, for heaven's sake. It's not like I was in my dance costume. Well, Maggie looked at me and said, "You look absolutely darling. I don't know what that old lady was thinking. And Travis, you look so handsome in that little white shirt and bowtie. I don't know Travis; you might have to beat the girls away." I laughed at that and Travis blushed, but I could see that he appreciated the compliment all the same.

We walked to the church and the first thing I noticed was the setting. It really was as beautiful and tranquil as it appeared from the crest of the hill when I first saw it. The second thing I noticed was a tall, nice-looking man, greeting people when they came in the door. Like so many others there, he was dressed in the style of the day. He had on a blue, Edwardian-style jacket, with wide, bell-bottom gray slacks. He had a white shirt with a beautiful paisley tie, with swirls of red, blue and gray, in a very fashionable pattern. He looked pretty sharp and seemed genuinely happy to meet Travis and me. He introduced me to a few other folks and then went on his way to greet some others, while I chatted with a few more of Maggie's friends.

Over the next few minutes, before the service was scheduled to begin, I looked over at greeter-man and it seemed that even though we were both involved in conversations, every time I looked at him, he would glance up at the exact same time and our eyes would meet. The first time it happened, I was kind of embarrassed and looked away quickly. But by the fourth time, I just looked at him and he looked at me, our gazes lingering longer than they probably should have. My heart did that little flutter thing and I scolded myself. We're in church, for crying-out-loud, we're not at some club. Concentrate Wendy, this isn't the reason you're here. But still, he was awfully handsome and very nice and welcoming. Maybe he's really a Christian, like Kevin was. Maybe God's really important to him, but you can't always go by looks. People aren't always what they first appear to be.

After a couple of minutes, we began to head into the sanctuary for the 11:00 AM service. I looked around for my new special friend, but I didn't see him. Oh well, he's probably sitting on the other side of the church. With any luck I'll run into him after the service. As I'm day-dreaming about this guy and how I'd like to get to know him better, I'm pulled out of my less-then-righteous fantasy by a voice I recognized. I looked up just in time to see a tall man, in a blue, Edwardian-style jacket with gray slacks, a white shirt, and a colorful red, blue and gray paisley tie. Mr. Handsome's up at the microphone greeting the people and he says, "I want to welcome you to church today. If you're new with us, let me introduce myself. My name is John Larson and I have the privilege of being the pastor of this wonderful church."

I sat there stunned. I think I had just fallen in love with the pastor. Oh nuts! What in the world am I supposed to do now?

Chapter 25

John

IT WAS ACTUALLY KIND OF EMBARRASSING. THIS beautiful blonde goddess comes walking in with Maggie, and suddenly I feel like a junior high kid who's just discovered girls. I think I was fairly professional when I met Wendy and her son Travis, but I was so taken with her, for all I knew I might have been babbling like an idiot. But whatever I said didn't seem to shock her or make her run away, so I must've been at least somewhat coherent. My palms were getting kind of sweaty, so I quickly introduced her to a few other folks and then drifted over to another group of parishioners.

I couldn't remember a time when I'd experienced so many conflicting emotions all at once. That just wasn't like me. I'm usually pretty conservative, almost a bit stoic in the face of some new information, or even danger. But all of that seemed to evaporate those few seconds I was with Wendy. I was smitten. I was scared. I was enthusiastic. I was concerned. I was joyful. I was puzzled. My emotions were all over the map and both shocked and excited me at the same time. Now I realized that these myriad of emotions didn't really make sense. It's not like I hadn't greeted many new folks over the last couple of months, and some of them were very nice looking young ladies. But this one was different. I felt this charge go through me like a bolt of electricity. Seriously, if I had been holding a lightbulb I think it would've lit up.

I moved on to other folks, but I found myself only half listening to the conversations. Mary Turnbull was telling me about her latest battle with her gout, and though I had inquired as to her health, I really wasn't all that interested. My mind was elsewhere. And that really concerned me and caused me to feel all kinds of guilt and shame. What kind of a pastor was I anyway? Here's poor Mary, pouring her heart out to me about her medical issues, and my mind's a million miles away, lost on a tropical island with this lovely creature, who's standing 20 feet away from me. Any self-respecting pastor would be riveted by the never-ending tale of Mary's "bout with gout," as I came to refer to it later. But not me. All the while Mary's pouring out her story of pain and woe, I'm wondering if Wendy would go out with me if I asked her. Talk about shallow. I should be taken out and shot for my lack of empathy at the moment.

Still, I'm who God made me to be, right? Hadn't I just been thinking about the future? Hadn't I just been dreaming about someday having a wonderful wife by my side, and maybe a few kids, and a dog, and a little house, with a charming white picket fence? We could minister together, hand-in-hand, and accomplish great things for God. The Kingdom would be greatly enriched to have us working together as a team. Yeah, sure, that's it! This daydream I'm having about this first-time visitor is all about the work of the Kingdom. It's all about doing God's work.

Who am I trying to kid? This isn't about doing God's work. This is about a very real, very heart stopping attraction to my new parishioner. I wonder what the "Pastoral Ethics Board" from my church would think about this one. Well, I'm never going to find out, because I'm never going to tell them. I quickly came to the realization that maybe this should be something that God and Wendy and I work out together, just the three of us. I think that as far as the "Pastoral Ethics Board" is concerned, maybe the old saying really is true: "It's better to ask forgiveness, then permission." At least that's what I'm feeling now.

The thing that gave me some hope that perhaps she was attracted to me also, was the fact that every time I turned, ever-so-slightly, to look at her, she was looking back at me. Now, the first time it happened I just looked away quickly and figured it was a coincidence. I mean, let's face it, she's new to the church. Of course she's going to scope out her new surroundings. When our eyes met that first time, she was probably checking out where the bathrooms were. Or, maybe she was interested in finding a sign that indicated that we had a class for her son, Travis. Or, maybe she was just looking at the decor, to see if we had some decorative taste, or were we just satisfied with a what-ever-we-happen-to-have mentality. Fortunately, our church decor is done tastefully, with much thought going into how it would make a visitor feel. What would their first impression be? The committee for "Church Appearance," had done a great job, and so I wasn't worried about that.

But four times our eyes locked, and each time we looked at each other a little longer. Finally, on the fourth time, when it seemed neither of us was going to break the spell and avert our eyes, I realized I had to break it off. The 11:00 AM service was scheduled to begin in four minutes, and I still had to get back to my office, grab my Bible and sermon notes, and make my way up to the platform by 11 AM, on the dot. I never started a service late. Even if people were still out in the narthex gabbing and catching up with each other, we still always started on time. I was insistent on punctuality for all of those involved in the service.

I got to the platform at 10:58 and sat down in my chair behind the wooden pulpit. I let my eyes wander over the congregation, most of whom were seated, for the most part. Everybody was in their normal seats; nobody was out of place. It's so funny how you can always look for a certain person on a Sunday morning because they always sat in their favorite seat and wouldn't change for anything. If you took a picture each week, you'd think we had assigned seating, but in reality, we're just creatures of habit.

So, with that in mind, I looked for Maggie in the fifth row from the front, stage right. And sure enough, there she was with her new friend, the lovely Wendy. Wendy wasn't looking at the platform, but was looking around the sanctuary instead. I got this little glimmer of hope that maybe she was looking for me. Maybe she wasn't just checking out the building, trying to get a handle on how things worked here. Maybe she was actually looking for me and was trying to figure out where I was. I decided that I was being a bit presumptuous, but as hard as I tried over the next two minutes, I couldn't put the thought out of my mind. I was trying to send some kind of a telepathic message to her to look up at the platform, but I got feeling all guilty because that was just a little too "New Age" for us.

At exactly 11 o'clock I stood up and welcomed the people to church, especially those who were with us for the first time. I saw Wendy's head turn towards me when she heard my voice coming over the sound system, and I must say she looked pretty shocked, especially when I introduced myself as the pastor. I realized then that Maggie had never told her who I was. And being who she is, Maggie just called me "John" when she introduced me. Maggie was kind of informal and never put too much stock in titles, and so I was always just "John" to her. And that was fine with me. I never put a whole lot of stock in titles either and simply wanted people to call me whatever they felt comfortable with. Some of the folks who came to church out of Catholic backgrounds had a hard time breaking the habit of calling me Father, or making the sign of the cross after the pastoral prayer. Well, that was fine with me. I don't think it's a problem when we pray in different ways, or express our devotion differently than the person next to us. I always assumed that God could sort it all out when it needed to be, but that in most cases God was cool with it. God was much less concerned about the method and manner of our worship, than He was the true nature of a person's heart. So they could call me Father instead of pastor. They could cross themselves, or get down on their knees in front of the pew and genuflect. They could worship God any way they chose. The only thing I was concerned about, and in fact mentioned quite often, was the condition of their heart. Did they love God and want to follow Him forever? If so, welcome to the family.

So, Wendy looks up at me, a little shocked, but with a hint of a smile forming at the corners of her mouth. And I knew what she was thinking. Or at least I thought I did, to some extent. She's probably wondering how any of this was going to work. You see, by this time, we both knew that we were checking each other out. I think we both felt an immediate attraction, at least I was hoping so. If she didn't feel anything, the move I was already planning would leave her embarrassed, and leave me looking like a number one dork. But judging from all the furtive, and then not so furtive glances, I think we were on the same wavelength.

The service continued on through the hymn singing, and the little section designated for choruses. The organ backed off, and the guitars came out and began to play in the quiet, folk style of some of the newer "Jesus People" songs. All in all, the worship music was very inspiring and always made preaching so much easier. When I stepped up to the pulpit, I whispered a silent prayer for the anointing of the Spirit to be upon my words and my delivery. I also prayed that the visitors would be blessed and want to come back. It sounds very spiritual now, but to be honest, the visitor I was most concerned with was Wendy. She's the visitor that I really wanted to come back. Did I want all of the visitors to come back? Sure, of course. Where was Wendy in terms of the "Welcome Back to Visitors" list? Honestly, she was right at the top. If I could get her back to church, I would be singing the "Hallelujah Chorus" all the way home.

Truth be told, I couldn't wait until the next Sunday. I had to find out more about this beautiful woman who had walked into my life. And even though she shook my hand on the way out of church at the door, as everybody knows that's just not the time and place for long, intimate conversations. You've got a few seconds to say "hi", and then there's somebody else coming through. And that keeps going right up until the last person leaves the sanctuary. By the time the last person left, I was looking around frantically for Wendy. She had left with Maggie evidently and so I was left alone in the church. It wasn't the end of the world because I knew, from our brief conversation, that she lived and worked at Maggie's Country Diner. I determined right at that moment that sack lunches were out from this point on and that a little diner food would probably do wonders for my overall health. After all, the Bible says that our "body is a temple" and to me, that means that maybe I ought to keep it up and in good shape. And what better way to get in shape than to walk the six blocks to the diner, have a good, healthy meal, and walk the six blocks back again. You see, that's really taking care of the temple, the body. And if going to the diner every day was going to help me in this very spiritual endeavor, I would give myself fully to the task. And if a certain waitress was there at each shift, I would just consider that to be another God-given opportunity for outreach and evangelism. So, all in all, you couldn't get much more spiritual than that. Billy Graham would be so proud.

As I'm beginning to close up for the afternoon, until the evening service, I heard a noise behind me. I turned around and an immediate thrill ran through me. It was Wendy, standing right there in front of me. Maggie and Travis evidently had gone on ahead, and it was just Wendy and me. I smiled and said "Hi." She looked at me and said, "Hi" back. I asked her what had brought her back, and she told me that she had accidentally left her purse in the pew and had come back for it, but didn't want to disturb me. I assured her that she wasn't disturbing me at all. I went over and stood in front of her, leaning against the pew in back of me, and told her that actually, I was happy to see her. She looked at me kind of funny like, and asked me why. Well, at that point, I realized that maybe I'd gone too far. As preachers often say, maybe I had preached myself into a corner. I wasn't sure how I was going to get out of this. And so I told her that I always like to touch base after church with all the visitors. Her face fell just a bit and then she asked, "All of them? You wanted to touch base with all of them?" And I said, "Well, to be honest, not all of them." And she innocently inquired, "Which ones?" And I said, "Well, only one, really." And Wendy said, "Only one, huh? And which visitor did you most want to touch base with?" I looked at her and smiled and said, "You." She opened her eyes wide, in a pretend look of surprised innocence, and she said, "Me? Why would you want to touch base with little, old me?" I looked Wendy right in the eyes and said, "Because you're the girl I'm going to marry!"

Chapter 26

Wendy

"YOU'RE THE GIRL I'M GOING TO MARRY." Wow! I didn't see that coming. It's one thing to be attracted to someone and feel the chemistry between the two of you. It's another thing to be talking marriage the first time you're alone together. It's funny, isn't it? Most guys I'd run into over the years wanted all the benefits of marriage, and yet, marriage was the last thing on their mind. They wanted all the fun, but none of the responsibility. I had grown to accept that over the years, at least until I met Kevin. He was different. He genuinely seemed to love me for who

I was. And then to find out that he was planning to propose that awful night of the accident, just served to reassure me that the love we felt for each other was real and lasting. In fact, although I may have been attracted to a few men here or there, I knew it couldn't compare to what I felt with Kevin. But now this?

When Pastor John made that startling declaration that I was going to be the girl he married, my first thought was, this guy must be crazy. And so, I told him so. I looked at him and found myself smiling. Smiling? Why would I be smiling? This guy I had spent a total of three or four minutes with, suddenly thinks he's in love with me. I'd never heard anything so outlandish in my life. The only problem was that I had felt the same kind of attraction myself. Hadn't I been day-dreaming about him throughout the one-hour service? You bet I was. I knew I wasn't there for that purpose. I knew Maggie invited me to church so that I would meet some new people and begin to feel a part of the community. But I wasn't naïve. I also knew she invited me because she really felt I needed to reconnect with God. After I told her my story, and had poured my heart out to her, I think the answer to my longing and searching was pretty clear to her. I needed God, and I needed the people of God in my life.

So, that's what was supposed to have happened. I would go and meet some really nice people, and at the same time I would become re-acquainted with the God I had given up on. What I couldn't figure out, however, was if Maggie had a third possibility in mind. Did she think that John and I would make a good couple? Maybe she did, but how she arrived at that notion I'd never know. Talk about opposites. Here was this nice looking, clean-cut pastor, who had probably been pretty straight-arrow for all of his life. I didn't know anything about him, but I could guess easily enough. I had this picture of a squeaky-clean, Pat Boone-type of guy, who grew up in a wonderful Christian family, and attended Christian schools, and went to Christian concerts. I, on the other hand, couldn't have been more different, and my experiences so far removed from his reality, that they could never really truly mesh together.

All of those thoughts were running through my mind as I was standing looking at John and trying to know how to respond to his brave, and I believe, sincere declaration that he and I were someday going to be married. And so, I looked up at him and smiled a bit and said, "You're crazy." I guess it was kind of mean to say that, but he didn't seem to be put off by it. I think most guys would've been so offended at that comment that they would have said, "Fine! Have it your way." And then they would have walked off, nursing their bruised egos. But that's not how John responded at all. When I told him he was crazy, he just laughed and said, "Well, maybe so, but would you go out with me anyway?" And, believe it or not, I heard myself say, "Sure." I still don't know why I said that exactly. All I can say, in my defense, is that it just seemed good, at the time. I also thought that it might be fun, in a clean and innocent kind of way, and truth be told that kind of appealed to me. I'd been out with a lot of dirt-bags over the years, so maybe somebody completely different would help restore my faith in humanity, while giving my self-esteem a much-needed boost.

Well, John jumped on my answer of "Sure" right away. This guy wanted to nail something down immediately before I came to my senses and backed out. He wanted to know what was good for me. He already knew that I was working for Maggie and that I was carrying a lot of shifts, while she was looking for an additional waitress to help.

And so, I told him what free nights I had, as well as the free time I had during the day. He checked a little calendar that he kept in his jacket pocket, and together we finally agreed to go out that next Thursday night. He was off on Fridays for the most part, and I didn't start until the evening shift. We could go out Thursday night and not have to worry about being up at the crack of dawn to get to work. When he mentioned about not having to be up early, that kind of surprised me. It sounded like he was just expecting that we might spend the night together if things worked out good and the attraction held. But then I realized I was still thinking in Chicago mode and was stuck with my past memories and experiences. I knew this would be different and that gave me a wonderful sense of value. That's the only way I can describe it, I guess. For so long I had felt cheap and of little worth to anyone, but Travis. But now, with John, I felt a little glimmer of hope that maybe I wasn't as worthless as I'd been led to believe.

We made the date and agreed that John would come and pick me up at 5 PM on Thursday. I didn't know what we were going to do, but I knew he'd have it all planned out. I just figured that anybody who could run a church of 400 people and keep things working smoothly would certainly be capable of planning a good first date. And so, I started to walk away and head back to the diner to be with Travis and Maggie, already kind of nervous and excited about our date. But just as I turned to walk away, John lightly touched me on the shoulder. I turned around and looked at him, and saw a little crease in his forehead, like he was worried about something. I looked at him and asked him if anything was wrong. And he assured me that, on the contrary, all was right, extremely right. It's just that he was a little bit worried about his spontaneous prophecy of our eventual marriage. He told me that he didn't want me to think that he really *was* crazy, or that he made those kinds of statements often. He assured me that I was the only one with whom he had ever been so bold and brash. He told me that he hoped I wouldn't see that as being some kind of weird pickup line, or a way to mess with my head. I assured him that I thought what he said was sweet. Kind of crazy, but sweet. I also assured him that I was truly looking forward to our date Thursday night. After all, it's not every day that a girl gets proposed to before she and the guy have even had a first date.

John chuckled, and said thanks for taking a chance on him. I smiled, and said that I was pretty daring and loved to take brave but somewhat foolhardy chances. But I had a feeling that I could trust him completely and really looked forward to our date. It didn't seem foolhardy at all. It seemed like the right thing to do. And after reassuring him that I enjoyed our talk, I turned around and headed back to the diner.

When I got back to the diner, Maggie and Travis were playing a board game at one of the tables in the dining area. They both looked up when I walked in and asked me if I had found my purse. I showed them that I had it tucked safely under my arm. I thought that would answer their questions adequately and then Travis and I would go upstairs and change. I had planned to go for an afternoon walk with Travis around the town, to better acquaint ourselves with our new home.

Maggie didn't open the diner until the 5 PM dinner shift. I asked her why she didn't open up at noon and take advantage of the Sunday church crowd. She told me that she had decided, a long time ago, that she wanted all of her workers to have the opportunity to go to church on Sundays, rather than having to come in and prepare the food early.

She and the Lord had engaged in a long talk about that idea. She knew that not being open on Sunday afternoons could lose her quite a bit of revenue. But she really felt the Lord had assured her that He would reward her faith and her desire for people to have an opportunity to worship every Sunday. Well, Maggie kept her word, and God kept His. The dinner hour on Sunday night more than made up for whatever loss she incurred from not having a lunch shift. People would come for the evening shift instead and would eat and socialize with each other, enjoying the time before Monday rolled around, and the new work week began.

I told Travis to go up and change and that I'd be up in a few minutes and we could go take a walk. Travis hurried upstairs and Maggie and I were alone in the booth. Maggie had this funny smile on her face and asked me how things were going. I told her that things were fine and I was looking forward to a walk with Travis. She asked me if I had any trouble locating my purse and I assured her it was right where I left it, on the pew. She looked at me and smiled knowingly and said, "You left it on purpose, didn't you?" Well, I was shocked at that accusation and I said, "Maggie, why in the world would I do that?" But then my honest nature got the best of me and I kind of smiled. And that smile grew and grew, until it stretched from ear to ear. Maggie started laughing and told me that she was very aware of my little plan to get some alone-time with her pastor. I said, "Maggie, how did you know that?" And she admitted that she had seen me pick up my purse, as everybody was leaving, but at the last minute, look around, and quickly tuck it into the corner of the pew. She knew all along what I was doing and she gave me the raised eyebrow look that made me think she was, in some ways, a co-conspirator.

She asked me how it went and I just blurted out the whole story. What is with Maggie, anyway? Any time we sit down to have a talk, I feel like my jaw is unhinged, and my tongue becomes lose, and I just spill the beans, on whatever topic we happen to be discussing. She has this ability to look right through me, and when she does that, I just open up and blab everything. I think it's knowing that she doesn't have a judgmental bone in her body that makes me feel at ease.

So, I admitted my little plan to get some time with John. I also let her know that he asked me out for Thursday night and I accepted. I also inquired if this would somehow be a problem for her, or the rest of the church members, for that matter. She assured me that people would be happy with their pastor dating. A lot of the older ladies had been trying to set him up with someone almost from the beginning. But he had always resisted. He didn't want to date a bunch of gals and gain a reputation as the Don Juan of Pleasant Pastures. Don Juan in a clerical collar just seemed wrong. That just wouldn't fly and would hurt the ministry. John had always stated that he wanted God to bring the right girl along, and then hit him, right between the eyes so that there'd be no chance of missing her.

I took all that Maggie said and processed it over the next few minutes of our conversation. He wanted God to bring the right girl along and then make it crystal clear to him that she was the one. What does that mean? Am I the right one God has for John? Are we supposed to be together? As much as that actually appealed to me, it also scared me to death. We come from such opposite backgrounds. We're as different as night and day in terms of our past experiences. I really liked John and was very attracted to him. But if he found out about my past, he would be shocked and very disappointed. And then I would lose him. I really didn't want to lose John. I wanted to be with him, maybe for life. So right then and there I made a decision. This is a brand-new start for me and Travis. I've left all the junk and all the garbage of my old life behind and a whole new life stretches out before me. The future looks very bright indeed and I'm not going mess it up this time. I'm not going to let John in on my secret past. I just can't. From now on, I'm going to be a whole new person. It may not be the most honest thing to do, but I have to think of the future for Travis and me. I've got a one - time shot at happiness and I'm not going to blow it this time. I determined right then, that John would never know about my past.

Chapter 27

John

THURSDAY NIGHT SEEMED LIKE SUCH A LONG time away and the hours seemed to drag by. I had gone out on a limb and asked Wendy, a parishioner of all people, to go out with me. Not only was she a parishioner, she was a first-time visitor. Technically, she wasn't really a parishioner; after all, she'd only been there one time as a guest of someone else, so I guess I didn't break my own rule of not dating my church members. On the other hand, maybe I should have already had a rule about visitors, but who would have thought I'd have needed a rule about them. And yet, I had gone and seriously flirted with one. What if she goes home, and thinks about the whole scenario, and comes to the conclusion that Pastor John, over at the Pleasant Pastures Community Church, is a certified wacko? What pastor meets a visitor at his church, goes off into a "love at first sight" fantasy, is crazy enough to ask her out, and then, has the audacity to tell her that she's the girl he's going to marry? Anybody else would hear that story and think that the pastor's been getting into the communion wine a little too often, and with a bit too much fervor. Of course, at our church, we used grape juice instead of wine, so what excuse do I have?

All of these random thoughts were whirling around in my mind, and I tossed them back-and-forth, trying to make sense of my words and actions. But then I came to a conclusion, and when I finally settled on it I began to relax. Yeah, it was kind of a weird thing to happen. And yeah, it was a first for me, that's for sure. And yeah, I probably wouldn't normally recommend my particular course of action to other pastor friends of mine. I suppose, I could go on and on, but one fact still remains. I've got a date with Wendy Baker and I'm as excited as I've been in a very long time. So, there's no sense trying to figure out every little nuance of this most unusual situation. However it came about, the end result is that I've got a date with the girl I'm going to marry.

There, I said it again. I can only hope that somehow, in some very unique way, God was leading, just as He has in so many other situations. None quite like this, admittedly, but what's to say He wasn't leading me now. I guess we'll find out soon enough.

Sunday night, after my brief but very satisfying conversation with Wendy, I went home after the evening service and continued to think about that next Thursday night. I tried to come up with all kinds of exciting scenarios that would impress her as being the all-time, super-colossal first-date that would absolutely blow her away. The only problem was that life in Pleasant Pastures wasn't what you would call super-colossal. I wouldn't say it was boring, but it's not the kind of town that's going to scream, "Come one, come all, excitement awaits you!" There just wasn't much we offered that could be termed exciting, or unique, or exotic, or the thrill of your life. The only venue in town that seemed to offer even a small dose of fun and thrills, was the new go-cart track, down at the edge of town. Some enterprising farmer thought that turning some of his land into a go-cart track would provide some extra income. It was a good idea, I suppose, but I don't think it turned into quite the gold mine he was picturing. There was a lot to do in keeping up the business. I'm not sure how long the, "Built for Speed" race-track, as it was called, was going to last, but for now it was still going. But, truth be told, I'm not really sure I could see that being a memorable first date.

Then I thought about going up to Leavenworth to one of the nice little restaurants in town, just having a leisurely dinner, and then walking along the streets, looking at all the different shops. That's always good and is certainly less noisy than the racetrack. I could see us stopping after dinner at the little ice cream shop that boasted 20 different flavors of homemade ice cream. We'd each get a bowl of some unusual flavor that appealed to us, leaving off the toppings because we'd want to be able to taste the true flavor of the ice cream itself, without all the extras. We'd each talk about how good it really was, and then offer the other one a taste. She'd dip her spoon into mine and I'd dip my spoon into hers and we'd both realize what an intimate act that really was. And if we really wanted the intimacy, I'd feed her a taste from my own spoon, and she would do the same with her spoon. Now, that would be romantic. Our heads would be close together and we'd share this intimate, ice-cream moment. The only thing that would ruin it was if one or the other wiped the spoon off first, to get rid of the germs. That somehow would just defeat the whole notion of enduring romance and adventure.

I even wondered about whisking her off to Seattle for dinner at the Space Needle. Now that would have gotten her attention. There's just something about being up there looking over the city, while the restaurant itself revolves. I've only been up there for dinner one time, and that was with my folks, about a month ago, when they came out for a little visit. They had wanted to see my new church and this little town that had such a "homey" sounding name, and so they made the drive out, enjoying the beauty of this land of ours all the way. They'd also wanted to see the big, thriving metropolis of Seattle, which seemed to be growing every month. And so, we took a couple of days and saw some of the typical sites. We went to Pike Street Market and watched them throw fish around at the seafood counter located there. We had crumpets at the little shop that specialized in those delicious, little hand-held tastes of heaven. We rode the Monorail to the Seattle Center and looked around at the various buildings that had been the site of the Seattle World's Fair a little over a decade ago. There was still a section for amusement rides, as well as the Food Circus, where you could get all kinds of different treats. But we didn't indulge because we had dinner reservations at the Space Needle, which truly was the highlight of the trip. It wasn't just the food though, it was the view. On a clear day in the Northwest, it's hard to find a more beautiful setting. And when the beauty of the area is set against the backdrop of the majestic Mount Rainier, it's just hard to take in all the magnificent sites and not want to sing, "How Great Thou Art." I think God's hand truly lingered a little longer when he created the Pacific Northwest.

But, as much I as I would have liked to take Wendy to Seattle, I knew that was going to have to be for another time. It's a 2 ½ hour drive one- way, and we just wouldn't be able to make it back. And so, as I continued to contemplate Thursday's activities, an idea came to mind that I thought actually might be a little more to our liking. I really didn't want to go for thrills, or shopping, or dinner at a fine restaurant. What I really wanted was to get some time alone with this beautiful, young woman, who had so captured my heart in a few short minutes. I wanted to go someplace where we could be alone, away from the crowds of people. Now granted, there weren't exactly crowds of people in Pleasant Pastures. It's just a small town of a few thousand people, but I figured that even one more person was a crowd. I wanted Thursday night to be just Wendy and me. I wanted to get to know her for who she really was. What made Wendy the woman she was? Where's she from? What's her background like? What kind of a family did she grow up in, and was her family in this area? What brought her to Pleasant Pastures, and how did she happen to meet Maggie? I guess I wanted to know everything I could about Wendy. I wanted to spend hours, just talking and sharing with each other, the details of our lives. Now, I knew that all of that wouldn't come on the first date, but we'd at least make a start. And I just knew, inside, that this wouldn't be a one-time event. We were going to have many more dates together, each one better than before.

I began to think about how much fun it would be to go on a little picnic, just the two of us. Wendy always spent her days serving food to her diner customers, and I thought how nice it would be for her to have someone else serve her. I suppose I could've just done the typical picnic food of Kentucky Fried Chicken and potato salad, but I wanted it to be special, things she really liked. And so, I came up with a plan. I was going to do a little recon and see what the lovely Wendy enjoyed. I wanted to make it very personal if I could. I'm not the greatest cook in the world, but I'm not a total klutz either. I learned a few techniques from my mom over the years, and I know how to follow recipes, for the most part. And what I couldn't make myself, I could maybe finagle a couple of the church ladies to work some of their culinary magic. No, on second thought, I was going to do the whole thing. That was a step of faith, believe me.

At noon, on Monday, I took the short walk down to Maggie's Country Diner to enjoy a bite of lunch. This wasn't a normal thing for me, and in fact, I think Maggie was a little surprised to see me walk in, but she just smiled and winked at me, with this barely perceptible nod of her head, that directed my attention to the other side of the diner.

There was Wendy serving a table at the far end. It was an older couple who probably had dropped in for their Monday afternoon lunch date. They seemed like a couple who had been together a long time. They were sitting on the same side of the booth with each other, rather than across. I thought that was rather sweet, after all these years together. They still wanted to be close to each other. And as I watched them and Wendy interact, I noticed that they were holding hands under the table, like two young lovers. A wistful feeling brought warmth within and I found myself longing to have that kind of close relationship that's built on decades of love and trust.

Wendy was talking to the couple and I could tell she wasn't just taking their orders. She was engaging in a conversation, that I pretty quickly discerned was about them and their relationship. They would smile at each other, and nod their heads, as they shared something with Wendy that seemed important to them. Wendy just did her best to fit into their world for those few moments, and she seemed to really enjoy their conversation. I could tell that Wendy was being genuine, even at one point reaching out and patting the gentleman on the shoulder, while they laughed about something funny that one of them had said. I knew she couldn't have really known this couple exactly, she hadn't been at the diner that long, but she just seemed to have this way about her. You would have thought that they had been lifelong friends, judging by the ease they seemed to have in their communication. She's quite a woman, I thought to myself. And then I found myself picturing her as a pastor's wife and I could see it. I really could.

Maggie seated me at a booth and pretty soon Wendy looked up and spotted me. I don't think she was expecting to see me there, and she raised her eyebrows in a look of surprise. She came over and greeted me, and asked if I came in often for lunch. I told her no, that actually this was my first time for the noon meal. I'd been here for dinner at times, but usually the day is pretty busy and I just eat at my desk or grab something at the 7-11 when I'm out on calls. She didn't look like she was too excited about the thought of eating 3-for-a-dollar hot dogs from 7-11 but that's a guy for you. We'll eat almost anything when we're young and single.

I told her that it was good to see her again and that she looked absolutely ravishing in her waitress uniform. She rolled her eyes and said, "Oh sure, I'm a regular Raquel Welch in this outfit. You can't get much more alluring than this." We both laughed and I said, "Well, you still look very nice. And by the way, I'm looking forward to our date on Thursday night." She assured me that she was also. She asked me if I wanted some lunch, and so, I ordered a burger and fries. Not too original, but it seemed perfect for lunch. I would have given anything for her to sit down and share it with me, but she was on duty. I was just going to have to wait for Thursday night.

When she brought my food back there was a little lull in the diner-action and so we talked for a few minutes. I asked her if I could get her opinion on something, and she said absolutely. I told her that we usually had several church picnics after services in the summer, and I wondered about the menu this year. This was true by the way; we really do have church picnics. But usually I never worry about the menu. It's pretty much a potluck with everybody bringing whatever they want, and then we share it. And sure enough, it always seems to work out just fine. So, I subtly asked what her favorite picnic foods were. And she told me that she was pretty traditional. She liked fried chicken and salads of any kind. She liked root beer on picnics, although she hardly ever drank it at other times. Root beer just seemed like picnic food to her. I told her that I thought that was kind of interesting, root beer only on picnics. And then I asked her about dessert and she said that she'd never met a dessert she didn't like, but she was especially fond of pie. I told her thanks for the input and that we'd have some great menus for the coming church picnics.

I finished my lunch and said goodbye, leaving her a generous tip. I'd always had a soft spot for single moms and I would have left a generous tip even if it hadn't been Wendy. But I have to admit, I enjoyed leaving the tip for Wendy, especially. She worked hard as a waitress and supporting Travis and herself had to be quite a challenge for her. I didn't know what her story was, but I figured I'd hear about it when she was ready. I guess I'd better slow it down a little bit; I haven't even had a date with her yet. We'll have plenty of time to talk and share about each other's lives.

I went home more excited than ever for date night. I blocked out my schedule for Thursday afternoon and planned my menu. I didn't have a deep-fat fryer, but I ran across a recipe in a Betty Crocker cookbook my mom had given me for oven-fried chicken. That sounded pretty good and looked easy enough. Plus, if I baked it, I could be sure it was done all the way through. The last thing I needed to impress Wendy was making her sick from undercooked chicken. How would you like to have that happen on a first date? Or any date, for that matter.

I also decided on a Minnesotan favorite, a dish that was a staple at every church potluck I ever attended. I was going to make a Jell-O salad with fruit cocktail. This would be very easy, and to my way of thinking, would be quite impressive, especially if I added a can of mandarin oranges for that extra punch. I'd have to do that Wednesday night, after prayer meeting, to give the Jell-O time to set up.

I also decided to bring some kind of potato chips. I couldn't really make those, so I just decided to buy them. I went to the store, and looked over the selection, finally deciding on something a little more exotic. They had some chips there that I'd never heard of before, but they were supposed to be kind of spicy. They used some kind of pepper to add a little kick to it. I think it was called a jalapeno, and as far as I could tell, it was just a regular green pepper that added a tiny bit more heat. Well, we might as well live dangerously. At least the chips might counter-balance the Jell-O salad which some non-Minnesotans feel is kind of bland. I don't know where they get that idea, but there's no accounting for taste.

And finally, I decided to make a pie. I've always loved cherry pie, and so I called my mom, and over a span of about 30 minutes, had her talk me through the process of making the crust, adding the sugar and preparing the cherries with a thickening agent, fitting the top crust on, and then crimping it. What a process. I had no idea it took that much fussing around. Once I baked the pie, again on Wednesday night to give it sufficient time to cool, I was pretty ready. The pie crust looked nothing like my moms, but it was going to have to do. It was pretty dark, but I'm sure it tasted better than it looked.

I started to prepare the oven-fried chicken on Thursday afternoon, and when the time for our date came, I was fully prepared. I had gone to the hardware store in Leavenworth looking for a picnic basket, and sure enough, they had a few on display. I guess even handymen get hungry.

I walked to the diner and picked Wendy up, the basket slung over my arm. Wendy asked me if that's what she thought it was, a picnic basket. I told her that I thought a picnic might be a good way to relax after her hard day at work. I wanted her to sit on the blanket I brought, and just let somebody else serve her, for once. She looked pretty surprised, but also very pleased.

We went down to a favorite spot of mine, by the little brook that flowed in the fields behind the church. Not too many people come here and I figured we'd have the place all to ourselves. If somebody was already there, we'd just move a little further downstream. There was always plenty of space in Pleasant Pastures. So, we got to the little bench and sat there for a few minutes, just chit-chatting and marveling at the scenery. The pasture land was a rich, vibrant green color and the surrounding foot hills were various shades of tan and brown, each with a beauty all of their own.

When we had been there a while, I suggested we should eat. She seemed ready to dig in, and so I opened the basket and took out the blanket I had packed, and laid it on the ground. Then I begin dish up a plate of food for her, all lovingly prepared by my own hand. Now, while we're on the subject, let me just get this off my chest, right away. The food was a disaster. I'm not trying to be modest and I'm not trying to be funny. It was a true disaster. The crispy, oven-fried chicken had totally lost whatever crisp it might've had. In fact, when I started taking the pieces out of the Tupperware bowl, all of the skin had stuck to the other pieces and immediately was pulled off. Great! Skinless fried chicken. What a treat. Isn't the skin the most important part of fried chicken? Well, mine was naked chicken.

The Jell-O with fruit cocktail salad was melting in the Eastern Washington heat. I never dreamed it would melt that fast, but by the time I opened up the container, it was well on its way to being soup. I looked at the Jell-O soup and thought that maybe I could at least redeem myself with the potato chips that had the funny sounding pepper name. I'd never heard about them in Duluth, so I just figured it was a Northwest treat. Both Wendy and I ate a few chips, commenting on how delicious they were. But then the heat came on, slowly at first, but building to a fiery intensity. I hurried and grabbed the bottle of root beer, quickly un-screwing the top to give her the first drink, in an effort to quench the fire. Well, evidently the bottle had bounced around a bit in the basket, and when I unscrewed the cap, the root beer sprayed out of the bottle all over her face and clothes. Wendy took it in stride and just simply wiped off the liquid with a towel I had in the basket. I'm really scoring points on this date.

We kind of joked about how the picnic was turning out, but agreed that it would certainly be memorable. And as I thought about future memories, I was convinced that, at least, she'd remember the cherry pie. It's got to be good. My mom walked me through it, step-by-step. How could it not be good, right? Well, let me tell you. When I first bit into that pie that looked so good, for the most part, except for a very definite shadow where the crust had gotten a little dark, I was shocked. That crust that mom walked me through on the phone, was hard as a rock. I'm not kidding you. I swear, I could have built sky-scrapers with that stuff. I tried to think back to what could have happened. And then I remembered something mom said, almost in passing. I heard her words in my thick head. "Don't handle the dough too much." That was it. That was my problem. The dough didn't look right. It didn't seem to be holding together very well, so I just figured I had to work with it to get it to fully blend together. So, I took that piece of dough and worked it with my hands into a round lump, the size of a softball. I may have even tossed it up in the air a few times, just thinking how perfectly blended and smooth the dough would become. Evidently, that is not the way to produce good, flaky crust. I'm surprised we didn't chip a tooth on it.

All the while, I'm dying inside. We're going from one disaster of inedible food, to another, and there's no respite in between. Wendy's being a trooper though. Finally, I said something to the effect that if we keep trying to choke this food down, they're going to find our bodies the next day. Cause of death? Picnic disaster. We would have been better off trying to eat the wicker basket.

I told Wendy that I was so sorry for the food. I really wanted this to be special for both of us. And she said that she still enjoyed herself, despite the food. And then she laughed and suggested that I never go to that deli again. I got a rather puzzled look on my face and asked her what she meant by that. And she said that whatever deli I got all this picnic food from probably wasn't going to be in business too long, because the quality wasn't the greatest. I looked at her and said, "Wendy, I wanted this to be special and personal. I made all the food myself, but I guess I'm not such a great cook." She immediately got tears in her eyes and said, "Oh John, you made all of this for me?" And I assured her that I did, but that I'd never subject her to that again, and I kind of chuckled. She leaned over and put her arms around me and kissed me on the cheek. "That is the sweetest thing I've ever heard. I've never had anybody put so much effort into trying to do something special for me. I will cherish this picnic with you for my entire life. Thank you for all your efforts and for caring that much."

From that point on, with the food disaster out of the way, we just began to talk. I told her about myself in response to her questions, and she talked about herself, in response to mine. It became apparent, pretty early on, that her life and my life were totally opposite. I knew that she'd had a hard time, on many different levels. I also knew that she was holding back, but I wasn't going to push it. I knew she'd tell me about herself over time. She was already amazingly honest, but some of the missing points to the story would just remain missing until it was time. And I was perfectly fine with that. I just wanted to spend as much time as possible with her because she absolutely made my heart sing.

It had gotten dark and had cooled off a bit. I looked at my watch and was surprised to see that it was about 11:00 PM. We had been at the picnic site for several hours, but they seemed to fly by, for both of us. I walked her home, carrying the basket in my left hand. She was on my right, and during the walk, she slipped her arm in mine. I can't begin to describe what a great feeling that was. It almost felt like she was, in some small way, claiming her territory. Maybe she didn't mean it that way, but that's the thought I had, and I was sticking to it.

I walked her to the door and looked deeply into those beautiful blue eyes. I remember thinking that someday I wanted to wake up next to her and see those eyes the first thing every morning. I put my arms around her and brought her in for a warm embrace. I pulled my head back just a little, lightly placed a finger under her chin, and tilted her lips up to mine. And then I bent my head and kissed her tenderly on the lips. It was a beautifully, sweet kiss, a kiss that I hoped would just be one of many in the months to come. There was a warm feeling of tenderness, flowing through my body, and I knew I wanted to love and protect this woman forever.

We finally said our good-nights and embraced each other one last time. Tomorrow seemed so far away and I was already missing her. I told her that I really enjoyed our picnic together and she said that she did also. I looked kind of surprised and she said, "No, really. I think we ought to do it again. But John, I'll bring the food next time.

Chapter 28

Wendy

A S FAR AS FIRST DATES GO, FROM A TECHNICAL
point of view, it was a disaster. It seemed that anything that
could go wrong with the food did. And when you're on a
picnic, food is a big part of the overall experience, obviously. So, the
food wasn't great. But you know what? I didn't really care; especially
when I found out that John had gone through all the trouble of fixing
it himself. He admitted that he wasn't a great cook, but he wanted
this date to be personal. He wanted some hands-on involvement in
the whole evening. He didn't just want to take me someplace to be

entertained or served by someone else; he wanted to be the one doing that. That touched me so deeply that I got tears in my eyes and had to try very hard to hold it together. If I had lost it and started weeping and wailing, he'd wonder what that was all about. It's only a picnic, for crying out loud. But John couldn't possibly understand the impact it had on me for him to be that caring. It was an experience that I just wasn't used too.

So technically, the picnic could be to termed a disaster. But relationally, it was a whole different story. There wasn't one time that I felt uncomfortable, or that I sensed I was heading down the wrong road, or that I discerned I could be in danger if I didn't behave according to my date's wishes. John was the most comfortable guy I'd ever been with. Even when the food was self-destructing right before our eyes, he didn't get angry and cuss and swear and stomp around like some guys would. He would just laugh and poke fun at himself in a very endearing manner. He made even the so-called disastrous moments fun and lighthearted. It was so amazingly refreshing that I hardly knew how to respond. What a wonderful evening, probably one of the best I'd ever had.

When we began to just lay back and relax on the blanket, I was determined that I wasn't going to allow the conversation to go too deep. I had already planned ahead of time how I was going to gracefully dodge any questions about my past. I would just suddenly turn the topic of conversation back to him. Everybody knows that guys love to talk about themselves, right? It doesn't take too much skill to get their attention off of you, and back on themselves, and their dreams and accomplishments. It was a great plan, full of pre-determined detours, and dodges, and rabbit trails. It was a great plan, but unfortunately, it bombed. John was like Maggie's counterpart. Both of these new friends of mine somehow had the ability to get me to spill my guts. I found myself saying things, that a few hours before, I was bound and determined would never come out of my mouth. And yet, here they came. I was beginning to think that both Maggie and John had worked as CIA interrogators in another life. I even wondered if they had planned my gut-spilling session together, to see if John could crack me like Maggie did that first day.

So, I was very surprised at what I heard myself sharing with John, and I marveled at his uncanny ability to trick me into opening up about myself. But partway through our conversation, a light bulb went on. It's like a switch clicked and the light bulb of understanding was suddenly shining, as bright as day over my head. This wasn't a plan, or a learned skill, or a plot that Maggie and John cooked up together. This was just one person caring about another person. This was just John genuinely caring about me. He wasn't trying to pull some trick of submission and control. It wasn't about him winning a contest to see who could get the most information in the shortest amount of time. This was about one thing and one thing only. John really did care about me, and that was a wonderfully secure feeling. I told John a lot about myself, but I didn't tell him the whole truth. I had a feeling it would come out someday, but I just wasn't ready. As much as I admired John, and as much as I knew that he really cared for me, I wasn't sure how he'd react to the idea that his sweet, beautiful Wendy, with the deep, blue eyes, had been a topless dancer and was just minutes away from being a professional escort, which was just a fancy name for a Call Girl, a lady of the evening. It scared me to death to think about him finding out about that part of my life. I was afraid that I'd lose him if I let that be known. I've learned before, from other so-called Christians, that grace only went so far. I found out, very painfully, that when a certain line had been crossed, grace didn't seem to be too popular. Judgment was in, but grace kind of took a backseat.

I think he knew I was holding back, but it didn't seem to concern him. We continued to talk anyway, and finally looked at our watches and saw that it was 11:00 PM. We didn't have to be up early necessarily, but we still had things on our schedules, and so felt that midnight might be a good time to bring our first date to a close. I think we both hated to part ways, but we also knew that this would probably be the first of many such dates to come.

We lingered a little more on the blanket, just looking up at the stars, and then we packed everything up and began to walk slowly back towards the diner. I took his arm, just because it felt like the right thing to do. I wanted to be closer to him, to touch him in some way and let him know I was glad to be with him. When we finally arrived at my door, he did what I was hoping he'd do. He kissed me in a very sweet, very respectful manner. It wasn't the kind of good night kiss I'd had from other guys in my past. This wasn't a kiss of raw lust and expectations. It was a simple kiss of tenderness and, dare I say it, love. I returned John's kiss and felt him respond with a gentle tightening of his embrace. We looked at each other, said our good nights, and then parted. I didn't even ask him to call me, I just knew he would.

Sure enough, John called the next day at a little before 8:00 AM. I was up, but just barely. I didn't go to work until the evening shift, but I'm not a late sleeper anyway. We both expressed how much we enjoyed the previous night and that we'd like to go out again. He asked me how I felt about going out to a movie in Leavenworth, after

I was done with the dinner crowd. I told him that I would check with Maggie about watching Travis, but I thought it would be fine.

I asked him if I was going to see him at dinner and he told me that normally he'd come by to eat, but he had to be in Wenatchee for a special meeting of the area pastors for most of the day. The pastors' meetings always ended with dinner at one of the local mom and pop cafés that had a back room where they could close their time in an hour of prayer. When he told me what his day was going to be like, I wondered how it felt to make your living talking about God and praying all the time. This wasn't just a Sunday gig for him, he did this kind of stuff every day, as near as I could figure. I found myself trying to imagine what it would be like for a preacher's wife. I'd never really known any preachers' wives before and there certainly wasn't one at Pleasant Pastures. What if I ever got thrust into that position, who would I take my cues from? How would I learn what to do, and how to act? I realized I was getting way ahead of myself, but John had declared his belief that we were going to be married someday so strongly, that I thought he might be right. It would be wonderful to be married, especially to a guy like John, but this preacher's wife thing scared the pants off me. What's the religion page for the local newspaper going to say? "Local preacher marries former hooker." Now there's an attention-grabbing headline! It seemed to me that Pleasant Pastures Community Church wouldn't be able to survive a scandal like that.

All these thoughts were tumbling around in my head and I hadn't even had my morning coffee. I decided to quit worrying over something that hadn't happened yet and, in all likelihood, never would. Once John heard the whole story, he'd realize that his prophecy about us getting married was probably just a moment of emotional fervor, a late spring fever kind of thing. He was probably lonely and feeling the need of someone in his life, and here I came at just the right moment. It must've seemed like a vision from God or something, but someday when he's heard the whole ugly truth, he'll come to his senses. I just hope that when he does, both of us will survive, because in all honesty, I'm falling kind of hard and fast for him. I've been hurt before, and I've survived. But this feels different. I'm not sure what the survival rate would be for something that feels this intense. Well, whatever happens, I'm going to enjoy the ride. I'm going to enjoy the road that John and I seem to be on. I just hope the road doesn't drop us off a cliff.

Chapter 29

John

I SUPPOSE I BROKE ALL KINDS OF UN-WRITTEN RULES when I called Wendy just a little before 8:00 that next morning. I'd heard that calling that soon, after a first date, is a dead give-away that you're very desperate, hard-up, lonely, pathetic and have no friends or social life. I'd heard all of those things, none of which are true. Oh man, at least I hope they're not true. I have a social life. Several weeks ago, the Tanks and I went over to Wenatchee and bowled for a couple hours. And if that wasn't exciting enough, we had dinner at the local Pizza Hut and I ordered mine with anchovies. The Tanks had never had anchovies before, and when they bit into their pizza, they gagged and accused me of being some kind of food sadist. What friend would trick another friend into biting into an anchovy? I didn't know what to say. I loved those little hairy fish and I'd been eating them since I discovered them several years ago. Of course, when your Swedish parents served pickled herring at all kinds of occasions, you just grew pretty used to it. The funny thing is, as time went on the Tanks developed a taste for those little fish, at least to some extent. As I mentioned before we'd sometimes have contests to see who could eat the most and not lose it all. Oh well, someday we'd grow up.

When I called Wendy at 7:56 that next morning I wasn't being desperate, I was just being courteous. I'd also read that it's very bad manners to wait too long before that first call. It's bad manners because it keeps the girl in suspense, wondering what she could have possibly done that would make her date hesitant to call again, if ever.

I guess I just didn't get the rules to the dating game. It seemed to me that if you really like someone, you'd want to spend more time with them. And I didn't know how to do that without calling and setting up another date. I didn't like all this talk about smart moves, and playing hard to get, and keeping the mystery alive by a little suspense. When did wanting to be with someone become all about manipulation and strategy? Last time I checked it wasn't a crime to enjoy another person's company. I didn't know where all that dating protocol came from, but I decided not to let those magazines at the checkout counter determine my destiny. If it was too soon to call, I guess I'd find out. Stupid games! I just wanted to be with her, where's the crime in that?

Anyway, despite my so-called social flub, she agreed to go to a late movie with me after her evening shift. When we got into the theater, we grabbed a small box of popcorn and a couple of cokes. I had already eaten at the pastors' meeting in Wenatchee earlier that evening, so I wasn't too hungry. And Wendy had already had some supper at the diner, so she was fine too. But we both felt that popcorn would be good to snack on. After all, what's a good movie without popcorn, right? Besides, sharing a box of popcorn would give me a chance to have a little physical contact with her when we'd reach into the box at the same time, and our hands would touch. It would feel so natural that when we finished, we'd move right onto holding hands. How's that for a bold, strategic move? I may be a pastor, but I can be suave and sophisticated. In fact, maybe I should be a writer for those checkout magazines at the counter. "The Popcorn Move", as I came to refer to it, was pretty slick and worked like a charm. We wound up holding hands for the rest of the movie.

After the movie, we both decided it was getting a little late and we should probably head back. I had to be at the Men's Breakfast at 7:00 the next morning, and she had to work the breakfast shift and be there by 6:00 AM. I began to realize how complicated life could get in terms of finding time to be together. Between her work hours, some of which were split-shifts, and my seemingly endless string of board meetings and committee meetings and so on, my schedule was a little full also. I decided to try to do something about that, at least on my end.

I begin to think about all those committee meetings that I attended. I asked the question," Why do I go? What do I really do there?" The people on the various committees were really quite capable of conducting the business, with or without me. Nobody ever said it was mandatory for me to attend, I just always assumed that's what pastors did. They had to keep a tight rein on those various committees because, after all, if they had too much decision-making power that could be disastrous for the church. Who knew what the "Ladies Kitchen Committee" might do if they weren't held in check. They might go out and buy new dishtowels, or a new coffee maker to replace the vintage 1950s one. Ghastly!

As I continued to think that over, I came to a decision. I was going to go to each committee, over the next month, and pass the mantle of authority on to them. I was going to assure them of my complete confidence in them as a team. They knew their particular ministry better than I could, so I was just going to bless them and turn them loose to set the proper direction and vision for where they wanted to go, and what they wanted to do. The only thing I asked was that if their plans and goals exceeded the amount designated by the annual church budget, they'd discuss it with me first. And if I thought it was necessary to do so, we'd check it out with the church board. So as long as they stayed within their committee's ministry plan, and they continued to be fiscally responsible, I'd have absolute confidence in their ability to run things very successfully, without me looking over their shoulder.

I met with every committee over the next month and the result was always the same. They were surprised at first, because after all, they've never done it that way before. By the way - "We've never done it that way before," - is the mantra of a dying church. I may have been young, but I knew that bold ministry would never happen if we weren't willing to step out and take a risk. Just because we've never done something that way before, didn't mean we shouldn't. And with that kind of challenge to them, every committee gratefully, though somewhat hesitantly, embraced their new marching orders of independence. I think they were excited about what could happen if they began to pray and dream about new possibilities, new ministries, which would make their particular calling more effective.

Well, let me just say that this new approach to ministry not only encouraged each person to use their various gifts in greater service to the Lord, it also freed up a ton of time for me. In the process of turning these very gifted folks loose to dream big and carry out their ministry with excellence, I was training them to become a church that was dependent on God, not on a man. I always figured that if I ever left and the church fell apart, I hadn't really done my job as a pastor. I needed to train people and then mobilize them for ministry. The church's success shouldn't be dependent on me alone. I was simply part of a greater team. We weren't just a bunch of committees; we were all a part of a team that had the same overall goal. We were dedicated to advancing the kingdom of God. So, with that thought in mind, I told the various committees that the only thing I wanted to do was to make a name change. From now on the Missions Committee was now the Missions Team. And the Worship Committee was now the Worship Team. The Kitchen Committee was now the Kitchen Team, right on down the line. Just that small name change carried with it a greater sense of purpose and possibility. The only snafu we had was with the committee that oversaw the church softball team. Now they would technically be called the Team Team. That was a little awkward, but I was confident that they'd come up with a good solution.

Needless to say, other than being on the church board, I was quite a bit freer to pursue some more time with Wendy. Plus, I had helped encourage the various teams to keep pushing forward in their respective ministries. So, all in all, it was good for all concerned. But I have to admit something to you. Letting go of all those responsibilities, which were not even part of my job description in the first place, was tremendously freeing for the various teams, as well as for me. While the teams were thinking about their specific goals and plans, I was thinking about mine also. And as non-spiritual as this may sound, a huge part of my plans and goals involved Wendy.

Now, I know what you're thinking. You're wondering how I could be called to be a pastor and to preach God's word and yet be so enamored and hung up on this woman who I'd only met a few days before. Preaching the word of God is an awesome calling and privilege. I'd always felt that way, and I suspected that I would for the rest of my life, but I also knew that there was a difference between my calling as a pastor, and what would eventually be my calling as a husband and a father. So, as I continued to think and pray about Wendy, and what I hoped would be our future together, I came to a conclusion. Life is full of opportunities, as well as duties and responsibilities. It's also true that whenever we're confronted with multiple options, we have to establish priorities. I mean, I can wake up on any day, and have multiple and varied options at my fingertips. Am I going to have a Pop-Tart on my way out the door, or am I going to take the time to fix myself a hearty breakfast of bacon and eggs, with a glass of orange juice to wash it down? Well, the breakfast might be better for me, but since I had to be at an early gathering of local pastors that met for prayer once a month, I'd have to prioritize. And on this particular day, I'd choose the Pop-Tart because I didn't want to be late for the prayer time, which was always a tremendous blessing. Life is always full of options, which in turn demands that we prioritize.

And so, I came to the conclusion that in the future I would have three major life-options available to me. The first was my personal relationship with God. That was always going to be a significant life-option for me. Am I always going to follow Him, or am I going to slack off over time, until God just becomes a small part of my life when I feel the need for Him? A second life-option would be my profession, specifically my calling to be a pastor. Would I always feel called to this profession, or would I lose steam somewhere down the road? And the third life-option would be family. What kind of a husband and father would I be? Would we be a tight-knit family who loved each other, or would other things get in the way, so that slowly over time, they would erode the intimacy that a family should share? Would my wife come to hate the ministry and the church because I seemed to care more about it than I did her? And would my kids wind up resenting me, because I never had time for them; I was too busy "serving the Lord?" Worse yet, would they grow up hating God, because He always took their daddy away? These kinds of thoughts were playing over and over in my mind, whenever I had a few minutes to myself. What were my priorities going to be in life? What path was I going to set for myself, hopefully in accordance with God's will? Priorities needed to be established before I ever had a wife and a family. If I could set them straight now, I would never have to re-think and question those three life-options again. And so, here's what I came up with as I was driving back to the church after making a hospital visit:

Priority 1: God - My personal relationship with God would always head up the list. Nothing would ever be allowed to take over that number one spot. Some people might object to that because they think that the family should come first. But I saw it differently. You see, if I made God my number one priority, my wife and kids were going to benefit greatly from that. I would be a better husband and a better father because I would be in a relationship with the One who invented marriage and family in the first place. So, there's absolutely no doubt about it. My number one priority was, and always will be, God.

Priority 2: Family - Now this might seem perfectly normal to most people. They can understand how family would come in at number two, just under God. That would seem to make perfect sense to them. At least it would make sense, until they saw my third priority. Then they'd get confused. But there was no confusion on my part. I knew that my second priority would be my family. My wife and my children would be a gift, given to me by a very loving and generous God, and I was going to do my best to honor and care for His marvelous gift to me.

Priority 3: Ministry - Now this is the part that gets people confused. And the reason they get confused is that they equate God and ministry as being one and the same. If God is my number one priority then obviously the ministry, and all that goes with it, is also at number one. But you see, what God had made crystal clear to me on that drive back to the church, is that God and ministry are not one and the same. God is the One I'll follow for the rest of my life. But ministry is my profession. I wouldn't have to be a minister to serve God. I could serve God no matter what I did to earn a living. It's just that God called me into ministry all those years ago and had allowed me to make my living doing what I loved to do, and that's share His word with others. I intended that ministry to be my profession for the rest of my life. But I also knew, very clearly, that even if I needed to change professions for some reason, I'd still serve God because I loved Him.

When those three priorities came to me on my drive back to the church, I suddenly felt a sense of calm and peace wash over me. I didn't fully know what was going on in my thinking, but I knew that I needed to settle something with myself before the relationship with Wendy went much further. There was a lot that was up in the air. I mean, I knew I believed with all my heart that she was the one for me. For heaven sake, I already blurted that out in the first few minutes I'd met her. And that hadn't changed. I still felt that she was the girl I was going to marry. How can you argue with love at first sight, right? But I also knew that we were from totally opposite backgrounds. My background was pretty good, with Christian parents who loved me and a church that, when I was growing up, made me feel part of an even larger family. But Wendy didn't have that, not at all. Hers was a very dark past and I knew I hadn't heard all of it. She had asked Jesus into her life when she first met Kevin and his Jesus People friends, but when he died she just wrote God off as being a heartless ogre. She figured that whoever this God was, He just didn't care. I knew it would take some time, and a little theological wrangling, but I felt that I'd be able to help her see the truth of God and His love. So, I wasn't really too worried about that at the time.

But as I looked into the future, I could see God bringing us together fairly quickly. He knew I'd been longing for someone to share my life with, and I was convinced that Wendy was the one. But the one thought that nagged at me was about priorities two and three. What would I do if Wendy and I got married, and things were going great for the first months or even years? But what if, down the road, Wendy grew tired of being a pastor's wife? What if she couldn't stand being what my black brothers-in-Christ call The First Lady? What if she felt that the pressures of being in the pastorate were just too much for her? What would I do then?

I thought about that a lot. You see, I loved doing what I do. I loved preaching and teaching the word of God. I loved helping cast vision for the church and coming up with different ideas and programs to grow the ministry. I loved it all. Well, I loved most of it. I could do without some of the little tiffs that every church has over disagreements that, in the end, don't really amount to a hill of beans. But I loved the ministry, I really did. But what if Wendy didn't? What if it just wasn't for her? What if instead of causing her to thrive, it became a source of heartache and despair? Well, that was hard to think about, and in fact, it was downright painful to even contemplate such a thing. But after the little talk that God and I had concerning priorities, my answer to all those questions was as clear as a bell. If I had to choose between my wife, and the ministry, I'd choose my wife every time, in a heartbeat. And I knew, beyond a shadow of a doubt, that God would applaud my decision and would be in my corner all the way, so I put those thoughts to rest, knowing that my priorities were established, and they were established for good.

Chapter 30

Wendy

IT WASN'T LONG BEFORE JOHN AND I FELL INTO A routine of sorts. And trust me; it wasn't one of those boring routines that put you to sleep. This routine felt pretty good because it relieved me of something I've felt for an awful lot of my life. The chaos was gone and was replaced by a comfortable ease of day-to-day activity. Where once my life had been full of poor choices on my part, and mean actions on the part of others, now I was simply going along enjoying a peaceful stability. I suppose some of my old friends back in Chicago would have thought my new life was about as exciting as watching cars rust, but I found it to be comforting. And yet, it was more than that. It wasn't just comforting and stable and peaceful. It was joyful. I felt a great deal of joy beginning to grow within me.

I told you before how I didn't really trust God, if He was even out there in the first place. And even if by chance He was there, He certainly didn't seem to care about me. And why would He? It's not like I'd been paying much attention to Him for the major portion of my life. In fact, the only time He and I were on speaking terms was when I was with Kevin. I was beginning to see a whole other side of God when Kevin was in my life. I asked Jesus to come into my life and felt that He answered my prayer. I truly felt different from that point on.

My few short months with Kevin were wonderful and I had fallen pretty fast for him. I spent a lot of time day-dreaming about my life and picturing a nice future for Travis and me, but in spite of my new faith and outlook on life I still had questions. For example, I wondered if God was, I don't know, blessing me in extra measure, to kind of make up for the negative things that happened in my life. I didn't know a lot about Him, and how He worked, and made decisions. I didn't have the foggiest notion of how He ran the universe and kept everything straight. In my thinking, the world was in a mess, with wars and famine and disease everywhere I looked. And I couldn't help but wonder where God was in the midst of all of that. Was He really in control, or did Christians just say that as a way to comfort themselves when something bad happened, or something that raised doubts and questions? I don't know how many times I'd heard people talking about a particularly difficult situation and, at the end, when there didn't seem to be any kind of answer or closure, they'd say, "Oh well, God's in control." And everybody would say yes or amen and then drop the subject and move on from there.

And as I was getting used to hanging out with them, I'd just go along with it and express the same kind of sentiment. "Oh well, God's in control" was an easy, no-sweat, no-pain answer for everything, right? Well, not exactly, at least not for me. I mean I didn't know much about Him, really. I hadn't been a Christian very long, at least not what President Jimmy Carter called a born-again Christian, so I was pretty much new to this stuff. But something didn't quite sit right with me and the whole God's-in-control idea. I guess I looked at that answer, the one everyone seemed to use, and wondered if it was actually true. Because it just wasn't making a lot of sense to me. On the one hand, that was an easy way to end the discussion when you couldn't seem to come up with an adequate answer for a really difficult situation. On the other hand, to use the word control seemed to indicate that God was behind it all, pulling the strings, so to speak, like the whole world was a puppet on a string. The thing that bothered me about that was that if it was actually true, then it made me feel that God wasn't doing such a great job. I don't want to be sacrilegious or anything, but there was some pretty nasty stuff going on in the world. And if all of that nasty stuff was going on because God was in control and somehow was behind it all, I wasn't sure how all of that fit with the whole "God is love" thing that we all talked about so often.

Kevin and I had been having conversations about what God was really like, and how all that fit in with the devastation and the pain and heartache that we saw in the world. I don't know if we ever got so far that we came up with any earth-shaking answers, but at least we were talking about it. I actually enjoyed those kinds of discussions because they let me voice my questions and concerns, and still feel safe about it. I realized after I'd asked a particularly blunt, and somewhat embarrassing question about faith that I was still standing. In other words, God wasn't ticked off at me for my questions and didn't strike me dead with a lightning bolt. So, even though Kevin and I didn't come up with some deep, theological answers, we at least had the freedom to ask the hard questions with no fear of a celestial reprisal. I may not have had all my questions answered, but I figured that I was a work in progress and would learn more as I went along. All I knew was that I was happier than I'd ever been before. And Kevin played a huge role in that happiness.

But then came the night of the accident, and my life just took a nose-dive. I didn't really care about anything else, other than Travis. I've often looked back on that time and wondered how Travis ever survived, living with a mother who was so broken and angry and defeated. All those questions Kevin and I talked about never really got answered. The only concept that stuck with me was the idea about God being in control. And if God was in control, then I guess that He caused all of this to happen to me. I guess this is what my Jesus Freak friends would call a part of "God's wonderful plan for my life." Well, if this was part of "God's wonderful plan for my life" I think it was mean and nasty. I think it's a terrible thing to plan for another person's life. And if that's what God does all day - sit up there dreaming up all these horrible scenarios - if that's what He does all day, I don't want anything to do with Him, if He even exists in the first place. It actually just became easier not to believe in Him anymore. Because to believe in Him left me no choice but to accept the idea that God did all of this to me, just because He could. That was harder to take than the death of Kevin.

But now I wasn't sure what was going on. I felt in some ways like I was reliving a part of my life. The similarities were a little freaky, in fact. Kevin was gone, but John was here. Both of these guys loved God and were actually sold out to Him, meaning that they considered Jesus to be their Lord. I'd learned a long time ago that the phrase "Jesus is Lord" that you'd see on bumper stickers, basically meant that He was their boss. Jesus was the One who called the shots and directed them where to go and what to do. And here's the really interesting thing. Both Kevin and John really believed that. They tried to live by that philosophy every day, in every way.

After several weeks with John, I realized that we were talking about some of the same questions Kevin and I had wrestled with so often. What was God really like? How much control did God really have? Just because God may be in control, does that mean that everything we see and experience is exactly as God had planned it all along? In other words, was it true that whatever we saw in the world could be traced back to God, who was the ultimate cause?

I think John was a little surprised at some of the questions I brought up, but it didn't take him too long to discern why those questions were on my mind. He realized pretty early on that I blamed God for all the devastation in my life. I blamed Him for my life of chaos and despair. I blamed Him for my low self-esteem and sordid activities that came as a result of that. I blamed Him for taking Kevin away from me in a cruel act of what I could only see as punishment for my sinful life; a life, by-the-way, that He brought about in the first place. I was stuck in a kind of circular thinking that kept leading back to a God who just didn't care. But it went further than that. It wasn't only that God didn't care, in my thinking, He actually enjoyed inflicting pain on His vast collection of puppets.

As John and I continued to date, he gently began to lead me down another path in my thinking. He told me very honestly and bluntly, that if what I thought about God was actually true, he wouldn't serve Him either. Who would want to serve a God like that? John began to show me instead about the true character of God. He used to always tell me that if I truly wanted to know what God was really like, I needed to look at Jesus, because after all, by His own declaration, Jesus was God in human form. Jesus was God, as John put it, with skin on. And so, I began to read through the Gospels, devouring what I saw in Jesus. At the same time, John and I would discuss the devastation that sin had brought into the world. We talked about the whole idea of free will, and how, on the one hand it was a marvelous risk that God took giving His creation this most prized gift. But, on the other hand, that free will, when used selfishly, led to all kinds of horrible, nasty situations in our world. God wasn't the cause; selfishness and sin were the cause. We talked about the devastation from natural things like earthquakes and floods and fires and so on. John talked about how even laws of science had been impacted by sin that entered the world and disrupted what God had originally intended. We talked about how Jesus had wept at the tomb of his friend Lazarus. And John told me that the idea of Jesus weeping gave him this picture of God weeping right along with us for the trauma, and the pain, and the devastation that comes into our world, in a way that should never have been. We talked about how God being in control doesn't mean He causes all things to happen, either good or bad. It just means that no matter what this sinful, selfish world dishes out, He can bring something good out of it. It means that no matter what "nature-gone-mad," devastating event comes about, God can and will turn it around and bring something valuable out of the whole experience. We also talked about how, in the end, God indeed is *ultimately* in control, and will win the battle over Satan's forces of darkness.

Now, I know what you're thinking. You're thinking that all of our dates and time spent together, were about as romantic as sitting in a seminary class talking about how many angels can sit on the head of a pin. Well, let me just say this. Make no mistake about it. Our dates were wonderful. They were fun, loving, romantic and always delightful. It wasn't so much a matter of what we did, as much as the fact that we were just together. It was the time spent together that so thrilled me. It was fun being together and it was fun having a man like John who I could share some pretty deep thoughts with. And yes, even though it might sound boring to some, having discussions about what God was really like, really added to the depth of feeling that I was having for John. It was actually romantic, in its own way. Because for John to take the time, and help me sort out some of my feelings, and fears, and huge misconceptions about God wasn't a matter of him trying to be the resident theologian in our relationship. No, it was about John being sensitive enough to know what was truly at the heart of some of my confusion about who I was. And he knew that as I would begin to understand about God and His love, I'd be able to love myself more. He also knew that when I began to really love God, and in turn, love myself, I'd be able to love him more deeply also. And so, we talked for hours over those first several weeks. He helped me to understand God, and understand myself. And sure enough, our love for each other grew very fast and very strong.

Maybe talking about God doesn't sound all that exciting, but in my book, I think it was the most romantic thing John could ever have done.

Chapter 31

John

I FOUND THAT MY THOUGHTS DURING THE DAY oftentimes drifted to Wendy. When I had to drive to a call, my mind might wander to a previous conversation we had. Or, I'd remember the lunch we shared the day before, or the walk we had taken in the cool of the evening that last Monday night. I found that I wanted to spend all my spare time with her. And, evidently, she felt the same way because we were pretty much inseparable on our off hours.

Sometimes Travis would come and we'd have dinner at the McDonald's up in Leavenworth. Or maybe we'd go to a German restaurant and try to figure out what spaetzli was, and if it had any flavor. I wasn't quite getting the hang of this spaetzli thing. They always talk about Swedes having some bland food, but I think Germans and their spaetzli might be right up there with the Scandinavians.

Sometimes the three of us would take in a movie, if there was anything decent playing of the PG-rated variety. But other times we might sit on the bench by the brook and talk about the school year that was coming up for Travis, and what activities he might be interested in. I was always impressed that Travis seemed to have no difficulty at all, talking to adults, and even enjoying it. Sometimes kids can be very shy or bored or rebellious or snippy and, sometimes, just plain rude. But Travis was just an all-around nice kid; very smart, very well-spoken for an eight-year-old. There were times I wondered if he was really eight, because his maturity level was very developed and his vocabulary would put a lot of adults to shame. In fact, as the Tanks got to know Travis a bit more from the boys Sunday school class they taught, tag-team style, they started calling him Einstein. Most boys his age had no idea who Einstein was, but Travis did. And he was quite pleased to have that as his nickname. I thought he might be upset and would want a nickname that made him sound like a Big Time Wrestler, but no, Einstein was just fine with him.

Most of the time when Wendy and I would go out or spend the evening at my place, Travis stayed with Maggie. They always had a great time together and Maggie was enjoying teaching Travis how to cook. She even taught him some of her secret recipes that I'd never known her to give out to anybody, for any reason. But, somehow Travis won her heart, and she taught him some of her favorite culinary secrets.

I was beginning to have a real soft spot in my heart for that little kid. He been through a few interesting challenges in his life, the latest one being uprooted from his home in the space of 30 minutes, and taken to another world entirely. I couldn't imagine Pleasant Pastures having much in common with Travis' previous home of Chicago. I figured it was pretty much different as night and day, but he adjusted amazingly well and it was a pleasure to continue building a relationship together.

I would make my way to the diner several times a week, sometimes for a meal, and other times just for a cup of coffee and maybe a piece of pie. The only reason I went so often was just to be with Wendy. I knew enough not to take up her time when the diner was busy, but when things were slow, she could sit for a few minutes and we could chat, and maybe make plans for the coming week. It didn't seem to matter what topic we were discussing, we could just about go on all night and talk for hours on end.

Now here's the thing that surprised me about the kinds of conversations we'd been having. I was beginning to pick up more and more tidbits of information concerning Wendy's growing up years, and the dysfunctional home-life she had somehow survived. I guess what surprised me so much was how resilient she was. A lot of people growing up in that kind of situation could wind up having major problems, either with relationships or with communication skills. But Wendy was very good with both. I knew that her self-esteem had really taken a hit sometime in the past, and yet here she was, pretty vibrant, with a joy and zest for life. I don't know. Maybe it was her newly re-discovered faith, or maybe she was in love with a certain 6'2" blonde pastor that kept hanging around. I hoped it was a little of both.

I wanted her to love God and I wanted her to love me, in that order. If she got the order right, the relationship we were developing had a much greater chance of success.

We had engaged in some pretty heavy theological discussions about the character and nature of God. I was very impressed by some of the questions that came up. I could tell that this wasn't just Wendy's way of getting to me. It wasn't her attempt to reel this young preacher in, like you would a trout. The questions she asked demonstrated some amazing insight and she wasn't afraid to address even the most difficult ones. Just to be able to articulate some of those questions showed how much thought had gone into them.

But as we talked over the coming weeks, I picked up a pattern with her questions. They all boiled down to whether or not she could trust God. Now, she never said that directly, out loud, but that was the underlying idea. It was the age-old question of why. Why, if God is so loving and kind, did this happen to me? Why doesn't God do something to stop all the world's problems; war, famine, nakedness, disease and so on. Not exactly lightweight questions, but they made for some very interesting and inspiring conversations. Any question was a go. We never set any kind of a boundary that made a particular question or topic off-limits. Now, we may not have settled all the questions, because after all, Christians haven't settled them in 2000 years. But we still gave it our best shot. So, whether we settled the questions or not, just being with someone who didn't have years of indoctrination by her denomination, was very refreshing.

Sometimes churches don't like their members to be asking questions. Some pastors feel threatened because they don't have a great answer either. Or, they may have good, solid, stock answers, but people who knew their Bible knew that in order to reach that good, solid, stock answer you'd have to ignore or explain away great portions of Scripture that would seem to support the other side. I'd personally learned several years ago that I'd rather live in the tension between two great, but opposing spiritual truths, than to totally embrace one set of scriptures, while ignoring the rest. Over the years that philosophy has served me well, particularly as a pastor of a community church where the doctrine and beliefs were a little more open to different views. There's actually great freedom in that, even though at first it might sound a little wishy-washy.

Anyway, with all the questions that Wendy would ask that had trust as the underlying foundation, I began to wonder if she trusted me. I knew that her trust in God was growing, but what about her trust in me? She had never given me any reason to think that she didn't trust me, but yet I still knew, deep inside, that she was holding back to some extent. You'd never know that, if you were a fly on the wall, listening into all our conversations, because our talk was very open and honest. But still, there seemed to be an area or two that she was bound and determined not to share.

I began to think of the various scenarios that could have made up her life previously. And knowing what she had shared made it easier to picture some of what she might be holding back. To be perfectly honest, even though I was still young in the ministry, I was convinced I had pretty much heard all the various scenarios. And so far, nothing was so shocking that I'd run out of my office screaming. People's lives were just kind of messed up. In fact, I think much of the Christian life is pretty messy. I'm not sure where we ever got the idea that church was for those folks who really had it all together. All I knew was that my flock at Pleasant Pastures came from some very interesting backgrounds. So interesting in fact, I think your hair would be blown back if you ever heard their full testimony.

I was very determined to let Wendy share her complete past with me when she felt it was time. I knew it would come someday, but I really wasn't sure when. She might be keeping something so personal to herself that she'd never want another person to know. But in Wendy's case, I decided to just let her be, and let the Lord work on her about it, when it was time for a little freedom. It's truly amazing how good a person can feel when the burden is lifted off one set of shoulders, and is transferred to several others. It's nice when other brothers and sisters in Christ come along and help carry the burden. Besides, I learned a principle a long time ago. And that principle basically says that if you bring something hidden out into the light, it takes the power out of it. And it's true; I've seen it with many folks. And I'm hoping Wendy will be one of those folks very soon.

One Thursday night we were sitting at our bench by the little brook, when without any fanfare, Wendy started to open up to me. Believe me when I say that she held nothing back. Before she started, she told me that she felt very deeply for me, and knew I felt the same. We had already declared our love for each other many times, and every time I heard those words from her lips, they made my heart sing all over again. I was confident of her love, and evidently, she was confident of mine because once she started I knew that she wasn't holding anything back. I knew that what I was hearing was the honest confession of someone for whom life had been extremely brutal. She told me all about diner-guy and the path that his comment started her on. She told me about how Travis's father could be any one of eight guys she had slept with, in a month-long fit of anger and disgust with herself. She told me about Nick and his strategy to move her from a go-go dancer, in a very skimpy outfit, to the topless venue that left even less to the imagination. My stomach churned as I pictured my beautiful Wendy, men leering at her and expressing crude, vulgar thoughts, with no thought of the emotional damage they were inflicting. And just when I thought I had heard the whole story, she told me how Nick had tried to convince her that prostituting herself for some very well-to-do customers of the club, would bring her so much extra income that Travis could have anything he wanted. She confessed that she had fallen so hard, after Kevin's death that she just didn't care anymore about whatever standards she still had. She related how she'd made her first appointment, as a professional, and was ready to park her car, but then she'd heard a voice inside saying that this wasn't her, this wasn't who she really was. She needed to run away and she needed to run away now. She knew that if she ran, it was very possible that Nick would find her and kill her. But she didn't have a choice, she had to get away. Travis and she hit the road and never looked back. She ended by saying that she was so thankful that God, a God she didn't even believe in back then, had brought her here to Pleasant Pastures. And she was so happy to have met me.

She told me how worried she had been that if she said anything about that part of her past, I would get disgusted and leave her, just figuring the she wasn't the kind of girl I should be having a relationship with. She was scared, but she knew it wasn't fair to hold back a story of that magnitude. She needed to be honest with me and get everything off her chest. And that was it, there was nothing more to confess.

I sat there for a few seconds processing all that Wendy had shared with me. I realized how hard that must have been for her to open up like that, but I was so thankful that she had. I couldn't play the I-can-top-that game to make her feel better. My life had been nothing like hers. I knew that she had been in some very deep and dark waters, but now she was finally able to swim freely, without her past dragging her down into the depths.

I slowly reached for her and took her into my arms. As I held her, I whispered softly, "Wendy, I love you more, right now, than I ever have before." With our arms locked around each other, she looked up at me as a tear rolled down her cheek, and rested her head on my chest.

Chapter 32

Wendy

I DON'T KNOW WHAT CAME OVER ME EXACTLY, BUT whatever it was it ended with me revealing the whole ugly truth to John. Several weeks before, I had determined that I would never tell him the whole story. How could I tell him that the woman he loved was just a few moments away from taking up the world's oldest profession? He's a pastor for crying out loud. The closest he ever got to seeing a hooker was probably on television, and I wasn't positive he'd even seen one then. John really tried to guard his mind, and so the Andy Griffith Show was probably about as edgy as he would get. Who knew what kind of risqué behavior Aunt Bee was up to? Seriously! John was so straight-arrow, I was pretty convinced that my story would send him packing. I was prepared for the worst; at least I hoped I was. It seemed possible that he'd listen, look at me sadly, and walk out. And who could blame him, right?

As scared as I was to tell John, I also knew that I had no choice. Even I knew that trying to build a relationship on lies and half-truths would never work. A lot of people try to do that and then are surprised when things don't work out. Well, it doesn't take a genius to know that absolute trust is the key to any successful relationship, but especially marriage. But if there's going to be trust, there also has to be truth. Without truth, the trust soon begins to fade. And once it's faded, it's very hard to recover it. It's not impossible, but it's very difficult.

So, when I came clean with John, it wasn't simply a matter of wanting to be truthful for my conscience sake. It was more than that. I wanted to be truthful because I'd fallen in love with John and was allowing myself the slim hope that maybe this would go someplace permanent. Being married to John seemed like a pipedream, but dreams sometimes do come true. At least that's what the Disney movies always seem to indicate. Wish upon a star and your dreams come true. It sure sounded good; I just wasn't sure in my case.

But my hopes began to rise when I finished the depressing saga of my life and John reached for me. And as his arms went around me and drew me into his embrace, I had a fleeting thought that this could go two ways. The first one was that he was holding me simply as a way to let me down easy. "There, there Wendy" (several pats on my back) "thank you for sharing your story with me, that was very brave of you. You should be proud. However, because of my position in the church, you must realize that this could never work between us. God bless you! Now take a hike." That's one way it could have gone, I suppose. But, in all honesty, I didn't think so. When you hang around a person, as much as John and I had been together, you get to know their character. And John just didn't seem to have the kind of character that would allow him to get holier-than-thou on me and give me the boot. I just couldn't really imagine him ever doing that.

But the second option made me a little more nervous. John could also embrace me out of pity, more than love. I'd watched him in action after church when someone would meet him at the front and pour out their story of woe on him. And even though I was in the back waiting, and wasn't privy to the actual conversation, I could see, by John's body language and gestures, that he was comforting the person in their trial. John had a great capacity for empathy and compassion. That's what made the people at Pleasant Pastures love him like they so obviously did. But that's not what I needed from John. I didn't need his pity, or his empathy, or even his compassion. I needed his love. And not the "love your neighbor" kind of love. I needed the mad, passionate love that only couples could share. I needed the kind of love that declared, with startling confidence, "It's you and me together, against all odds. And Wendy, together we can face anything." I needed a declaration of love that would see us through anything.

John reached out and drew me near, and reflexively, I put my arms around him. As we held each other tight, I felt a tear rolled down my cheek. I already knew what he was going to say. I think I knew it, because I knew him. And true to form, true to the picture I had developed of him over the months, he told me that he loved me, more now, than ever before. I can't tell you the flood of emotions that came over me in that instant. I felt totally, wonderfully, marvelously in love with this man and I knew that he felt the same way about me. I felt all kinds of warm emotions; all kinds of exciting possibilities flood my mind. But the feeling I was experiencing most intensely was safety. I leaned my head against his chest and felt absolutely safe and warm and secure. I can't express deeply enough what that did for me. It seemed as if years of chaos and abuse just melted away, and I was home. So good - so pure - so safe.

That night was a major step in our relationship. John knew all about me, and I knew all about him. And even though I sometimes kidded him about his lily-white, Swedish Baptist, pure-as-the-driven-snow upbringing, in reality I really envied him and wished I could have had that kind of experience myself. But John had another take on it. He told me that maybe God had brought us together because of the fact that we were so different. He had a view of people and their situations that was from a very distinct vantage point. I, on the other hand, could see things that he couldn't because I had a vantage point that was very different from him, almost totally opposite. He would tell me how valuable that really was in terms of dealing with the messiness of people's lives. There were even times that he asked a parishioner he was dealing with if he could bring me in on the conversation, simply because I could provide a different perspective. And whenever I had the opportunity to sit in, I always seemed to be able to bring a new thought or new view to the table, and that would help guide the direction of the conversation. Truth be told, I found it to be quite satisfying.

We continued to date and had reached our three-month anniversary. I didn't really have a time-frame in mind in terms of whatever steps forward we might take. We hadn't really talked that much about marriage, or moving the relationship along to the next step of engagement, but I wasn't really worried. By this time, I had learned to trust John completely. I thought he was the most honest, caring, and loving man I'd ever known. In fact, he had some areas of spiritual maturity and insight that I didn't even see in Kevin. Of course, Kevin had only been a Christian for a few years during the Jesus People Movement. John, on the other hand, had been following Jesus his whole life. I didn't want to compare the two, but it was interesting all the same.

Life with John was really wonderful, it truly was. Still…there was something that was kind of bugging me. And it was such a sensitive topic I didn't know how to bring it up, or even if I should. The reason it was a little sensitive is because it involved our physical relationship. You know what my past was like and believe me, I'd never want to go back to that. Never! But in my experience, the physical intimacy came about pretty quickly, no matter who I happened to be dating. I can't tell you how many times I had to fight off men who thought that I owed them a good time in the sack, simply because they had bought me dinner in a semi-nice restaurant. Most of the time there wasn't even a small attempt at romance. It was usually, "I-hope-you-liked-your-dinner-let's-go-to-my-place-for-dessert - heh-heh," raised eyebrows, pathetic grin. A lot of times I'd go because, after all, according to my now well-worn, self-esteem philosophy, that's all I really had going for me in the first place.

But now, it was such a relief not to have to fight this kind of philosophy and physical aggression by every loser that came along, hoping to score. John wasn't like any of these men and it was such a huge relief. He'd been very passionate with his declarations of love and the way he'd always protect me, or take charge of difficult situations.

It wasn't that he didn't think I couldn't handle something myself, it's just that he truly wanted to do things for me. He told me, many times, that it brought him great joy to serve me, whenever possible. Well hey, who wouldn't want that on occasion, right?

But here we were in our third month, and other than holding hands, walking with his arm around me, hugging each other, and kissing quite regularly, there was nothing else. Nothing! Nada! Zippo! I knew from past experience with Kevin that he had wanted to save our physical relationship for marriage, the way he believed God had originally intended when He invented marriage in the first place. And that was fine with me, it really was. And the way John was handling this was fine with me also. It was fine, yes, but it was also very confusing.

You see, the question that I had that I wasn't too sure how to ask, or even if I should ask, was this: "John, do you feel *any* physical attraction to me? I appreciate your desire to wait, and to do it God's way, but I just have to know. Is there a physical chemistry here? Are you fighting to hold back, or are you just not experiencing a battle in that area? Because John, I am. I'm fighting a battle like you can't believe. But you've never tried anything. You've never coaxed me to go further. You've never even "accidentally" brushed up against me in ways that could be termed sexual. I saw you looking down my blouse once, and I thought that was a good sign of a healthy, normal male. But then you pointed out the spider that had crawled in my blouse and I screamed and shook it out. Most guys would've used that as an excuse to go to the "forbidden zone" to rescue their girlfriend. But you didn't even do that. John, I don't know what to think. If we stay together, will we have any kind of a physical relationship? I mean, I know it's not the most important thing, but it's right up there."

You see what I mean by this being a very sensitive issue? As a Christian, who's hopefully growing every day, I'm glad I'm not having to continually fight an eight-handed octopus, but even a one-handed octopus would at least reassure me. This had been bothering me for quite a while and so I decided that the best course of action was, once again, telling the truth and confronting the issue head on.

I invited John over to the apartment one night for dinner. Travis and Maggie had gone to see Maggie's sister who lived on a farm over in Cle Elum. Travis was super-excited to see the cows and goats and chickens close up. Not only that, he was going to get to ride a horse. This was his first horse ride and he was really looking forward to it. He'd ridden a pony when the fair came to Wenatchee, but this was his first ride on a full-size, golden Palomino. John had bought him a cowboy hat at the Hat Shop in Leavenworth and he looked so cute as he walked to Maggie's car in his cowboy hat and boots.

John and I sat down to a wonderful dinner that I knew he would enjoy. John had a pretty simple palette really. Meat and potatoes were his thing. And so, I pan fried some thin, strip steaks, while popping some potatoes into the oven to bake. I had fixed a salad of mixed greens, along with carrots and onions, and then topped it all off with blue cheese dressing and bacon crumbles on top. We ate at a leisurely pace and really enjoyed the food and the conversation. It was fun to be at home, just the two of us. After dinner was finished and we had cleared the dishes, we went into the living room to let things settle a bit, before we had some of the pie I brought home from the diner. As we sat there on the couch, John looked at me and asked if something was bothering me. "You've got this scrunched up look on your face, just above your eyebrows, and that usually means that something's going on." Of course, John picked up on my body language right away. Like I said before, he was good at that kind of thing. So, I thought, well, I might as well just spit it out.

I looked at him and said, "John, you know how much I love you, don't you?" He nodded, somewhat hesitantly, with a concerned look on his face. And I told him that I loved him too, but that something had been eating away at me and I just needed to ask him a question. And, of course, he told me to ask away; ask any question I want. So, I took a deep breath and said, "John, you've never tried anything with me. Do you just not find me physically attractive?" Well, John had been in the middle of taking a drink of coffee when I asked him that question. What happened next was just not pretty, not at all. When I asked my question, that coffee came spewing out of his mouth, all over my clean, blue-and-white "Gunny Sax" dress I'd just bought. I was covered in it. I had no idea his mouth was so big and could hold what seemed like a pint of coffee. He looked at me, almost in shock, and apologized for making a mess. And then he grabbed me by the shoulders, looked me right in the eyes and said, "Wendy, you need to listen and you need to listen hard. Am I attracted to you? Am I physically attracted to you? You've got to be kidding! It's all I can do, every time I see you, not to rip your clothes off and take you right on the spot. Every time! I'm trying to hold back to honor you, and honor the Lord. But if it was just up to me, your clothes would be on that floor right now and we'd be on the bed. Does that answer your question?" He stared at me and I noticed he was panting very hard, a look of intensity in his eyes that I had never seen before.

"Yes John, that answered my question, quite clearly." I smiled and went out to the kitchen to cut the pie. Our relationship might be a little tame for now, but if we get married someday, watch out, a tsu-nami is going to be unleashed.

Chapter 33

John

I'VE ALWAYS BEEN A LIST- MAKER. EVER SINCE I'VE been in high school I made lists as a way of giving myself something to shoot for. That might sound odd to some people, maybe even most people, but to fellow list-makers we understand it completely. The basic idea behind this compunction is to write down all the things that you either want to accomplish, or at the very least, need to accomplish. That list can comprise everything from school assignments, to chores, to errands, to social events. In other words, all the details of what would comprise your day or your week, maybe even your year.

Let me give you an example. Let's say you come home from the Sunday evening church service. You're a high school kid and you feel you're pretty typical of most other kids your age. And you are, for the most part. But there are a few differences. A lot of high school kids would come home from church and...well, now wait a minute. I guess most high school kids wouldn't be in church on a Sunday night, so let me rephrase that. Let's say that you're a typical Baptist kid, from Duluth, Minnesota, who had parents who always insisted that the entire family go to church every Sunday morning and evening. Now, maybe that gives a little better picture of the situation.

As I was saying, let's say you come home from church after a Sunday evening service, and you've got a few hours before you should probably hit the sack and be up by 6:45 AM to get to school. Most kids I knew would start their homework right away. They certainly didn't want to waste their weekend doing homework. Heaven forbid! The weekend was meant to be enjoyed. So whatever homework they had would have to wait until the very last minute and only then would they sit down and knock out that essay or study for the quiz on Monday morning. Now that might be the M.O. of the typical high school kid.

Ah, but that's where the difference lies between list-makers and non-list-makers. A true, died-in-the-wool list-maker would never wait until Sunday night to do homework. That homework would be done by Friday night, before the evening began. Or, if Friday night was so tied up with school games or other major events, the homework would be finished by Saturday, mid-morning. And the reason for that is that list-makers like closure. They like to know that certain chores, or events, or obligations, and so on, have been completed and that they're free to move on to the next thing on their list. And I know that this might sound odd to some people who are not necessarily prone to living their life by what's printed on the daily or weekly list, but to those of us compulsive list-makers it makes perfect sense.

You see, to a compulsive list-maker, crossing an item off brings a great sense of joy. It also brings relief, a sense of accomplishment, a feeling of satisfaction, a much-needed closure and more. When you have a list you've been working from and you see a line through each item, all crossed off within the specified timeframe, it truly is a wonderful feeling. All is right with the world. Your goals have been accomplished; your duties and obligations taken care of. And with the completion of that list, you're now free to start working on your next list. What do you have on for tomorrow or for next week?

Most list-makers don't stop, however, with just chores and obligations and errands. The true-blue list-maker will jot down the movies they'd like to see, and maybe even put them in order of preference. They might make a list of places to visit in the next five years and in which order. They'll record their top 10 goals to be accomplished by age 25. Anyway, you get the idea. All kinds of things go on those little pieces of paper and when each paper is eventually covered in black lines or checkmarks, the papers are discarded and a new one emerges. It's really quite a nice sensation, although I'm sure to other people it sounds like some kind of daily bondage. But to those of us who know, it's anything but.

And so, after my latest exchange with Wendy, I felt compelled to write a few things down. I was so in love with this woman that I wasn't even sure I was thinking straight. That's one of the great things about making lists. It forces you to organize your thoughts into some semblance of order. And that's what I needed right now. I needed order. I needed to know what I was experiencing in terms of my deep feelings for this woman; a woman I'd really only known for a few months. I know that sounds crazy, but it made perfect sense to me, given the circumstances. So, I just took out a clean, white sheet of paper, and divided it in half. On the one side of the page I listed pros, and on the other side I listed cons. I realize that's not very original, and it's a method used by a lot of people, but there's a reason for that; it works.

I started off my list of pros. What was it about Wendy and our relationship that I felt was really positive? What were the qualities I saw in her that held such attraction for me? And what was it about the relationship itself that made me so interested in where it was going to go? And so, with that idea in mind, I just started to brainstorm with myself. I planned to just let my mind go and start jotting down what ever came to me. I would then go back and put the random thoughts in some kind of order that made sense and presented a clear picture. So, the following is the list of pros I came up with, in no particular order:

1. She was drop-dead gorgeous. I know that sounds shallow, but I can't help it. She was beautiful, and truth be told that's what caught my eye right off the bat. I may be a pastor, but that doesn't mean I can't appreciate the beauty of God's creation in female form.

2. She was very sweet. She had a very sweet, loving, and kind personality. I recognized it very early on. And knowing more about her background, after a little while, made me appreciate it even more.

3. She was funny. We always had a great time together and would spend a huge amount of time laughing, and finding the humor in every day experiences.

4. She was smart. She would ask me questions about faith, for example, that were a clear indication of how deeply she thought about such things. Sometimes she wouldn't ask questions so much as just challenge a particular theological belief I held. I'm the one who's got this supposedly great seminary training, but the arguments she raised made me have to go back to question some of my beliefs. And a couple of times, I have to admit, she won me over. There were times that this girl could think circles around me.

5. She was passionate. I still remember the time I had to go away for a two-day seminar in Seattle. I got back home about dinnertime on the second day and went immediately to the diner. I ordered dinner and ate fairly slowly, until all the other diners had left. When they were all gone, Wendy pulled me into the little stockroom off the kitchen, and kissed me long and hard. I decided right there that I was done with seminars. I'm not leaving her again.

6. She was playful. I was at her place one night and she told me that she wanted to play me one of her favorite gospel songs. And so, she put on a tape of some Gospel artist singing "Fill My Cup Lord." Wendy indicated that was her favorite song and she hoped it would be mine too. I thought that was a little strange, but it was a very nice song, and I'd always liked it. But I didn't think much about our conversation. At least I didn't think much about it until I walked into my office the next morning. I opened the door and saw what must've been several hundred, small Dixie cups, placed 1 inch apart, completely covering the floor of my small office. I couldn't get into my office. Wendy had set up the surprise with the help of The Tanks, who were always up for a good joke. When I opened the door, they had a cassette recorder rigged to start playing - you guessed it - "Fill My Cup Lord." I couldn't

help but laugh. I got a bucket and began to empty those hundreds of cups. But, within a few minutes, Wendy and The Tanks were there to help me. I saw the twinkle in her eyes and I loved her playfulness.

7. She was a great mom. She adored Travis and he adored her. And on the rare occasion when she'd have to discipline Travis for some infraction of the household rules, she always did it in love. She also made sure that he understood why she was doing this, and how this was really for his own good. She'd always follow through with the discipline, but in a very controlled, appropriate and loving manner.

8. She was honest. At the beginning I knew that there were things about her past she was choosing not to share with me. And I was fine with that, I really was. The reason it didn't concern me all that much was because I was beginning to know Wendy and her character. I knew she'd tell me when it was time. She was just too transparent not to share the complete story. And sure enough, she told me everything, even the part about Nick wanting to use her in a hooker/pimp relationship. She was so honest and transparent with me, it was shocking and yet tremendously endearing at the same time.

9. She was hard-working. Wendy had a great work ethic and it was obvious to anyone who observed her at the diner. She was always on time, looking fresh and vibrant. Her uniform was always clean and her smile always welcoming and hospitable. She took great care to make each customer feel special and cared for. Now, I knew that when customers felt that way their tips would be larger, but that wasn't the issue for Wendy, at least not totally. Vern Hodges came into the diner every night for dinner and everybody knew he was a cranky, stingy, old man who probably never left Wendy a tip. I'd overheard Vern saying one time: "I worked my whole life in the grocery business and

no one ever tipped me." So, I knew Wendy wasn't getting great tips from old Vern, if any at all. But I watched Wendy give Vern the best customer service possible, just like she did everyone else. I asked her why she did that and she just told me that she thought he was probably lonely. His wife had died 15 years before and he'd never remarried. She felt kind of sorry for him and tried to brighten his day a little bit when he came in.

10. She was compassionate. I knew that from the way she handled Vern. But I also saw it in so many other ways. There was a food bank in town whose workers always stood outside the doors of the small grocery store down at the end of the block. And people would bring out a jar of peanut butter, or maybe some of the Top-Raman packages that were 10 for a dollar. But there wasn't one time that I was with Wendy that I didn't see her drop a bag of groceries into the bin. I knew as a single mom that couldn't have been easy for her, but she did it anyway, because she knew people were hurting and needed help.

I started on my list of pros and never finished. I could've gone on for a much longer time and created a much more extensive list. But about midway through my list of pros, and before I had listed any cons, I suddenly stopped. It hit me like a ton of bricks. What's wrong with you John? Can't you see what's so plainly right in front of you, staring you in the face? You are madly, passionately, head-over-heels in love with this beautiful woman. What's the next item on your list? When you discover what a wonderful person she really is, and all the qualities that go into making Wendy the person you've fallen in love with, what's the next item on your list? Come on John, this isn't rocket science. What's the next item on your list?

I took my pen and made a third column on the page that read "Action Steps." I jotted down my next step and then sat back and smiled. I only had one "Action Step." I was going to ask Wendy Baker to marry me, and then my list would be complete.

Chapter 34

Wendy

I'M NOT SURE HOW TO DESCRIBE IT EXACTLY, BUT after our little conversation about physical attraction, things seemed to pick up a bit. Don't misunderstand me. John was still very respectful of me and very much dedicated to the idea of keeping our relationship pure until such time as we were married. But I could tell that it was getting more difficult to maintain the right balance between appropriate, romantic expressions of love and affection, and crossing the line in such a way that we'd have been uncomfortable. It's quite weird, really. I never thought I'd be one to think about "crossing the lines." I'd crossed so many lines in the past that I wasn't even sure what the lines were. All I knew is that for once I really wanted to do it the right way. So, we were keeping a pretty tight rein on the physical relationship. I knew it was frustrating for both of us, but at the same time, we knew it was the right way to go.

But still, after that initial conversation the intensity of the relationship seemed to go to another level. I didn't know if it was just the conversation about physical things or if it was something else. It might've been a combination of factors for all I know.

John began to talk about some of the good qualities he'd seen in me. It was almost as if he had made a list at some point and wanted to share them with me. I even asked him about that, and he admitted that he had indeed made a list of the pros and cons of our relationship, as well as the character qualities he saw in me. I didn't have the heart to tell him that the idea of a list wasn't the most romantic notion I'd ever heard, but it seemed to mean a lot to him, so I was fine with that.

I asked John what he'd come up with on that list and he began to share some of his findings with me. As I listened, I experienced several different kinds of feelings all at once. On the one hand, I was kind of embarrassed when he would give the character quality, which I thought was really nice, but then he'd expound on it. He'd tell me how he recognized it and what kind of a person it made me. He'd give me examples of how he saw it lived out in my life and what those actions meant to him and to others. His comments were very nice to hear, but at the same time rather embarrassing. I knew that no matter what he might see, I was aware of my failings and faults, and believe me, there were a bunch of them. But on the other hand, if he wanted to believe all those wonderful things about me, who was I to stop him? Maybe love is blind, but I'm in no hurry to give him 20/20 vision.

John went right on through his list of about 10 pros that he had come up with. When I complimented him on such a thorough, and might I add, flattering job he did, he assured me that it wasn't even complete. I asked him why he didn't finish his "Wendy Project." Did he just run out of time? He told me that time wasn't the issue. He could have gone on writing for quite a bit longer, but that he had an epiphany of sorts. All he could think of were the pros and, in fact, he could've kept going. But when he tried to list the cons of our relationship or of my character, he couldn't think of a single one. And again, like I said before, I know love is blind, but I think John was so in love with me that he wasn't seeing clearly or thinking straight at all. He couldn't see a negative here, no matter what.

When we said goodbye for the night, I slipped into my bed feeling warm and fuzzy all over. It wasn't the summer heat, it was something else. It was the wonderful feeling you get when you know that someone you care about deeply has the same depth of feeling for you. To know that you're loved by another person, who absolutely adores you, is a source of great delight. And when I let my mind go, after John's recitation of my good qualities and the strength of our relationship, I couldn't bring it under control again. I was so happy and I was pretty sure where this was going to lead. In fact, John had been making overtures to marriage over the past several days. I wasn't sure he was quite ready yet, but he was at least testing the waters a bit.

I had to really think this idea through. I mean, the only time that I had come anywhere close to marriage before was when I was with Kevin. We hadn't been together that long, but I just had this feeling, this impression that he was going to ask me. And sure enough, when they checked his pockets after the accident, they found the ring. I still hadn't quite come to grips with that horrible tragedy, but I'd been healing a little bit at a time over the years. And my relationship with John was obviously helping. I was through blaming God, but I was still a bit un-nerved about the future. When you get badly burned, you have a tendency to be quite a bit more cautious around fire.

I lay in my bed that night thinking about all that had gone on in my life. I thought about the chaos of my childhood and the kind of environment I grew up in. I thought about how diner-guy's words to me had set me on a path of destruction and sexual promiscuity. I thought about all the men I'd been with and all the customers I exposed my body to. I thought about the fact that Travis's dad could be one of eight guys and I had absolutely no idea which one was the father. I thought about how I was almost ready to jump into the prostitution racket and how, at the last minute, I backed out. My mind was racing, and I was darting back-and-forth between some very dark, random thoughts - thoughts that I hadn't struggled with for months now - but they were back, with a vengeance.

I fell asleep into a rather fitful state. The interesting thing is that when I first went to bed I was happy. John had spent the evening telling me how wonderful I was and how much he loved me. He extolled the virtues of our strong relationship together and even hinted about marriage. With all that, I should've been ecstatic, full of joy and hope for the future. And I was, at first. It was a marvelous feeling to know that John loved me and could really picture us together for the rest of our lives.

But as I was drifting off to sleep, my thoughts began to go to some pretty dark places. It surprised me because I thought I had already dealt with those dark thoughts and sent them packing months ago. But no, they evidently hadn't disappeared, or at least not completely; they were back again, more disturbing than before.

When I would think of one of the wonderful character qualities John saw in me, I would see the word in my mind. It would make me feel good and special, for a second or two. But then, as I continued to see the word, it would actually begin disintegrating, right before my eyes. It's like when you go to a fireworks show for the Fourth of July and watch an awesome display. And then towards the end maybe they have a special firework that spells out USA or America or maybe even the name of your own town. And it looks really good at first, but after a little while it starts to burn itself out and the letters begin to disintegrate; little pieces of letters dropping off until there's nothing but darkness left, where once a bright light shone.

That's exactly what happened to the character qualities John had told me about myself. I saw the word and felt good, but then they disintegrated. And as I was in the twilight zone between sleep and consciousness, I saw every one of those wonderful qualities he saw in me just drop off, until there was nothing left. When the last piece of each letter would flutter to the ground, a voice out of the darkness would say to me, "Who do you think you are? Do you really see yourself this way? This isn't you. It's never been you. Those qualities that John sees in you are an illusion in his mind. You may have fooled him so far, but he'll find out the real truth pretty soon and then they'll be nothing left. The relationship will be over and you'll be alone, just like before."

I can't tell if I'm dreaming, or if I'm in a semi-conscious state and I'm losing my mind. There was such a sense of darkness and despair I wasn't sure how I was ever going to pull out of it. The longer these thoughts played over in my mind, the more convinced I became that I would never escape them.

Finally, I drifted off into a troubled sleep and was plagued with yet another frightening scenario. But this time it was a dream. And it was a dream that to me felt very real, and maybe should serve as a warning. If I didn't heed the message of both the random thoughts about me and the dream itself, I was going to cause irreparable damage to the man I deeply loved.

In my dream, John proposed to me in a beautiful setting that was so peaceful and tranquil. I recognized at least parts of it as being by the little brook that runs through the pasture in back of the church. It was similar to the setting and yet different somehow.

John told me how much he loved me and I did the same. He brought out this box and I knew right away what was in it. As he opened the box I saw a beautiful ring, with a brilliant diamond in an antique-gold setting. He once again told me how much he loved me and that he knew I was the one for him. He asked me to marry him and I accepted immediately because I loved John with all my heart.

I could envision our life together and everything I saw, and every thought I had, was about as near perfection as I could possibly imagine. I saw the three of us, like the Three Musketeers; together, one-for-all and all-for-one; John, Travis and myself, a force to be reckoned with. Together, we could handle anything that came our way.

I then saw John and I sitting in the morning service at church. John was up in the front, at the pulpit, preaching his heart out. People were saying an occasional Amen when a point particularly hit home. And when the service was over, and people were expecting to hear the benediction and then leave to the postlude music of the organ, John said that he had a little announcement. People stood there expectantly and waited for what could possibly be some very exciting news. John took a deep breath, smiled, and then announced our engagement and wedding date. People erupted in applause and there were hugs and handshakes all around. Some of the older ladies were crying, and even some of the guys grew a little misty around the eyes. Words of congratulations rang out, as together, we walked out hand-in-hand, thoroughly enjoying the results of this surprising announcement that had brought joy to so many people. In my dream I was smiling from ear to ear and could hardly wait to begin our new life together.

But, in my dream, the scene suddenly changed. We were sitting in church the very next Sunday after the big announcement. The mood in the room was tense and angry, with a strong feeling of hostility. In one week the tide of public opinion had turned, and John and I were on the proverbial hot seat. Someone in the congregation had taken it upon themselves to do a little research on me. She had relatives who lived in Chicago and knew my family. She asked them to do a little snooping, for the good of the church, of course. You can't be too careful when you're dealing with a person who is virtually unknown to the congregation. Within three or four days the relative had called back and informed her of my upbringing, home life, life of promiscuity, and my career as a topless dancer and brief flirtation with prostitution. This woman who had a raunchy and sordid past was going to be the pastor's wife at Pleasant Pastures? Not on your life! This marriage has to be stopped. Pastor John probably has no idea of the kind of woman he's about to marry. She has no right to even consider herself as being qualified to be the pastor's wife. That position is one of great influence, especially on the younger women of the congregation. Well, that marriage is never going to take place, that's for sure.

As the dream continued, the crowd got more and more angry. With all the evidence that had been given as to the highly questionable character of his fiancée, John wouldn't be moved. He loved me and that was it. He wasn't willing to compromise, or change his opinion, let alone his course of action.

Members of the congregation rose to their feet, almost in unison and began shouting angry, abusive, horrible words at both me and John. The chairman of the church, who in my dream was a faceless, un-known person to me, stood up and addressed the congregation with a sense of pious superiority. He stated very formally that this kind of atrocity could not be allowed to happen. It would tarnish the reputation of Pleasant Pastures Community Church for years to come and would make a mockery of God's house. This must be stopped, and it must be stopped now. He then informed the congregation that, as of this very moment, Pastor John is relieved of his position as senior pastor of the church. Together, John and I stood up, and walked the aisle, hand in hand as we had last Sunday. But today, one week later, we walked out to jeers and shouts of derision.

I woke up from my nightmare crying, but so relieved that it had only been a bad dream. Nothing had changed. John and I still loved each other and things were progressing beautifully. I knew he was probably going to asked me to marry him very shortly and that was an answer to my prayers. But a nagging thought kept scratching at me, biting me, chewing its way into my guts. What if this nightmare was, in reality, a warning? And what if it was a warning from God?

Chapter 35

John

H ERE'S THE DEAL ABOUT ME. ONCE I MAKE UP my mind on an issue, I don't like to let a lot of grass grow under my feet. In other words, if I'm convinced about something enough to actually commit action steps to paper, I'm going to get working on that right away.

I know that some people aren't quite like that. They'll take weeks, or months, or maybe even years to mull something over in their minds. They look at the topic at hand from every possible angle. They analyze it up one side and down the other. They pull it and push it and turn it inside out trying to wring out every bit of information possible concerning the issue, and the next possible course of action. They'll even go to their friends and special confidants to get their take on the matter. They do everything in their power to see the matter at hand as clearly as possible.

I admire people like that, I really do. Sometimes I wish I could be a bit more like that. I wonder sometimes what it would be like to see a situation from a hundred different angles. But you know what? That's just not me. As much as I try at times to sit back and just let things develop slowly, over time, and with great amounts of time and energy spent in reflective analysis, it just doesn't work for me. I see a situation and right away begin to think and pray it through. And after what I think is an appropriate amount of time and personal reflection, I go ahead and make a decision. And I have to tell you something. Most of the time that decision is right. And if the decision turns out to not be right, I'll usually know it pretty early on and can adjust a few things and rescue it. So, I say all of that to let you know that though I'd been praying about the relationship with Wendy and me, to most people it would probably seem like I was kind of jumping the gun. After all, this whole romance only began about three months ago. But look, when you know, you know. It's as simple as that.

Now, some people might question my claim to have prayed about our relationship enough. I mean, it's not like I would go off and spend an hour every day just praying about Wendy's and my future together. I spend significant amounts of time in extended prayer every week and our relationship is certainly part of that. But to me some of the most important prayer we can engage in happens in the natural course of every day.

Let's say that I've got to make the 30-minute drive into Wenatchee for the monthly meeting of area pastors. I suppose I could turn on the radio and listen to music, but that's not what I usually choose to do. During times like that I'll usually just try to have a conversation with God; a conversation that goes something like this: "Well Lord, here we are again. You know what's on my mind and I think I know where we're headed on this one, but Lord I need to know what you really think. This one is big Lord, and I don't want to blow it and make a mistake. There are too many people that could be impacted by my actions. So, what do you think, Lord? Did you bring Wendy into my life to be more than just a parishioner? To tell you the truth Lord, I'm not sure I could ever view her as just a parishioner. There's something about her that caught my attention from the start. And it wasn't just the fact that she was beautiful, although, I must say, you really did a good job with her. She's one of your best creations, really! But it's not just that. It's everything about her that captivates me. It's the total person that's won my heart."

"Lord, I remember when I first heard her story. She was so honest with me. Now, I know it took her a while to lay the whole story out, but it's not the kind of story you share with just anyone. Lord, her background, her growing up years made me want to cry. The way she's been treated by men through the years made me angry; especially the route that Nick wanted to take with her. When I heard that, I was angry and nauseous, all at the same time. It's a good thing that Nick wasn't in the room with us. I think I would have lost my Christian testimony, real fast!"

"So, Lord, here's the deal. I love Wendy with all my heart. There's actually no doubt in my mind that she's the one I want to spend the rest of my life with. But Lord, you know me. You know how I think. You know my tendency to want to have answers for the various issues or opportunities that come up from time to time. I personally think that I've nailed this one Lord, I really do. I think Wendy is the one you have for me and I think you'll bless our marriage and our life together. I think you'll let me learn how to be a good dad to Travis and that he and I will have some great times together. I know there will be times of struggle and adjustment for both of us, just like there is for any couple. But I also know that you'll be with us all the way. You've never let me down. And even when hard things came my way, you were right there beside me, whether I could feel you at the time or not. The fact is Lord, even during the hard times you've never bailed on me."

"So, here's what I'm going to do. I'm going to make a plan on how to ask Wendy to marry me. I don't want to spend months in planning, but I do want to give it some thought so that it will be special. Not over-the-top fancy, but rather simple. That's how I see us together… not fancy, but simple, in a wholesome, healthy way. So that's what I'm planning to do, Lord. But Lord, if I'm going in the wrong direction change me around. If this isn't right and good, or if I've missed your timing or your purpose, please show me clearly so that I don't mess up a lot of lives here. I think I'm walking in your will, but if I've missed it somehow, smack me on the head and let me know. You know me Lord; I want your will above everything."

That's how I'd spend the 30-minute drive to Wenatchee or the 20-minute walk to the gym. The Apostle Paul would call that "praying without ceasing." I just call it talking with God. Whatever you want to call it, it's always worked for me. It's informal - no bowing my head and closing my eyes - that's not a good idea when you're driving or walking down the street. It's just talking to God and listening for that still, small voice answering back. I don't know about you, but it works for me.

So far, I haven't heard anything to the contrary from God. In fact, the impression I get inside of me is full steam ahead. I think God's all over this one and so I'm starting to make plans. Like I said, I'm not going to spend months on this. I'm going to think this through, talk to a few other folks, get some dates and times down in my mind, and then go for it. I'm also pretty sure that she's going to say yes because I know she loves me. And besides, I've been hinting at the possibility of being married someday. We've never had a definite, formal conversation about it; it just seems to come up on occasion. And when it does, it seems like the most natural thing in the world.

The first person I wanted to talk to was Maggie. I figured if anybody knew Wendy in this town, other than me, it would be her. And so, I arranged for Maggie to come to my office one day for a little talk. Now, I know that she was under the impression that we were probably going to talk about the new fall Sunday school program that she was always a part of. It was always about this time that the church leaders would get their heads together and see what kind of a lineup of adult classes they might want to offer. And so, I just figured that instead of the usual discussion, I'd surprise her with talk of engagements and weddings and watch her reaction.

When Maggie walked into my office that morning she had a strange little smile on her face. I looked at her and she looked at me and I knew something was up. This didn't feel like a normal fall planning session. And so, I looked at her and, after a few seconds of mutual staring, I said, "What?" And she said, "What do you mean, what?" And I look at her again and said, "You've been giving me this weird look ever since you came in. What did you do, win the lottery or something?" Well, she assured me that she hadn't won the lottery. But then she said something that shocked me. She said, "No, I didn't win the lottery, but I think you might have." I raised my eyebrows and shot back, "What are you talking about? You know I don't gamble." And Maggie looked at me slyly and with a little grin said, "That's not the kind of prize I'm talking about, John. I think you may have won the prize already and you're just waiting for the right time to claim it."

I knew then that this idea of talking about the fall program was no more on her mind than it was on mine. I knew that somehow Maggie was on to me. She knew that this little secret meeting wasn't about Sunday school, this was about romance and love and rings and wedding bells. I asked her to clearly lay it out for me. I asked her to tell me, in no uncertain terms, what she was talking about. She got up out of her chair, came right up to where I was sitting, pointed a finger at me and said, "You're in love with Wendy and you're going to ask her to marry you. And you're not going waste any time about it. You're going to ask her in the next week or so. Am I right or am I wrong?"

I don't mind telling you, I was flabbergasted. How in the world did she know that? Nobody could've tipped her off. For crying out loud, I'd only come to that conclusion the day before and I hadn't shared it with another soul. And so, I said, "You're absolutely right. I'm going to ask her to marry me. But how did you know that? I didn't even know that until just last night." Maggie looked at me and said, "Oh John, you got so much to learn. Anyone with an ounce of brains and insight could see where this was heading. You've been walking around with this silly grin on your face ever since you met Wendy.

Maybe nobody else has picked up on it, but I sure have. And when you asked me to come in, which is about two weeks early by the way, I just knew. Don't ever try to play poker John, you'd lose every time. You are so open and transparent, if you were a spy for the government we'd all be doomed. You couldn't hide your feelings if your life depended on it."

Wow! I'm not quite sure what I felt about her description of me and my less-than-perfect poker-face, but then I figured there could be worse things than not knowing how to hide the truth. I asked Maggie to be honest with me and tell me what she thought. What were her impressions of Wendy and me together? Knowing what she knew about both of us, could she see this relationship working? In fact, could she see it not just working, but actually thriving? Could she see me being a good husband and father? Did I have what it takes to be the person Wendy needed me to be, or would I simply be one more guy in a string of disappointments? I knew I loved her with my whole heart, but I also knew that if I didn't have what it takes to be the kind of loving, supportive, life-long marriage partner she deserved, I didn't want to promise her something that I couldn't deliver on.

I poured out my heart to Maggie. I admitted that even though from the pulpit I came across as strong and confident, deep down on the inside I harbored doubts about myself. I'm pretty sure that everybody does, and I'm no exception. I'm not sure that people can understand how even up-front people who come across as confident and sure in themselves, can actually have trepidation in certain areas. When you're up in front all the time you have to come across with a certain air of confidence. Now that confidence isn't arrogance; nobody wants to see that. But it's a confidence you want to exude, even if you're shaking in your boots. It's not an act of selfishness. In fact, it's quite the opposite. Coming across confident sets your audience at ease. I mean, you know how you feel if the person up in front seems unsure of himself; it's uncomfortable for everyone. So, I've learned how to do that as a pastor. God helps me with that and it's usually not a problem.

But when it came to asking Wendy to be my wife and becoming a father to Travis, I knew that this was no time for false bravado or a carefully cultivated picture of confidence. This needed to be the real deal. And so, I asked Maggie to be honest with me. I knew she would because it was obvious to me how much she loved and appreciated me, not only as her pastor, but also as her friend. And I also knew that she had developed a very special place in her heart for Wendy, right from the very start. And Travis? Well, there wasn't a little child on the face of this earth that Maggie didn't love. But Travis was right up there at the very top. He'd won her heart the very first time he had tasted her wild blackberry pie. His eyes got big and round and he looked like he had discovered heaven on earth.

Maggie looked at me and said the words I was truly longing to hear. She said, "John, I know that you'll make an exceptional husband and father. I know the capacity that you have to love people. I've seen it in action with our congregation. And some of us aren't the most lovable people in the world and we both know it, don't we? But as much as you love your congregation, the love you have for Wendy is so apparent to me. I've watched both of you very closely since the beginning. I've seen your faces light up when you come to get her for a date. I've seen her get a little extra spring in her step when she sees you walk into the diner for an unexpected meal. I've seen her give you a little extra ice cream for your pie or come to top off your coffee just a bit more often. I've seen the way you look each other in church. I've seen you look her way when you're preaching, especially if you're talking about love and marriage. I've watched her looking at you, intently, while you're preaching. I always marveled at what a serious student of the Scriptures she was because she was following your sermon so closely. In fact, I commented one time to her on how interested she seemed to be in what you had been saying and I asked her what her favorite part of the message was. But she got embarrassed and admitted that she had no idea what you had just preached on. She was too busy looking at your deep, blue eyes and thick, wavy blonde hair. Sorry John, you're a good preacher, but her mind was elsewhere."

I suppose I could've gotten upset at that revelation, but it actually made me feel great. I knew that Maggie approved of my plans for Wendy and me and that was more important than I realized. She knew both of us very well and if she thought that everything was good, that's all the encouragement I needed.

Over the next couple of days, I made plans. I drove into Wenatchee and spent several hours looking at rings. I had seen how Wendy dressed and what kind of jewelry she wore. I felt that I knew her taste well enough that I could pick out something she'd really like. I noticed that several of the diamond rings were gold, with a black antiquing applied, and I knew she would love that. It was different enough to say that she was very special and unique to me in her own way. Now, I wasn't making a ton of money as a pastor, but I'd been able to save up some over the past couple of years.

I eventually settled on an exquisite antique gold ring with a 2/3 carat diamond in the middle of a beautiful rose setting. I took the ring home and put it in the back of my dresser drawer. I also determined the day I was going to ask her and came up with a list of potential wedding dates, to be decided together, of course. In addition, while I was in Wenatchee, I went to a travel agent to see how much a 10-day honeymoon in Hawaii would cost. It wasn't cheap but I thought I could swing it. I told the travel agent that as soon as Wendy said yes, I'd be back to set up all the arrangements. The gal who helped me smiled and wished me luck and said that she hoped to be seeing me real soon.

As I drove home that day I couldn't help but thank the Lord for all He had done in bringing us together. Friday night was going to be a life-changer, that's for sure.

Chapter 36

Wendy

SOMETIMES MUCH OF LIFE SEEMS LIKE A SERIES OF contradictions. Have you ever noticed that? It's like when you're a kid. You really look forward to the last day of school. You're so excited about the summer and all that it promises. Maybe you get the chance to sleep in later each morning. Maybe you get to spend time at a pool or a lake with your friends. Maybe it's about having slumber parties with your girlfriends, or riding your bike all over town just exploring. Even though my childhood was pretty chaotic, I still got to experience these kinds of summer adventures, at least to some extent. So, by the time June comes along you're counting down your last days until you're free for the summer.

Finally, the day arrives and you and your girlfriends run out of the doors of the school and start heading for home. Someone starts up the chant: "No more papers, no more books, no more teachers' dirty looks." Pretty soon everyone's joining in and it feels great. After nine long months you're finally free to experience all that summer has for you. And it's a wonderful feeling, isn't it? Freedom! Independence! Celebration! There are truly some great days ahead.

But as the summer rolls on something changes. It's a subtle change but it's definitely there. You start coming into the middle of August when school is just maybe two or three weeks away and you find your-self getting a little excited for the first day back. You're shocked at that because you were so happy a couple of months ago to finally be done. And yet, here you are, a relatively short time later, with a totally opposite attitude. You find that you miss your friends. You're looking forward to seeing everybody again. Well, almost everybody. There are some kids you'd just as soon not see again because they were mean and snotty and spread rumors about you. But with your newfound attitude you figure that you can handle that better this year. You're older and wiser now; you're not a little kid anymore. Besides, maybe you'll luck out and they'll have moved over the summer and won't be attending your school. Well, whatever happens, you're just excited to be start-ing back.

You see what I mean by life seems like a series of contradic-tions? June comes along and you're so excited to get out of school you're ready to bust. September comes along and you're excited about going back to the very place that three months ago you couldn't wait to leave. That's what I mean by life's contradictions. You experience one thing and a little while later you experience something totally different. They're exactly opposite and yet you find yourself embracing both. Life is full of contradictions.

If you've experienced anything like what I've just been talking about, then maybe you can understand some of what I've been going through lately. Talk about contradictions; I think my life right now is stuck in a huge one, and frankly, I'm not sure how it's going to resolve itself. And, when it finally does resolve itself, is it going to be good? Will everybody involved live "happily ever after" or is everything just going to blow up and leave bits and pieces of our lives, our souls, lying scattered along the side of the road?

I love John so much, there's absolutely no question in my mind about that. He's the kindest, most loving, compassionate, stable man I've ever known. Now maybe using the word stable doesn't sound too exciting to you but when you come out of a life of chaos like I did, stability is a definite plus. It's not only a plus, it's a major requirement. If there's one thing I've observed over the years, it's that love can't truly grow and flourish in an atmosphere of chaos. When everything is just flying around you with no sense of direction, or purpose, or planning, true love can be pretty elusive. True love takes energy to maintain, but chaos sucks all the energy right out of it, dumping it into a huge black hole and then love hardly stands a chance.

I love John with all my heart. I love everything about him. I get very excited about a possible future with him. And here's the really exciting thing; I know he feels the exact same way about me. This man truly loves me. Regardless of my past mistakes, my chaotic, dysfunctional childhood and my less than stellar choices of the past several years, he still loves me. Sometimes I have to shake my head and think what's wrong with this picture? It doesn't make any sense. Talk about contradictions; this is one for the books. A fine, upstanding, straight-arrow pastor falling in love with a girl from the opposite side of the tracks. A sweet, dedicated, and somewhat sheltered pastor, loving a gal who's seen and experienced more of the raw side of life than anyone ever should. Contradictions. Opposite attraction. Black and white. Oil and water. However you want to describe it, it's there in front of me and I just can't shake the feeling that it's too big to ignore.

Is love really enough to see us through? Can love really somehow bridge the gap that exists between us? When we're together I get the sense that the gap is being bridged already. But when I go to sleep at night, something rises up within my subconscious that totally destroys what I experience in the sunshine of a new day.

The dreams I've been having are getting more pronounced, more bizarre every night. There are a variety of scenarios, a variety of sub-plots, within bigger plots, but all of the storylines have the same ending. Though our love starts out strong and sure, ultimately, in the end, it's the very thing that destroys John's life and ministry. And, after one of these terribly anxious dreams, I wake up in a cold sweat, shivering beneath my covers. And the question that invades my semi-conscious state has to do with selfishness. If John and I being together would ultimately end in him losing his ministry and people's respect in the church, and in the Christian community as a whole, then how could I possibly let this relationship go on? If everything these dreams are telling me wind up coming true, then staying with John would be the most selfish choice I've ever made. And let me assure you, I've made quite a few selfish choices in my lifetime.

So, here's the dilemma. During the day I'm happy as can be with John. I feel lighter and brighter and more joyful than I ever have before. But at night, that all changes. There's a darkness that comes over me that actually makes it difficult to breathe. I wake up in a state of anxiety, something very near panic. My chest feels heavy and sometimes I wonder if I'm having a heart attack. The impression I get in those dark moments is that if I'd just leave, everything would be fine. Life would go on for me and I'd spare John years of misery, both personally and professionally.

I've tried to figure out why so many of my dreams seem to end with John and I being cast out of the church I've grown to love and appreciate so much. People seem to like me and they certainly have taken Travis under their wing. I know some of the little ladies at the church are watching their pastor and me very closely to see if something's developing there. It's really kind of sweet and I always enjoy their kind words and warm hugs. That's why what I experience in the day at church or at the diner is such a contradiction to what I experience at night. Why am I so anxious? Why do my dreams always end up with John and me being thrown out of the church and having to take a walk of shame down the aisle and out the doors? How could this loving congregation do that to us?

But one day, as I was between shifts and having a cup of coffee in a rare moment of solitude, it suddenly became clear to me. I thought back to that church in Chicago I tried to go to for Travis's sake. It was obvious that I didn't belong there because of the way I looked, the outfit I was wearing, perhaps even the attitude I was giving off. Whatever it was, the lady that talked to me afterwards made it crystal clear that they didn't want me in their church. I left, and as you know,

I met Kevin, which of course takes us to another major piece of the story. But the thing that hit me when I was drinking my coffee was that maybe the reason they're so accepting of me at Pleasant Pastures is that I haven't given them any reason not to.

I take great care in making sure that I'm always dressed modestly. I always make sure that my language is appropriate. I've never sworn like a sailor on a regular basis, but I have been known to slip out with a few choice cuss words, if the situation seemed to warrant it. But that's pretty much a thing of the past. As far as the church folks know, I'm just a nice, sweet, hard-working single mom who came to live in their quiet community and join their church. So far so good, right?

But how would they be if they knew about my past? If they knew my background and the pretty horrendous choices I've made in my life, would they be quite so accepting? Would they begin to worry that I would corrupt their pastor and maybe even the entire church over time? If they truly knew everything about me would they see me as a Jezebel, a woman sent from hell itself to destroy the work of the Lord? Would they wind up being like the people in that church back home that rejected me and basically told me to get moving? Maybe all Christians feel that they need to guard the purity and sanctity of their fellowship from some of the riff-raff that occasionally wander through the doors of their church.

These thoughts were running around in my head as I sat there with my coffee. Maybe the folks at church have accepted me because they don't really know me. What would they do if they heard the whole story? Well, I could pretty much guess what they'd do because I'd already experienced it; different church, yes, but the same Christian faith and, I presume, the same Christian standards. If they knew the whole story I'd be banned. I'd be asked to leave. I'd be told in no uncertain terms to quit trying to corrupt their pastor. They weren't going to let me get away with that. And sure enough, the dreams I've been having would come true. I would be the person responsible for ruining John's life and ministry. As much as I loved him and wanted to be with him, I just couldn't let that happen.

I heard the bell above the door ring indicating that I had a customer. It was the midafternoon crowd and I knew I'd be busy for a couple of hours. I worked until about 4:30 PM and then went up to take a short nap and get ready for an evening out with John. It was Friday, and whenever my work schedule permitted it, we would try to go out for dinner, or a movie, or maybe just a walk around the town.

After a 20-minute nap, I showered and redid my hair and makeup. I heard the knock on my door at exactly 6:00 PM. John was always very conscious of time; he never wanted to be late for anything. Travis was spending the evening with Maggie who had promised him that they were going to try a brand-new recipe of some kind, one that he would love. Maggie was so sweet and thoughtful. She had come to me a few days before and told me that she needed a little "Travis Time." She suggested that John and I might want to spend Friday night together since things had been so hectic recently and we'd hardly seen each other. Well, before I even got a chance to talk to John about it, he called and suggested the same thing.

He seemed happy to be done with his work week and was looking forward to spending the evening together. I knew that at some point I would need to talk with John about my feelings, and fears, my anxious nightmares, and what I felt they meant. But I didn't want to ruin the evening and just figured I could put off that conversation for a while. John had hinted about marriage on occasion, especially in the last week or two, but I still assumed that he was just kind of testing the waters for something at a much later date. After all, we really had only known each other for a few months. I honestly felt that I had more time to figure this whole mess out. I loved him and would never do anything that would hurt him, even if he couldn't understand my reasoning at first.

I had a lot on my mind when he picked me up, but I tried to put that all aside and concentrate on having a good time. John told me that he'd just rather take a walk instead of going to a movie and I told him that was great. So, we left the diner and walked back towards the church. We took the little trail that leads to the brook in back of the church. It was always one of our favorite spots. It's so quiet and peaceful there and it's always been a wonderful place to sit and talk and do a little dreaming together. It's also a very romantic place to hold hands and kiss a little; very sweet, very pure.

The evening was going beautifully and when John told me that he loved me, I said it back to him. We'd both been saying those words for a few weeks now. I knew that whenever those words left our lips, we meant them with our entire being, and tonight was no exception. I truly loved this man, but underneath that love was the sense that in spite of it, I was going to wind up hurting him deeply. I tried to put that aside, but I still couldn't shake the picture of being cast out of the church, John's life and ministry in ruins.

I chided myself and determined to enjoy the moment. And I was just about there in my mind, when suddenly, John slipped off the bench, presented me with a ring and asked me to marry him. Panic set in immediately. This was happening much faster than I ever imagined.

Somehow, I had missed the cues leading up to this moment. All the nightmares I'd been experiencing over the last week came flooding back into my mind. My breathing grew labored and it felt like my heart was going to fly right out of my chest. He looked so happy and I felt so horrible. My fear was growing with every second and I felt that if I didn't get away soon I was going to explode from the inside out. This was the moment of truth. Did I want John and this fairy-tale romance so badly that I'd allow him to risk everything for me? Was I so selfish that I would ignore the obvious warnings that had been so clearly invading my dreams, night after night? If I'm willing to ignore all of that and let John risk everything, is that really love in the first place? Right then and there I decided that I just couldn't do that to the man that I loved.

I looked at John, trying desperately not to break down, and I said the words that would change both of our lives in a split second. I looked at him, tears glistening in my eyes, and I said *no*. And before I could break down and change my mind, I turned and ran away. I ran away from the only man I would truly love for all eternity.

Chapter 37

John

SHE SAID NO. WHEN I GOT DOWN ON MY KNEES, and pulled out the ring, and joyfully asked the woman I deeply love to marry me, she said no. I didn't even have a chance to try to convince her otherwise. After she said no, she ran off, and in all honesty, I didn't have the strength to follow her. I broke down in tears and wondered how I was ever going to get over what truly was a broken heart. In fact, I don't think broken is a strong enough term. My heart wasn't broken; it was smashed, destroyed, obliterated, and shattered beyond hope.

I realize how dramatic that sounds. I also realize that some folks would think that break-ups and separations and divorces are all just a natural part of life – everybody experiences these kinds of things once in a while – so buck up, get on with your life and you'll survive. That's how some folks would view my current situation, I'm sure. Well, there may be some truth in what they say and advise, but I'm not feeling it right now. My heart felt like it had been hit by a Mack truck and was lying in bits and pieces all over this highway of pain and suffering. I really had no idea how, or even if I'd survive.

After I had sat for a period of time by myself on the bench, I thought that perhaps I just needed to go over to Wendy's and talk with her. Maybe she just got scared. Maybe some painful memory in her past triggered a deep-seated response to committing to loving one person for the rest of her life. Perhaps never having seen a successful marriage in all of her growing up years, as well as in adulthood, left her feeling hopeless about the institution of marriage in the first place. There could be any number of factors that came into play here. A lot of people didn't trust the institution of marriage anymore, because they'd never seen a good one modeled. It seemed like so many young couples were just beginning to live together because, after all, as they put it, "Who needs a piece of paper if our love is real?"

All of these thoughts were swirling around in my head as I sat there on the bench, wondering what I should do. And as I sat there, I came up with a plan. I originally wanted to go over to the diner and knock on Wendy's door and get this thing settled tonight. If she was afraid of commitment, we could take it slower; we didn't have to get engaged right now, we could wait until she felt ready. If she had questions about the concept of marriage itself, we could read some of the excellent books that were on the market concerning the gift of a Christian marriage. Or, we could go to a marriage and family therapist to help us work through some of the issues together. There were any number of pathways we could choose that would help us move ahead.

As I said before, I'm not a guy who likes to let any grass grow under my feet. When I make a decision, or come up with a plan of action, that's it, I want to get it done now. But just as I'm ready to jump up off the bench and head over to Wendy's, and try to rescue this disaster from total, eternal destruction, it suddenly hits me, that maybe I should give this a little time. Maybe I should give this enough time to let the dust settle a little bit. Maybe both of us needed a cooling off period so that our emotions had time to get on a more even keel. Jumping the gun, in the past, hasn't always worked out that well for me. I've discovered, over the years, that getting something done in record time may allow me to cross one more item off my list, but the speed in which I did it sometimes affected the success of the overall project or idea. In other words, if I had sat back and thought about something a little more deeply, or prayed about something a little longer and with more openness, the result would've been much better, much more effective.

So, I decided to do something that I'm not really very good at. I decided to simply wait. I wasn't going to go over there and attempt to get this thing settled. I wasn't going to confront her and demand an answer as to why she said "no" when, from all indications, she clearly loved me. I wasn't going to go over and cry and beg and throw myself down on the floor in an emotional tantrum. I wasn't even going to go and try to show her, through biblical evidence, why we should be together. Using the Bible to prove my point about our love, and God's desire for us to be together forever, would have been stretching it a bit, and she was smart enough to catch on really quick. The Bible's definitely pro-marriage, yes, but trying to prove that it was referring to us specifically? Well, let's just say that I'd have to jump through some real theological hoops to make my point.

No, I decided that the best course of action would be to wait and let the emotions settle down. That was going to be extremely difficult, because I hate when things are up in the air, so to speak. List-makers like closure, and I'm the king of the list-makers. But in this case, I felt it was better to wait, all in the hope of having a better outcome, eventually.

So, I didn't go over there that night, nor did I call her. I didn't sneak over and tape a note to her door or put one in her mailbox. I didn't go into the diner the next day, even though I knew she always worked a double shift on Saturday. Give her some time, and she'll come to realize all that she's giving up, and in the next few days, she'll recognize the fear and negative memories that triggered her response. Give her some time and this thing will work itself out.

I got to church on Sunday morning, not having seen or talked to Wendy since Friday night's disaster. I wasn't sure if she'd be in church on Sunday, like she always was, but I was holding out hope that she'd be there. I decided on Saturday to change my sermon for Sunday. I was just preaching through a variety of topics at that point and so no one would know that I changed it at the last minute. I was originally scheduled to preach on hope, but I decided instead to preach on disappointment. That's a topic I could really relate to.

I went to my files and found a sermon I had preached at First Baptist a couple of years ago, and it was on that very topic. I had preached it at a time when our church was going through a very difficult season. People were beginning to grumble about Pastor Charles and how he didn't live up to their expectations as to what a pastor should be. My desire, of course, was to help our congregation recognize that disappointments can be turned around if - and this is a *big* if - they can be turned around if we trust the Lord and let him lead in every situation.

Obviously, I didn't refer to the situation the church was currently experiencing with Pastor Charles. I was filling in for him while he was away at a conference, and I was always very careful to give nothing but positive comments about the church, and how it was going. I didn't refer to the church situation; I simply talked about the disappointment that all of us feel at times when things don't go the way we thought they would. It was actually a pretty good sermon, and a lot of people thanked me for it, and said that the principles helped them to navigate whatever difficult situation they were going through at that time.

I took this sermon out of my files, re-worked it a bit, and made sure that there was nothing in there that could give anybody the idea that I was referring to my own disappointment with the events of Friday night. It was a very heart-felt sermon that talked about what a great capacity we as human beings have for pain and heartache. But it also gave a message of the hope that we have in Christ, who "makes all things work together for good." My hope was that Wendy would hear the message and realize that I wasn't angry with her. My greatest prayer was that she'd hear the message and truly read between the lines. Out of our mutual disappointment and heartache, could come something absolutely beautiful; stronger and more precious than ever before. Wendy would know that I was sending her a very personal message, in the guise of a sermon; our own secret code, if you will.

But Wendy wasn't there. And, as I looked out over the congregation, my heart sank as I realized that I may never see her beautiful face again, staring at me intently from the pews. It just didn't feel right, and her not being there affected me more than I thought it would.

I told you before how a preacher has to get up in front, giving off a certain level of confidence, even if he's shaking in his boots. That sense of confidence is what puts people at ease. If a preacher isn't confident, people begin to worry about what he might say, or what whacked-out thing is going to happen during the service, or if he's going to go off on some strange tantrum that has nothing to do with the topic at hand. So, in order to put people at ease, I always try to look and act confident, but in a spirit of humility. Confidence and humility are not contradictory. True confidence comes when we humbly rely on Jesus, and His power and strength.

That's what I always wanted whenever I stepped up to the pulpit to share the word of God. But Sunday morning, looking out over the congregation, the confidence just seemed to evaporate. That is the last place I wanted to be. The absolute last thing I wanted to be doing was leading a bunch of people in a worship service, and then break open the word of God to them. It's hard to describe the pain that's involved in trying to convince everyone that God will help us handle the disappointments that come our way, all the while doubting the very message you're preaching. Intellectually you believe it, but inside you're just not feeling it.

I think that was the longest service I've ever been in. Granted, it was only 75 minutes, just like every other service we have, but it felt like an eternity. The odd thing was that when the service was finally over, and I was greeting people as they left, so many of them remarked about what a touching and powerful message it was. They remarked about how it seemed to really come from the heart. Boy, if they knew the truth, I think this sermon would have meant even more.

Finally, the last parishioner had left the sanctuary to go home, or perhaps out to a restaurant for their usual Sunday dinner. I went back to the pulpit to gather my Bible and my notes, and as I was walking down the stairs I saw Maggie standing near the back. I called her name and she came walking down the aisle toward me. We met somewhere in the middle of the sanctuary, and as I walked up to her, I kept telling myself to hold it together. But when Maggie reached out her arms in comfort to me, I lost it and the tears began to flow. Maggie held me and just let me cry. After a few minutes of sobbing, I finally got a hold of myself and tried to stop the water-works. They always talk about the stoic Scandinavians; somehow, I must've missed out on that gene.

When I was finally able to speak, I thanked Maggie for her loving concern, and for letting me totally soak the shoulder of her blouse. She laughed and said, "Oh, that's all right John. Wendy soaked my nightgown Friday night, when she came home." I questioned her and said, "Really? Was she really upset?" Maggie looked at me and replied, "Of course she was upset. The last thing in the world she wanted to do was hurt you, John. She loves you and she always will - at least that's what she said - she'd always love you." So, in light of that, I questioned Maggie about what the problem was. I mean, if she loves me, and I love her, shouldn't that pretty much take care of this situation? If we could just sit down and talk, maybe we could work this out and get on with our life together. I got excited about that possibility and suggested that maybe I should go over to her place right now, and we'd get this whole thing settled, and see where we wanted to go from here. If the idea of engagement and marriage was too soon, I'd be willing to wait. I'd wait forever, if that's what it took to be with Wendy. Whatever it takes, I'm ready for it. Just tell me what to do and I'll do it.

I got a smile on my face and my heart was feeling vibrant with hope and expectation. Wendy's place is just a few minutes' walk from the church. We could be back together by this afternoon, with a new course of action. We can slow it down, or speed it up, or just let it drift a while. I didn't really care; I just wanted my beautiful Wendy. So, I looked at Maggie as I shared my thoughts and I finally said, "What do you think?" I waited for her answer, with great anticipation. But then Maggie looked at me, with concern etched on her face and said, "Well, that's just it, John. Wendy's gone."

Chapter 38

Maggie

LOOK HERE! I THINK IT'S ABOUT TIME THAT I HAD add my two cents worth. I know John and Wendy, probably better than anyone in Pleasant Pastures. I watched John come as our new pastor all these months ago and I liked him right at the very start. Not only was he good from the pulpit, more importantly he was good out of the pulpit. And, what I mean by that is that the person you saw in the pulpit was the same person you met at the grocery store, or at my diner. He was real. He was genuine. And I always appreciated that in a pastor.

And then that day Wendy arrived in town, it didn't take me long to get to know her either. You can know a lot about a person just from the way they work. And gracious, was she ever a worker. In all my years of running a diner I'd never seen anything like it. That first day, when my two other waitresses left because of a family emergency, Wendy just jumped in like she'd worked there for 20 years. This gal knew her stuff when it came to waiting on customers and giving them excellent service. And, over the last four months, as I've gotten to know her and Travis more closely, they've become two of my most favorite people in the world. I have a lot of friends; some are customers, some are church members, and the majority of them are both. But my three favorite people in the world are John, Wendy and Travis. And when I began to see that, when I looked at these three people who I'd grown to love in a relatively short period of time, it didn't take me long to come up with the brilliant idea that they needed to be together. You don't have to be some kind of a genius to recognize that certain people may do well on their own, but you put them together, and watch out. They're going to be dynamite. I think I saw that in the first month, probably sooner than they ever did.

Now, I've sat back these last four months and haven't really said much to them about that. I haven't really had to, because it seemed to me, that they were coming to the conclusion on their own. It wasn't hard to see all the signs of love and the pieces of a romantic relationship falling into place. It was really fun to watch. And I did whatever I could to help the relationship along. I'd take care of Travis, so that they could go out. I'd give Wendy the option of trading shifts occasionally, so she'd be free on John's day off, or one of the nights when he didn't have some church function. I did everything I could to lend some background support, so that they could be together.

It was obvious to me, particularly this last month, that things were progressing pretty fast. In fact, I was convinced, dollars to donuts, that John would propose fairly quickly. And just between us, I'll let you in on a little secret. My sister Ruth, who lives on a farm in Cle Elum, has been to church with me once before when she was visiting. She saw John from the pulpit, but actually never got a chance to meet him because he was busy at the altar after the service, praying for person who was in distress. But a few weeks ago, she had gone to Wenatchee for an appointment at the hospital there. She got to Wenatchee early, and instead of sitting in the waiting room for those 45 minutes, she decided to take a walk and look at some of the shops that were just a block or two from the hospital complex. As she rounded the corner, she saw Pastor John. Just as she spotted him, he walked into a jewelry store. So, being the super-snoop that she is, and realizing that he didn't know her from Adam, she just stepped into the store to browse. The guy behind the counter seemed to recognize him and affirmed that the special order had come in. She began to subtly make her way towards the same counter, and then glanced over at what was taking place between the salesman and Pastor John. He opened the box, and there was one of the prettiest engagement rings she had ever seen. It was gold, with black antiquing applied to it. John said something about hardly being able to wait to give it to her that next week. The salesman asked John the name of this very special woman. John told them it was Wendy Baker, but he hoped to change that to Wendy Larson, very soon. The salesman wished him well as John walked out. Then he turned to my sister and asked how he could help her, and she told him that she was just looking. And after a few minutes she left the store and went back for her appointment. But as soon as she got home, she called me and spilled the beans. I told her to shush up about it; we didn't want to spoil the surprise.

So, I knew that a proposal was coming up pretty quickly in Wendy's future. And I figured that as soon as he asked her to marry him, she'd be on cloud nine. I know it's what she had wanted, almost from the first day she met him. Now, she thought it was kind of odd that he told her his intentions that first day he met her at church, but he was so open and sincere, she thought that he might be right. Time would tell; and it did. He proposed and all should have been well. To me, at least, it's exactly what was supposed to happen. He would propose with great anticipation; she would accept with tremendous joy and enthusiasm; and pretty soon they'd be Mr. and Mrs. John Larson, and perhaps be on the way to providing Travis with a little brother or sister. Sorry - I guess I'm getting a little ahead of myself.

Anyway, when she came home that Friday night and ran into her apartment, I knew something was wrong. I had put Travis down for bed and he was sound asleep. I went up and knocked on her door and she said, "Who is it?" I thought that was kind of odd. I mean, who else would it be? But when I told her it was me, she opened the door and said, "Oh, I thought it might be John and I don't want to talk to him." I knew right away that, obviously, something was up. Whatever happened that night didn't go well, and she was in a great deal of pain.

I sat with Wendy for the better part of an hour and tried to get her to share with me what had happened. She told me all about their relationship and the fun she had with him. She expressed the delight she always experienced when she was with him, and how she never thought, in her wildest dreams, that someone like John, could ever be interested in someone like her. Someone like her. That should've been my first clue as to what was really going on. She assured me that she loved him with all her heart, but things could never work out with them. When I asked her why she felt that way, she said something to the effect, that true love and permanent relationships were probably a myth anyway. And even if there was true love, a person shouldn't pursue it if they knew that it was ultimately going to harm the other person. That should've been my second clue.

I asked her what she was going to do. What were her plans? She shocked me when she said that she was going to leave Pleasant Pastures the next day, and that she and Travis would have to find a new place to live, maybe across the mountains in Seattle. That sent me into a panic, because once she was gone, I might never see her or Travis again, and that weighed heavily on me.

I looked at Wendy and reminded her that her whole life had been one of chaos and dysfunction. And a lot of that chaos and dysfunction was brought on by either herself, or someone else, making very unwise, spur-of-the-moment decisions, in the heat of an emotional challenge. I encouraged her to fight that tendency and to give it some time, before she made any permanent move. I told her to go in and take a shower, let the water soothe her, and then come out and let's have some tea. She agreed to do that and went into the bathroom, where I heard her quietly weeping.

I went back down to my apartment, directly behind the diner, and called my sister. I told her the story and asked if she and Travis could come and stay for a few weeks, while she tried to get her thinking straight and come up with a good plan. She agreed that the idea was a good one, and when I offered to pay for their food, she told me not to worry about it. She had enjoyed having Travis that one day when I brought him for a visit, and that she would love to have both of them.

By that time, Wendy was out of the shower and I brought each of us a cup of tea. I told her what I had done, not as a way of controlling her life, but just to give her some breathing room. She needed a little space in which she could sort out her thoughts. Wendy thought it over for a few minutes and then smiled at me, rather weakly, and said that she appreciated my thoughtfulness. She also said that a couple of weeks at the farm should be enough to get her head on straight.

The next day was Saturday and I knew she would be leaving. Thankfully, we had hired and trained a couple of new waitresses, who could fill in for Wendy until she came back. *If* she came back – I really wasn't sure what was going to happen. Anyway, she and Travis left Saturday morning and drove to Cle Elum and settled into my sister's place. When I would call over the next several days, Ruth told me that Travis was really enjoying the animals and was even helping her in the kitchen. She told me that I had trained him well, and she was pretty surprised at his skill. But when I asked her about Wendy, she just said that she had been pretty subdued and quiet. She was always helpful around the place, but the joy and the energy she had seen in Wendy before, just wasn't there. She had a heavy heart and it was as plain as the nose on your face.

Wendy had been there for a little over two weeks, including three Sundays. When I went to church those three Sundays and heard John preach, I realized that the average Joe who walked into the church probably wouldn't necessarily pick up on anything, but I knew John.

He preached very well, very strong, very forceful and emphatic. But the subject matter had changed. John normally preached on topics such as God's love, or His calling in our lives, or how to become more Christ-like and so on. But the first week that Wendy didn't show up, John preached on, "Disappointment." The second week he preached on, "What do you do when God doesn't show up?" And the third week he preached on, "Tragedy - is God to blame?" I was afraid that if things kept going like this, we might come some Sunday morning and the topic would be, "Hello God - are you even out there? Do you even exist?"

After hearing three weeks of sermons that might've been fine for some people, I, on the other hand, could read between the lines. And as near as I could tell, neither John nor Wendy were making any headway. They were both heartbroken, down-trodden, depressed and lacking any sense of direction.

As I sat at my kitchen table one Monday morning, after having my prayer and devotions, I suddenly sat up straight and tall. I felt that God had given me an idea. And this idea wasn't just a nice little thought you have when trying to make sense of a tough situation. No, this idea was quickly morphing into a plan— a plan that would hopefully get John and Wendy back together, and the universe back on track, the way it was meant to be. It was a bold plan and required me to call out the big guns. And so, I got up, reached for the phone and called The Tanks.

Chapter 39

Max Sherman a.k.a. Tank 1

WHEN MAGGIE CALLED ME TO LAY OUT HER plan, I knew Ryan and I would be all in. What you need to understand is that though we're both pretty big guys, and we work in a fairly rough occupation, alongside of some seriously tough characters, both Ryan and I are a bit soft on the inside. When the Lord changed our lives, he didn't just change our circumstances and our behaviors. He actually changed our hearts. In fact, I've come to the conclusion, that it was the changed heart that actually wound up changing our behavior.

I know for myself that when I came back from 'Nam my heart was like a rock. I was angry and short tempered, and wanted to be left alone. I was miserable, but couldn't quite figure out what to do with that. I just figured that I was going to be in this state of mind from this point on. Nothing was ever going to get better, because there *was* no better; and to pretend otherwise was a myth.

But when I came to the Lord, the first thing I noticed was a difference on the inside. The anger was gone and the desire to fight and hurt others wasn't there anymore. For lack of a better term, I had grown soft, but soft in a good way. I was still tall and strong, and in great shape. I could wrestle logs all day long at my job, and still kid around with my logging buddies. But deep inside, something had changed. My heart had grown soft. It wasn't hard anymore; I actually had feelings and emotions and the ability to feel pain, right along with another person. It was a strange new sensation for me, but to tell you the truth I loved it. It actually made me feel more human, and I hadn't felt truly human for a long time. Of course, I came to understand later, that it wasn't really a matter of feeling more human, as much as it was feeling like the perfect representation of what it *meant* to be human. I was feeling, and thinking, and acting more like Jesus every day, and you can't get a more beautiful example of what humans are supposed to be like than Him.

I went all out and embraced as much of this new life and outlook as I possibly could. I joined the church and began to grow in my faith. People began to see certain gifts in me, as well as my heart for the Lord, and eventually I was placed in leadership positions, which I took very seriously. I studied the word of God with great enthusiasm, and tried every day to learn some new thought, or new principle that would help me to be a better Christian.

And let me say this: Maybe you get the idea that somebody my size, 6-foot six and 300 pounds of pretty solid muscle, would be all brawn and no brain. That's the kind of stereotype guys like me have to fight all the time, especially when we work in an occupation like logging. But I work in logging because I love the outdoors, and being cooped up in an office would kill me. I say all of this to let you know that my brother Ryan and I are pretty smart, and could do any number of things to earn a living. But we thrive in the outdoors, and our size makes logging an excellent occupation that not only pays the bills, but also keeps us in shape physically. We may be big, but we definitely don't fit the stereotype.

So, when Maggie approached us about her concerns about John and Wendy, we were already tracking with her. I could feel John's pain over the breakup, and had prayed with him about it a couple of times in the last three weeks. But with Wendy being gone, he had no idea what to do. He knew she was safe, at least for the moment, and that she was using this time to try to gather her thoughts and straighten out her thinking, but he still worried nevertheless. He wanted her to be safe, but he wanted her to be safe with him.

As Maggie and I talked, and she shared her idea about a last-ditch effort to get them back together, I could see how it might work. Maggie sensed that Wendy was on the verge of making a decision to leave the area for good, and then the opportunity would be over. She also shared that though Wendy was pretty closed-mouth about why she left, she still loved John and had actually left John for his benefit. Neither Maggie or I, or Ryan, when I shared it with him, could figure out what this was all about. All we knew was that all three of us were absolutely convinced that they needed to get together and talk about it, honestly and openly. The problem was that neither one of them felt that was the right thing to do, at least not right now.

John felt that Wendy needed space - she needed time to sort out her true feelings - feelings about a lot of things, including her past experiences, as well as her desires for the future. We could understand how John would feel this way, because he's always been a big proponent of people having the freedom to let God work in them, in His own unique way. And we all agreed that this was good. Wendy certainly needed to have her time to pray and seek the Lord. The only problem was the fact that John didn't know that Wendy was probably about ready to make a more permanent move, one that would make an eventual reconciliation even more difficult.

Now Wendy, on the other hand, had been as miserable as John had been the entire three weeks now. She knew she couldn't stay in Cle Elum forever and yet she felt no definite leading of the Lord to move on. The only thing she felt was that John and she should be together. But every time she began to feel like that, she just chalked it up to her emotions. As we came to find out later, she felt that it would be very destructive to go back to John; destructive in the sense that it would eventually destroy John's ministry, and his life. And because she loved him so much, she just couldn't do that to him. Though we didn't know it at the time, the nightmares she'd been having about her and John both being rejected because of her past, were continuing and just made her resolve to leave even stronger. What kind of a love would it be if she wasn't willing to sacrifice her happiness for John's ministry?

We didn't know all of this when we hatched the plan. All we knew was that we were convinced that God wanted them together, and that not only would it be good for them, it would also be good for the Kingdom. We were also convinced that God was calling us to step in and help Him accomplish His purposes. So, with that divine calling in mind, we began to hatch a plot that we felt would either do the trick, once and for all, or blow the whole thing apart. We figured it could go either way, but we felt peace about it and sensed that the Lord was going to use our rather simple and yet bold plan to accomplish something truly wonderful.

So, here's how it went down: Maggie wanted to visit her sister Ruth, in Cle Elum, and had let Wendy know she was coming down. She also suggested that the whole group should go on a little hike and take a picnic lunch with them. The trails were beautiful this time of year, the squirrels and rabbits and other wildlife were plentiful, and fun to watch. Travis would love an afternoon of this. They could pick wildflowers and berries that grew along the path. And then, at some point, after hiking for a period of time, they'd un-load the backpack and lay out the food they had brought, all on a red and white checkered cloth Maggie had purchased, just for the occasion. It would be a very lovely, old-fashioned picnic and might be one of the last times they could all be together.

Wendy thought that this would be a marvelous idea, especially when Travis started jumping up and down when she told him. He had really missed Maggie and looked forward to seeing her again. He was also feeling a little cooped up on the farm. There was always plenty to do and see, but he thought it would be great fun to hike, and have a real picnic in the wilds. So, it was all set. They'd leave that morning about 11 o'clock and spend the day out in nature.

Now, unbeknownst to Wendy, Ryan and I had been talking with John. We had spent some time with him on Wednesday night and knew that he had Saturday completely free; nobody was sick in the hospital-no weddings-no funerals-no emergency counseling sessions-completely free. And so, I told him that Ryan and I wanted to take him on a little hike on a trail that we had discovered, just off of one of the old logging roads. It was an amazing hike, with gorgeous views of the pastures and foothills. We'd also discovered an old train trestle that was safe to walk across, and was actually quite a rush from being up so high. When John began to hem and haw about the hike I said, "Come on John. Don't be such a pansy. If you're scared to go across the trestle, I'll hold your hand. You're looking a little pasty John, you need to get out in the sunshine and fresh air." Well, I knew John, and he wasn't going to let anyone call him a pansy. And so, we made plans to spend the day hiking on Saturday.

Maggie, Ryan and I had planned to meet at a predetermined spot at about 1 o'clock in the afternoon. We checked out this trail before and knew that very few people were aware of it, except the loggers. And they certainly weren't going back up into the woods on their day off.

So, Maggie and her group drove the few miles and began their hike on the trail. Ryan and John and I hit the trail from the other side. Both groups were hiking towards each other, but only the three of us schemers knew it.

Maggie and her group got to the picnic site a few minutes before one, and begin to lay everything out on the checkered tablecloth.

At Maggie's suggestion, Wendy and Travis took off their shoes and waded in the little stream that ran along the trail and pooled a few feet from where they were having the picnic.

At the same time my group had crossed the train trestle and was walking along the trail. I told them that we were going to have to cross the stream to get to the trail on the other side. It was too wide to jump across, but there was no choice, we had to cross over if we wanted to continue our hike. John started to object, but both Ryan and I jumped on him immediately and said, "Ah, come on John. The best is just up ahead. You don't want to miss it. Why don't you lead the way?" So, John took off his boots and started to cross the stream. All of us had decided that we didn't want to complete the hike with wet boots and socks, so off they came. Except, after John got in the water, Ryan and I kept our boots on and waded across. When John had gotten across, he bent down to dry his feet and put on his boots, and that's when we attacked. I grabbed his boots and socks, much to John's surprise. I think he figured we were just going to toss them back-and-forth, like kids do on a playground when they play "keep away." He started laughing and began to get up from his stooped position. But just as he was beginning to straighten up, Ryan rushed at him, all 6'8", and 350 pounds of solid muscle, and picked John up like a ragdoll and threw him over his shoulder. Then we took off and a few minutes later we rounded the bend and came upon the picnic scene. Wendy and Travis had just come out of the water and were sitting on the cloth. When Wendy saw us, she looked shocked. And when she realized that Ryan was carrying John over his shoulder like a sack of potatoes, she was even more shocked. Ryan dropped a surprised John on the tablecloth, right next to Wendy.

Maggie, Ryan and I approached the others and looked them squarely in the eye. Maggie took the lead and said, "Okay, John and Wendy, you look here. See this sack? Well, your shoes are in there. And we're going to take this sack and we're going to head up the trail a ways. You can't follow us, because the trail is full of rocks and thorns of all kinds and it would tear your feet up. So, here's how it's going to go. We're all leaving and you're going to stay here on this cloth until you talk this situation out. If two people were ever meant to be together, it's you. Don't be a couple of knuckleheads. Talk it out - work it out - yell it out - we don't care. But we're coming back in about two hours and you'd better be kissin' and smoochin'. If you're not, we're leaving you and we're taking this sack of boots and socks with us. And then you're on your own. We're on a divine mission from God, and we don't aim to fail. Now get a move on."

And with that, we all took off and didn't come back until 3 o'clock that afternoon. We gave them two hours to get the Lord's business accomplished. And sure enough, when we quietly tiptoed back, they were doing exactly what Maggie had told them to do. They were locked in each other's embrace, kissing with a beautiful tenderness. We watched quietly, for several seconds, as the tears rolled down our cheeks.

Chapter 40

Wendy

I T'S VERY DIFFICULT FOR ME TO DESCRIBE MY INI-
tial thoughts and feelings, when I saw the Tanks come rounding
the bend. And when the load Ryan was carrying turned out to be
John, and not a large tent or a huge back pack full of camping supplies,
I just about jumped out of my skin from the shock. I couldn't believe
John would even let himself get in that position, slung over Ryan's
back, totally helpless. But, on the other hand, it's pretty hard to fight
off 350 pounds of rock-solid muscle. Ryan was huge, and saying no to
him probably was an exercise in futility.

The feelings and thoughts in those few seconds were fast and furious. But I have to say, in all honesty, when they dropped John rather un-ceremoniously on the picnic cloth beside me, my thoughts came together in a split second. I felt like I had just been reunited with my long-lost best friend. It felt so good, so right to have John beside me once again that I began to choke up. But before I could break out into a full-blown weep-fest, Maggie started shouting orders with the voice of a drill sergeant. And she told us that, in no uncertain terms, we weren't going to leave that spot until we had worked everything out. They were messengers on a divine mission, and they weren't about to let down the God of the universe.

Well, I thought that was a little dramatic, but I really appreciated their effort at trying to fulfill their mission. The whole event must've taken an amazing amount of planning, to get the details and the timing down so perfectly. It was so perfect in execution, in fact, that I seriously considered the idea that perhaps there really was divine intervention involved. But, however it all came about, the thing that made my insides stir with a little hope, was that maybe there could be a workable solution to the separation: a separation that had caused me sleepless nights for three weeks straight.

But just as hope began to rise up within me, I remembered why we were in the situation in the first place. The separation from John, this wonderful man who I truly loved, was a reality precisely *because* I loved him so much. If I didn't care so much about him, I would've just continued on with him and let the chips fall where they may. But I just couldn't do that to John. When you truly love someone, you'll always be willing to sacrifice your desires, and your wishes, and even your happiness, for their greater good. If loving John meant a rejection by his church, and a blot on his ministry, there was no doubt what I had to do. If my past was going to destroy his future, then the only loving choice I had was to break it off.

Those kinds of thoughts were once again playing in my mind, and yet, having him so close beside me, was making it difficult to think clearly. It felt so right, and yet, to my way of thinking, it was so wrong. John can't marry a girl from the opposite side of the tracks, who's a poster child for damaged goods. No church is going to want their beloved pastor to be in a situation like that - love or no love. Nothing had really changed; the hopelessness of the situation was still there, staring me in the face.

When Maggie and the rest of the group left, John and I sat there for a few minutes with a quiet, but uncomfortable silence between us. But then John turned and looked at me, and softly told me that he loved me, and always will. I lifted my eyes to his and told him that I loved him too. We sat and stared at each other for several seconds, until John finally addressed the proverbial elephant in the room. We were going to have to address the issue, because it certainly wasn't going to go away, or just resolve itself. The only thing that was going to take away the awkward presence of that stupid elephant was an honest discussion. And, it appeared to me at least, that now was the time to share the whole story.

So, when John asked me to be honest, brutally honest, and tell him why I said no to his proposal, I took several minutes before I could respond. I was locked in an inner battle with myself, first going one way, and then going the opposite way. But, after a few minutes, I decided that the only way to send that invasive elephant packing was to tell the truth. And so, I did. I just started talking, and John sat there and listened intently.

It didn't really take too long to explain my actions. I started out by reminding him of my past, and the pain I had grown up with from living in a very chaotic and unstable home. I talked of the insecurity I'd always felt in my life, simply because my self-image had always been in the gutter. I reiterated my own poor choices and unwise decisions as an adult that simply added to the pain and heartache of a life that was, in essence, a waste. I told him how there were times when I felt like I was taking up space, and using up valuable resources, when I had given absolutely nothing back.

I continued on like this for several minutes, but then got right to the heart of the issue. I looked at him and told him why I said no and ran away. He may not believe this, but I did it because I loved him so much. I told him that I had been having a series of dreams that always began with us loving one another, and wanting to shout it from the rooftops. Our love was passionate, and yet, tender. It was exciting, and yet, felt comfortable, like well-worn slippers. It was what I would consider to be a perfect love. But in every dream the scene changed. The congregation found out about my past, and decided that their pastor deserved someone better – someone whose life was more stable and well-suited to the role of pastor's wife. And if he was too spiritually blind to see their viewpoint, then he shouldn't be in the ministry at all, let alone at Pleasant Pastures.

As I finished my story of the dreams, and my inner turmoil about the potential for inflicting pain and misery on him, I finished by telling him plainly, so he couldn't misinterpret what I was trying to explain to him. All the while, I was trying to control the tears of pain that were running down my cheeks, but it was a losing battle. So in between sobs and heavy sighs, I said, "John, I said no and ran away because I didn't want to ruin your life and your ministry. I love you too much to do that to you." And with that admission, I just sat back and shut up, hoping and praying that he would understand the wisdom of my actions, and the intensity of the love those actions were grounded in.

He sat there for a few minutes and didn't say a word. I figured that he was trying to come up with just the right way to thank me for my sensitivity to this very important and potentially life-altering dilemma. I knew John loved me, but I also knew he loved serving the Lord. The ministry was his first calling. I, on the other hand, came along years later. I was pretty sure that, in thinking it over, John would see the painful, but honest reality of what I had expressed to him.

Finally, after several moments of silent contemplation, John spoke. John reached out and turned my face toward his, and he began to speak in a very quiet and controlled manner. I could tell that he was serious, and that he felt he had something important to say. He looked at me and asked me to let him speak, without interruption, because he didn't want to lose his train of thought. I agreed to just sit silently and let him share what was on his heart. I really wondered how he was going to wind up agreeing with my side of the issue, and yet try to build me up in the process. John always wanted to build people up, even when he had to share uncomfortable truths with them.

But as John began to speak, what he said to me took me by complete surprise. He started out by telling me how much he loved me. Now, that wasn't a surprise, I had known that all along. He also told me what a wonderful person I was, in so many areas. I was pretty, and kind, and a hard worker, a wonderful mom, and I was a lot of fun to be with. But one of the things that most impressed him was how smart I was, how insightful I was, in a variety of situations he had observed me in. Here it comes, I thought. Here's where he's going to agree with my wisdom and insight into the futility of mixing our love, and his ministry. He's letting me down slowly and gently, but that's John for you; that's just what he does.

But he surprised me when he said, "Wendy, you're very smart, very insightful, but I have to tell you, in the strongest terms possible, you missed this one by a country mile. You couldn't be more wrong on this issue, and I'll tell you why. First of all, you're really short changing the folks at church. You're believing your nightmares. You're believing what you see at night, instead of trusting what you've seen in the daylight. These are wonderful, loving folks. Some of them might be a bit quirky, but who isn't at times? Secondly, you'd be surprised if you heard where some of these folks have come from. I've heard some of their testimonies of their life, before they came to know the Lord, and without trying to downplay what you been through, their life stories would make yours almost pale in comparison. Seriously, I'm just telling you like it is. Thirdly, you're putting too much trust in your dreams. I know you've had some interesting messages from God, in a variety of ways, and I really believe that God speaks to us that way, even today. But there are other explanations for those dreams. Not all dreams are from God. Some are from the enemy, who's on a mission to mess with your head. Now, I'm no psychiatrist, but they could also simply be a result of the fear of rejection you've had your entire life. And the rejection you felt from getting kicked out of that church could really be the culprit here. Wendy, those nightmares could be from any number of sources. But I can tell you right now, they're not from God. You know how I know? Because the two major points are just not true. Number one: the people at Pleasant Pastures aren't like the people in your dream. And number two: even if they did reject us, my ministry wouldn't be ruined. In fact, if it ever did happen that way, and we left the church in a spirit of grace and humility like Jesus, God would have an even greater ministry for us. One negative church experience that's based in wrong thinking and false accusation, doesn't negate your calling. If anything, it just makes you more gracious, more compassionate, and better equipped to serve. You see what I mean, Wendy? And while I'm at it, let me say one more thing. And this is probably the most important, and so I don't want you to miss it. If, by some chance, you were right about the folks at church, and they rejected us because of your past, I can tell you right now that I would be the first one to leave. If that's what the folks were truly like, then I would know, beyond a shadow of a doubt, that I was in the wrong church. That's not the Jesus I know. And that's not the way He taught us to live. If that's what the church was really like, I'd be gone in a minute. They couldn't pay me enough to stay there."

I was staring intently into his eyes and I knew, without a doubt, that he was absolutely serious. There was no joking - no little smile - no twinkle in the eye - no nonchalant toss of his head. John was as serious as I've ever seen him. He looked deeply into my eyes and told me once again how much he loved me, and wanted to spend his life with me. I was so thankful to hear those words again that I just broke down and sobbed. And when he reached out and wrapped his arms around me, I nestled deeply into his chest, so thankful to be there once again, in the arms of the man I loved. He tenderly asked me again to be his wife and I quietly, but joyfully, told him yes. Whatever happens, we'll face it together. I want to be married to this man, more than anything else in the world.

As we cried and continued to hold each other, he asked me if I was still worried about the congregation's view of me, if they should ever find out the truth. And I admitted that I was, to some extent. Not as much as before, maybe, but it still concerned me, and made me feel a bit anxious. I knew that John loved me and would stick by me no matter what, but even though I wasn't worried any longer about his ministry being ruined, I still didn't want him to be embarrassed or suffer disgrace because of me. I told him that, and he was quiet for a few seconds, but then said that he had a solution. And this solution would put my fears to rest, once and for all, one way or the other. He then asked me if I wanted to hear his suggestion. And admittedly, with a bit of trepidation, I said yes.

John laid out his plan for me. It was a simple plan really; at least simple in principle. Following through with it, however, was a bit daunting, but I could definitely see how it would answer my fears and questions quite clearly in a short period of time. The idea was that I would give my testimony to the congregation at a service, a week from tomorrow. We'd let people know that we felt it was important for the spiritual health of our church, for everyone to know the future Mrs. John Larson. They needed to know all about this husband-and-wife ministry team that would be leading the Pleasant Pastures Community Church for years to come. I swallowed hard and gave him a thumbs-up.

We sat there holding each other and kissing, until we heard Maggie and the other folks tiptoe back. We looked up and smiled, and they broke out into cheers and applause. We told him that we were going to announce our engagement during the church service tomorrow, and they cheered and applauded once again. We didn't tell them about the plan to share my story that next Sunday. We'd let them hear it tomorrow, with the rest of the congregation.

I went to bed that night, knowing that in a relatively short period of time, I'd be Mrs. John Larson, the pastor's wife. I knew our marriage was going to be amazing, passionate, heartfelt, tender, successful – the adjectives just kept coming. I also knew that our ministry together was going to be powerful and effective. The part I didn't know for sure was where our ministry would be. Eventually, I fell asleep accepting the truth that the future of our ministry at Pleasant Pastures lay in the hands and the hearts of the people. Did they have enough love and grace to accept me? I wondered.

Chapter 41

John

HAVE YOU EVER HAD AN EXPERIENCE WHERE you thought you knew someone pretty well? You'd spent quite a bit of time together, and shared many opinions and insights, personal goals and triumphs, victories as well as failures - all the kinds of things that go into making for an honest and open relationship. But then one day a piece of news comes out concerning the person that you thought you knew so well. And the news wasn't good. Maybe they'd had an affair. Maybe they were discovered to be abusing their children. Maybe they had embezzled funds from their employer.

Maybe they'd been caught trying to shoplift an item from a store at the mall. Whatever the situation was, it just didn't seem to fit what you felt you knew about this person. The only answer you could give when confronted with the news of their actions is, "Oh, that can't be. They would never do that. That doesn't sound like them at all." That's your answer. That's your take on the situation, and you're 100% sure that you know the truth, better than anybody else. But then, to your complete astonishment, they come clean and admit that they, indeed, were guilty as charged. You're both surprised and devastated. That just doesn't fit with the person you thought you knew.

If you've ever had that kind of experience, then maybe you can get an idea of the anxiety I was feeling after suggesting my plan, my solution, to Wendy concerning her fear of rejection. After Wendy admitted that she ran off from me because she was afraid that she'd ruin my ministry if the congregation found out about her past, I suggested that she simply go before the congregation and share her story, honestly and openly. I was convinced that the good folks at Pleasant Pastures would listen with grace and understanding, and then accept her with open arms. I knew my congregation, and I'd observed them readily embrace a host of war-torn travelers who came through our doors. Life can have a tendency to beat you up, and Pleasant Pastures seemed to be a place that provided hope and rest to the weary soul who had experienced much of life's pain.

That's how I saw my folks; that's what I felt I observed in my congregation. But the question that nagged at me was: What if it was different in Wendy's case? What if they heard Wendy's story, and certainly had sympathy for all she'd gone through, but felt that in this case, they couldn't let it go? What if they truly felt that a pastor's wife should have a greater degree of positive life experiences, and possess a much deeper understanding, a deeper grasp, of the Christian faith? How's she ever going lead others, if her life has been such a mess?

Part of me was convinced that I knew my congregation very well, and that they would live up to my expectations. Still…I'd been surprised by people's actions before. I kept thinking about how shocked I was to watch people, who I thought I knew very well at First Baptist suddenly turn on each other, and say some pretty nasty things to people they had worshiped with for years, and in some cases decades. So, as sure as I was, there was still a bit of nervousness. I didn't share that with Wendy because I knew she was having her own struggles with the plan. We decided together to just pray and let God lead us, and hopefully, the congregation.

The next day in church, I made the announcement about our engagement. I started off by saying that God had a divine plan, from the very beginning, that brought people together in this wonderful relationship we call marriage. And although, as the Apostle Paul says, not everyone is called to it - that everyone has different gifting's - still, most people find marriage to be high on their list of desirable experiences.

I think the people just felt that this was an introduction to the morning message, because I didn't announce anything until it was time to preach. But, after I gave a few words about marriage, and the wonderful idea God had at the beginning, I then asked Wendy to step up to the front. And as she came up to the pulpit area, I took her by the hand, smiled, and simply said, "I want you to greet the future Mrs. John Larson. I proposed yesterday, and she said yes." The congregation broke out in thunderous applause, and even some cheers. It was great fun, and both Wendy and I had a marvelous time basking in the encouraging shouts and well wishes.

Finally, when the applause had died down, I told them that we wanted to do something a little bit unusual. I reminded them that Wendy had come, with her son Travis, about three months ago from back East. And though they had immediately received her and Travis into the congregation, still she was a relative new-comer. I told the folks gathered there that we both thought it would be good, and in fact necessary, if they knew her story. I looked out over the congregation and told them, very honestly, that Wendy had come from a very difficult background - a background that was pretty rough, pretty messy. I told them that it was only by the grace of God she survived it at all; life could've gone much differently, in a much darker direction. And because of all of this, we felt that it was extremely important for everyone to hear her story, in order to truly know their pastor's wife. I invited them to come for the evening service, a week from tonight, and listen as Wendy shared about her past. I also told them, that because of the nature of some of her testimony, we would be having a special children's event in the fellowship hall during that time. This was going to be an evening of painful, but honest testimony.

Well, the crowd had quieted down until you could've heard a pin drop. And so, to break the tension, I said something to the effect, "Hey guys, listen, don't get so worried. She's not from Mars - she's not an alien for heaven's sakes - she's just got a testimony we think you need to hear." Thankfully, that broke the tension a bit and I was able to get on with the message. I preached about having joy in our Christian walk, and how that joy should spill over and touch people, wherever we go, and to everyone God brings our way. I then closed the service with a benediction, and both Wendy and I left to say goodbye to the folks at the door. Of course, as they were leaving, so many told us how exciting it was to hear about our forth-coming marriage. In fact, several of the little old ladies, as I like to refer to them, told us that they had been praying up a storm for, "a really good girl" to come along and snatch up their pastor. We both laughed and said thanks, and told him to keep on praying, because we're going to need it now maybe more than ever before.

Wendy and I stayed until everybody had gone and then started out walking toward the diner. Maggie had taken Travis home with her to start fixing lunch. We were all going to eat together, but we weren't due there for another hour, and so we decided, at the last minute, to take a detour through the pasture and go sit on our bench for a while. Sometimes it's good to have a bit of time to decompress after the service, particularly one like today. As we sat there on the bench, we rehashed the events of the last hour. I asked her how she was doing and she said fine. I asked her if she felt that I had said too much in terms of explaining that her past was a bit messy. But she assured me that she felt it was just right. It gave them something to think, and hopefully, pray about in anticipation of next Sunday night. She thought the comments about her not being an alien from Mars were effective in easing the situation a bit. The only thing that would have made it perfect is if we could have arranged ahead of time for our sound guy to play that weird music from "The Twilight Zone" when I was talking about aliens. Alas, it was in ad-lib, so the opportunity was lost. But it was still a good morning.

I took Wendy into my arms and kissed her. We had to be careful with displays of affection, particularly now that everyone knew. It didn't seem very wise to be seen falling all over each other in public. I wasn't sure what that would say to people who witnessed it. Would it just say that we were a couple that was deeply in love, or would it give them the idea that their pastor was some kind of a lecherous scoundrel, who couldn't wait to have his way with the fair, young maiden? We could kiss, and we could hug, and we could hold each other, within certain limits, and that was fine. But I have to tell you; I was getting very anxious for our wedding, and looking very much forward to celebrating and expressing our love, the way God intended. Personally, I think that was one of His better ideas!

The week passed fairly quickly, and though we were looking forward to finally getting things out in the open, there was still a bit of anxiety about the whole evening. For Wendy, of course, it was about the idea of baring her soul so honestly, so nakedly. When someone would give a testimony of God's love and grace in their lives, everybody received it warmly, because that's what our faith is all about. Jesus changes lives! That's the essence of the gospel message. But it's one thing for the average Joe sitting in the pew to share his broken past, but it's quite another thing for the pastor's wife to do that. So, we were both excited, and yet, a bit nervous, not really sure what the outcome would be.

Sunday night came, and after praying together in my office, we went out just a minute before the service was scheduled to begin. We walked out the side door, directly onto the platform. Normally, we would have been visiting with the folks ahead of time, but we felt it would be better to spend the time praying and focused on the task ahead.

Harley Logan led the folks in a few songs, accompanying the congregation on his guitar, and then it was time. I stood up and introduced Wendy as my future wife, and then reiterated why we felt it was important for her to share her story. I wasn't planning to introduce her, because after all, everybody in the church knew who she was already. But as we were singing, I looked out over the congregation and realized it was larger than normal, much larger in fact. And as I ran my eyes over each row, I saw people from the community that I had never seen at church before. It's then that I began to realize that the word had gotten out that something interesting was going on down at the church. And since all services were open to the public, here they all were. I wasn't sure what I thought about that. I mean, Wendy's story is pretty intimate, and the way she's planning to share is honest and raw, no holds barred. It's one thing to bare yourself in front of your church family, but it's quite another thing to do that to just anybody who walks in off the street. So, as I stood there introducing Wendy for the benefit of our visitors, I simply prayed, "Lord, this is all in your hands; may your will be done. And when this is all over Lord, may it become abundantly clear to us, what your plans will be for our future." And with that, I handed the mic to Wendy and sat down.

Chapter 42

Wendy

WHEN I WAS DANCING TOPLESS AT NICK'S club in Chicago, it got to the point, after a while, that I could just zone out and go to a different place in my head. I couldn't do it all the time, because someone was always getting a little too rowdy, and would have to be ushered out by security. Or, some other guy, who had imbibed a bit too much alcohol, would try to jump up on the platform and dance with the girls, but that usually ended with him missing the step, and falling on his face, or security would grab him just in time. Either way, it would distract me and pull me back from my private island of escape. But most of the time I was able to block what was happening around me, and just moved to the music coming through the sound system. I made it through each evening by retreating into "The Zone." When you're standing there naked in front of people, you have to have "The Zone" if you're going to survive. At least, I needed it.

Well, tonight I was going to be standing there naked again, in front of a bunch of people. But this time, I was going to be baring my soul, instead of my body. And, as strange as this may sound to some people, I think this evening was more nerve-racking than the others. I'm not sure how to explain it exactly, except to say it was really about the customer, the audience if you will. You see when I was dancing, I didn't care about the customers. I wanted their patronage, yes. It was their patronage that put food on the table for Travis and me. It was the act of opening their wallets and filling the tip jar, or slipping the bills to me personally, that paid for some of the extras in life. So, customers were always important. But, in all honesty, I didn't really care about them, beyond their wallets. Why would I? As much as I might try to connect with them from the stage, it was all about tips. There was no real relationship going on, no matter what the guy was imagining and hoping in his mind.

But baring myself in front of this church family I'd grown to love, and even cherish, was a whole different story. These folks weren't customers. I suppose a cynic could look at the situation and disagree with me. They might point out the fact that, yes, in essence, they are customers because, after all, they give their tithes and offerings, some of which go to pay the pastor's salary. And pretty soon, as his wife, you're going to be reaping the benefit of that salary also. So, in essence, they are like your customers.

I suppose a cynic, who doesn't understand, could say that, but he would be wrong. These people aren't customers; they're family. And they don't give their tithes and offerings to us. They give them to the Lord, through their church. The church financial team then distributes those finances to the various ministries, and professional staff they have. So, as the pastor, John gets a salary that is voted on and approved by the congregation. It's not a huge salary, but it's certainly adequate. And it doesn't matter how hard he works, or how many extra hours he spends on an emergency situation, or launching a new program, his salary remains the same for that year. So, there are no tips for paying special attention to this customer or that customer.

These folks are not customers; they're dear friends and family. So, as much as I think they're going to accept me, in many ways they're like any other family. Something could set them off, or hit them the wrong way, or send them into a fit of despair. Any number of things could happen, with any number of potential outcomes. Christians, after all, are people. And people can wind up being pretty unpredictable at times. Look at Jesus' 12 disciples, for heaven's sake. Who would've thought that when the chips were down and He needed them most, they'd all run away and leave Him to face the cross, all alone. With friends like that…

As I started to share my testimony, my story, of a life redeemed from the pit of hell, I noticed a lot of unfamiliar faces. Not unfamiliar exactly, just unfamiliar here at church. I'd seen most of them, of course, at the diner, but never in church. I wasn't sure what to think about that. I just figured that they heard that something dramatic was going to take place at the church, and they wanted to come along and see it. Small-town entertainment, I guess.

I started to speak and I could tell that my voice was kind of weak, and a little bit quaky. But I shot up a quick arrow prayer that basically cried, "Help me, Lord." And you know what? He did. He absolutely came through and allowed me to get through my whole story, with a strong, sure voice, and an even stronger spirit. I really sensed the Holy Spirit speaking through me and I absently wondered if that's how John felt when he preached.

I was watching the people as closely as I dared. I had to be careful because many of them had tears running down their faces, and I knew I'd lose it if I watched them too closely. I knew they were tracking with me all the way. I saw it, for example, when I mentioned diner-guy's demonic word over me about having nothing worthwhile to offer, but my body. I saw several women shake their heads, and I wondered how many of them had experienced similar kinds of abusive words from men in their past. I also noticed several guys who grew angry, and unconsciously made a fist, as if they wanted to protect me. I heard a small gasp, when I got to the part of being a topless dancer for several months. And who could blame them? Who wants to think of their pastor's wife being naked in front of a bunch of leering men?

I saw sympathy, and in some cases, empathy, when I shared about doing all of this for my son's sake. People there understood how much parents are willing to sacrifice for their kids, even if we get mixed up at times and try to do it in ways that are just not healthy. I could tell that some of them were thinking back to their own parents, and the rough, abusive life they had dished out to their kids. I could see the pain on some faces, as they wondered what it would have been like to have parents who would sacrifice for their kids. They didn't have that, and I could read it on their faces as plain as day.

I looked at the clock in back of the sanctuary and realized, much to my amazement, that I had been up in front for 45 minutes. I got to the part in my story where Nick reminded me that I owed him, and if I didn't agree to meet some of the more important customers, on the side, he'd kill me. An audible murmur went through the crowd as they processed what that must have felt like. Fear suddenly came flooding back, for just a second, as I remembered how frightened I was for Travis and me. And when I told them, that out of fear, I set up my first appointment in a hotel room with a very prominent businessman from Chicago, the room became deathly still, the people barely breathing, wondering what I was going to say next.

I told him how I kept circling the block, and finally decided to go in. What choice did I have? I was scared, and I just wanted to get it over with. But then I heard that voice. I heard God's voice assuring me that this wasn't me, and I needed to run now. I needed to escape now. I described how I went home and packed and was gone, in under 30 minutes, determined to get as far away as possible. I told them how, after driving all that way, thinking I would go to Seattle, I accidentally took a road I didn't even know was there, and wound up in Pleasant Pastures. I shared with them that it felt like I'd come home the minute I began driving down Main Street. And when Travis spotted the sign in the window of Maggie's Country Diner, I just knew that it couldn't be a coincidence that she needed a waitress. It felt like God was leading me all the way. But I still wasn't sure I believed in Him, and if I did, I think I was still pretty angry with Him. I confessed how very mixed up I was when I got here, but I wasn't anymore. God had done a marvelous job.

I finally closed with a few words thanking all the folks for their kindness, but especially Maggie, for all her support over these months. I confessed my nervousness at speaking so honestly, but it had to be done. They absolutely had to know the kind of background I came out of, if I was ever going to have the privilege of ministering alongside of John. I told them I loved them all, but I would absolutely understand, if they felt my past disqualified me as being a leader in the church.

And with that, John came up and joined me on the stage. He put his arms around me and kissed me on the cheek. Then he whispered in my ear, saying that he was so proud of me and that I had done great. We turned and faced the congregation, tears streaming down our faces, and John asked a very open, and somewhat dangerous question: "Well, where do we go from here?" Nobody said a word - complete silence - my heart felt like it had stopped beating. Just then, Virginia Crupp stood up, and with all eyes watching her, she walked up the aisle and out the door of the sanctuary. The folks began to murmur, and I thought someone else was going to say something in response to Virginia's leaving, obviously upset at what she'd heard. But then we heard the sanctuary door open, and in came Virginia, carrying a wad of Kleenex in her hand that she had collected in the women's restroom. She walked down the aisle and up to the pulpit area, and gently dabbed at my eyes. And then she turned to John and did the same thing to him. She was crying, and she put her arms around both of our necks, drawing us close to her, her rose-scented perfume invading our senses. I never liked the scent of roses in a perfume before, but after Virginia's demonstration of love and acceptance, it became my favorite.

Within a few seconds, we were surrounded and embraced by more people than I could count. And people who couldn't get close to us stood in the group and hugged the other person next to them. Pretty soon, Max began to pray, and as always, I was amazed at how eloquent his prayer was; not something you would expect from a guy named Tank. Other folks prayed also, and they were beautiful prayers about love and acceptance - about mercy and grace - about hope and healing - all the well-known gospel themes that Jesus demonstrated for us throughout His life on earth.

As I stood there, I realized that I was experiencing quite a miracle. Not only had God turned my life around and brought a wonderful husband-to-be into my life, He also had brought me a whole congregation of new friends - friends who would stick by me, no matter what. And as I watched, and emotionally embraced all of this, I wondered what it would be like, from this point on, to minister right alongside of John. What would it be like to see people come to faith in Christ? What would it be like to see them leave their life of emptiness and begin to follow Jesus? As I stood there, embraced by so many, I whispered a prayer to God saying that I was so excited to see that happen in our ministry.

I didn't have to wait long. Sometimes God moves slow, like a mighty glacier. And other times, He's quick, like lightning. Just as I whispered my prayer to God, we all heard a man's voice - a little weak, a little shaky, but definitely a voice that had something to say. We all turned to see who it was, and to our amazement, that voice belonged to Vern Hodges. Besides being one of the crankiest men in town, as a waitress, I knew that he was the worst tipper on the face of this planet. The reason I knew that is because he's never left me a tip, not once.

I wondered what he was doing here, because he certainly had never darkened the door of the church before. But regardless of all that, Vern had something to say.

He stood in front of us and spoke for just a few minutes. He looked at us and said, "When I was just a little boy, growing up down south, my daddy died, and from that point on we became pretty poor. We were the family who the church always had to help. I hated that, because they always made it very clear to us how much effort they had put forth on our behalf. And then I got older, and I got into a little trouble at school and around the town. Nothing too bad, but I was definitely going in the wrong direction. Well, I guess they felt that the trouble I was in, combined with our financial woes, left them no choice, but to make it very clear that we weren't welcomed in their church any longer. It broke my mama's heart, but she found another church, in time. But I just couldn't. All I could think of was how they treated us, and I determined as a young man, never to have anything to do with church again. In fact, this is the first time I've been in a church, since I was 15. But when I heard rumors about this gal, Wendy, telling her story, I just had to come. I know Wendy from the diner. And if you know me, and most of you do, you know how cranky I can be, and pretty tight-fisted. I'm ashamed to admit it, but I've never given her one dime as a tip. But you know what? She has always treated me with nothing but love and kindness, always going out of her way to give me wonderful service. I've looked at her so many times and wondered if that's what Christians are supposed to be like. To me, she always seemed to live like I imagined Jesus wanted His people to live. I still didn't come to church, but it got me thinking. And then, when I heard about this meeting, I decided to sneak in the back and take a listen. The rejection she felt from that first church, brought back all kinds of painful memories, and I said to myself, "You see Vern, it's like that all over." And when she finished, I watched Virginia leave. And it just added more fuel to this angry fire inside of me. But then, here comes Virginia, right up onto the stage, and she wipes their eyes, and hugs them. Then I realized, there's no rejection here, that's just pure love and acceptance. And then all the rest of you came up, with the same hugs, and encouraging words, and honest, beautiful, prayers, right from the heart. And for the first time, since I was a teenager, I talked to God. I told Him that if this gal Wendy was anything like Jesus, I wanted that. And if these people were anything like He wanted them to be, I wanted that too. I guess what I'm really asking, is can I become a part of this church too? I've never seen anything like it."

By this time, of course, we're all blubbering like idiots. God had used this time of testimony and prayer to bring one man closer to the kingdom. I watched all of this unfolding, and I wondered if this is what ministry with John is going to be like? Because if it is, we're in for quite an adventure. And I want to experience every minute of it!

Epilogue

RED AND WHITE CHECKED TABLECLOTHS DOT-
ted the freshly mown lawn of Pleasant Pastures Community
Church. The tables were decked out in a simple, but beautiful picnic theme. Each table had a small Mason jar containing a bouquet
of wildflowers, lovingly gathered from the foothills, by Virginia Crupp
and the ladies of the Martha Circle. There was also a lovely basket of
fruit on each table, all from the bounty of the Eastern Washington
harvest. Each table was perfectly arranged by the ladies of the church,

as a gift of love to Pastor John and Wendy, who would be married in the next few minutes.

People began bringing all kinds of dishes to this rather unusual, yet somehow totally appropriate picnic wedding. The entire church had been invited, and what better way to serve a crowd of 400 than by sharing the gifts of food that came from the kitchens of the members? There were several trays of golden-fried chicken, the aroma making mouths water. There were bowls of potato salad, baked beans, string bean casserole, and the ever-popular Tater-Tot hot dish. And then, there were the pies. The assortment of berry pies was enough to send a person into a sugar-frenzy, just from looking.

The men of the church were in charge of providing the meat. Brisket, which had been smoked for over 14 hours, was the main staple, along with hamburgers and hotdogs for the kids. All in all, this was destined to be the best potluck picnic the folks at Pleasant Pastures had ever seen. People were going to be heading home full, and bottles of Tum's were going to be retrieved from medicine cabinets all over town.

But in spite of the vast array of marvelous foods, and beautifully arranged table decorations, everybody knew the real reason they were there. Today, they would all have the privilege of witnessing the uniting in marriage of Pastor John Larson, from Duluth, Minnesota and Wendy Baker, from the wrong side of the tracks.

It was just three weeks ago that Wendy had shared her story of pain and chaos - of fear and dysfunction - of glimmers of hope, and the darkness of disappointments. But her willingness to bare her soul, all the while trusting in the loving grace of the church members, spoke volumes to everybody who witnessed that truly touching event. There was not a dry eye in the house. And when it became abundantly clear that not only was Wendy not going to be rejected, but rather more fully embraced than ever before, everybody knew that a wedding celebration wasn't going to be too far off in the future. And sure enough, within one week, the entire church membership, as well as the patrons of Maggie's Country Diner, all received invitations to attend.

So, here they all were, 400 strong, seated around the tables as the ceremony began. Pastor Josh Miller, from the Faith Presbyterian Church in Leavenworth, would be officiating. He and John had shared many hours of prayer, as well as several lively discussions on the topic of predestination. They were never going to agree on all aspects of their theology, but they were great friends, nevertheless. A love for Jesus was their unifying factor. The rest would all be figured out someday, in the "sweet by and by." Neither of them was sure they'd even care by then. Once you're with the Lord in heaven, what's there to be arguing about?

John and Wendy approached the designated spot and stood facing Pastor Josh. The beautiful strains of Noel Paul Stookey's, "The Wedding Song" filled the air, as Harley Logan sang it with tenderness, and fairly-controlled emotions. He was very touched to be asked to participate in this wonderful event. He had tears in his eyes and yet, he was able to hold it together, even having the breath-support to sustain the long phrases. To John and Wendy, Harley had never sounded better.

Pastor Josh gave a short meditation and then guided John and Wendy through their vows. Both of their voices cracked as they made those enduring vows, purposely composed to last a lifetime. When the vows were completed, and the rings exchanged, Pastor Josh pronounced them husband and wife, in the name of the Father, and the Son, and the Holy Spirit. He gave a lovely benediction declaring God's smiling face to be upon them from this time forth, and then closed with an Amen. After the bridal kiss, which provoked a few whistles, he had John and Wendy turn to face their friends and declared with a loud voice: "It is now my privilege, to be the first to introduce to you, Mr. and Mrs. John Larson." And the minute those words escaped his lips, there was near pandemonium. People stood up and cheered and applauded enthusiastically, while John and Wendy walked over to a little table to sign the license.

The reception began and the bride and groom were the first in line, followed by Travis and Maggie, and then The Tanks. Travis had been the ring bearer and was very careful to guard it with his life. Maggie was the matron-of-honor, and considered it a real blessing to be asked. John couldn't decide who was going to be his best man, and so he took the easy way out and had both of his good friends stand up for him. The Tanks had been with John since his first weeks at the church, and John felt that although it was a bit unconventional, why not have both of them fill the best man slot? Besides, given their size, it wouldn't be very wise to get either one of them upset with him, right? But, sure enough, when they got to the vows, John glanced over at his best men and saw tears running down their faces. Man, what a couple of pansies, crying like little girls. And he loved them for it.

As the reception was coming to a close, and the cake had been cut and toasts had been made, Harley Logan came up to the mic and sang, "The Hawaiian Wedding Song." When he was finished the people shouted for an encore. John and Wendy didn't know this, but that had all been staged. Harley went back to the mic and sang the song, "Blue Hawaii" with a distinctly Elvis sound. It brought the house down, and both John and Wendy thoroughly enjoyed it. It was very special to them, and they appreciated the sensitivity of their friends. They had wanted to honeymoon in Hawaii, specifically the islands of Maui and Kauai, but the money just wasn't available. Maybe someday, but not at this time.

After Harley sang "Blue Hawaii," Vern Hodges got up to say something. Now this was a bit of a surprise, because he only been a part of the church for three weeks, ever since the night Wendy shared her testimony. But he got up to the mic and told them that the people had taken up a collection, over the last two weeks, to help them out with their honeymoon expenses. John and Wendy were planning to head out on Monday, after spending the next two nights at the Enzian Hotel in Leavenworth, and then just make their way down though the Washington and Oregon coast. They had heard that was a beautiful trip, and they were excited to experience it.

But what Vern Hodges said, and did, at the mic, changed all their plans in a split second. He acknowledged how they had heard that their first choice of a honeymoon destination had been Hawaii, but that wasn't possible because of the finances. With that, Vern took out an envelope and gave it to John and Wendy. They looked at each other, and both felt a growing sense of excitement, as they thought about the songs Harley had sung, and the comments Vern had made. This couldn't be, could it? They looked inside the envelope and there were two folded sheets of white paper. They opened the first sheet of paper and saw two tickets on Hawaiian Airlines to both Maui and Kauai. They gasped when they saw the tickets, and immediately choked up at the generosity of their friends. Vern then encouraged them to open the second sheet of paper. They opened the second sheet, looked at the paper, and discovered that it was a letter from the Sheraton Hotels on Maui and Kauai, confirming a one-week reservation in each, beginning Monday afternoon, with check-in at 3:00 PM.

John and Wendy were absolutely humbled by the love that was being expressed to them. In all honesty, they didn't feel like they deserved it, and it made them marvel at God's goodness to them, expressed through His people. They thanked everybody profusely, but were a bit perplexed when they all just stood there, many with peculiar smiles on their faces. Without knowing it, both Wendy and John were wondering what that was all about. And just as they begin to wonder, Vern stepped up to the mic, yet again, and told them that they had one more thing for them. And with that, he took out a manila envelope and encouraged them to open it. They slowly took the envelope and looked inside, astonished to find it full of smaller envelopes that said *Honeymoon Surprise*. They didn't open the envelopes until later that night, and when they did they discovered that the envelopes contained cash, in ones, fives, tens, and twenties. This was all from people who work hard to make it financially, and yet wanted to bless their pastor and his new bride. The total amount came to just a little over $400, money that could be used on their honeymoon.

But there was a special envelope among all the others. This one was a light shade of blue, in contrast to the others that were white. It had a note scrawled on the front that said: *Please open last.* Wendy took the last envelope and opened it. The first thing she saw was a short note. She read the note out loud to John and it expressed joy for them and their new marriage. The writer also apologized for being so cranky, and for being such an old tight-wad. Obviously, this note was from Vern. The last line simply read, "Wendy gal, I hope this can make up for all the tips I never gave you." They both looked inside the envelope and there was a $500 check, drawn on Vern's bank account. They sat there stunned, just beginning to understand how quickly love had changed this one man's heart.

John and Wendy traveled the short distance to the Enzian Hotel and spent the night, and most of the next morning, expressing their love in the way their Heavenly Father had designed. On Sunday afternoon, after a marvelous brunch at the hotel, they took off for the Hyatt Regency that was located on Highway 99, just a few blocks north of the Seattle/Tacoma Airport. They got up early the next morning and took Hawaiian Airlines to Maui, where they spent a wonderful week snorkeling, lying in the sun, reading mystery novels, and of course, making love. They even took the Jeep Wrangler they had rented and drove the long and windy road to Heavenly Hana. Quite a trip, but well worth it.

They flew off to Kauai after a week and thoroughly enjoyed the rich, lush beauty of the Garden Isle. They spent many hours on Poipu Beach, jumping in the surf, floating on air mattresses, and just relaxing by the pool. Kauai was such a laid-back Island and had what the hippies would call a "mellow vibe." It was all wonderful, but they found themselves getting anxious and excited to go back and start their life and ministry together.

They got back late Saturday afternoon and were looking forward to being in church on Sunday. John wasn't scheduled to preach, since he was getting back so late. But Max was filling in for him while he was gone, and according to everybody, had done a superb job. In fact, as John listened to Max preach, he wondered why he was still in logging. This guy could really get his point across.

At the end of the service, before everyone was dismissed, John and Wendy stood up at the front and thanked everybody for making their honeymoon so special, beyond their wildest dreams. John said that it was wonderful to get to know Wendy, in such a close way. Some of the people began to giggle, while Wendy turned several shades of red. "Well, that is to say, it's been a joy to get to know her more intimately." A little more giggling – "to spend more time and get to see more of her" – outright laughter. Wendy looked over at John and said, "Honey, I think they get what you're trying to say." John looked kind of sheepish and said, "Yeah, I guess you're right." That started people laughing again, but it was all in good fun.

As John and Wendy looked out over their beloved congregation, they rejoiced at the thought of what God had for them in the coming years. What can we do together as a church that would make a real difference for the kingdom? What lives will be changed as we go forward? And as Wendy looked out over these people who had so lovingly and warmly embraced her, she was truly touched by all that God had done in her life. She wasn't the same person as she had been a short five months ago. Here she was, a child of God and involved in ministry with her husband. As she looked out over the crowd, she wondered what marvelous new plans God had for them. She could hardly wait for what lie ahead.

She lovingly looked over at John, her wonderful husband. She looked at her precious son Travis and rejoiced that he now had a devoted father. And, at that moment, Wendy realized that she did indeed have her own TV family – with one exception. Hers was real.

Quietly, in her heart, Wendy celebrated the marvelous truth, that after her long and painful journey, she had finally come home. Home to Pleasant Pastures.